REBEL'S BLADE

THE AERMIAN FEUDS

By

Frost Kay

Copyright

Dedication

To my mama, who always told me that I could do anything I set
my mind to. I love you.

The Kingdoms

Table of Contents

Prologue

This was it.

Escape was impossible and death inevitable.

Leering men surrounded her; the stench of their rotting teeth and filthy clothing assaulted her senses. Black spots dotted her vision as she struggled to maintain consciousness. She couldn't let herself slip away though, or think of what they'd do if she did.

Sage had been trained for this sort of thing, had been told pain was in the mind and, while she could push *some* of it away, her body was only so strong. It was impossible to remain unaffected. She blinked, clearing the tears and blood from her eyes, only to catch the dark, empty ones of her captor studying her with amusement, seeming to enjoy her every wince or whimper. Biting the inside of her cheek she steeled herself; she would not give him the satisfaction.

If by some miracle she made it through this alive, he was on her list.

Her body screamed in pain as someone pushed her forward, her toes skimming the floor seeking purchase. Her hands, slick with sweat, slipped from the chains, shifting the entirety of her weight onto her manacled wrists. The metal bit into her abused flesh, though she had thankfully lost feeling in them some time ago. Tremors now wracked her nearly naked body.

How much longer could she hold on?

She peered at the ringleader, a sadistic man named Serge. He appeared to be moving his lips, yet all she heard was the high-pitched ringing in her ears. The edges of her vision blurred, and every sound seemed distorted—almost as if she was underwater. She would die here and her family would never know where to find her. Bitterness and regret then filled her. She should have killed the crown prince when she had the chance. This was his doing, she knew it. If she made it out alive, she would bring Aermia down around his ears.

Chapter One

KING MARQ

The toes of his boots hovered over the air. Marq stood on the ledge of a massive open window and gazed down at the waves crashing into the jagged cliffs below. The wind whistled softly, carrying the scent of salt and seaweed through the window. It caressed his face, ruffling his charcoal-colored woolen cloak. Gulls cried over each other amid the roar of waves and the sharp voices of the fishmongers' wives as they haggled prices. Despite this cacophony of noise, it was peaceful here. Pulling his gaze from the boiling sea below, he turned his attention to the port, its ships decorating the harbor, bobbing like toys. Fishermen, merchants and traders marched to and fro like ants.

He sighed. His wife had loved walking in the market, always

looking for new treasures or herbs to bring home. Her eyes would round and light up with excitement over some trinket. The woman had also harbored a deep love for the sea. A soft smile brightened his features thinking of the first time he saw her. He had turned into a bumbling idiot. He had taken a walk below the castle at low tide, as was his custom, and had reveled in the quiet time to think.

When he'd caught sight of her, it stopped him in his tracks. She was completely oblivious to the world, with her arms thrown high and her palms facing the sky—almost like she was worshiping the sun. As she tilted her face to its rays, her midnight hair cascaded down her back, kissing the waves as they lapped just above her knees, her dress fluidly twirling about her legs. He had seen nothing more beautiful. As a boy, his nana used to tell him stories of sea nymphs and Sirenidae, and he wondered, could she be one of them? He was afraid she would disappear if he looked away even for a second.

Then she'd dropped her chin, running her fingers along the frothy waves, a tiny smirk playing along her mouth.

That's peculiar, he had thought, *what's she smirking about?*

His eyes snapped from her full pink lips to soft purple eyes. All he could do was gape. Purple eyes? Incredible.

"You know that's considered rude; to stare in most places." She had grinned at him expectantly, yet he still hadn't moved a muscle. He couldn't. Rolling her eyes at him, she had gestured for him to come closer. "Come introduce yourself."

He recalled how he had wanted to run to her, but that wouldn't do. He was a prince, and princes were dignified, so instead he had collected himself and strode toward her attempting an air of confidence. But it was just his luck that on the first step he'd caught his boot on a rock, stumbling and flailing his arms as he attempted to catch his balance. However, he had instead somehow entangled his feet in seaweed, landing on his stomach with a face full of sand.

Curses and sand had spewed out of his mouth. Marq growled and clenched his jaw, the sand crunching between his teeth.

"Figures," he grumbled to himself, "there goes any chance of wooing her."

Female laughter, interspersed with an occasional wheeze, had then tickled his ears, bringing his attention back to the woman. He'd been so embarrassed that he rolled over and threw an arm over his face. Perhaps if he couldn't see her, then she couldn't see him. If only life worked that way.

A cool drop of water had plopped onto his face. *What the devil was that?* Moving his arm, he'd squinted up at the purple-eyed beauty who was at that very moment leaning over him. His heart stuttered, which surprised him. *Is it supposed to do that?*

She had shoved her hand out at him, laughter dancing in those unusual eyes of hers. "I'm Ivy," she had stated. "You should have seen my fall in the forest last week. I tripped on nothing, nothing at all. You figure out how that happened. I can tell you one thing, it was not pretty!" she'd continued.

He'd blinked. She talked fast. Marq didn't think she had taken a breath.

She'd grabbed his hand and pulled him up, "Here, let me help you up!" Her impish grin had enchanted him, making him feel right at home. She'd changed his life that day, for in her he had found something he didn't even know he needed.

The vivid memory faded, and the present came creeping back in. Marq's gaze once again sought the waves below. Without Ivy, he was weary of his empty life. The passing of time had not diminished his ache for her. And as each day passed, his memories of her faded bit by bit. He couldn't remember the sound of her voice anymore and it killed him. Self-loathing bubbled up at his uselessness; he didn't recognize himself anymore. Thirty years of love and memories haunted him every day.

Again, the waves seemed to beckon him. He knew it would be easy to take just one step. If he was a weaker man, perhaps he might have. He scoffed, thinking the ocean would likely just spit him back up.

He pondered what the future would hold: how was he to die? Would he go to sleep one day never to wake up? Or would he instead bleed out on a battlefield somewhere, sword in hand? How would he be remembered?

The quiet scuff of a boot roused him from his morbid reverie, and he internally groaned. Lord save him from one of his son's 'interventions'.

Without turning around, he asked, "To what do I owe the pleasure of your visit, son? Decided to check up on your old man, have you?" Ivy had called her father 'old man', and the memory brought a smile to his face.

He already knew what his son, Tehl, would say, so he shook his head, instead answering his own question. "No, I think not." He reached out and rapped his knuckles on the window frame. "I highly doubt this is a social visit as it's been a while since you last visited me." His eldest son was pragmatic and logical, putting duty before all else. If he were visiting, then it had to do with Aermian business.

Marq turned to study his oldest boy. A strong, azure gaze met his own. He supposed Tehl was not so much a boy anymore.

"What is it you need, son?"

Tehl was casually leaning his broad shoulders against the cold stone wall, one black brow arched, the spitting image of his mother. At least Marq could have a little piece of Ivy in his son, he mused. He had grown into a handsome man. Maybe one day he would get some adorable grandbabies out of him. Ivy had always wanted to be a grandmother. He rubbed his chest; perhaps if he rubbed hard enough some of the terrible grief could depart and he'd no longer feel like someone was squeezing the life from his body. Marq shoved down the pain and focused on his son.

"You must have heard about the revolts. Are you having trouble pinning down the leaders? If it isn't handled soon, it will turn into civil war," he commented.

"You know of the recent revolts?" Tehl asked.

Marq released a heavy sigh. "It's of no consequence. Tehl, get on with it. I haven't seen you in three weeks, and I am not getting any younger. I know you have no desire to see me, as you've made clear, so you must need something. Am I wrong?" His son's expressionless face stared back at him, mute. He grimaced, pressing the heels of his hands to his weary eyes. Sometimes his son made rocks seem downright chatty.

"I am surprised you're not out patrolling the city or chasing skirts. That seems to be your only pastime these days, other than avoiding me," he muttered.

Tehl scoffed, pushing off the wall. His son strolled over to his side and peered out the window. "No, that's Samuel's job, not mine. He chases enough women for the both of us." Tehl's lips pulled down. "I don't chase. If I want one, I say something and either the female accepts or declines. I don't have the time for chasing." Tehl's hands fluttered in the air. His son's dark blue eyes focused back on him after a moment. "I have too many responsibilities to engage in something so frivolous. *Your* responsibilities," Tehl added, his tone bitter.

Marq shook his head. "Your mother would be disgusted to see your brother's treatment of women. I only wish one of you would finally pick one, then I might at the very least have grandchildren to keep me occupied." He and Ivy had always liked the idea of being grandparents. Maybe they would fill the blasted hole in his chest, he thought.

Sadly though, Marq didn't expect that to happen soon. Sam loved all women so much it seemed he felt no desire to settle down with any one woman, while Tehl was too busy trying to save the world to notice anyone at all.

"Your mother always wanted you to find someone that made you happy," he hinted.

"You don't know how Mum would feel because she isn't here," Tehl remarked, as if he were speaking of the weather.

Marq gasped, the barb stealing the breath from his lungs. In fact, it would have been less painful if Tehl had punched him in the face.

His son's face fell, remorse evident. "Forgive me, that was uncalled for." Tehl's gaze dropped to his cloak, and he added, "But she is gone and you need to let her go."

"I will never let your mother go, a companion like her is rare, and I can only hope you might one day find what I had in your mum. If you're ever fortunate enough to find a woman like her, you'll understand," Marq said, gruffly.

His son stared, his eyes narrowed in disbelief. "What you had only happens in fairy tales." Tehl's face pinched. "And look at what her death has done to you. You're unable to even care for yourself, much less Aermia. You are wasting away. I can't even recall the last time you left the castle walls. Our people are starving and why? Because it seems you're incapable of halting this steady descent of yours. The Scythians steal into our kingdom to despoil the land, burn our crops. Aermians are disappearing along the border."

Marq's eyes widened. "Scythians?" he repeated, trying to make sense of his son's words. Over the last nine hundred years, a few outcasts of the Scythians kingdom had sought refuge, but they kept to themselves. He shuddered, thinking of the warriors—more monster than man—that they created. He scrutinized his son. "What do you mean by Scythian?"

"Exactly what I said. It wasn't the rebels causing the trouble along the border, it was Scythia."

"You have confirmation?"

"Yes, there were survivors this time." Tehl's face hardened. "If you can call them that. They will be scarred for life, children." Pain filled his son's eyes. "Our kingdom needs you but you sit in this godforsaken tower and do nothing."

Having vented his frustration, Tehl's shoulders slumped. The pain and anger his son was struggling with became evident with his every word. Marq felt it as if it were his own. Did Tehl not understand how much he was trying, fighting every day? His only companions of late were sadness, guilt, and anger.

"Don't take that tone with me, son. You cannot fathom how it has been, having lost the woman who owned my soul. She was my helper, friend, and companion. My other half. When she died, it may as well have been me," he replied. Every word was a slash to his tortured soul.

"I understand that you miss Mum, but..." Tehl trailed off, his head cocked as he seemed to take note of his father's belt, his eyes narrowing.

Marq looked down, attempting to discover what had caught his son's attention. Before he could discern anything, Tehl reached out and snatched the dagger from under his cloak. Marq gritted his teeth and tilted his head toward the open rafters of the great stone ceiling above. Lord give him patience. "Why did you do that?"

Tehl ignored his question, instead replying with one of his own. "What is this?"

Marq observed his son run a careful finger along the edge of the blade, wondering what in the world he was about. "What does it look like, son? I am certain you're in full possession of your wits?" he inquired, exasperation coloring his words.

Tehl's face was impassive even as his hand clenched the hilt of the blade. That one display of emotion was enough to make Marq scrutinize his son. His son rarely showed emotion of any kind. Why was he so furious?

"You *know* you're not allowed any weapons in your possession," Tehl hissed.

Ah, he thought. *So that's what this is about.*

Tehl was worried he might hurt himself again. There had been one instance following Ivy's death he had cut himself. He had been numb, unable to feel a single thing; not anger, not guilt, nor joy. He couldn't even cry. What sort of human being was he, to be incapable of mourning his loved ones? And even as he made that miniscule cut in his own flesh there'd been no pain. He'd still felt nothing.

"I have always carried a blade," Marq reasoned, attempting to placate his son. "This is not unusual. In fact, it is essential for protection."

"I am trying to protect you from yourself."

That stung. "It was only the one instance, son, we'd barely buried her, but I am in no such danger now," he reasoned. "I have no wish to die."

"Death is a weak man's tactic to escape problems. You, as the king, ought to be stronger than that. No person should hold that much power over you."

Those words pained him but, as they weren't unfounded, he could not fault his son for them. "Then you ought to understand that it is only for protection. You shouldn't worry."

Tehl glanced away from him in disgust. "I can't save you from yourself, and I'm done trying. Mope around your little fortress, lose yourself in your precious memories, or drink yourself into oblivion. Hell, you can sit in this tower and rot or jump out the damned window if that's preferable. I am not your guardian." Black smudges rested beneath his son's eyes. He looked exhausted. Tehl sighed, "And you were correct in guessing this was not a social visit, as enlightening as it has been. It seems Sam and his sneaks have found new leads on the rebellion leaders. My men and I will investigate. We will find them soon."

"Always the dutiful son, aren't you?" Marq asked, not expecting an answer. His son kept himself so engrossed in his duties to Aermia that his life was slipping past him and he didn't even see it. Tehl needed someone to shock him out of his rut, this relentless routine he kept up. "You need a wife." The accompanying look of absolute horror on his son's face made him chuckle. Biting back a grin he continued, "You need someone to help you. It's time to find a woman."

"A woman?" Tehl repeated, stunned. His face soured, disgust evident as he stared at Marq, his arms crossed. It was rather akin to the look his son had given when he was little and had wanted pudding but received spinach instead.

"I don't need a wife. I have a higher chance of being struck by lightning than being married." Tehl appeared thoughtful. "If I took a mistress, would that appease you?"

Marq scowled at his eldest son. "No! That would be disgraceful."

Tehl's lips twitched.

Realization dawned: his son was teasing him. His scowl deepened. It seemed sons were more trouble than they were worth. Why couldn't Ivy have given him daughters? He crossed his arms and his scowl morphed into a smirk. "You may joke now, but just you wait. At your age, I had rather the same attitude, but I received a large slice of humble pie." Tehl looked at him as he continued: "Your mother."

Tehl paled and backed away as if he had some disease. "I have to go. Take care of yourself, father. The next time we meet I will have good news about the rebellion." With that his son turned on his heel and left the chamber.

That boy was headstrong, yet Marq knew he would make an exceptional king. He knew it. He slumped against the stone wall. It seemed their conversation had taken a lot of out him. He hadn't experienced that many emotions in a long time. And yet...maybe things were looking up for him. As soon as he had thought it, he winced. Hope was a dangerous thing.

Chapter Two

TEHL

The king was living in the past. It seemed like he wanted to lose himself in his memories and never come back. Tehl tucked his father's dagger into a sheath at his waist, moving down the corridor.

Where does he keep getting these weapons?

He needed to increase the security on the armory. You would think someone who wasn't lucid more than half the time would lose some of their cunning, but not his father. One thing he could say, it seemed King Marq did not dull with age.

Tehl scanned the chilly hallway that led to the part of the castle his father inhabited. He shuddered, it unnerved him. Between the dim lantern light, the chill from the drab, gray stone, and the puddles of darkness, it felt like something out of one of the horror stories Sam would read to him. Goosebumps broke out on his arms and the hair on the back of his neck prickled. He hated it up here.

Light winked at him from the bottom of the stairway, and Tehl picked up his speed, ready to leave the gloom behind him. He stepped into the bright hallway, glad to have left behind the dreary turrets. How could his father stand it? He resided in the darkest, ugliest part of the castle, and Tehl couldn't see why.

Tehl loved their castle. It was a true feat of architecture, having been built from the stone bluff on which it rested. White marble columns stretched toward the high, arched ceiling where shimmering gold stars twinkled in the sunlight as it streamed through the windows. It danced over the stained glass, casting murals of colored images onto the smooth white walls. The kaleidoscope of colors helped to soothe his frayed nerves after the depressing conversation he'd had with his father.

He reluctantly turned from the peaceful scenes as he caught sight of a familiar head of curly, golden hair.

"Samuel," Tehl shouted. "Are the Elite ready for our stroll through the Sanee?"

Sam glanced over his shoulder with an innocent smile that made Tehl pause. There was nothing innocent about Sam. That look boded mischief. He eyed his brother, wondering what he was up to.

His brother turned with militant perfection and executed a courtly bow. "Why yes, my lord. Everything is almost in place, my worshipfulness."

A deep sigh slipped out of him. "Dear God, Sam, cut it out. I can't take any of your teasing this early in the morning." He needed a drink of something strong to cope with Sam at the moment.

His brother's face morphed into a blinding smile of white teeth, which only irritated him further. It was too early to have that much energy.

"Well, I knew you were off tracking down Father Dearest earlier, so I figured you would need something to brighten your day. It seems I was not far off. I'm sure I saw a dark cloud hovering over you as you approached. Quit being so serious and angry. We have to be on our best behavior enough as it is. Smile, live a little."

Tehl frowned. "I smile," he argued. Perhaps not as often as Sam, but he wasn't droll all the time. It wasn't in his nature to be as carefree as Sam.

Or rather, he mused, *as carefree as Sam pretends to be.*

"You do enough of that for the both of us," Tehl retorted. "Do you ever take *anything* seriously?"

"Not if I don't have to, that's something *you* do for the both of us, brother," Sam joked, slapping him on the back.

In spite of himself, one side of Tehl's mouth tipped up. As the second son, his brother had always been granted so much more freedom. While Sam ran through the palace, wailing like a banshee, playing pirates or dragons, Tehl had to sit quietly, listening to his father and his advisers. After a time, though, Sam ended up sneaking in, choosing to sit with him through all the long boring talks. It bonded them. Samuel didn't need to sit there, and yet he did, so Tehl wouldn't be miserable. Tehl couldn't even imagine not having his brother around.

Besides their behavioral differences, they were also like the sun and the moon in appearance. Their only shared feature was their eyes. They had the same deep sapphire eyes, so dark they made the midnight sky green with envy. The striking eyes were framed with such thick dark lashes that his mum had always been envious.

But that was where their similarities ended, for Sam was light to his dark. Sam's curly blond hair, sunny disposition, and boyish smile had an endless stream of women falling at his feet throughout the years, while he'd had a much harder time of it, even with his exotic looks. Despite what some people said, it seemed personality made quite the difference.

Tehl flicked his eyes upward to his own unruly black waves. He had his mum's hair, so dark it almost seemed highlighted with blue. His strong jawline, high cheekbones, and dimples all came from his father though. Tehl smiled as he remembered his mother telling him they were his father's secret weapon. Dimples—who would have thought women loved them so much? A secret weapon, yes, but one would have to smile for you to see them. His smile dimmed. After conversing with him, women would run for the hills. So he chose not to say anything. You can't embarrass yourself if you don't speak. He didn't feel comfortable talking to strangers anyway. Tehl was the 'serious' one to Sam's 'fun-loving' personality. He didn't have time to chase women; his duty demanded too much attention.

Tehl eyed his brother, contemplating the difference between the man he knew Sam to be and the persona he encouraged. While Sam held the title of Elite Commander, it was Gavriel, their cousin, who fulfilled the duties, although this was not due to any negligence on

Sam's part. Rather, it served a purpose for his brother's true talents: information acquisition and manipulation. A more befitting title might have been spymaster, he was possibly the most qualified man to have ever played that role. He had a million different faces for the myriads of circumstances in which he found himself. He was a master of disguise.

However, Tehl thought, *Sam doesn't have the weight of starving, angry people on his shoulders, nor the threat of revolt, war, and invasion looming over him.*

Just contemplating it was enough to give him a throbbing headache and send his heart pounding. Because his people were unaware of the true extent of his father's deterioration, it was impossible for them to understand how Tehl was floundering in a vain attempt to remedy everything unaided.

The sound of Sam's voice penetrated his reverie. "Sorry?" he said, blinking to clear his thoughts.

"You still in there?" Sam teased, knocking the side of Tehl's head. "You didn't hear a word I said, did you? Perhaps you were dreaming of that sweet little thing vying for your attention last night? She was gorgeous and curvy in all the right places!" Sam waved his hands in the shape of an hourglass and waggled his eyebrows.

Tehl cringed at the memory. The harpy had thrown herself at him, despite his obvious lack of interest, finding a miraculous number of opportunities to do so again and again throughout the evening. Vain was an understatement.

"For hell's sake Sam, get your mind out of the gutter. She was pretty until she opened her mouth." Tehl shuddered. "When she smiled at me, it was like looking at a leviathan. She seems needy and manipulative, and I have no desire for her to sink her claws into me. Also," he continued, wrinkling his nose, "she had so much rose oil on her I could barely breathe. I haven't survived elite training, battles, and assassination attempts only to die by stupid rose perfume. I don't care if she is Jaren's daughter, I won't spend another evening with her."

Sam tilted his head, thinking. "It would be rather poetic, wouldn't it? To die by a rose? Just imagine the tragic retelling: oh, poor Crown Prince Tehl Ramses perished, not by the sword, but because he suffocated by a set of rose-oil-saturated breasts!" Unable to keep a straight face, Sam let out a snigger.

"Not on your life," he muttered darkly. "I'm grabbing my cloak and then I will meet you on the city streets."

Sam's face sobered for a moment. "Be careful. I still don't know what it is we're dealing with. I know it is to be an exchange, but I'm unsure how many parties will be involved. Keep your eyes and ears open—though I will stay near you most of the time." His brother paused, his eyes glittering in challenge. "Let's see if you can locate me among the crowd this time." Sam then swaggered off toward the armory.

Tehl once again continued down the corridors of the castle, noting again how much things had changed since his mother died. It seemed all the vibrancy and warmth left with her and now, despite the impressive architecture, the place felt empty and hollow. The flowers had all but disappeared and the cheerful tapestries replaced with dull, muted ones.

He planned to change that though. And it wasn't the castle alone which required restoration. The kingdom did as well. It had been three years since the last festival. This year would be different. Aermia needed something to look forward to, and he would give it to them.

As he pondered these hopeful changes, he couldn't help the frustration which also came. Whenever he thought of the changes his mum's death had wrought, anger seemed to bubble up at the injustice of what he had been dealt. Not only had he lost his mother, but in the aftermath, he'd lost his father and his youth. And if that wasn't enough, now he had a rebellion on his hands.

He ground his teeth, exasperated with the shortsightedness of those responsible for its incitement. They were ignorant of the havoc and grief their rebellion brought on Aermia and her inhabitants. Shaking his head, he attempted to clear his thoughts. Maybe today would be the day he received answers. Tehl clasped his woolen cloak, slipped on his hood, and departed the palace, completely unnoticed.

Chapter Three

SAGE

Setting aside her tools, Sage stretched her cramped fingers. She loved creating new pieces, but setting a couple hundred black seed pearls was not her idea of fun. She stood as she placed her hands on her hips and arched her back, sighing with satisfaction. Being hunched over for so long had made her feel like she'd never be able to stand straight again. She limped over to the window and attempted to rub the feeling back into her stiff legs. Sage poked her head out to gauge the time and noted that the sun was high in the sky. She needed to hurry up.

Sage set about gathering up her tools from where she'd left them. The sweltering heat from the forge made her hair stick to her damp neck as she meticulously placed her tools in their proper place. She valued the heavy fall of coffee-colored hair plaited down her back, but days like today made her want to hack it all off. She swiped at the sweat on her brow with the back of her hand and appraised the broad sword she'd painstakingly created.

The sword was beautiful; too extravagant for her own taste but a creation to be proud of.

Sage lifted the sword and placed two fingers under the hilt, testing the balance. She knew the balance was perfect, but she still checked it every time out of habit. It sat still and straight atop her fingers, neither end outweighing the other. The light caught its finely sharpened double edge, gleaming wickedly. She drew her thumb gently across the blade's length and watched with satisfaction as the line of blood appeared there.

Perfect, utterly perfect, she thought, *and made by a woman to boot.*

Sage sighed, content, knowing if she and her family were frugal, the coin this brought would keep them fed for a good, long while. They'd need it too. Fine swords were not in high demand anymore. Ever since the Sickness had swept through the land, many swords-smiths moved on, seeking greener pastures in which to ply their trade. She was thankful Colm Blackwell, her papa, had made a name for himself prior to the devastation. They still received commissions from all regions of Aermia due to his renown, albeit less frequently. Their faithful customers and their referrals had kept them afloat. Without them, she'd no clue what they'd have done, and although Sage wished she could forge fine art more often, few requests such as this came.

Holding it before her, she again examined the blade, and a triumphant grin spread across her face, as she let herself admire this deadly weapon she herself had forged. It was truly a work of art. A black dragon adorned the pommel, its sapphire eyes glittering up at her. The dragon's tail circled up the hilt, and the dragon appeared to be perched there observing the world. The black seed pearls used for scales added luster to the fearsome beast's hide. She'd outdone herself, and it would fetch a hefty price from whatever nobleman commissioned it.

As a young girl, Sage had always been fascinated with swords and the forge. It was incredible to her that her papa started with a boring lump of metal and could create something useful, beautiful, or deadly. While her brothers, Seb and Zeke, chased each other with sticks she grew up always by her papa's side. Her mum always tried to get her interested in things more appropriate for a girl of her age, yet Sage always conveniently lost her dolls and sewing needles, instead ending up back in the forge. Her papa took to calling her 'his little shadow'. This began her long journey in learning how to forge weapons.

As she grew, he was always willing to pause and teach her things here and there. One day, he handed her a wooden sword, and she remembered looking at it unimpressed. Chuckling at the look she gave him, he patted her head and told her a secret that day. One couldn't know how to craft a fine sword if they didn't know how to use one, and use it well. He'd then tapped the wooden sword and said this was where she had to start.

At the tender age of five, he'd trained her in sword wielding, and

Sage loved every moment. Even when her arms quivered and her body screamed, she was powerful. As she grew, so did the swords her papa made for her. When she came of age, he'd allowed her to fulfill the duties of an apprentice, despite her mum's chagrin. Her mum was disappointed she didn't have lady-like aspirations yet her mum accepted it and loved her no less.

Over the next five years, she'd worked hard in her father's forge, perfecting her skills. No one ever suspected it was Sage who made their swords, and not the famed Colm. Men were fickle that way. They ate up her work, but if word ever spread that a woman had made them, her swords would be considered unsuitable for a warrior. It was rubbish. She loved designing new pieces. Being the secret designer didn't bother her if it meant she could keep doing what she loved.

Their business had continued to flourish until the queen died. While their king mourned the loss of his beloved, the kingdom slowly deteriorated in his absence. Bandits attacked the outskirts of Aermia, burning crops, and pillaging villages. Business slowed for their finer work, so they adapted and changed the focus of their wares to tools and farming equipment. Though it lacked the complexity and challenge she craved, Sage knew it put food in their bellies, something few people had.

When her papa became ill, it was by far the worst thing they'd faced. The Sickness started slowly, but eventually he began to waste away. It attacked his lungs, weakening him and stealing away his energy. Her heart broke to see him so ravaged. Their roles reversed after that. Sage ran the smith while he, instead, sat watching her. He and her mum took care of the customers, while she continued to work in the back. She was exhausted at the end of the day, but still thankful that her labor prevented them from sleeping with hollow stomachs and kept a roof above their heads.

It was these circumstances that culminated in a decision which altered her life over the past year. With just one meeting, her entire life changed.

***

The day was like any other. She'd hiked to her favorite spot, a hidden meadow, and there she practiced her swordplay, as like every other morning. In the middle of an intricate set of steps the forest stilled. Halting, she listened, not one sound could be heard, even the trees were silent, unnaturally so. Sage scanned the forest spinning in a circle. She kept her sword angled in front of her, ready to defend herself. The hair on the back of her neck prickled; she was being watched.

Just come and get me.

"I know you're there. Show yourself," she commanded.

A figure emerged from the forest, approaching at an almost leisurely pace, gliding silently in her direction. He was tall, with a warrior's build, his dark cloak flowing behind him. His arms were loose at his sides, completely at ease, yet she didn't doubt for a second he was dangerous. She'd bet her family's smithy on it. No one glided without extensive combat training.

She peered at his cloak again, noting the green color. Camouflage, that was brilliant. Sage lifted her sword, warning him to stop. Despite the ten feet between them, a trickle of unease slithered down her spine. He wasn't a typical thief; but something else entirely. The deep cowl of his hood prevented her seeing his eyes, but she still sensed him measuring her as she took his measure. Unease crept over her as she waited for his next move.

"Little one, I am not here to harm you," he rumbled softly. His voice was deep and smooth like whiskey, with a hint of a growl.

"Says the wolf to the lamb," she retorted, her gaze never wavering.

One side of his lips pulled up. "You are right to be cautious of men in the woods. It's not safe for you to be here alone. You should be in your home where you belong," he admonished.

Sage bristled and squared her shoulders. What right did he have to tell her what to do? "You are neither my father, nor brother, nor husband. You've no right telling me where I should be. It's you who is not safe. Leave my meadow."

"You and your family have suffered much," he stated. "We have been studying you for some time, Sage. Your skills would prove useful for Aermia, to heal her and protect her."

Her guard went up. *What was he about? Was this a trap?*

Sage glanced around the meadow searching for others, chills skating down her arms, her unease tripling. "You have been watching my family and me?" she probed, licking her dry lips. Time to go. But first, she needed to shift his focus off her. "Who is this 'we'?" she questioned, stepping toward the forest.

He dismissed her question and answered with one of his. "What do you see as you walk through the city?"

What an odd question. "I don't understand what you are looking for," Sage replied steadily. Another step closer to her escape.

"Our people go hungry while our land's dying. Meanwhile, trouble stirs along our Scythian border. No doubt you've heard whispers of those disappearing along it, though none know for sure why or where they've vanished." He paused, considering for a moment. "Are you aware that this most likely means they've been taken? Why would someone steal another person?"

"No," she breathed, not hiding her shock or disgust. Stars above, he was talking of slaves. Being torn from your home and forced to God-knows-where sent a chill up her spine. Scythians were the stuff of nightmares, barbaric and ruthless, with no shred of conscience. History books from every nation corroborated the fact they hated outsiders, besides anyone who didn't fit the model of 'perfection' to which they aspired. A 'perfect' Scythian had yet to cross the Mort Wall in the last five hundred years, not since the Nagalian Purge. Why would they steal people?

"And how long do you say this has been going on?" Sage inquired, her suspicion clear, all the while edging toward the forest border.

"The reports of missing Aermians go back the last four years, as far as we understand. The commander has sent a few soldiers, but the pathetic attempts always come to nothing." Controlled anger laced his words.

It seemed he wasn't so calm and collected. That told her he most likely believed what he was telling her. Sage pursed her lips, trying to discern if he was being truthful. He didn't come by her on accident; he sought her out for a reason. Sage's instincts told her he was dangerous, but she thought he wasn't interested in harming her. He also had shown no signs he was touched in the head. So what did he want?

Sage gave him a hard stare and spoke her mind. "What do you want from me?"

"Change. You'd be a great asset to the restoration of Aermia and its people."

"An asset?" she scoffed, how impersonal. Whoever he was working with viewed people as tools and not individuals. "An asset to whom?" she drew out the question, staring unflinchingly at him, awaiting his answer. There were only five more feet until the forest edge, and she fought to keep from sprinting into the woods. Something told her he would be onto her before she could scream, even if she made a run for it.

"The rebellion." Noting her position, he angled his body toward her. "I will not hurt you, but if you run I will catch you."

Sage froze, not so much from his threat as the phrase he'd just thrown out there. The word echoed in her mind, yet he had said it like it was of no consequence, as if it didn't have the potential to change everything in her life.

Rebellion.

She had heard whispers over the years, but had never given it another thought. It had always been young hotheads spouting off treasonous nonsense, acting like that made them heroes of some sort. But never had she seen actual proof of an organized rebellion. That would be a HUGE secret. The rebellion would have to be well trained or very new. Sage scrutinized the mystery man and highly doubted he was wet behind the ears.

This is what their king had driven his people to: treasonous meetings in the woods. The king's grief superseded the needs of his people. Aermia was rotting from the inside out. Why had no one stepped up? It wasn't as if he didn't have two sons that could at least have tried to fill his place, his sons' inaction made them as guilty. The time for mourning had passed.

Now was the time to fight.

If she joined the rebellion, she could make a difference, but she also wasn't naïve. Sage wasn't about to commit to something until she had all the facts. That meant knowing those she was dealing with.

She tilted her head, considering. She could lose everything by agreeing. If caught by the Crown she'd be tried as a traitor and hung. That would leave her family helpless and destitute. She couldn't be the only one with something to lose—he needed to have a stake in this too. Her heart raced as she decided. "I don't make deals with strangers, show me your face and actual evidence that what you say is true. Then we'll talk."

From beneath his hood sounded a rumbling chuckle. Goosebumps ran down her arms. If his looks matched his laugh, she was in real trouble. Sage held her breath as he reached up and pulled his hood off, revealing a mane of black hair.

No. Not quite black, she thought, *rather a deep red.*

It reminded her of a dark wine. Not once in her lifetime had she ever seen hair that color before. He also had a strong chin, and thick eyebrows accentuated unique eyes the color of citrine, so bright they looked like liquid gold. A thin scar ran from the end of his right brow, passing dangerously close to his eye, and ended at his chin. She realized he was quite an attractive man, despite the scar. In fact, the scar added to his dangerous air.

"What do you expect from me and when do I get to meet your 'we'?" she asked, eyebrows lifted.

"Soon," he said, and a dazzling smile transformed his rugged face. He was beautiful in a wild sort of way. "I will be in touch, little one, then all your questions will be answered." He bowed, then turned to walk away.

Swamp apples. That wasn't an answer, and he never gave her his name. "That's not good enough! I'm not going into this blind. I need a name!" Sage shouted at his back.

He looked over his shoulder and locked onto her with his odd, mesmerizing eyes. For a moment, they stared at each other, until he winked and broke the spell. "Rafe. I'll be seeing you soon."

***

She let the memory fade away as she stared down at the broadsword still carefully clutched in her hands. Lifting a hand, Sage rubbed at her temple, glancing out the window. Realizing just how much time had passed while she was daydreaming, she let a curse slip out. She should have left a quarter of an hour ago. Sage placed the sword in its bed of velvet and rushed to grab her black cloak from the wall.

Opening the door which connected their home and the forge she called out. "Mum, I'm slipping out. I will bring back meat if I can find anything edible at the market. If not, it will be fish."

"Be safe, my love. We will hold down the fort," her mother trilled back and then decided she needed admonishment. "Try not to get your clothes so filthy this time. It took hours to get the stench out of them last time."

Sage looked at her collection of blades, snatching her favorite and attaching its sheath to her waist. With sarcasm evident in every word, she retorted, "Yes mum, you know how I strive to get pushed into puddles if only just to spite you."

"Don't get sassy with me, Little Miss, and try to be home before dark please."

Sage smiled at her mum's words and tone. "I will. If not, don't worry. I can always spend the night with Elle and be home early in the morning." Sage poked her head out the door, scanning left and right. People milled along the lane but it seemed no one paid her any attention so she casually meandered into the flow of people. If she didn't hurry, Rafe was sure to wring her neck.

Chapter Four

TEHL

Sanee was once a thriving, beautiful city. Now it was rotting. In every direction, buildings were adorned with decaying wood and chipped paint. Porches sagged and troughs had green algae growing in them. Rotting fish permeated the air. His city desperately needed care. It was disintegrating before his eyes, but he didn't know how he could stop its decline.

Oddly enough, in spite of the smell, a sense of peace enveloped him as he walked down the open lane. The familiar sound of pots clanking, donkeys' braying, and the crashing of the waves on the shore surrounded him. Tehl preferred this to the whispers and delicate giggles of court. The symphony of sounds reminded him of trips to the market with his mum as a boy, and he still found that comforting.

Once he looked closely, though, noting the state of his people, his small moment of peace left him. He had always known the merchants to be jovial, and perhaps plump, yet now they were thin and haggard, ghosts of their former prosperities.

The further he trudged into the city, the more depressed he became. The people in the fishing district were the worst. Their hollow eyes tracked his movements, and the looks they were giving him made his skin crawl. Tehl clenched his hand around the sword hilt each time he met any pair of eyes that seemed hostile. Perhaps the warning in his gaze would discourage them from trying anything.

Beggars littered the streets. There hadn't been half this many a couple months ago. It was the children who caught his attention. Most of them sat on crates and bins, staring listlessly at the filth-strewn streets. Where were their parents? Their thin little bodies made him ashamed of what he had left at the table this morning. As soon as he returned to the palace, he would put something in motion to care for the children. It was appalling how long it took to build up a successful kingdom—yet how quickly it seemed to fall around your ears.

He spotted Garreth casually leaning against a post, supposedly dozing, so Tehl moved on, noting familiar faces as he went. Tehl looked to the left and glimpsed a familiar set of eyes beneath a straw hat. Gavriel. He looked so different that if it wasn't for his cousin being a mere eight feet away, then he might not have spotted him. It was incredible how the Elite blended in. Samuel and Gavriel's training had paid off.

Scanning the vicinity, Tehl paused when a small, faint carving caught his eye. A wooden door showed a rough version of his family crest: a black dragon spewing flames. Rather than clutching the sword in its claws however, they had depicted the dragon with the sword piercing its heart. His brows lifted, surprised at the boldness displayed by whoever had the audacity to openly mock the Crown. He committed the symbol to memory and noted the sign hanging above the door which read *Cobbler*.

How original of them.

So, the shoemaker was a resistance sympathizer. Though he doubted the man knew anything useful, he made a mental note to have Sam investigate.

Tehl glanced at the sky and blew out a frustrated breath when he realized he'd already wasted a considerable amount of time wandering the streets. He'd be cutting it close. As he navigated the streets and alleyways, darting around horse droppings and the occasional puddle, he kept his eyes and ears open, picking up on snatches of conversation. It both irked and baffled him how little the people understood current events. His brother had hoped to nip this kind of talk in the bud but gossip remained unconquerable. Hearing their hushed conversations of so called heroic deeds, he scoffed. Heroic, his ass. Try self-serving.

People were so careless. If he were so inclined, they would be tried for treason and their whole family would lose everything, all because of a casual conversation. He smiled to himself as he noted with interest that at least one Elite had slipped into each group.

He put the thoughts aside; gossip was the least of today's worries. The current priority was catching any of the rebel leaders.

The capture of even one of their high-ranking officers could be the break he needed, and it would be an enormous step in the right direction. He rather hoped they'd put up a good fight though. He'd been itching to brawl for some time.

Tehl arrived at their exchange location, Lavender Alley, and examined his surroundings with distaste. You'd think a street named Lavender would at least have the decency to smell as delightfully as it was named, but no. Death and decay filled the air, and he didn't want to know where it was coming from.

As he moved farther into the dank alley, the stone cobbles beneath his boots were black and slippery, and he spotted red beady eyes peering at him from the shadows. Long little pink tails and whiskered noses stuck out of every nook and cranny.

Rats.

God, he hated rats. They were so vile. It was all he could do not to stumble when one darted past his foot.

Do not slip and fall because: One, the rats will eat you, and Two, you will catch a disease, and die a horrible death before you even make it back to the palace.

With these gems rattling around in his head, he pressed forward.

To his left, there was a perfect hiding place. He cautiously made his way to it and faded into the small dark space between the stone walls. Somehow, the smell became stronger here. What was that anyway? Tehl tried not to breathe through his nose, but it seemed to slither into his mouth and squat on his tongue. While trying to keep from gagging, he jerked a cloth up over his mouth and nose. He may have experienced nasty things in his life but this was one of the worst.

It seemed fitting that the rebellion would pick this place. Rats enjoying the company of other rats.

A moment later, movement left of his shoulder alerted him to another. Surveying the shadows, he noticed little whiskers twitching at him from a hole in the wall a mere six inches away.

Damn! Nothing went his way today.

Tehl tried not to move, calming his rapid breathing. Tehl never panicked in dangerous situations. Yet throw in one stupid little rodent, and it was all he could do not to flail his arms and take off running.

He steeled himself. Mind over matter. Logically, he knew that he was way bigger than a rat and he needed to calm the hell down. Just when he gained control, it began creeping toward him.

Gritting his teeth, he hissed at the rat. "Psst...get out of here!"

The furry menace would not be deterred. It scampered right onto his cloak, pausing briefly to sniff it. He hoped he smelled so offensive the whiskers would be singed right off its dingy face. But he had never had good luck. The rat continued crawling across his shoulder, sniffing here or there.

Don't get comfy, he thought to it. His cloak would *not* become its next home.

A flutter of activity distracted him from the creature invading his space. Two cloaked figures approached from the dead end of the ally.

Where did they come from?

It was a dead end. Something exchanged hands, and words were spoken in hushed tones, much too soft to pick up. He strained his ears, trying to catch their conversation, but his mind went blank when a tiny nose nuzzled his neck. He shuddered.

Disgusting.

Needle-like claws scratched along his neck as whiskers tickled his ear. It was imperative that he remained stock-still. *Stay calm, stay calm, stay calm,* he chanted in his mind.

If any of the Elite—or my brother—hear of this, I'll never hear the end of it.

He realized he'd been so preoccupied by the nasty vermin making its new home at his neck, he'd missed the meeting. One figure disappeared into the dark while the other cloaked figure paused for a moment, and then started toward him, taking soundless steps on the diseased cobblestones.

The little bastard then sniffed his ear again. Goosebumps broke out on his neck, and he shivered. Abruptly, sharp pain exploded from his ear. The little bugger bit him! Pain and heat radiated around his ear, down his neck, and across his cheek. Tehl shook his head once, dislodging the fiend from his ear and hissed out a breath. *Stars above that hurt.*

At the sound, the rebel making his way toward him paused. The figure cocked his head as if listening.

Tehl forced himself to hold his breath, praying that his position hadn't been compromised. He focused on blending in.

Be one with the stone, be one with the blasted stone.

The rebel wasn't very tall or broad shouldered, petite even, childlike. His thoughts screeched to a halt. The rebellion wouldn't use children...would they? The idea made him sick. The figure before him could easily be a boy of thirteen or fourteen, and the more he turned it over in his mind, the more it made sense. What a perfect way to pass messages. No one ever paid much attention to where children ran off to, and no one would suspect a child as a rebel informant. It'd be brilliant if it wasn't so disgusting. If that *was* the case, which he suspected it was, he'd have to be very careful. He could never hurt a child.

He inched his hand into his cloak, clutching his dagger. Maybe he could instead scare the youth into doing what he wanted. All he needed to do was convince the child that he himself was not the enemy.

The cloaked rebel scanned the alley. After a moment, the young rebel began moving toward him again, ignorant of the danger lurking in the shadows. His whole body tensed. He didn't want to threaten the boy but he wasn't sure he had any other choice. If he fought, he risked injuring the child.

As the rebel passed, he stepped behind him, wrapping his right arm around the rebel's neck and pulling upward in warning. His other wrapped around the boy's ribs and pressed the tip of his dagger against the rebel as he whispered, "You will come calm and quietly or things will not be looking good for you."

"My coins are hanging from my belt on the right side," the rebel replied in a higher register. "Take them and leave."

The boy's reply surprised him, for the child's voice never trembled or wavered. He must be brave or stupid to not have any fear with a blade involved.

"I do not want your coins, son. What I need is information. You can help me with that. After what I observed, I think you may be the one to get me what I need. What do you know of the rebellion?"

The rebel stiffened, shaking his head in an emphatic *no*. "Don't involve me in your treasonous affairs with talks of rebellion. People are hung for less, and I'd rather not be found guilty by association. I want no trouble." Conviction rang in his voice.

Had Tehl not seen the exchange himself moments before, he was sure he would've been inclined to believe the boy. His lips thinned. "Lying to a new friend makes a horrible first impression." Tehl pushed aside the boy's cloak with his own dagger, revealing a shiny blade. "I doubt you'll be needing this. I would hate for you to hurt yourself...or me," he said, relieving the boy of the dagger.

"I'm *not* your friend," the rebel hissed.

The boy was angry. No one enjoyed being powerless.

"Release me," growled the rebel.

At that inopportune moment, little whiskers poked the back of his neck. With all the excitement, Tehl had forgotten about that fuzzy tyrant taking up residence in the hood of his cloak. Momentarily surprised, he loosened his grip around the rebel's ribs, and that was all the opening the boy needed. He thrust his hips backward, knocking Tehl off balance, and ducked his chin, escaping Tehl's hold.

For a second, Tehl only gaped at his empty arms. How had that happened? The boy attempted to flee, slipping and sliding along the cobbles. Tehl scrambled after the boy. "Oh no you don't!"

The rebel was quick, but Tehl had longer legs. He reached out, grabbing a handful of his cloak and yanked the boy back. All the frantic movements were enough to dislodge the rat from his cloak and send it sailing through the air, after which it landed in a dank puddle of sludge with a splat.

Serves the menace right, he thought.

The boy twisted and tugged on his own cloak as he tried to dislodge it from Tehl's fingers. A chuckle slipped out. Like he'd make it that easy for him. The boy growled and stopped tugging.

The blow came before he could block it. A foot clipped him hard enough on the chin that his teeth clacked together. Copper flooded his mouth. Damn it, he had bitten his cheek. Tehl spat blood on to the ground and wiped the back of his arm across his mouth, appraising the boy. He grudgingly admitted that it was a perfect round-house kick and said so.

"Are you hungry for more?" was the arrogant reply.

Tehl managed to stop himself from rolling his eyes. With a mouth like that, he wondered how many fights the boy got himself into. He watched as the rebel shifted sideways to defend himself. Tehl eyed the boy's form and adjusted his stance even while he sighed. He didn't want to play this game with a child. He tried to stamp down his frustration with the boy and imagined what Sam would say in his position. "Cease and there will be no repercussions. I will not harm you."

A disbelieving laugh burst out of the lad. "You held me at knife point, so excuse me if I don't believe the words spewing from your lying trap."

"If you don't come willingly things will get rough. I promise you, I won't be the only one bleeding." He bared his bloody teeth. The hood of the young rebel's cloak slipped, revealing part of a smirk. Tehl narrowed his eyes at the cocky boy in front of him. He was much too confident for his own good and someone needed to knock him down a peg or two...though for a lad he sure had odd-shaped lips.

The boy's smirk grew into a full-blown smile, showing all his straight white teeth. "I would love to see you try," he taunted, launching into a sweeping kick.

Tehl stepped to the side, avoiding the kick and onto the lad's cloak as it brushed past him. The boy turned around trapping himself in his own cloak. Tehl seized him by the shirt and pulled him up onto his toes. "Listen here you little cur! Stop this before you get hurt. What would your father say if he saw you?"

The child's smile turned into a sneer, "I wouldn't know. He left my mum before I was born."

Pity pricked Tehl—until a fist drove into his ribs. He tightened his grip on the boy as his breath whooshed out of him. Fine. If the lad was hankering for a fight, then he'd get one. Tehl jammed a knee into the boy's lower stomach. The young rebel bent toward him, letting out a groan of pain, and a sliver of guilt bubbled up at the sound. It faded though as the boy jerked his head up and knocked him in the face. Pain exploded from his nose, his eyes watering. He glimpsed thinned lips before small forearms wedged in between his and smashed outwards breaking his grip.

The young rebel ducked out of his range to assess him, and Tehl knew the exact moment the boy decided to go on the offensive starting with a swift jab. Instinctively, Tehl lifted his forearm to block the blow though he noted for someone so small the lad had a lot of power. He could give it no more thought though as the rebel continued his assault by twisting his hips and throwing a cross punch followed by an uppercut. He blocked each blow with ease, his training paying off. The rebel then hesitated a second, and it was all the opening he needed.

Tehl threw two hooks, putting his body weight into them, yet the lad deftly blocked both blows. And when he jerked his knee upward, the boy curled forward, avoiding his knee, dancing out of his reach. He was impressed; few men his own weight could hold their own against him. He was quicker than Tehl, and he knew how to use that to his advantage. The rebel lashed out with a couple kicks that he swatted away. It took a moment, but Tehl detected a pattern in the boy's movements. He'd first dance in to trade a few blows, before slipping out of his reach and attacking with a few kicks, and it was a good strategy. The fluid way the boy moved suggested that he had training. He needed a good grip on him. But for some odd reason he was enjoying himself.

He followed the boy's movements, expecting his next kick. Sure enough, the rebel attempted to sidekick him. Tehl caught the lad's leg, grabbed the front of his shirt, and pushed him backward into the stone wall, pinning him there.

"You had enough yet, son?"

The answer he received was a snarl and a head to the face, followed by a sickening crack, and pain blasted through his face. Warm liquid gushed down his lips and chin, dripping onto his chest. His nose was broken!

Through his blurry eyes, he could see the boy's mouth grinning at him, smug.

"You sure you had enough?" the young rebel mocked. He didn't know when to stop. The boy tried to head-butt him again, but his elbow blocked the boy's head. The young rebel's head snapped back into the stone wall behind him with a sharp cry.

Damn, he was a little too rough with the child. He spun the dazed boy around to face the wall, so he could inspect the wound and bind the boy's hands. He couldn't analyze it because of the hood, but although blood seeped through it, it was not at an alarming rate. Messy but not too bad. The lad would live.

Blinking his eyes to rid himself of the tears his injury brought, he searched for a length of rope to bind the boy.

When that was done, Tehl then cautiously ran his hands inside the boy's cloak, looking for weapons; he didn't feel like getting stabbed. One dagger at the waist.

The boy slumped against the wall. He didn't want the boy concussed. Tehl jostled the boy. "Stay awake, you will need to be examined by a healer. You hit your head pretty hard." He turned the boy back around and used the wall to help hold the youth up.

"I didn't hit my head. You pushed my head into a stone wall," the boy slurred but somehow still managed a dry tone.

Tehl still hadn't seen the lad's face. It was disrespectful to wear your hood up when someone was talking to you. He reached over and grasped the boy's hood. The boy struggled weakly against him.

"Hold still," he admonished, "I only want to see your face."

At first nothing made sense. What was going on? He expected the round face of a young boy, but an angel stood before him instead. Big emerald eyes glared up at him, framed by long black lashes.

A woman.

Chapter Five

TEHL

He stared and gaped like an idiot.

The boy was a woman.

Tehl leaned closer.

Yep, still a woman.

Wait. The rebellion was using women?

"Get off me!" she yelled, startling him.

He was so close to her, he felt the woman vibrate with anger, yet despite all the blood and yowling, he was entranced. He stared, mapping out high cheekbones, a heart-shaped face, and creamy skin. Somehow one of his hands reached out to touch her smooth skin only to have her teeth snap at him, trying to remove one of his fingers. Tehl looked aghast at the offending appendage. When had it moved?

"Don't touch me!" she screeched.

He focused back on the wriggling woman he was pressed against; his brain finally caught up with his eyes. "You're a woman?" Tehl asked, stupidly.

"Last time I checked," she retorted, hotly. A mocking smile spread across her face. "Not so quick, are you? Let me repeat it for you. I am a woman," she drew out, lengthening the word, so it sounded like *woooomaaan*. "How is that broken nose treating you?" she taunted.

"About as well as yours," he baited, tweaking her button nose.

Her big green eyes immediately welled up. Crystal tears glistened on her black lashes. Tehl frowned feeling like a beast. Why did he do that? An apology was on the tip of his tongue, until saliva exploded across his face. There was nothing more disrespectful than being spat upon. It was not only disgusting but degrading. As Tehl had already been bitten by a rat and his nose broken why not add being spit on to the list?

Meticulously, he wiped the blood and spit from his chin, all the while keeping her pinned, and by the time he finished he had calmed down.

"I have never met anyone stupid enough to spit on me," he said, appraising her. "You don't realize the danger you put yourself in. Lawfully, I have every right to kill you."

Tehl met her green eyes and lifted his hand, wrapping it firmly around her delicate neck. He squeezed once for emphasis. Her face never wavered from the bland, bored expression she was wearing, but the swift staccato of her pulse under his thumb told another story. She pretended she wasn't afraid but her pulse announced her a liar.

She took shallow breaths, her gaze never wavering from his. "You don't want to hurt me. You held yourself back. Several times you could have hurt me but you blocked instead of striking. Also, you pulled your punches. That leads me to the conclusion you need me. I will bet my mum's ruby necklace you won't kill me." She looked up at him with a calculating glint in her eyes. "Your threats don't scare me."

What an interesting female—so unlike the women of his court. "Everyone fears something," he reasoned. "Are you sure death doesn't scare you? What if I squeezed my hand, cutting off your air?"

She didn't so much as twitch.

"Pain for long periods of time?"

Her impassive mask still didn't alter.

"The death or torture of a loved one?"

Still nothing.

Tehl was impressed; most men would have panicked by now. He moved his thumb across her pulse, causing her to jolt. He did it again, and she hissed at him. *Why did she react to that?* She didn't like him touching her at all, but it wasn't just because of the skin on skin contact. It was the *type* of contact.

A plan formed in his mind but he wasn't sure he could pull it off as he had never been much of a womanizer.

"You sure are a pretty little thing. So much beauty hidden under that cloak." He locked eyes with her before raking his eyes down her generous curves. Her attire surprised him. She was wearing brown leather trousers, a linen shirt, and a leather vest. He lazily stared at her leather trousers. No wonder women weren't allowed to wear trousers. The way they hugged her hips and thighs was indecent. She was gorgeous. Too bad she was a traitor.

Tehl had to fight his scowl, he needed to maintain his persona, but it was unfair she was so beautiful. It was just wrong. She should instead have had the common decency to have some gross imperfection. He swallowed the lump in his throat and made a show of ogling her body. Humiliation, anger, and a touch of fear bled through her impenetrable mask.

"*Tsk tsk*, a woman wearing trousers... So naughty," Tehl drawled. "It sends the wrong message to men around you, my dear. It gives them ideas."

In increments, he closed the remaining distance between the two of them, invading her space. He lifted one finger and skimmed it lightly around the shell of her ear and down her neck, touching the v of her cleavage—all the while looking into her eyes. Her's widened, and her heart picked up speed as she panicked.

"GET OFF ME, YOU PIG! DON'T TOUCH ME! HELP! HELP! HELP!" she yelled, her green eyes wild.

He craned his neck toward the entrance of the alley. People scurried by, but no one stopped. Cowards. Tehl looked back to the frantic woman struggling in his arms. He needed her information. She could lie all she wanted, but he had seen the exchange with his own eyes. She hadn't reacted to any of his other forms of intimidation. He would have to scare her into giving it up.

He'd never forced a woman and he never would. Just the idea made him sick to his stomach. But she didn't know him. Tehl's heart was heavy with the knowledge of what he had to do. He morphed his face into a leer and flashed her a lascivious grin. Tehl tightened his grip on her neck and pressed his large body harder into her, sandwiching her between the wall and himself.

He planted his lips softly along the column of her neck, allowing a low hum to escape. A small whimper escaped her lips. Tehl clenched his jaw, disgusted with himself, and forced out the words lodged in his throat. "I could have you here, and now, no one would look twice," he crooned, into her ear.

Her breath quickened, and her heart raced against his chest. He felt like a total lecher and a creep. At that moment, he was. Tehl turned his head and skimmed her jaw with the tip of his nose. She smelled like cinnamon. Why did she smell like cinnamon?

He shook himself out of his stupor and focused on the task at hand. "This is what you will do." He nuzzled her once more, and then leaned back, placing a finger beneath her chin, forcing her eyes to meet his. Her glassy green eyes brimmed with tears almost crumbling his resolve. Tehl hardened his heart against her and gazed at her evenly. "You will come along like a good little girl, quiet and docile. No more kicking, screaming, or head-butting. If you do that, then I won't leave you damaged and broken in this hellhole."

She jerked her chin out of his grasp and looked away. Why did acting like a monster get things done? The world should not be like this. Sometimes, like now, he felt so dirty and low.

"Do you accept?" He purred in her ear, hoping she didn't call his bluff.

She trembled in his grasp and dipped her chin once. That was what he was looking for. Tehl released her face and moved his beaten body back a hair, just enough for her to take deep breaths without their chests touching.

She shivered, but fire still glinted in her eyes. She would cause him more trouble, despite what she'd told him. He grabbed her biceps and pulled her from the wall to the center of the alley.

"How can I trust you won't hurt me if I do as you ask?" she demanded, eyes filled with hate.

She deserved reassurance, and he could give her that much. Tehl looked down at her, "I give you my word you won't be hurt when I take you to the palace."

She barked out a laugh while a tear trekked a path down her dirty cheek. "You're a liar and a lecher." She looked at him, disgusted. "If you take me, you won't like the outcome. Someone will miss me; you can bet on that. I promise you will regret the day you were born because my brothers, crooked as they may be, will hunt you down."

He forced a chuckle since, even tied up and helpless, she was making threats. Raising his eyebrows, he smiled. "You're not in a position to be making threats. Threatening your future king is hazardous for your health."

Her reaction did not disappoint. She stilled, and what color she had, drained from her face. He slipped his hands up her arms and settled them on her shoulders. "I imagine you are quite attached to your neck, and so am I, if I am honest." She shuddered at his comment. "So pipe down," he added.

"You disgust me," she spat and wrinkled her nose at him, like he smelled offensive. Thinking about it, he probably did. This whole situation had him sweating like a pig.

"Your father has left us all to starve. I *had* hoped his son would make a better king but here the crown prince stands, threatening to rape me if I don't give him information on something that I am not part of." She leaned toward him, anger sparkling in her eyes. "Your mother was an amazing woman. If she saw you today, she would be appalled!"

She flinched back, closing her eyes, when he lifted his hand toward her. He watched as she swallowed thickly. Did she think he would hit her? He frowned. He would never hit a woman. She was right though. His mother would be ashamed if she could see him frightening the poor girl.

"You know nothing about my m-mother—" he stuttered as her lips parted on a breath, capturing his attention. He knew he shouldn't, but he couldn't help himself. He grabbed her face and gently brushed his thumb across her bottom lip. They were so smooth and soft.

What was wrong with him?

Tehl went to withdraw his thumb when she lunged at him, biting his finger. He cursed and ripped his thumb out of her mouth, shaking his hand. "Gods, woman, why would you do that?" Tehl inspected the small wound. There were actually teeth marks.

Her eyes popped open, and she grinned at him. She arched an eyebrow at him and howled with laughter. What was so funny? Was it the blow to the head affecting her? Was she touched in the head?

"What's wrong with you?" he asked perplexed.

"Why *wouldn't* I bite you is the question."

He was not going there; he deserved it. Her information would be worth all the pain. Tehl eyed his feisty captive, they had wasted enough time and needed to leave. The mutinous look on her face promised a fight. He needed to take her by surprise. Tehl struck and slung her over his shoulder before she knew what happened. He grunted as a sharp pain shot through it and down his arm, making his hand tingle. When had he injured it?

From her new position, she let out an undignified little shriek that gave way to cursing. His lips curled at her creative verbiage.

She thrashed, making it difficult to keep a hold on her. Nothing about today would be easy. He lifted a hand and swatted her on the butt. "Knock it off, or I will end up dropping you on your head. If you hadn't tried to escape, I would've let you walk. You and I both know you won't be reasonable." More curses floated his way. Guess that was his answer.

He gingerly picked his way to the entrance of the alley, keeping his eyes on the treacherous cobbles beneath his feet. A burning pain in the middle of his back jerked him from his thoughts. He'd only experienced pain like that once before in his life, and it came from a very nasty horse.

"Did you just bite me?" he growled, incredulous.

"You took all my weapons and tied my hands. What was I supposed to do?" she mumbled into his back.

The bloody woman had bitten him.

"Lord, you're more harpy than woman!"

"If you let me go you'd never have to deal with me again," she reasoned, her tone syrupy sweet though she was anything but.

"I thought women were sweet and gentle." He wondered out

loud. "What kind of woman are you, anyway? Running around in trousers? What ever happened to being a lady?"

"Never said I was a lady."

He snickered. She was right there. "Well, with a vocabulary like yours you could make sailors blush."

Having reached the end of the alley he scanned the busy intersection, searching for his men. A familiar laugh drew his attention to a group sitting on barrels, playing dice. His brother's blue eyes met his. Tehl jerked his chin, signaling it was time to go.

Sam stood with a flourish, tipping his hat to his dice buddies, and meandered over to them.

"Did you get what we came for?" Sam assessed the bundle draped over Tehl's shoulder and glanced back at him with confusion. "It's smaller than I expected."

"I assure you we got *more* than we bargained for." He said wryly. "Look for yourself."

Sam walked around and lifted the woman's face and then bit out an oath.

"My God, Tehl, what are you doing with a woman?! Did you do that to her face?" Then in a soft tone he added, "Are you all right, sweetheart?"

Tehl felt her shake her head: no. *Ah, here comes the sob story.*

"That precious woman," Tehl interjected, "is the rebel you sent me after, and she gave as good as she got."

"No, I am not all right," she cried over him. "This man has threatened to hurt my family or torture me if I don't give him information. But I don't know what he is talking about," she sobbed into his back. "I want to go home! Please help me! Don't let him take me." She pleaded rather loudly.

What a world class performance.

Sam walked back around and eyed her hog-tied hands, then lifted his gaze to Tehl's. "What's your name sweetheart?" Sam asked.

"It's...it's Ruby," she stammered out.

He had broken her nose, threatened her, and had basically accosted her yet she didn't shed a blooming tear until the end, and he suspected it was more from anger than pain. Now she was a completely different creature. Apparently, besides fighting like a she-demon and cursing like a sailor, she was also an actress.

He opened his mouth in defense, but closed it as he caught sight of Sam's face. His brother was not buying it. Sam quirked up one side of his mouth and raised an eyebrow. There was no fooling Sam. An amazing actor she may be, but he was sure his brother was an even better one. He was not the spymaster for nothing.

Sam made a show of studying her bound wrists. "What happened to your hands, darling? They have cuts all over them!" he probed as he ran a finger over her bloody knuckles.

"I was trying to protect myself from him." She sniffed.

Tehl distinctly remembered it was she who had first attacked. *He* had done everything in his power to keep them from fighting.

Sam lingered on her hands a moment longer and then continued to investigate. "Did you not have a weapon to protect yourself?"

"I did! But he disarmed me," she wailed, her whole-body shuddering with her cries.

Unbelievable. "Her blade is in my belt."

Sam reached into his cloak and plucked her dagger from his

waist, inspecting it. He ran his finger along the detail of the worn hilt and circled back to her, remarking on the blade. "What a unique dagger. It's well made. Why, the attention to detail is stunning! How did you come by it?"

She sucked in a breath, trying to control her crying. "I took it from someone."

"Now, I don't believe that." Tehl heard the triumph in Sam's voice. "Because I have also seen daggers like this on all the other rebels I've come across. You are not what you seem darling. Only one thing's certain: you are a traitor to the Crown and dangerous."

The wailing and sobbing stopped. "You learn to be tough when you live on the streets. Why don't you come closer and I will show you how dangerous I can be?"

"No thank you. I like all my body parts just the way they are. Now that's all squared away, Ruby, we can get you settled in your new abode!"

"Hell no!" she screeched at Sam, struggling again.

"Would you please do something about that?" Tehl complained, trying to keep the bothersome wench in his arms. "My ears are about to bleed from all this shrieking."

The girl sneezed and then demanded, "What did you blow in my face?"

Sam ignored her question and sauntered back into view, brushing his hands off. His brother winked at him and patted one of the many pouches he always carried at his waist. Tehl would bet his next pair of boots it was Ashwanganda powder.

"How much longer does she have?" he asked in a low voice.

"What! What was that? Did you poison me? Put me down!" Even

as her yelling continued, her body went limp. "Oh God, you drugged me. You are both going to regret..." she trailed off like she'd forgotten what she was talking about.

And she probably had, courtesy of the Ashwanganda.

She pressed her face into his back and rubbed her cheek against it. "You have hard muscles, like a rock," she said in a sing-song voice.

Sam smirked at him. "Not one word, Sam. Not one word."

"*Sam*. What a nice name," she chirped. "Is it short for Samuel? That is a strong handsome name," she slurred while poking him in the back with her nose. "I want a nap; I am so tired."

She would give him whiplash with her quick subject changes. Her body finally succumbed to the sedative and went limp against him. For someone so tiny she had weight to her. Tehl carefully pulled her off his shoulder and into his arms, tucking one arm beneath her knees and one around her shoulders.

Sam stepped closer, inspecting her face. "She is a beauty underneath all the blood, bruises, and grime."

Tehl's stomach soured. He was the cause of each cut and bruise marring her relaxed features. His brother cleared his throat, and Tehl raised his eyes to Sam's face. He lifted an eyebrow in question and, after a beat, asked, "Well, what is it? Why are you staring?"

Sam flashed a blinding grin, "Seems you're studying her a little closely, brother," he drawled. "Me thinks you might like her."

Tehl scoffed at this ridiculous accusation. He'd only just met the woman. Pretty she may be, but she was also a criminal.

"You know me better than that Sam. The fairer sex only cause trouble." His gaze bounced to her, then settled back on his brother.

"I feel bad I hurt her. Look at her bloody face. No woman, no matter how trying they are, deserves the beating she received."

"Why is she so battered?"

He cleared his throat. "I thought she was a man."

Sam scoffed. "She doesn't look like a man. Your eyesight needs checking."

"She disguised herself," Tehl defended.

Sam studied her face first, then his. "She isn't the only one with a few marks. She put up a hell of a fight."

"That she did." His eyebrows furrowed. "The moves she executed weren't anything she'd have learned on the street. She had training. I've never come across her fighting style before. If she'd had her blade, I'm sure I'd have come out of this with a stab wound or two."

"I thought only men did the stabbing," his brother deadpanned.

Of course, Sam would make an inappropriate joke right now.

Tehl grunted and shot his brother a crooked grin. "There's something wrong with your mind.

Sam's serious face shifted to a mischievous grin. "What can I say? It's a gift."

"Not a gift I want." It still boggled his mind that they were from the same parents when they were so different. "I still say you were adopted."

"Oh! You always say the nicest things," Sam tittered, sending him a coy smile that disturbed him.

Gavriel approached them, tipping his straw hat back to reveal an amused grin. "You never cease to surprise me Sam."

"Whatever do you mean, cousin?"

Gav rolled his eyes at Sam's innocent expression. "I hate to break up this entertaining exchange but people are getting restless." Gav nodded toward the girl. "We need to leave before the urchin wakes up."

Tehl surveyed the people surrounding them. Most were casting scared and nervous glances in their direction. A few young men stood grouped together, glaring their way. The last thing they needed was the hotheads starting a fight.

"Lead on, then."

Sam slapped him on the shoulder, gave a short nod to Gavriel who turned, making eye contact with their men among the crowd. Simultaneously the Elite gathered in loose formation around them. Gav nodded once more, and they began their journey home. Although Tehl noted several concerned looks thrown at the unconscious girl carried like a sack of potatoes, no one dared approach.

Tehl turned his attention to the man at his side. Gavriel's eyes never stayed in one place. They were always sharp, ever alert to potential dangers. Gav was an interesting study in contradictions. He was a soldier through and through, but he also had immense talents in healing and the sciences. There was none more fierce on the battlefield, yet he never lost his temper and had a compassionate heart.

Tehl considered Gav a brother, for his cousin had been raised with them since childhood. Gav also favored his mother's side of the family so the black hair, straight nose, and wide shoulders meant he resembled Tehl more than his actual brother. But Gav inherited what he didn't: the amethyst colored eyes that ran in his mum's side of the family.

Tehl squinted at the ridiculous thing atop his cousin's head. Gav had yet to rid himself of the absurd straw hat adorning his head like a giant bird's nest. He couldn't help but stare. His cousin's unusual-colored eyes flickered over to him, and a small smile touched Gav's mouth.

"Staring into my eyes, cousin?" Gav teased. "And so intense… If I didn't know any better, I'd think you were mooning over me."

Sam sniggered at this comment.

"Have you *ever* seen me moon over someone?" Tehl asked with a grin, only half serious, scouting the area, noting anyone who looked suspicious. You could never be too careful.

"Honestly? You don't know how to moon, neither can you woo, seduce, nor charm anyone."

Tehl considered that for a moment. There was truth to that. His people skills were abhorrent. He didn't know whether he was insulted or impressed his cousin knew him so well, so Tehl settled on narrowing his eyes and glaring. Gav shrugged a shoulder and continued his survey of their surroundings.

"Hey now," Sam broke in, "no need to point out the obvious. He needs a little training from yours truly." Sam pointed to himself.

Now they were ganging up on him.

Tehl glanced at the Elite who were pretending they weren't listening in. Nosy bastards. He shifted the girl in his arms. "I am the only one with a woman in his arms."

Sam choked out a laugh and held up a finger. "But you had to render her unconscious to get her to stay with you so…she doesn't count. If you would listen to my advice more women would stick around."

Tehl attempted to infuse some of Sam's attitude in his voice and failed. "I don't need any of that. All I have to do is snap my fingers and they come running." He sounded like an idiot.

"Right," Sam drew the word out. "Because that's how women desire to be spoken to: I am man, I drag you by hair to cave, you like." Sam dropped his shoulders like a wild man grunting.

A short laugh burst out of Gav. "That doesn't work in real life, although if it did, it would be heaven, pure heaven," Gav replied with a twinkle in his eye. "Life would be so much simpler."

"Ah don't lie, you haven't taken a woman to bed since your wife passed," Tehl stated, looking down at the sleeping woman in his arms. Silence greeted him. He whipped his head up, eyes darting between Sam and Gav.

Both his brother and cousin were looking at him, silent. His eyes continued to bounce back and forth between them as he tried to figure out what he'd said wrong. He'd stated the absolute truth. Gavriel didn't care about women anymore. After his wife died, it was like the fairer sex didn't even exist to him. They might flirt and smile, but he never noticed. When propositioned, it seemed to shock him, almost like he had no clue why they would be interested.

Tehl opened his mouth, preparing to ask what he had done, when Sam cut in.

"Are you incapable of watching what comes out of your mouth? Why would you say that to Gav?" Sam hissed, anger evident. "You will have some serious issues as king if you can't learn to be more diplomatic and at least a little sensitive."

Tehl grimaced as he took in the pain Gav was trying, but failing, to hide. It clicked then why his words upset his cousin. He cursed his ignorance. Gavriel still missed Emma, so the subject was a painful wound which his words had scraped open again.

"I'm sorry Gav," he offered, remorse coloring the words. "I know how much you loved Emma. We all miss her and wish she was still here." Tehl cleared his throat to get rid of the large lump lodged there.

All three of them grew up with Emma and loved her dearly. They all met her one day as children. She was working in the stables at the time, and he remembered how she threatened each one of them with the loss of a limb if they *ever* hurt one of 'her' horses. After that, they'd grown attached to the fiery girl. She may have been plain in appearance, but the light she had inside shone so bright that all who knew her thought her lovely. It was Gavriel she had adored though, from the very moment she laid eyes on him. The law for royalty to marry common blood had worked out for them. Everything had been right...until her accident. It broke them all when she died. It was devastating to lose Queen Ivy and Emma so close together.

Gav gave him a sad smile, which spoke in itself of his immense loss. The hurt his friend was experiencing pained him, adding to the weight he already bore.

"I miss her Tehl. She was it for me. And you're right, there are no other women and there won't ever be." He took a deep breath and glared at the cobbles beneath their feet. "I can't believe Emma left me alone to care for the child. A little girl no less! I know nothing about her care. She...she needs her mother. And so do I."

All three fell silent when Gav's voice broke.

Isa. Gavriel's child. He couldn't remember the last time he saw the little girl. Tehl sent Gav a curious look. "When did you see Isa last?"

Gav tilted his head back, staring at the sky. "It's been six months since I've been to my keep." He paused. "I need to take a leave soon and go visit."

"Six months, Gav? You haven't seen Isa in *six months*?" Tehl asked, shifting the unconscious woman in his arms. If it had been him he was sure he wouldn't want to miss a single moment with his daughter, all the more so had she lost her mother.

"You're missing everything! Your keep is only a two-hour ride from here." Sam's censure was loud and clear.

Gav turned back to them. "Don't judge me, Sam," he said evenly. "You don't understand how hard it is to go back there. It kills me. Everything there reminds me of Emma, most of all Isa."

That Tehl related to. Didn't the palace feel empty and desolate without his mum? He couldn't imagine losing a spouse. An idea then struck Tehl. Why none of them had considered it baffled him.

"You could bring her here to live. Then you could spend time with her without all the haunting memories of your home." The more he pondered it, the more Tehl liked that idea. He would love to have his little cousin close by, perhaps it would even sooth his own heart's wounds.

Gav looked at him thoughtfully. "That's a good suggestion; I will consider it. My only worry is removing her from somewhere she's already familiar with. Her mum's death has confused her enough as it is."

Sam speared Gavriel with a serious look. "I bet she is more confused that she's lost you *as well* as her mum."

Gavriel's shoulders slumped, and silence descended on them as they each drifted off into their own thoughts. Just thinking about sweet little Isa made him feel lighter, more buoyant. She had been a precious baby girl with big violet eyes like her papa and unruly red hair like her mum. He didn't want a wife but he liked children. Would they look like him? He shook his head at the thoughts he had no time for and headed toward the dungeon on the west side of his castle.

It was time to show the rebel her new home.

Chapter Six

TEHL

As Tehl approached the door, two guards saluted and opened it for him. When he crossed the threshold, a flutter of movement had him glancing down at his unconscious captive to find green eyes scrutinizing him.

"It's awake," he called to his brother and cousin.

"And it has a name," she snapped. "What did you do? I still can't feel my arms or legs…" Seeming to realize she was still in his arms she demanded, "Put. Me. DOWN. You have no right to hold me."

Gav's eyebrows rose to his hairline. "Correct me if I am wrong, but I was under the impression that attacking the crown prince is against the law." Gavriel stared, daring her to argue with him. She glared at all of them as they continued their descent.

"Well, I didn't know he was the crown prince." She huffed out an annoyed breath. "I thought he was a thief and I was protecting myself. Why aren't my legs working?" she asked again.

If only it was her mouth she couldn't feel. "It will wear off with no permanent damage," he supplied, hoping it would quiet her.

"I am so grateful there will be no permanent damage, my prince," she mocked, lip curling.

What a terribly vexing wench. If she wanted to irritate him then he'd return the favor. Tehl squeezed her against his chest, lowering his head. A low hum rumbled in his throat as he grazed her temple with the tip of his nose.

"I like the way you say 'my prince.' Say it again for me." Tehl lifted his head and took in her reaction. Her face was pinched and her lips clamped shut so tightly they were turning white.

Well that shut her up.

A smile played about his mouth as he continued, "Shall we go and explore your new home then, my love?"

"I'd be delighted, my pet," she hissed through clenched teeth.

"Pet... Interesting word choice. What do you think about that, Sam?"

His brother glanced over, biting back a grin. "There are so many things I could say, but alas—" Sam sighed. "I suppose I shall control myself."

Gav scoffed, "There's a first time for everything."

The girl's brows wrinkled in confusion. "What's wrong with the word 'pet'?"

Tehl arched a brow. "Would you like me to show you?"

Her face cleared as understanding dawned and her eyes

widened in horror. She lifted her chin. "Not on your life."

The little rebel stiffened in his arms as Sam coughed—a lame attempt to cover his snicker.

Having reached the base of the stairs, they approached a sturdy-looking desk where the Keeper was scribbling away furiously, their boots splashing in shallow pools covering the stone floor.

The Keeper, an older man by the name of Jeffry had a wicked sense of humor and Tehl considered him a close friend. The man had a scruffy gray and white beard, and deep wrinkles bracketed his charcoal eyes. As he was rarely outdoors, his skin was so pale he almost resembled a specter.

At their approach, he abandoned his scratching, meeting Tehl's eyes, before sliding his gaze to the woman in his arms. He sat back and laced his fingers across his stomach as they stopped before his desk.

Tehl gave the older man a warm smile and lifted the girl in his arms. "I have a new one for you, Jeffry."

Jeffry's gaze settled back on his new prisoner, and he quirked an eyebrow in question. "Well, isn't this a surprise," Jeffry commented, staring at Sage with interest. "I don't believe I've had the pleasure of housing a woman down here. It's a delight to meet you missy." Jeffry stood as he spoke, his chair creaking. He reached over his wooden desk and gently patted the woman's arm.

He then pinned Tehl with his off-putting eyes. "You're positive you've got the right one? This isn't fit for women."

"She's the rebel we were after this morning. You can imagine my surprise as well when I realized it was she we came for."

Jeffry continued to eye him and then addressed the girl. "Are you dangerous, little miss?"

"Come nearer, and I'll show you," the rebel purred.

Jeffry grinned. "Well. This shall be interesting, my dear. Welcome." He then opened one tomb atop his desk and dragged a finger down the page.

"Jacque," Jeffry called, lifting his head. "Please put her in cell two-zero-eight." He rubbed his silver eyebrows and inquired: "What was your name, miss? It's imperative I keep my records well organized and up to date. I'm sure you understand."

The rebel stayed silent.

"It's Ruby," Sam offered.

The Keeper jotted down her name and swept his arm in a grand gesture toward the sharp-faced Jacque. "Jacque will show you to your new home! Be seeing you soon, my dear." The Keeper then ridiculously fluttered his fingers at Ruby as Tehl departed with her.

Jacque peeled himself from the wall, moving passed them as the stoic guard led them deeper into the dungeon.

"I am not your 'dear'!" Ruby called over his shoulder.

"Always a pleasure," the old man called back, adding to himself, "She is delightful. Absolutely delightful."

Tehl allowed himself a small smile at Jeffry's antics. He was eccentric, but he was a hard worker and extremely loyal. The Keeper had been one of his father's closest companions. Jeffry was present at both princes' births. The Keeper had sat with his father outside their mother's chamber, helping to calm him while he awaited his sons. Previously a member of the Elite under King Marq, his age had eventually prevented him from fulfilling his duties. Although he could have retired to his keep, he instead opted to continue his service to the Crown here saying that although he wasn't as able as he was in his youth, he still had a lot to offer. And he was right. The Keeper was one of the few he considered family.

Tehl watched as the girl absorbed her new surroundings. Iron bars and mossy stone encased them. Each cell was small, sparse, and drab; either cloaked in shadow or shrouded with complete darkness. Some cells boasted a window but that was not necessarily a blessing. Hearing the crashing waves outside and knowing freedom was so close yet unattainable seemed like another kind of torture. It was a depressing place to spend one's time.

Jacque had stopped ahead of them and was unlocking a cell, swinging open the door with a screech. A rusted two-zero-eight hung above the door, and Tehl gauged its interior dimensions at around nine feet by nine. Its only contents were an old cot and a bucket in one corner. In the center of the floor, emitting a putrid stench, was a sturdy metal grate.

Tehl stepped through the doorway, carrying the small rebel like a bride over a threshold. Her eyes found his, pleading with him not to cage her in here. A flicker of uncertainty gave him pause.

What if I'm wrong?

He mentally slapped himself for these thoughts. No matter the lies she spouted, it did nothing to change what he'd seen with own eyes; she was a rebel supporter.

He strolled in and unceremoniously deposited her on the cot, quickly exiting the cell. He allowed the cell door to shut behind him, ringing with a sense of finality, before turning around.

Tehl stood with the three men, rolling his shoulders, and shook out his arms as a million pinpricks traveled down them. They had fallen asleep holding her for so long. The men regarded the motionless woman, waiting, but she only stared at the ceiling blankly. Tehl had expected a lot more shrieking and cursing based on her prior behavior, but she stayed silent.

He gripped the iron bars and cleared his throat. Her green eyes dispassionately wandered to his chest, lacking their previous fire. Why wasn't she looking him in the eye? "Ruby, I would think long and hard about your life choices. If you help us, things will be a lot easier for you. If not…" He paused long enough for her to meet his eyes. "There will be consequences for your actions."

She stared at him stonily. "You promised not to hurt me. Are you so dishonorable to go back on your word?" Her gaze drifted over the other men. "You ought to be ashamed of yourselves, taking part in this madness. Do you take pleasure in his unjust actions and threats?"

None of them responded to her bait. The girl's attention then swung back to him. As he suspected, she was quite the actress. Here she was trying to manipulate them from her cell. Tehl detested lying, and it was all she'd done since first opening her big mouth. Had she been honest, even once, things might have been different.

"The devil's in the details, love." Her eyes narrowed. "I said no harm would come to you *when* I took you to the palace, not *while* you're *staying* here."

"Staying?" She let out an unladylike snort. "You talk as if I'm some honored guest and not a prisoner trapped in the dark belly of your home."

"It's rather like we're living together. Don't most men keep their mistresses hidden?" Tehl needled.

Her pale cheeks colored to an alarming shade of red, her ire raised. She closed her eyes and blew out a breath, dismissing them. Her impassive mask slid back in place.

"Be seeing you soon."

Still nothing.

She was in her own little world. He would need to make it difficult for her to ignore him at their next interaction.

Tehl pushed off the bars, nodding to Jacque. The wiry guard took the lead, guiding them through the dungeon. Its design ensured those attempting escape would have a hard time accomplishing the feat, most likely losing their way among its various twists and turns. Gavriel's steps echoed behind him yet his brother's steps were noticeably absent. Sam moved like a griffin in the darkness, silent and predatory. When they reached Jeffry's desk, Jacque strolled to his usual position behind it, leaning against the wall.

Tehl nodded to them both before heading back up the stairway. He needed to get away. The rebel wench was still messing with his mind. Pushing up the stairs he broke into a run, thighs burning as he burst through the door like the devil was on his tail. In the dim courtyard, his breath seesawed out of his chest.

Why can't things be black and white? He hated gray areas.

Sam and Gav caught up with him, faces showing their confusion. Odd, since nothing surprised Sam anymore. What had he done wrong this time?

"Why are you looking at me like that?"

Sam opened and closed his mouth a couple times before saying anything. "I'm not sure where to start." His brother sighed, covering his face with his large hand, and glanced at his cousin. "Do you want to go first, or shall I?"

Gav grunted. "You."

Sam held up one finger. "First, I have never heard you call a woman 'my love'. Not in jest and not in seriousness. Brother, you hardly even *talk* to women, let alone bestow an endearment." Sam shook his head. "Of course, you'd start with our minx of a prisoner, who is guilty as sin."

He gave his brother a black look. "I meant nothing by it. I was only trying to irritate her."

Sam looked at him skeptically, holding up a second finger. "Second, did or did I not hear you flirt with her?" He turned to Gav for confirmation.

"Yep that happened," Gav drawled.

Tehl blinked. "No, I didn't." What were they talking about?

"I've only heard you use innuendo a handful of times our entire lives, and I have *never* seen you flirt, not even once." Gav grimaced. "It was odd."

"Ass." Not his best retort.

"No more than you were today," Gav quipped.

"Touché," Tehl conceded.

"Third," Sam interjected, holding up three fingers, "you were acting out of character. Why were you playing the lecher? *None of us* have touched a woman without invitation. Why would you make her think such?"

"She wasn't afraid," Tehl explained. "She wouldn't stop fighting me, though I tried everything. I tried to be peaceful and speak with her. When that didn't work, I threatened her and her loved ones but still *nothing*. I had to do something." Both men were visibly upset by his explanation. He pointed a finger, first to Sam, then Gav. "Don't you two give me those looks and don't be hypocrites. I've observed both of you interrogate, and I know some of the things you've said or done because you understood it necessary for *them* to cooperate."

Sam opened his mouth, but the look on Tehl's face must have made his brother reconsider his comment.

"No, Sam. She is *still* our enemy, regardless of her gender. Everything she represents threatens our families and the safety of the people in our kingdom. I did what I had to. I used what scared her to our advantage."

"So, you're saying you want us to threaten to ravish her?"

His brother locked eyes with him. Sam was serious. It was times like these when he remembered just how dangerous Sam could be. He would do anything to protect Aermia and its people.

"No, Sam." Frustrated, Tehl kicked a rock with the toe of his boot. "I scared her by crowding her and leering, but that's as far as I want to take it. The entire time, I was only trying to scare her into cooperating, but my stomach churned. When I think about it, I feel sick," he confessed. Her terrified eyes flashed through his mind. Boredom, shock, irritation—yes, all of those. But never fear. He lifted his head and stared at the inner wall, eyes distant. "We don't need to give the rebels any more reasons to hate us. We may need that information but not enough to incite a riot over our tactics."

"You think that could happen?" Gav asked.

"I do. I have never met a woman with skills like hers. No doubt someone will miss her and perhaps already has. I think it wise for one of us to always have an eye on her. We need to make certain none of the men cross a line they shouldn't."

Both nodded in agreement.

"It's what makes us different from the criminals; we have honor and we have morals." Gav then turned his head and stared pointedly at Sam. "Well, at least some of us have morals."

Sam stared right back and, to Tehl's shock and amusement, a slight blush crept up his cheeks. "Hey now, I have morals. I do my duty as commander, I am excellent at being sneaky, I treat women right, and I *always* respected my mother." Sam crossed his arms, mock-glaring at them both.

"I think you and I have a very different view of morals, my friend." Gav said lightly, regarding the guards moving through the training yard and barracks.

Sam retorted something but their voices soon faded to a dull buzz as he tuned them out. The sun had already begun its descent behind the palace, throwing jagged shadows across the courtyard. Nothing had gone as planned today and while his head throbbed, his entire body was a giant bruise.

He tuned back into their conversation, looking their way. Apparently, they were still bickering about morals with Sam losing. The corner of his mouth lifted as he listened to them. They argued like an old married couple.

"So…" He began, raising his voice so they'd hear him over their debate. They both paused, looking at him expectantly. "I will go and get cleaned up. In the meantime, I'll leave Jeffry to take care of that Ruby girl until we're ready for her interrogation." He turned his back to them, already starting toward the palace when Sam's words stopped him.

"You mean the rebel, right?" Sam asked.

Tehl's brow furrowed. *What?* He peered over his shoulder. "That's what I said."

"No, you said Ruby."

"That's her name, is it not?" Tehl intoned. A flicker of annoyance ran through him at the delay of his warm bath. "Out with it, Sam."

"In using her name you're establishing a connection to her." Sam gave him a searching look. "She's nothing but a wealth of information. An asset. A prisoner. Maybe you need to keep your distance."

He didn't care if Sam handled this. That meant one less thing on his list to take care of. "If that's what you think is best, Commander," Tehl murmured, emphasizing Sam's title. He shifted impatiently from one foot to another. "Are we done?"

"Yeah, we are. Go take a bath. Lord! You reek. I can smell you from here." Sam wrinkled his nose. "What in God's name did you get into, anyway?"

Tehl sent a rude gesture Sam's way, nodded to Gav, and made his way back to the palace.

Chapter Seven

SAMUEL

"He doesn't know what he is getting into with that woman," Gav declared as they watched Tehl limp his way to the palace. "She's a distraction he doesn't need."

Sam couldn't agree more; the girl was heaps of trouble wrapped in a tantalizing package, one that even his brother had noticed.

"She's dangerous, that one, and in more ways than I can count. Tonight, I'll be having a little chat with her to get a feel for what we're working with here. I have a feeling she isn't the type to break easily. It'll take just the right touch."

Gav turned his startling purple eyes on him. "If you hurt her, he will be livid," Gav admonished him. "If you don't tread carefully, this will come back on us, you understand that?"

Sam nodded, but Gav's words rankled. He wasn't a bumbling idiot or wet behind the ears. Sam clasped his hands to his chest and smirked at his cousin. "I don't know what you're talking about. Women love me! She'll be putty in my hands in no time." He pasted on a smug grin full of male confidence.

"She's not your typical woman. I bet she will see through anything you throw her way."

"We shall see about that, we shall see. Care to bet on it?"

Gav rolled his eyes and followed Tehl's example, heading back to the palace.

Sam rubbed his hands together. He eagerly anticipated this new challenge. Puzzles were his specialty, and Ruby was a puzzle that could solve more than a few of their problems.

Chapter Eight

SAGE

The clank of the closing door reverberated in her mind. Any freedom had left through it.

Sage was trapped in a stone box.

A wet stone box.

What to do now? Her thoughts whirled at a frantic pace, flipping through ideas. She squeezed her eyes shut, trying to regain her cool. She could only thank the stars she had nothing condemning on her when she was taken.

When the prince first grabbed her, she had thought he was an everyday pickpocket. Sage wasn't even concerned; it wasn't until he'd started in about information she felt something was amiss. After that, it became clear she needed to escape. And yet, despite her vast skill set, there was only so much she could do against a man who outweighed her with a hundred pounds of muscle.

She hadn't doubted herself before, often going head to head with men in training. Sage never needed to, she always succeeded. Dueling with the prince, though, gave her a little more perspective. It also bruised her ego. Rafe had told her there would always be someone who was more skilled, trained, or stronger than her. The key, however, was to be more *prepared* than your opponent in those instances and she had met no one who fell into that category until today.

Sage opened her eyes and stared at the drab ceiling above her. If the crown prince had his way, she would become well acquainted with this cell. And yet...she had been so captured by his dark blue eyes she'd stared into them several times. The crown prince was dangerously handsome. Wide shoulders, broad muscled chest and dimples...the dang dimples. Such a shame his insides didn't match his exterior.

Even thinking of his behavior made her shudder. He was more animal than man. Sage couldn't imagine what would happen if he ascended the throne. It was a frightening thought.

Sage closed her eyes and exhaled a long sigh, realizing she couldn't even wiggle. She'd humiliated the prince, he wasn't likely to let it go. Men were fragile creatures when it came to their egos so he would come for her; it was only the matter of *when*. What was their plan? That question concerned her. She cringed, remembering his nose running along her neck. Her heart pounded, breath seizing, as the unpleasant memory flashed in her mind.

Calm down, she commanded herself, *he's not even here.*

She took a measured breath through her nose and held it, letting it out slowly to release some of her tension and continued until her heart had slowed.

After a time, feeling crept back into her digits and Sage tried to move her feet and hands. The best she could manage was a slight wiggling of her toes and fingers. Sage clenched her jaw, frustrated at being so vulnerable. She hated it.

What drug had they used? She hoped it wouldn't have any permanent effects. Sage knew they probably wanted her undamaged. But one could never be too sure. The Crown was dangerous. Most likely they needed her healthy, so they'd have a better chance of getting her to talk. It was a brilliant move, but it wouldn't work on her. They hadn't been trained by Rafe. He had shown her that pain was in the mind. Now, for the most part, she could turn it off. Despite this, a million what-ifs played out in her mind.

Focus Sage. Focus on what's most important.

Trust. She needed to trust the training she'd received, she could get through this. Her first task was to stop worrying and assess the situation. What resources were at her disposal? Sage flopped her head to the side, scrutinizing her temporary home.

Just terrific.

Her surroundings were depressing. Green lichen covered the damp gray stone walls and ceiling. A large grate in the center of the floor emitted a foul odor, and a faint gurgling sounded below it. A lone, wooden bucket sat in one corner, most likely to piss in. Her fingers twitched against the rickety old cot, she was surprised it hadn't collapsed beneath her.

Having completed the first step, she moved on to the second. Find a weapon. She could probably pull apart the cot and make a pike or club of sorts. Sage chuckled darkly. She didn't need a weapon, she *was* one.

Sage moved on and assessed her cage again, this time searching for any weaknesses. A tiny window faced the sea, gracing the room with a small beam of sunlight. There was no way she would fit. And even if she could, she would have to figure out how to deal with the five-hundred-foot drop into the sea below. Her gaze dropped to the grate—that, as well, was too small.

Last, Sage examined the iron bars making up the door and one wall. Stupid things didn't even have the decency to sport a rusty spot or two. The damn thing looked impenetrable, and it heightened her frustration. She wouldn't be breaking out tonight.

Pinpricks rushed up her arms causing her hands to clench. Relief swept through her at the movement. Finally, she was regaining mobility, and as soon as she recovered full movement she'd do a more thorough inspection of her cell.

Time crawled as she waited for more feeling to return in her extremities, counting the stones in her ceiling. How much time had passed? Minutes? Hours? Sage had no clue. After a time, her rambling thoughts were interrupted when a horrendous throbbing began in her head and pulsed along her body. The drug had been a blessing in disguise as it had been blocking all her pain. Sage rolled her neck but, rather than helping, dizziness assaulted her.

Get up Sage, you need to get up.

After a couple tries she managed to sit, the room spinning around her. She braced a hand on the stone wall when nausea slammed into her. Saliva flooded her mouth just before she heaved until her stomach was empty.

Once her stomach settled, she tried lifting her head again. Even the small movement was painful now that she wasn't focused on throwing up. Sage gingerly touched her bruised face, trying to map out her injuries. When she brushed the bridge of her nose, she cringed. It was swollen and crooked.

"Well, that's just great. A broken nose," she muttered to the empty room.

She continued her exploration, discovering a bruised cheekbone, a cut in her eyebrow, and a fat lip. She ran a hand along the back of her head and jerked in pain. Sage examined her hand: blood stained her fingertips. That explained the dizzy spells.

Gritting her teeth, she continued, next probing her ribs with her bloody fingers. Each time she pressed down, her breath whooshed out as the pain struck anew. Sage blew out a relieved breath. If she had broken them, she wouldn't have been able to sit. She grasped her linen shirt and pulled it up over her shoulders with painstaking slowness. Sage ripped her threadbare cloak into strips and bound her ribs. By the time she finished, she was aching everywhere and more than irritable. To make things worse, the cold air on her bare skin had her shivering. Sage squinted at her shirt and hesitated, cringing at the idea of trying to put it back on.

She still needed to straighten her nose though. No reason to stain her shirt even worse than it already was. Both feet dropped to the floor as she straightened. Sage blew out a deep breath trying to psyche herself up for what she had to do.

On the count of three, one, two, three!

Grasping her nose, she simultaneously pulled up on the bridge and down on the tip of her nose. Tears washed down her face as white spots danced across her vision.

Hot liquid dripped down and mingled with her tears, painting the stone floor with crimson spots. Sage tilted her head back and reminded herself to control the pain. If she focused hard enough on her anchor, her family, Sage could turn it off.

What would they do when she didn't show up? How would they run the forge?

They would search but it wouldn't matter. They'd find no trace of her. The Elite were too careful to leave evidence of an abduction and with her disguise no one would have recognized her. Dying her hair black with squid ink turned out to be a good move. Even if her parents asked someone who had seen the Elite haul her away, their description of her wouldn't match her parents'. They wouldn't connect a black-haired boy with a brunette woman. Thank God she'd also given the Elite an alias. Now they couldn't track down her family. From this point on she *was* Ruby.

The faint sound of shuffling steps sounded from the corridor. Sage pushed through the pain and donned her shirt, only able to finish enough buttons to keep it closed.

The whisper of leather against stone drew nearer to her cell. Sage straightened, patiently awaiting whomever was paying her a visit. Sage clenched her hands, preparing for a fight.

To her surprise, the old man from the desk came into view. Sage noticed again his striking coloring. She couldn't decide if it was attractive or off-putting.

He stopped in front of her cell, watching her through the bars. There was something about his eyes that disturbed her, and she tried not to squirm under his intense gaze. She opted instead to stare right back.

Without thinking, she blurted, "Do you ever scare yourself when you glance in the mirror?" Sage lifted a hand to cover her mouth. *Why did she say that?* She had to get it together, she needed to sell her act.

An amused grin peeked out from his wiry, gray beard, his eyes twinkling with mirth. He clasped his hands behind his back and straightened. "Can't say that I have. Sure as hell have scared others though. It's one of my preferred pastimes." Glee was apparent in his voice.

"Well that's comforting," she grumbled. "What do you want? If you've come to scare or intimidate me, you'll be disappointed. I don't do frightened very well. I leave that to the high-class ladies."

Jeffry, Sage remembered his name, took two shuffling steps closer to the iron bars.

Why is he shuffling like an old man?

She'd bet her finest pair of daggers that those shuffling steps were all for show. Her lips fought a smile. She wasn't the only one playing games.

She circled her hand once for him to continue; yet he remained silent, giving her a look she didn't quite understand. If he thought he was going to unnerve her by staring, he was sorely mistaken. Her green eyes stayed focused on his metallic ones as she stared back in a silent challenge.

He gave her a toothy smile full of white teeth and cocked his head. His eyes traced her face and body. "Underneath all that grime and blood my dear, I believe you are quite the stunner."

She sucked her cheeks in, trying to reign in her anger at being ogled so openly. She pushed down the anger, slipping into character. Sage batted her lashes and fluttered her bloody fingers at him like she had seen the strumpets do.

"I can stun you all right," she purred, in a smoky tone. "If you come and join me, I'll show you how much." She winked, saucily.

His smile widened.

"I bet." He shook his head at her, amused. "Trouble, that's what you are. Pure trouble." He chuckled and then continued, "The princes won't know what to do with you, that's for sure. It will be enjoyable to watch."

"I don't even know what I'm doing here. Surely the princes won't hurt me?"

"You aren't getting any information from me, missy. I wanted to see how you were settling in."

She scoffed. "Every man who's ever said he wanted to make sure a woman was 'settling in' wanted much more than that. I know how this particular drama ends."

The old man gurgled. Was he dying? He tipped forward and slapped the bars, startling Sage. Lifting his head, he wiped tears from the corners of his eyes. Her concern melted into irritation. He was laughing at her!

He eventually caught his breath and looked her dead in the eye. "Aye, missy, you're a beautiful woman, one many men would want." Pointing to his chest, he continued: "But this old man has no desire for you. I already have a wonderful woman waiting at home for me." He eyed her again and shook his head. "For heaven's sake. I have granddaughters your age! Every time I look at you, I only see them." He sobered, his previous carefree persona melting away. "Listen, tonight will be rough. I have strict instructions you're to receive no food, water, nor blankets so prepare yourself my dear. Tonight is your first night in purgatory. Good night."

She watched him shuffle like an invalid until he'd disappeared around the corner. Sage couldn't help but roll her eyes at the whole shuffling bit. She would eat her shirt if he wasn't in better shape than most men half his age.

Sage dismissed him from her mind and focused on her newly discovered predicament. No blankets? She eyed the window. It might be her salvation during the day but it would mean her death during the night. She fingered the remains of her threadbare cloak. Were they trying to kill her or did they enjoy others suffering? Sage would figure something out; she had to.

Chapter Nine

TEHL

As Tehl made his way toward the infirmary, Sam's words replayed over and over in his head.

You're connecting with her.

Sit this one out.

Tehl didn't necessarily agree with Sam, but his brother understood emotions better than he did. That little spitfire may be a huge part of his problems but she could very well be the solution.

Ruby. The name just didn't match the impression she'd left. When he'd discovered that cloak had been hiding a beautiful woman, he'd barely covered his astonishment. And it was still difficult to reconcile the fierce opponent she had been with the stunning girl before him. But her face didn't fool him. She was tough and bloodthirsty.

Who could have trained her? No one learnt to fight like that overnight, yet he didn't know of any masters willing to take on female apprentices. Skills like hers only came with grueling years of training and dedication. It must have been in secret or he'd have heard tell of her. So, the question was, how did she acquire such skills? Why hide them? To have any chance at uncovering her identity they'd first need to find her master.

Reaching the infirmary, Tehl headed through the open door to Jacob, the palace's most-prized healer: the Healer. The older man had held the position since well before either prince had been born. He stood now with his glasses low on his nose, squinting at herbs. Without thinking, Tehl tossed himself onto one of the many pristine cots, hissing in a breath when his ribs protested the rough treatment.

That girl sure didn't pull her punches.

The pungent scents of basil and lemon permeated the room, causing his nose to twitch. Absentmindedly, he rubbed it as Jacob completed whatever he was working on. Jacob scrubbed his hands, turning as he dried them. He paused as he took in Tehl's injuries, his thick spectacles magnifying the coppery-hazel of his eyes. He smiled crookedly. "What happened this time?" He moved closer to Tehl, examining his face. "You've been beaten to a bloody pulp." His owl-like gaze awaited an explanation.

Tehl grunted. "A woman." He watched the other man attempt to contain his obvious amusement even while he continued cataloging injuries.

"You win some, you lose some, I suppose. Not all women fall at the feet of royalty, my lord."

"You're hilarious," Tehl deadpanned. "I'm worn out and desperately in need of a bath. Would you make this quick?"

Jacob leaned closer, sniffing. "You're correct there, my lord."

Tehl rolled his eyes. He appreciated his old friend's sense of humor but he had other priorities—his swollen nose for instance. Pointing to it he told the Healer, "You will need to reset my nose. She might have broken a couple of my ribs, but I'm still fairly mobile so they're more than likely only bruised."

Jacob's eyebrows furrowed as he drew closer and probed the bridge of Tehl's nose. The Healer clucked his tongue. "Your nose is broken. Let's take care of that before I examine anything else. On three I will straighten it. One, two—"

Pain exploded in his face. Tehl glared through his watery eyes. "What happened to three?"

"It sets better if you aren't expecting it. Stop whining. It's not like this is your first time you're experiencing a broken nose." Jacob chided.

"Still hurts."

The Healer ignored him. "Lift your shirt."

When Tehl painstakingly lifted his shirt over his head, he heard a familiar voice say.

"It's fun to get a little rough but your little woman may have taken it a bit too far."

He deposited his dirty shirt on the clean cot next to him and lifted his head to scowl at Sam and Gav.

"What?" His brother raised his hands in mock innocence.

Tehl disregarded the pair, turning back to Jacob who was still inspecting his body.

"A woman. She must be some kind of hellcat."

Tehl frowned as he noted the glimmer of awe evident in Jacob's voice.

"And you should see her! She is a curvy little pixie," Gav put in. "You'd never think she had it in her."

Tehl's head whipped around, glaring at the obvious admiration in Gav's words.

Eyes glinting, Sam chided, "Add to that the fact he had at least seventy-five pounds on her, yet she still beat him bloody. Brother, you've let yourself go. If you were in better shape that woman couldn't have bested you."

Tehl rolled his eyes, refusing to dignify his brother's ribbing with a response. He knew Sam's comments were good natured though, so he wasn't bothered overmuch.

Ignoring his irksome brother and cousin, Tehl focused instead on Jacob's movements as he cleaned each injury. At some point, Jacob had stopped trying to maintain his blank face; he was now smiling broadly.

Tehl cleared his throat. "Found something amusing, have you?"

"I have, thank you. I had thought, as you got older, these crazy injuries would eventually lessen but it seems—" Jacob paused mid-sentence, examining his back. "Did she bite you?!"

Tehl glanced up in time to see Sam and Gav trade glances. Sam vaulted over the cot for a better look. His three friends peered at the circular welt on his back. The silence shattered as both Sam and Gav burst into peals of laughter. Tehl narrowed his eyes at Jacob who was chuckling underneath his breath.

"It's not that bad," he mumbled, creating another round of laughter behind him.

"Sam look! You can see all her bitty teeth marks!" Gav chortled.

"I'm all for a well-placed bite on occasion, and we've all marked our territory at times but, brother? That's just brutal." Sam plopped down next to him, jarring the cot and, subsequently, his ribs. Tehl sucked in a shaky breath only to have it whoosh out of him when Sam bumped him with his shoulder. "However did you come by it?" Sam probed, brimming with curiosity.

He sighed, knowing his brother wouldn't leave the subject alone without the full story. "When I threw the blasted woman over my shoulder, she attempted escape by any means possible, thus the biting."

After staring for a beat, Sam shook his head and stood, twisting from side to side as he tried to work out the stiffness. "Sitting on barrels all day has left its mark. My back's all kinked," he sighed, adding, "What I wouldn't give for a hot bath right now."

Tehl shot his brother a dirty look. "Yeah…because sitting all day is just so hard on your body," he said sardonically, thinking of every ache afflicting his pummeled body.

Jacob noticed the blood on his shoulder and mangled ear. "Bloody hell, Tehl! How'd you come by this?"

"A damn rat bit me."

Gav's brows furrowed, and his cousin opened and closed his

mouth several times but Sam spoke up first. "How did that even happen? What was a rat doing on your shoulder?"

"It's a long story." Tehl was not keen on doling out an explanation; exhaustion was riding him hard. He closed his eyes as Jacob continued his ministrations, smearing smelly stuff on his neck and inspecting his lip. Jacob pulled it down, and checked Tehl's gums, letting out a resigned sigh when he'd finished. "I'll need to stitch it. Your teeth have cut clean through." Uncorking an amber bottle, he portioned some of the liquid in a cup and on a rag, handing Tehl the bottle afterward. "Take a couple swigs. It will help clean the wound and numb some of the pain."

Tehl brought the bottle to his lips and took a healthy gulp, before Jacob swiped the outside of his lip with the whiskey soaked rag. The liquid burned a hot trail down his throat and warmed his belly. The Healer threaded a needle, ready to stitch the botched lip. He cringed. He'd always hated this part. People were not meant to be stabbed with sharp objects.

"This will sting."

Gav shifted closer, watching Jacob with interest. Without looking away, he addressed Tehl. "So you're telling me you were bitten by rat and a woman, got your nose broken, had your lip busted, and are suffering bruised ribs, all from a pint-sized woman?"

Tehl huffed. "She's tougher than she looks."

Sam nodded. "My plan was to let her stew, maybe a couple of days, then I'd work my charm on her." Sam smirked. "But now I can't bear to wait that long. I believe I'll collect all the information we need by the end of the week."

If anyone could accomplish that it was Sam. Tehl was sure his brother could charm the knickers off a nun. "Good. The sooner the better, honestly."

Jacob leaned over to retrieve a small pair of clippers and cut the string that was tugging Tehl's lip.

"There you go. I put in ten stitches but it should heal quickly. Try not to agitate it though by rubbing your tongue along it." Jacob picked up a couple herbal packets from his desk and made a few notations. He handed them to Tehl, motioning to the green. "Mix those into your wine tonight before bed and they'll reduce some of your pain." He pointed to the purple herbs. "Use the lavender in your bath. It will help you relax and, hopefully, fall asleep. You'll need the rest. Also, when you're done with your bath, wrap your ribs with that gauze. If you need anything, you know where to find me." Jacob gathered his remaining herbs and ambled toward the door. He stopped in the doorway, and smirked over his shoulder. "If you need anyone to teach you what proper foreplay with a lady is, I suppose I'd be willing to help you out." He winked and slipped through the door.

Tehl's jaw dropped in horror.

"Did he give us love advice?" Sam grinned through his own shock. "I want to be him when I grow up."

Tehl squeezed his eyes closed, attempting to erase the image that had sprung in his mind. Putting that aside he steeled himself for the laborious trek ahead to get to his rooms. Tehl slid off the cot and he shrugged his shirt back on, ignoring the buttons for now.

Gav rocked forward onto the balls of his feet and clapped his hands. "Well..." he drew out, "after that remark, I need a drink. Want to join me?"

Sam rubbed his hands together in anticipation. "Yeah, I'm coming. And maybe, while we are at it, we can scare up some enjoyable company of the female persuasion." Gav smiled at Sam's antics and moved toward the door. Sam looked to Tehl expectantly.

He clasped his brother on the shoulder once with a slight smile. "No, you go. I need to clean up so I'll catch up with you in the morning. Also, I need you to get any information you can on Ruby and report it as soon as possible."

The three flights of stairs leading to his quarters just about killed him. When he finally reached his own floor, he paused to catch his breath. Tehl leaned against the wall while listening for the sounds of anyone approaching. God help him, if anyone caught him slumping against the wall like an invalid.

Once his body let him breathe again, he covered the remaining twenty feet to his room and went straight to his bathing area. To his delight steam was already wafting from a hot bath that had been prepped before his arrival. He stripped and dumped the herbs in the tub. Tehl lowered himself in and sighed as the warm water enveloped him. Immediately, his muscles relaxed.

Best part of life right here.

Tehl closed his eyes and drifted off. The next thing he knew, he was choking on water. He jerked up, sluicing water everywhere as he coughed. Time to get out. Clumsily, he climbed out of the tub, still sputtering on water. He wiped the water from his eyes and peered blearily around his room. Why did his bed seem so damn far away?

He stumbled back to his main quarters and collapsed onto the bed, still soaked. He thought about what his mother would say if she knew he had climbed into bed while wet. She would have skinned him alive and fussing over the state of him, the mattress, and the sheets. He could imagine her scolding him saying, "You'll catch your death you silly boy!"

He smiled and floated away into the recesses of his mind. His thoughts turned to a raven-haired beauty. Why did she intrigue him? Trouble. She was only trouble, he reminded his sleepy self. He closed his eyes and dreamt about warrior angels with green eyes.

Chapter Ten

TEHL

Tehl cracked his eyes open and blinked to clear the sleep from his eyes. How did he get to bed? He sat up; the blankets fell to his waist, exposing his skin to the chill of the morning air. The last thing he remembered was being in the bath. At least he didn't drown. Rolling his head back and forth, he took stock of how he was feeling: sore, but much better than yesterday. His stomach rumbled, reminding him he'd missed dinner last night.

Tehl threw on some leather breeches, a linen shirt, and a dark blue velvet vest. He may be royal but he would not primp and dress up. He ran his hands through his disheveled hair, not looking at the mirror, and rushed down to the dining room.

Gav was munching on a piece of toast while reading something, and Sam was digging into his mountain of food. "So much for manners," Tehl commented dryly.

Gav grunted, and Sam didn't spare him a glance, too intent on his horde. A servant placed a plate in front of him with everything he loved. The delicious smell of baked hot cakes, eggs, and buttery goodness teased his nose. His mouth watered, taking in the deliciousness laid before him. Tehl ignored everything but his food and dove right in.

His mountain of food speedily disappeared, much to his disappointment. Tehl took the last bite of his last hot cake, savoring the taste as it melted in his mouth. Opening his eyes, he looked down the table toward Gav, who was reading while sipping his coffee. Tehl flicked his eyes to Sam, who sat across from him. Sam had his head tilted back against the chair with his eyes closed.

"Rough night, Sam?" His brother didn't move or respond. "I know you're not asleep, if I hadn't seen you destroy half this table of food five minutes ago, I might have believed it."

"Give me a moment," Sam grouched, glaring at him.

"Out too late last night?" Tehl smirked. "That's what happens when you are chasing women."

"If that's what he was doing, he sure as hell would be in a better mood," Gav remarked from behind his book.

His brother leaned his head back and closed his eyes and muttered, "It *had* to be a woman!"

"What do you mean by that?" Tehl asked, curious.

"What I meant was *that woman* has caused a ruckus already. Most of the Elite and Guard saw us bring her in yesterday, so naturally they were curious. Last night, a group went to investigate.

She goaded them into a fight and they opened her cell."

"Did she escape?" Tehl growled.

"No, they kept her caged, but she took out five of our men last night! *Five*, with no weapons. Unbelievable! I slept down there to make sure no other men attempted to satisfy their curiosity," he shouted.

"She took out five of our men?"

"Well, she didn't kill them if that's what you're wondering," his brother snapped. "She rendered them unconscious and then stole their clothes."

Gav spewed his coffee and hacked. Tehl slapped him on the back and turned to Sam. His lips twitched at the irate coffee covered man.

"Great," Sam blew out. "I am done with this day and it only just began."

"Why did she steal their clothes?" Gav sputtered, between coughs.

Sam stabbed a finger at Tehl. "He told Jeffry she wasn't to have any food, water, or blankets until he said so. I guess she figured she would help herself to their clothes to keep warm. She deserved them if she took down five guards."

Tehl smiled down into his cup of coffee while listening to his brother rant. "One little woman did all that? I am surprised she got the best of your guards. It seems they need better training," he needled.

Sam stood, knocking his chair back. His brother placed his hands on the table and leaned forward. "That is no woman! She is a damn warrior disguised as an angel!" Sucking in a deep breath, he continued. "We have a problem if all the rebels have received the same training as the woman. Ruby was seventy pounds lighter than those men, and she *still* got the best of them. We don't know what we are dealing with. They aren't a handful of unhappy farmers. The resistance is organized and trained. They pose a real threat."

Tehl turned this over in his mind. Ruby had surprised him with her prowess in battle. Were there other women who were trained? What was the rebellion planning? Her information was vital.

"We need her information, sooner rather than later. You need to break her. We need the resistance taken care of. They don't understand the severity of our situation or who is knocking at our borders," Tehl said, gravely.

Sam looked him dead in the eye, "I will pay our lovely captive a visit this morning to see how well she slept. You'll have what you need in the next couple of days, my lord." Sam bowed and stomped from the room.

"She wound him up. I don't think I have seen him lose his temper like that in a couple years. I forgot that he even had one," drawled Gav, still sipping on his coffee. "If he interrogates her when he's angry, she could manipulate him."

"He is the best at what he does, he won't go in blind," Tehl defended. "He won't let her manipulate him."

"Women are different creatures than men. They play by a different set of rules. She will be more difficult than Sam expects."

"Would you like to deal with her?"

Gav shook his head. "Not particularly, but it would be better with both of us there."

"Then your main priority is to deal with Sam and Ruby."

Gav stood and set his coffee down. "It's been an eventful morning. I will apprise you of the situation later," he said tossing the words over his shoulder. His cousin strolled out of the room like he had all the time in the world.

Time...that was the one thing Tehl didn't have. Hopefully they would get what they needed today.

Chapter Eleven

SAGE

Sage's eyes flickered open as light filtered through the window, dancing across her eyelids. The window allowed just enough light to warm a small portion of the otherwise icy floor.

Sage cursed, irritation and alarm surging through her. She'd fallen asleep without realizing it. Last night had been rough.

She shivered in the damp cold. It seemed her recent wardrobe additions were not enough to ward off the chill, but the memory of their acquisition had her smiling in spite of herself. She'd mopped the floor with those idiots, and stealing their uniforms for warmth was icing on the cake. When their commander arrived after the fact, his expression had been priceless. Sage smirked. She couldn't wait to tell Rafe.

As terrifying as it had been initially when the men came for her, she'd enjoyed putting them in their place. It was an image she wouldn't soon forget; the Elite sprawled across the floor, naked.

The commander, or Prince Samuel, had retrieved his men with muttered curses, all the while attempting to burn a hole in her head with a dark glare. As he left, she'd heard him bellowing at Jeffry; he was obviously displeased. Her glee was short lived, though, when he camped outside her cell shortly thereafter. The cursed man had stayed all night. Unlike her, the cold stone didn't seem to bother him at all for he began snoring as soon as he lay down. Sage had stayed awake, knowing she couldn't allow herself to be so vulnerable in his presence.

In the middle of the night, she'd glanced to where he'd been sleeping to find he was now watching her. Not to be cowed, she'd stared right back, watching him watch her, neither of them speaking a word. For hours, they'd stayed that way, until the fingers of dawn trickled through the window. He'd then silently rolled up his pallet and disappeared down the corridor. Sighing in relief, Sage had leaned her head against the wall, only for a second, and that was the last thing she remembered.

How could she be so careless?

Sage shifted and winced with the movement. Pain coursed through her, reminding her how bruised her entire body was. She unclenched her hands and noted they looked a little blue. It was stinking cold down here. Sage scooted into the sunlight, exhaling a happy sigh as sunlight warmed her back. Stars above, she hated being cold. Sage took a slow breath in and closed her eyes.

"Enjoying yourself, I see."

She stiffened at his voice but wouldn't give him the satisfaction of seeing her discomfort. Her eyes snapped open as she stared unflinchingly at the commander standing before her cell. He moved like a damned cat, quickly and quietly, nothing to warn her of his approach.

"Jumpy are we?" he mused, leaning a shoulder against her cell. "Never fear, I don't bite too hard...not unless you ask me to that is."

Oh, he was the epitome of arrogance. It was even in his posture, his stance. But there was also a cunning glint to his eyes, and that gave her pause. She'd have to tread carefully with this one. Rumors were circulating about the young commander; he was cunning, ruthless, an incredible strategist, and an accomplished womanizer. A deadly combination, for sure.

Two could play his game though, and she doubted he'd ever encountered an opponent of her level. The 'helpless, innocent woman' wouldn't work; she'd blown that cover to smithereens after taking out his men. The trollop however...now that had potential. She mentally grimaced at the idea of pulling it off though.

Seductress, how unoriginal, though simple at least. Men. All you need is a little skin and they become so stupid.

Preparing herself, she lowered her lashes and peered through them with a smile.

Let the games begin.

She uncoiled from the floor and arched her back to allow the sun to halo her figure. She watched as his eyes skimmed her curves.

Bait set.

Sage unbraided her hair and ran her fingers through the raven tresses like she'd seen the women of the night do. Her silky waves cascaded down her back.

"See something you like?" The words were ash on her tongue though she maintained the façade.

"Quite a few things actually," he crooned back.

"Oh?" she inquired, letting a sensuous smile slide across her lips. Hips swaying, she sidled close to the bars, pausing just out of reach. Sage gestured lightly to his face and quirked a brow. "And how did you come by that scar?" She took one step closer and pointed to his face again, making sure to cock one hip.

Meeting her eyes, he grinned broadly. "Boys being boys, we engaged in a fierce snowball fight but, sadly, the losing team felt it necessary to pack theirs with stones."

Well, that was an unexpected response.

The commander extended his arm in between the bars, brushed a piece of hair from her shoulder, and traced a line of scar tissue at her collarbone. Every fiber of her being rebelled against his touch, and she clenched her teeth to keep from shoving him away.

"And how did *you* come by *this scar*?"

She debated lying and yet...perhaps a little truth would keep him talking. "Boys will be boys. I guess we have something in common. Whenever the boys played at swordplay, I wanted to join. So, one time they gave me one of their wooden swords but ganged up on me. I walloped them but one managed to crack me on the collarbone, gifting me this little token." After falling quiet, Sage brushed her fingers down his temple, tracing his scar. His breath hitched at her contact, and she inwardly grinned, satisfied that things were so far going as planned.

"It only adds to your beauty," he breathed, slipping his hand from her collarbone and into her hair. She looked from the scar to his eyes and froze. His clear blue eyes were frosty. Unease crept up her spine. His actions and words didn't match the ice in his eyes. Sage tried to slip back and out of reach, but his hand tightened just as quickly.

"Where are you going? Why don't we keep discussing your childhood? I'm very keen to learn all about you."

She tugged harder only to be pulled roughly against the bars. What an idiot she was; she should've known better. Sage had meant to play him but he'd turned it around and played her even better. She'd sauntered right into his web thinking she was the spider not the fly. Rafe would rebuke her for such an idiotic mistake.

Prince Samuel leaned toward her. "First rule of hand-to-hand combat: never allow your enemy to get a good hold on you."

She grinned, feigning confidence. "It seems we've reached an impasse. You have to open the door to get to me." Her grin shifted to a feral smile. "And when you do, I can fight and maybe I will end up with your clothes to keep me warm as well."

His eyes gleamed and a wicked smile split his handsome face. "Gav, stop lurking and help me. That's what you're here for." A tall violet-eyed man emerged from the darkened hallway to the left.

How long has he been there?

These two men moved like blasted wraiths.

"Open the door and cuff her, please."

The other man opened the door to her cell and moved toward her. Fighting, Sage clawed at the commander's arm but his grip stayed fast. She went limp, hoping her dead weight would catch him off balance and give her a chance. Instead, the commander reacted not at all, and it accomplished nothing, except for ripping a few hairs from her neck.

"Stop fighting. If you don't you'll just hurt yourself further," the other man growled from behind her. Sage could not let them pin her. She shot her foot back, connecting with his shin. He grunted in pain but wrestled her arms behind her back, and she writhed against both men, angering her damaged ribs. Before she knew it, cool metal clasped her wrists and closed with a faint click. Cuffs. She tugged a few times against the metal restraints but nothing. She was well and truly caught.

"If you stop pulling at the restraints, you'll spare yourself bruised and bleeding wrists," the one called Gav warned. His touch was firm but not unkind. He moved to her side and leaned against the bars, staring down at her.

She couldn't stop staring at the unique coloring of his irises.

Purple eyes? Who had purple eyes?

"You have the most incredible eyes," Sage blurted. Her face heated. *Where the hell had that come from?* Heavens above she needed to get a grip.

His eyes widened, crinkling at the corners. The commander's snickering caught her attention as she faced forward.

"Ah damn. And here I thought you fancied me." Prince Samuel's knowing smirk infuriated her. She would wipe that smug expression right off his face as soon as she had the chance.

Sage gave up her pathetic role as seductress and allowed her disgust to manifest itself. "I wouldn't fancy you if you were the last man in the whole of Aermia. I'd venture to say you're more a woman than I am. How much time do you spend before your looking glass?" She mirrored his smirk.

His smile dropped. Leisurely, his eyes skimmed her face and hair. "You're not wrong but perhaps next time you're attempting to seduce someone you ought to glance in the mirror yourself. Dirt, blood, and bruises provide little appeal."

Her cheeks burned once again for it was true, she was a mess. Sage had been so focused on escaping she hadn't considered the state of her face. Prince Samuel let go of her, and Gav gripped her bicep, moving her toward the cell opening.

"Where are you taking me?" she demanded.

"You'll just have to see," was Samuel's flippant response.

Again, she threw herself to the floor, but Gav's grip didn't budge. He hauled her up, giving her a stern look. "Ruby, are you going to fight us the entire way?" Gav looked quite exasperated.

Her fake name surprised her for a moment, but recovering she hissed at him. "Until my last breath."

The two men exchanged looks. The purple-eyed man slid his hand underneath her armpits, and the commander reached for her legs. She got in one good kick before her legs were secured and she was suspended midair. She bucked, but it helped her not at all.

Prince Samuel jerked his chin toward the other man, and they began to move. She registered pain in almost every part of her body. How would she escape now?

There was one thing she hadn't tried, distasteful as it was. It was a last resort, but there was no honor in being dead.

So, she screamed.

At the top of her lungs.

Men rushed from the dark corners of their cells to their doors and began bellowing at the commander and his man. A chorus of shouts—*"Leave her alone!"* and *"Don't touch her!"* and *"Let her go!"*—filled the corridor, repeating over and over, but neither man was even phased. They ignored the prisoners' clamoring and continued. When they stopped at a dark chamber, her heart pounded in her chest. Chains clanked, and cool metal embraced one of her wrists. Sage yanked on her other arm and swung wildly. A large calloused hand caught her wrist and returned it to its shackle. Samuel dropped her feet, and she stumbled back into the stone wall.

She blinked several times, hoping her eyes would adjust to the dark. She heard the strike of flint and soon a flare of light burst from the lone lantern stationed on a sturdy-looking table. The floor beneath it was stained a dark brown.

Huh? She thought, *Why is the—*

Suddenly everything clicked.

Blood and lots of it. Blood stained the floor and table.

Bile burned its way up her throat, and she forced it down.

How many people were hurt in this room?

She tore her eyes from the stain and noticed a pristine porcelain cup placed upon the filthy surface. It was filled to the brim with some sort of golden, frothy liquid. A scent like apple pie wafted over and teased her nose, sweet and crisp. She knew it had to be drugged but her body didn't seem to care, her mouth watered.

When was the last time she had a drink? Yesterday morning? Was this one of their tortures?

Sage forced her eyes away from the cup and back at her two jailers. They stood shoulder to shoulder watching her. Why was everyone always staring at her? She was so sick and tired of being stared at. She wasn't an animal in a menagerie. "Well, gentleman? Get on with it already."

"Are you done with all that screeching?" the commander inquired tugging on his ear. "Damn, woman. My ears are still ringing."

She would have found it funny if he didn't have her in chains. "I suppose...for the time being anyway."

Prince Samuel gestured to the cup. "Would you like some?"

"No, thank you."

"But Gavriel made it specially for you."

Sage scoffed. "I'm sure."

The commander retrieved the cup and sniffed it. With a shrug, he took a couple of sips.

Well it's not poisoned at least.

Looking back at her over its rim, he asked, "So? Would you like some?"

Is this a test? she wondered. *What reaction was he looking for? Best to not appear too eager.*

Sage raised her eyes from the cup and noticed his grin. It made her want to punch it right off his stupid, smug face.

"No, thank you. I wouldn't want anything that's touched your lips to come into contact with mine. I don't know where they've been," she sneered. His grin widened. Why was he still smiling?

"You should ask your mother since they kept her busy all last night."

Her jaw dropped, and she stared at him.

"Wha—what?!" Sage sputtered.

His sapphire eyes crinkled in amusement. "What is it, Ruby? Cat got your tongue?"

This was the man everyone feared? "Did you—" she paused, incredulous, "Did you just joke about bedding my mum?"

His smile now reached epic proportions. "Let me assure you, there was little sleeping involved."

Sage once again sputtered and gaped like a fish.

"Oh, come on," he teased, "You've got to admit you walked right into that one."

She gave Gav a disbelieving look and frowned. *"This* is the man with whom the king has entrusted Aermia's safety? Is this a joke or something?" she continued, shocked. "This is ridiculous. I must have died. Only in hell would someone joke about tumbling my mum."

"You're not dead," Gavriel stated. "But you might be soon if you don't drink what Commander Samuel is offering you. You need liquids."

"What is it?"

Samuel approached her and placed the cup to her lips.

"It's cider, plain and simple. Now open."

Sage eyed the concoction but couldn't detect anything because of her damn broken nose. The commander had already taken a sip yet he appeared to be fine, so she opened her mouth. More gentle than she expected, he poured the brew down, and it slipped refreshingly down her throat, coating her taste buds with its sweet and tangy flavor. Sage closed her eyes and savored it. Her parched throat rejoiced, and she gulped down as much as possible. In her haste, a portion of the precious liquid spilled, dribbling down her chin.

"Slow down or you'll end up throwing it all up," Samuel chided.

He tipped the cup up and she got every last drop. Opening her eyes, she stared curiously back at him. His famed midnight eyes matched his brother's but there was something about the commander's that intrigued her. His eyes were prettier than his brother's and probably held more secrets too.

Wait, what? Why was she even thinking about this?

She blinked once slowly and took stock of her body. She felt giddy, yet a part of her registered that this wasn't normal.

"What did you put in my drink?"

"We put nothing in it."

"Liar," she retorted.

It wasn't possible, for her body was going soft on her. The commander returned the cup to its table and faced her. Both men seemed to be waiting for something. She looked to Gav. He looked like he was carved from stone. Why was he so serious all of a sudden? It struck her as funny and a giggle burst out of her. Oh dear, that was not a good sign. She needed to reel it in.

"What's happening?"

"Gavriel has a sort of talent with chemistry. He discovered a manner of fermenting an apple, which alters its reaction in our body. Gav has a special name for it, but I always forget. But, anyway, after experimenting we've found that when administered in the right proportions it acts as a truth serum."

She couldn't feel her face well, but Sage was sure her eyebrows were raised. They had to be joking. There was no such thing. "You're lying. I'm positive nothing like that exists."

Think, Sage, Think!

Were they just trying to mess with her head? She needed to focus on her training. Closing her eyes, she repeated what Rafe had taught her.

Be the lie.

Live the lie.

She was not Sage. She was Ruby.

Vaguely, she registered Samuel speaking. Sage opened her eyes. "What's that, handsome?" she asked with another giggle.

"What's your real name?" the commander--or rather, as she liked to think of him, *the prince*—asked.

"Ruby. Like the gem, you know? All shiny and red. My mother used to have a necklace with rubies all in it." Leaning forward, she strained against the chain and whispered, "But it wasn't hers. She stole it!"

"Where is your mother now then, Ruby?"

"Oh, she died a while ago, when the Sickness came through. I don't miss her much though. She said I was old enough to take care of myself, anyway. My brothers were just lazy bags of bones, but not me. When she kicked me out I learned to fend for myself. On the streets, I toughened up real quick and learned how to fight dirty." She smiled. "You might have seen some of my work on the crown prince's back?"

"And what of your brothers?"

Sage shook her head trying to clear the fog blanketing her mind. She needed to focus on her story if she wanted to make it out of this alive. "Filthy pirates is what they are. I haven't seen them in ages," she slurred. "Dirty rotten thieves, I tell you. They're not important." Her body tingled, so warm all over.

"And what part do you play in the resistance?"

She sniggered, "Resistance? Darling, I know nothing about that. Gossip on the streets spreads like fire in a drought. If there was a resistance, I would have heard about it already. There's no such thing."

Samuel pulled her dagger out of a sheath at his waist and laid it on the table. "Then why did you have this?"

Sage peeked over at the dagger. "Seriously? Is that what all this is about? A silly dagger? I'll give it to ya straight then. I filched it off of an unsuspecting idiot about six months ago. Don't know who he was though, and honestly, I don't even remember what he looked like either."

The two men in front of her blurred together into one: a curly blond-haired man with purple eyes. The cuffs at her wrists chafed.

Damn! They're so itchy.

She pulled and tugged at them.

"So, you're telling me you stole this, and it's not yours?"

Her head lulled to the side. She blinked, and there were two men again. "It's mine now. Do I look like I could afford something of that quality?"

Neither man said a word in response as the room spun, making her stomach lurch. Her eyelids drooped as her mouth slackened. This was not good; she'd never eat apple anything ever again.

"Sam? She's going to pass out," muttered Gav.

Samuel leaned closer, looking her over, and swore. "How much was in that cup?"

"Enough to make her talk."

Sage was numb. She felt nothing and crashed onto her knees, held upright only by the metal at her wrists.

How peculiar...

A strange euphoria spread through her as warm liquid ran down her arms. The dark one wrapped a strong arm around her waist, hoisting her up as the blond one with the devastating smile unlocked her wrists.

Maybe they'll stop itching now.

Her head flopped against Gav's shoulder, and she stared blearily at him. He was a stunning man. She kissed his neck and breathed in his leather and musk scent. Sage looked up into his unique eyes when he stiffened. "You really do have the most beautiful eyes. I think we would have gorgeous babies."

Surprise flashed on his face just before it blurred. Then everything went black.

Chapter Twelve

TEHL

When will this day end?

Demari, the Aermian steward, was currently droning on about expenses for the Midsummer Festival. The budget was already set. Why were they still discussing it? It was times like these that he felt his mother's loss; this had always been her forte.

"Your Highness?"

Tehl snapped out of his thoughts. "Yes, Demari?"

"What colors would you like us to use in the decorations?" His thin steward stared at him, awaiting an answer along with twenty other sets of eyes.

"Colors?" Tehl grimaced and addressed the small crowd. "I don't care, do what you will. I already approved the budget, so, if you have questions, ask Demari and he can assist you." The thin and graying steward then smiled at the rest of the household servants. "That will be all." They bowed and scurried after Demari.

It had been such a long day. He'd been sitting in the wooden chair for so long he'd begun to ache. Tehl was inclined to just eat in the private dining room as it was much more comfortable, however, he hadn't eaten with the court in three days so he'd have to brave the shark-infested waters.

***

He should've gone to bed; there was absolutely nothing worth his time or attention in this room. Sam and Gav never showed up for dinner so Tehl found himself surrounded with less than ideal dinner companions. Men and women alike engaging in droll and vapid conversation. Looking down the table, it seemed only feathers were visible. The reason women dressed to resemble distorted birds eluded him. Where they'd gotten the idea that it was somehow appealing to men remained an even greater mystery.

A hand on his arm forced his attention back to the lady seated at his side. She was leaning toward him with a dress cut so low he was worried her breasts might actually tumble out of it. Her face wore a practiced smile as her lashes fluttered, her peacock-feathered hairpiece tickling his face. Tehl leaned back and pasted on a smile although the feathers put him in mind of strange antennae. It was ridiculous.

"Your Highness, I had heard tell that you bested a nefarious foe yesterday, and that you fought valiantly despite having sustained injuries. I wanted to be certain you weren't permanently harmed in any way, and should you require anything at all I would be more than willing to provide assistance." A seductive smile slipped across her face as she stroked his arm and leaned even closer, if that was possible. "I hate to think you might suffer in any way." More eye-batting.

His jaw slackened. Could she possibly be saying what he thought she was saying? He swept his gaze down the table and spotted her father giving him a disturbing smile.

"She is an expert caregiver. I'm sure she'd be at your disposal any time you need."

Was she being thrown at him by *her father*? The Aermian nobility knew the old laws; he'd only marry a commoner which meant this man was, what? Offering his own daughter as a mistress to the crown prince? Filled with revulsion, Tehl's eyes darted back to the girl who continued to eye him. If he ever had a daughter, he wouldn't let a man near her without honorable intentions. And even then, no guarantees. He neither understood nor wanted anything to do with such a dishonorable man.

He covered her hand with his and whispered, "I very much appreciate your concern but I am well-cared-for by our healers. Good evening." Tehl shoved back his chair and fled, more than happy to leave the sniveling court behind.

***

When he returned to his chambers, a fire was already crackling in the hearth. He fell more than sat on his bed and painstakingly pulled off his boots, followed by his vest and shirt, tossing them all into a corner. Raising his eyes to the mirror across the room, he warily took stock of his reflection. Well hell, he looked terrible. His skin was black and blue in multiple spots, and the bite on his shoulder looked pretty damn ugly.

A knock sounded at his chamber door, interrupting his thoughts. "Enter," he called.

Sam and Gav entered looking just as ragged as he did. "Get anything out of her?" Tehl asked, exhausted.

They traded looks before responding. Not a good sign. Sam sat on the corner of Tehl's dresser and propped a leg up. "You first, Gav. I feel like I've talked enough today. Your turn."

Gav grimaced, brushing imaginary lint from his sleeve.

"Not well?" Tehl guessed.

"Your brother used his usual charm, and she played right into him." Gav's expression remained solemn. "She fought us the entire way afterward, and we had to chain her. She'd taken neither food nor water, as per your orders, so Sam offered my ester cider, which she wanted not as she assumed it to be poisoned, but long story short: Sam tried it first, and she was thirsty enough to drink the whole cup."

"You used the serum then? And how did it go? Did it work?" Excitement raced through him. The serum Gav created was a stroke of genius; they'd managed to get even the toughest of men to blubber out their life stories with it.

"Well..." Gavriel seemed unwilling to continue so Sam interrupted:

"It didn't work."

Gav glared at his cousin. "Hey! What happened to me telling the story?"

Sam shrugged. "You were taking too long."

"Wait," Tehl cut in. "What do you mean 'it didn't work'? It's worked on everyone we've tested it on so far."

"Well, I'm sorry to inform you it didn't work on Miss Ruby." Sam pulled a face. "I drugged her out of her mind but she never once stumbled or slipped."

"Then what was her story?"

"She said her mother named her Ruby after some necklace she'd stolen. Later, her mum threw her out on the street where she's been supposedly living ever since. She also said her mother is dead and that her brothers are now pirates, and she stole the dagger from a random man about six months ago," Sam finished with a strong dose of skepticism.

"So, why don't you believe her, Sam?" Tehl asked.

Sam stood and began pacing. "First, she doesn't look like a 'Ruby'. I mean she's not even a redhead!"

Sometimes he couldn't follow his brother's logic. Tehl glanced to Gav and his cousin rolled his eyes. "What does red hair have to do with it?"

Sam tossed his hands in the air. "Everything and nothing. I guess that's beside the point so let's leave it for now. Did either of you notice how her words would change as she spoke? She constantly shifts from proper, educated speech to slang. When I spoke of how the ester was distilled she had no difficulty following. A child who grew up on the streets, uneducated, would've had more questions and general confusion." Sam paused, considering. "I also found it interesting that she didn't divulge information unless prompted. Generally, after administering the ester, we can't get them to shut up, but not so with this girl. Not once did I have to redirect the conversation."

Tehl looked to Gav for confirmation. "Do you agree?"

"Unfortunately, I do. I've no idea how she lied to us, but I'm certain she did," Gav bit out.

The room fell silent as each contemplated the implications of this.

"How long was your interrogation?" Tehl

"Until she lost consciousness," Sam deadpanned.

"Why the hell did she pass out?" Tehl growled. "That's not even supposed to happen."

"Ask our brooding alchemist."

Tehl arched a midnight eyebrow at his cousin. Gav folded his arms and returned their looks with a scowl. "It was a bit of an overdose. I made adjustments for her smaller size, but somehow it was still too much." Shrugging, he added, "She's slept the rest of the day but at least she didn't die or anything."

"I am greatly pleased to hear you didn't kill our solitary tie to the resistance," Tehl said dryly. "So, what now?"

Gav glanced between the two brothers. "It pains me to say this, but I think there may be continued benefit in restrictions on food and water. I'm not interested in hurting the woman, however, I'm also hoping two days of isolation might provide the incentive for her to be more forthcoming."

Tehl looked to Sam. "What do you think? This is, after all, your area or expertise."

Sam shook his head. "Honestly? She'll be a problem no matter what, but I believe Gav's suggestion has merit. She seems to come alive with company so isolation may just do the trick."

"It's settled then. Keep an eye on her but without her knowledge, stay out of sight. First, though, go and rest, both of you. You're dead on your feet."

Mumbling their farewells, each departed for his own chamber as Tehl watched the flames dance in the hearth, soothed by the comforting sounds of crackling wood. After a moment, he stripped himself of any remaining clothing and fell into bed with a sigh. Tomorrow would be a better day.

***

It was too much to hope this day would be an improvement from the last. He'd barely finished breakfast, and he already had a list of issues demanding his attention. When he said he didn't care how the festival came together it seemed no one listened. Who gave a rat's ass if the linens were white or ivory? He certainly didn't. And who knew that the colors in his theme had the potential to either elevate or offend various nobles? What a crock. If a color scheme offended you then you really had no business representing a kingdom.

In addition to this, it seemed every invitation required his personal signature. After the first hundred, his hand cramped. Shaking it out, he glared at the sea of invitations still taunting him. Groaning he laid his head on the desk. Was this what his life had come to? Picking colors and signing invitations? He would complete the invitations, and with efficiency, but he briefly allowed himself a moment to indulge in a bit of wallowing.

Suddenly, his door burst open. The noise startled him enough that the pen in his hand scratched a hole in one of his pristine invitations.

"Damn it," he growled, glaring up at the intruder. "Ever heard of knocking? Look what you made me do!" Tehl waved the ink-marred invitation before his brother. "It's ruined. Now I'll have to sign another of these stupid things. I'm going to be here forever."

Oddly enough, Sam had not interrupted his invitation tirade and allowed him to finish before speaking.

"I am sorry, my prince, but I have urgent news."

Tehl sat up taller. His brother rarely used his title and usually only to tease him or when addressing him on matters of great importance. "What is it?"

"I've just received word that the Scythians have broken their borders and attacked. This time, however, they did not return to their own borders, but have instead set up camp in Silva."

All color drained from Tehl's face. "What of the people?"

"They took care of anyone capable of resisting and enslaved the rest. If those captives cross their border, there's no chance of recovery. As Silva's a farming community, no garrison is stationed there. What would you have me do?"

Tehl's fists clenched, his voice hard. "It seems they're looking for war. I will not allow my people to suffer and die in Scythia. What are the enemy numbers?"

"My current information says around twenty-five soldiers."

"Gather a company from the Elite, and we can depart immediately."

Sam shook his head. "I believe we would be better off if you stayed. We ought not risk both of our country's princes at once. If things go south, we need someone to handle things here."

Tehl shot up and placed both hands on the desk. "I understand your concerns, but these are my people and they need me. My place is not sitting here, waiting. I will fight for them, you know this."

Sam studied him and nodded. "I will ready the men."

"Please saddle Wraith."

"It will be done."

Spinning on his heel, Sam departed. Tehl stared after him trying to calm the fury that had overtaken him. It was the Scythians. He loathed any dealing with the damned kingdom.

They were barbaric warmongers. Dark eyes, dark hair, and olive skin characterized the entire nation, not because of some geographic isolation but rather owing to their disturbing practice of removing any born who did not fit the established standard. Even contemplating it had Tehl's stomach turning sour.

He strode to the armory, determined to strike fear into their dark hearts. No one attacked his people and got away with it.

Chapter Thirteen

TEHL

As the company made their way to the border, Tehl observed the passing countryside with appreciation. The rolling fields had always enchanted him as a boy whenever they rode this way. The golden wheat gleamed and swayed in the wind, almost as if it waved a greeting as they galloped by.

His eyes wandered to his brother riding beside him. He looked to be made of stone, his expression severe and his jaw set. It was hard to believe this was the same man with whom he'd joked and teased earlier that morning.

"Are you going to stare at me the entire way?" Sam asked without even sparing a glance in Tehl's direction.

"I wasn't staring at you," he fibbed.

"Sure you were." Though he continued to scrutinize the landscape, the corners of Sam's lips tipped ever so slightly heavenward.

Mollified at having achieved at least a little reaction, Tehl changed the subject.

"How long 'til we arrive?" It had been a long time since he was near Silva.

Sam squinted at the sun and then to the forest. "We have a couple hours until we get into position, but it will be dark before we reach the trees. After that it will be slow going once we enter the forest." Sam's voice drifted over the thunder of hooves toward Tehl.

Tehl nodded and focused back on the trail ahead.

When they finally reached the forest boundary only a sliver of the sun remained over the western mountains. Sam slowed his mount and raised a fist, signaling all to slow their approach. The company followed at a trot as he led them to a small creek and dismounted, gesturing for the Elite to follow suit.

As Tehl swung off Wraith, he was stopped short by a sharp pain in his calf.

Damn leg cramps.

Carefully, he flexed his foot back and forth until the pain subsided. Stepping from his horse Tehl stretched, clicking his neck and back.

Sam, noticing Tehl's discomfort, sauntered over with a grin. "Stiff, brother?"

"I'm sure that's what Daisy asked you last night," Tehl shot back.

Sam whistled. "Two innuendos in a week. I think I might finally be rubbing off on you."

"Let's hope not," Tehl retorted, attempting to gnaw a hunk of dried venison.

Sam grimaced. "That's disgusting! For God's sake, close your mouth. Our tutors beat matters of etiquette into us, so how is it you've retained such an awful set of manners?"

Tehl responded by opening his mouth and displaying more chewed food. "Does it look like there's anyone to impress out here? I'm pretty sure the men and the horses don't care so I'll eat however I damn well please." He finished his tirade by shooting a meat-filled grin in Sam's direction and, though he obviously fought it, his brother's lip still twitched. He loved that about Sam; no matter their situation, he never lost his sense of humor.

Sam rifled through his saddlebags, eventually producing a canteen, which they shared, the cool water refreshing them after their hard ride. Tehl closed his eyes and inhaled deeply, enjoying the crispness of the evening air but paused when something familiar tickled his nose, stirring up childhood memories. Glancing around, he noticed the forest floor was littered with little herbs. With a soft smile, he bent down, skimming his fingers across the ruffled leaf. Lemon balm. His mum had always kept it in her solar, so wherever she went the scent clung to her skin and garments. Sam squatted next to him, mirroring his smile. Tehl broke off a leaf and passed it to his brother. Sam rubbed the leaf and brought it to his nose.

"Smells like Mum."

Tehl nodded, no other words needed. He leaned back and stared at the night sky. A few stars had appeared, shining like diamonds on blue silk. In the distance, he could see the fields of wheat had softened from the brilliant gold of day to a soft silver in the waning light.

Sam too peered up at the sky and muttered, "It's time. I'd prefer to have the moon for a bit of light but we'd best head out now." Standing, he commanded the company: "Prepare to depart."

Sam eyed his men with pride as they followed his orders with efficiency, each checking their tack and gear before mounting up. They were ready within moments.

"Listen up," Sam called. "You all know how many lives depend on the success of this mission so I'm sure I need not tell you how essential a soundless approach is. Be alert. It's going to be a tedious few hours so prepare yourselves."

Sam then kneed his mount forward, approaching the tree line.

Tehl noted that, in the faded light, the shadows of the forest seemed a bit sinister. As a boy, he always treasured this forest; the trees stretched their limbs over him like giant protectors. Tonight, though, they seemed more like reapers, limbs reaching to steal your life from your body.

Sam raised a hand and motioned, signaling the company forward. Tehl directed Wraith beneath the leafy canopy and tried to shrug off the feeling of foreboding creeping over him. They would do their best and hopefully it'd be enough.

Wraith sensed his unease and tossed his head, sidestepping, so Tehl forced himself to relax. Unclenching his hands, he tried to shake the tension from them and ran a soothing hand along Wraith's glossy neck.

Ahead, Sam stopped, raising a fist. Everyone froze, scanning the darkened woods around them. Silently, Sam dismounted.

"The village is not far from here. The Scythians are camped out in the town's center with the survivors being held slightly north in an old silo." Sam's eyes shifted to three men right of Tehl. "Jethro, Garreth, and Sethen: accompany the Crown and make your way toward the prisoners, but be cautious. The Scythians have already made it clear that if any step out of line, the silo will be burnt to the ground along with everyone inside."

Shocked, the Elite whispered curses of outrage to one another.

"Be certain every Scythian is dealt with." Sam looked each man in the eye. "Form your groups. I'll lead from the east, Jaxon from the south and Luchas from the north. Stealth is our ally. Execute this both swiftly and silently, but await my signal to begin our strike on the square. Fight honorably for Aermia's people, and I'll see you all on the other side."

Tehl slipped from Wraith's back and clasped his brother's arm. Sam gave him a crooked grin. "Don't die. I'd really hate to take your place, forced to sit for hours through all those bloody meetings."

Tehl mirrored his brother's grin. "You don't need to worry about me." Releasing his brother, Tehl addressed Jethro, Garreth, and Sethen. "Let's rid ourselves of these animals before they have a chance to hurt anymore of our people." Each nodded, exchanging feral grins, eyes lit in anticipation.

"Let's go."

Chapter Fourteen

SAGE

Sage blinked and rubbed her eyes, trying to clear the sleep from them though they felt like a bag of sand had been poured over them. Her tongue, thick and dry, stuck to the roof of her mouth. She lifted her head and surveyed herself but was surprised to see nothing was tying her down. Why weren't her arms and legs moving? Squinting at the stone wall across from her, she tried to remember what had happened. Slowly, little pieces of yesterday resurfaced in her mind. A cup full of apple cider...violet eyes...and blond curls.

They'd drugged her, *again*.

How long had she been out? Minutes? Hours? How much time had she lost? Her breathing picked up as her heart pounded. She was panicking, which was pointless.

Calm down, you're okay.

The drugs were still in effect so it mustn't have been long since they were administered. Hence, they'd likely wear off after a short time; she needed to be patient. Sage dropped her head back on the cot and began counting the gray stones in the ceiling to pass the time. At around stone one hundred and seventy, her eyes became heavy, and she finally dropped off.

***

Sage jerked awake and bolted upright, painfully jostling her ribs as she did so. The sudden movement also had the dark room spinning around her. Her entire body was sticky and over warm. Panting, she placed her fist to her mouth, wanting to retch from the various unsavory smells that seemed to be pressing in on her. Sage grimaced and leaned against the wall, the cool stone bringing relief to the heat in her feverish skin.

Pale moonlight now shone through the bars of the small window. She'd slept quite a while but at least it meant the truth serum had worn off. She noticed a small tin cup glinting in the dim lighting, and she remembered how dry her throat was. With a groan, she hoisted herself off the bed and staggered a few steps to pick it up. Her legs shook, threatening to collapse. Sage tried not to spill a drop of the precious liquid as she stumbled back to the bed. She needed a healer.

Just as she was about to bring the cup to her lips it occurred to her that something could be amiss with it. She sat, debating whether to drink it or not. She swirled the water in the cup and eyed it. Sage dipped one finger into the cup, tasted a drop and then waited.

Nothing.

She didn't know how much time had passed since she drank the cider, but she was definitely suffering the effects of dehydration. She needed to drink this. But was it worth taking the chance of being drugged again? She'd never been helpless before yesterday, and it wasn't a feeling she relished. This time, Sage sniffed the cup, just to see if she detected anything out of the ordinary, but she smelled nothing. Her tests so far didn't mean it was safe to drink but she couldn't survive without water so she'd have to take the chance. Sage brought the cup to her parched lips, and she took a small sip, letting it wet her mouth and soothe her dry throat. She took another small sip, trying not to gulp it all down at once. She decided it was enough for now and hid the now half-empty cup beneath her cot. Who knew when she would receive more?

Sage's stomach cramped and let out a large growl. It seemed the water had awakened her appetite. When had she eaten last? What day was it?

Don't focus on it, think of something else.

Instead she tried to recall everything she had told the commander during the drug-induced interrogation. She needed to keep her story straight, or they'd hang her with it. The memory of it was still a blur, but Sage was fairly certain she hadn't revealed anything important.

A frigid breeze floated off the ocean and through her cell window, caressing her overheated skin. The room was freezing, but she felt as if she was sitting beneath the sun. Her linen shirt clung to her skin in a sticky mess. Was this an after-effect of the concoction they'd given her? Or was she actually ill? Sage examined her wrists. Already, they were swollen and tender to the touch. Angry red lines mapped her wrists. Sage winced. She didn't doubt an infection was starting.

Her head pounded like someone had kicked it, so, rubbing her temples, she lay on her side, cradling her head in one arm. Hopefully, with a little rest, she would sleep off the pain. Vaguely, she was aware of metal clanging nearby but didn't rouse enough to open her eyes. Damn noisy prisoners.

Out of nowhere, a strong hand covered her mouth while other hands clasped her ankles, sufficiently rousing her from her daze. Her eyes flew open, and she found herself surrounded by four strangers. She tried to jerk from their grasp but, in her current state, was too weak to accomplish anything. The man whose hand enveloped her face yanked her head back with her hair, bringing her to him. His rancid breath washed over her as he leaned closer. "You sure are a pretty little thing underneath all those bruises, aren't ya?"

She glared at him and bit down as hard as she could. He yanked his hand back cursing her. "Vicious little wench!" he spat.

She bared her teeth in response.

"Get her up, and quickly. I have pressing matters to attend to," remarked a tall man with a haughty voice.

Sage bucked her hips, trying to dislodge the bruising fingers pressed into her skin, until a massive fist hammered into the side of her face. Tears pricked her eyes as everything blurred and darkness swirled around her. Sage shook her head, trying to focus, but only succeeded in nauseating herself.

Tight metal cuffs encased her wrists, and her body swung through the air. Sage's ribs screamed as someone wrenched her arms above her head. Her body dropped painfully, the restraints biting into her already sensitive wrists. Her toes brushed the floor as she scrambled for purchase.

Sage dropped her chin to her chest, heaving in a breath as she tried not to retch. She stared at the grate below her and thought grimly that it wasn't for waste but to wash away the crimes of this room.

Shiny, brown leather boots interrupted her study of the floor. Sage lifted her head and met the eyes of the man who was no doubt her executioner. His primary characteristic was his unusual height—he had to be at least five inches over six feet. Apart from that, though, he seemed rather ordinary: brown hair, brown eyes. Utterly forgettable. Not what she'd pictured death to look like.

"What do you want from me?" she croaked. "I've already told Commander Samuel everything." Sweat dripped from her temples into her eyes.

"The commander didn't think you were entirely honest with him, so here I am." He stepped up to her with cold eyes and fingered her sweat-soaked shirt. He watched her face as he languidly slid his hand from her ribs to the hollow of her waist and then to her hip. Her blood froze in her veins as a cruel smile crossed his face.

"Men's clothing? Interesting choice. So improper. You have to know the ideas you inspire when you showcase your body in such a manner." He squeezed her hip. "I am sure your mother wouldn't approve."

"I wouldn't know, she's dead," she replied.

"Now, now. Let's not lie to each other. Wouldn't want to start our relationship with lies, would we?"

He dropped his hand, reaching for the blade sheath at his waist. Her eyes tracked his movements as he removed the knife from its sheath. She would stay calm. She would not allow them the satisfaction of breaking her. He brought the blade to her face and scraped the sharp edge to where her pulse hammered in her neck.

"Let's start this again, shall we? My name is Serge. I will ask you a question. You will answer me—truthfully, I might add—or there will be consequences."

Sage tried to remain as still as possible. One flick of his wrist and she would bleed out in seconds.

"What is your name?"

"M-my name is Ruby." She held her breath, awaiting his next move.

He lifted his lips in a mocking smile and replied sarcastically, "I appreciate your honesty."

He moved his dagger from her neck to the opening of her linen shirt, catching it with the blade. He flicked his wrist, and her shirt fluttered open. Embarrassment and rage battled inside her, but she stamped both emotions down. If she gave them one inkling of her feelings, she knew they'd run with it. She could show no fear.

Sage raised her chin and gave Serge her haughtiest and most

disdainful look.

"Oh! I can be so clumsy sometimes," he whispered. Leering, he leaned forward and placed the knife tip between her leather trousers and hip. With another tug, it cut through them like butter and they fell flimsily to the floor. Even the pain radiating through her body wasn't enough to distract her from the embarrassment of being stripped in front of four men. Their eyes crawled over her skin like insects, leaving goosebumps in their wake. Sage focused on a stone behind him and steeled herself. She would *not* show fear.

The tall man pushed away the shirt from her stomach with the tip of his dagger and seemed to survey each mark or bruise marring her torso.

"The crown prince knows how to punch. A pity that your beauty had to be marred by his hands." He grinned, which only made him look more deranged, and clapped his hands once. "Next question, what do you do for the resistance?"

"I've already said I don't know what you're talking about. I didn't even know about the resistance until the commander spoke with me. What would the resistance want with an orphan? I don't have any skills to offer."

"Not quite what I was looking for."

He ran his eyes down her legs and back up her thighs. He caressed the front of her legs with his rough fingers, and she couldn't contain a shudder of revulsion.

Serge raised his eyebrows. "This appears to be the only spot untouched. Probably the best place to leave my mark." Lazily, he slashed along the front of her left thigh. Pain exploded in her leg, and she hissed out a breath but maintained a blank face.

He cocked his head with a smirk. "I do enjoy symmetry."

After a moment, the pain in her leg worsened, burning like hell. Her whole body trembled, and she bit back a whimper as blood dripped down her leg.

Time passed, and Serge continued his line of questioning. He also proved to be a sadistic bastard. Sage drifted in and out of consciousness until a sharp crack across her face whipped her head to the side, her face throbbing in time with her heartbeat. Serge grabbed her hair and yanked back her head, and his other hand wrapped around her neck with a squeeze.

"No falling asleep on me, dear."

"I am no one's 'dear'," she choked out, her swollen lips making speech difficult.

"Your fire is incredible," Serge mused, "and I rather enjoy the idea of breaking you. Perhaps I'll keep you around as a mistress."

"Not on your life," she spat vehemently, throwing every last bit of energy she had into the words. "I would die first." His smile dropped as hers appeared.

"That can be arranged, *dear*," he sneered, tightening his grip on her neck.

Sage tried to suck in a breath but none came. She would die after all. She hoped her family would be okay without her.

Her thoughts were interrupted when someone shouted, and, suddenly, the pressure on her neck disappeared. She sucked in a breath—only to cough so hard she was sure her lungs were coming out.

Someone wrapped their arms around her waist and lifted her off her wrists. Like a fire, pain consumed her entire body. She opened her mouth to cry out but only choked on it, instead emitting a shaky wheeze. The fetters were peeled from her wrists and her arms flopped limply to her side.

What was happening? Sage peered up and saw amid the swirling room two spots of violet. "Gav?" she coughed out. Did she already die?

The purple eyes stared down at her, concerned, and a deep voice pleaded with her to stay awake. "Ruby? Keep your eyes open for me, darling."

He gently pushed her bloody hair from her face and gave her a gentle smile. The purple eyes left her and the voice snapped at someone else. Another voice answered just as sharply, and that voice too seemed familiar, only at the moment she couldn't place it.

A ghoulish figure appeared above her. A specter with silvery hair, gray eyes, and a myriad of wrinkles.

She must have died. Nobody looking like that would exist in this world.

The voices seemed to urge her to do something, but she couldn't understand what. Their words faded as her pulse pounded and lights dotted her vision, followed by darkness. Smiling, she gave into the blessed void of nothingness.

Chapter Fifteen

TEHL

Tehl sat, watching as the sun peaked over the horizon. As its rays shed a dusky light on the ashen silo before him, his thoughts returned to the events that had transpired the night before...

***

Initially, all had gone smoothly. They'd been well prepared. Between Jethro, Garreth, Sethen, and himself, they'd managed to subdue the Scythian guards. It happened with such unusual ease it both surprised and troubled him.

He was not prepared, however, for what greeted him as they broke open the silo. Tehl had halted as the stenches of urine, body odor, and blood assaulted him. Filthy women, children, and the elderly trembled on the ground, terror evident in their eyes. The children whimpered, hiding themselves within the skirts of their mothers. All bore evidence of the Scythian's cruelty, each one bruised and battered. His heart broke within his chest, simultaneously growing hot with rage. They would not get away with committing such atrocities.

"Peace," he whispered. "We mean you no harm. We are here to free you from this prison. My men and I are removing the Scythians to ensure your safety." At his words, some burst into tears while others seemed to say prayers under their breaths.

"Safety?" an incredulous voice cut through the air.

Tehl searched the group of villagers for the owner of the voice. He stopped when he saw a young woman kneeling with two small children. She stood to face him with narrowed eyes. She was a tiny thing; he doubted the top of her head reached even his shoulder, yet her chin jutted out defiantly and her fists clenched. She was the owner of the angry voice.

"Does it look like we're safe?" she hissed, gesturing to the people. "Where were *you* two days ago? *You* let this happen, *you*..." She swallowed and continued roughly: "*you* let our loved ones die."

An older woman placed a hand on the girl's shoulder. "Dear one, don't blame these men. That's simply not fair. They didn't harm us. They are here to help."

Lips tight with anger, the young woman shook her head and stabbed a finger at him. "No! What isn't fair is that our king didn't protect us! And now? Now our families are gone forever." She blinked rapidly, fighting back tears, and glared.

"I am sorry for your loss," Tehl offered, hating how generic his words sounded. He meant it, every word.

She dropped her head. "That won't bring them back." The young woman sucked in a breath and pinned him with eyes full of unshed tears. "Finish this," she growled. "Not one of them deserves to live."

"Never fear on that account, lady. It will be done." Tehl's promise was sincere and deadly.

She'd studied him a moment and dipped her chin in dismissal. The young woman scooped up the little ones at her feet and buried her face in the downy fuzz blanketing their heads.

Tehl had grappled with himself. He wanted to rage through the village, destroying anything Scythian he could get his hands on. Turning to his men he registered his own shock and anger mirrored in their faces—clearly, they too were struggling with this.

He had turned back to the villagers and offered the group a smile meant to inspire confidence. "Stay here until we come for you and don't worry; you're safe now."

An unladylike snort exploded out of the young woman. Her blue-gray eyes locked onto him. "Mmhmm. Because we have been *so* safe here previously!" she mumbled. "Are you really going to leave us defenseless? Without even weapons?"

Tehl reached into his boot. Plucking out a dagger, he held the hilt out to her. "You do know how to use one of these?"

She scowled at him as she passed one child to the elderly woman beside her. "I am well acquainted with daggers, thank you."

"Good. Do you require anything else, my lady?"

She ran her finger along the blade and a ghost of a smile touched her lips. "No, that will be all, I'm sure."

A smile tugged at his lips. She was feisty, in a way, reminding him a bit of Sam. "What's your name?"

"Jasmine, my lord," she tacked on the title with a bow, or as much of one as she could execute with a small child on her hip. It seemed her anger toward him had waned, a little.

Sethen stepped inside. "The commander has signaled."

Tehl jerked his chin at Jasmine. "Protect your people." Her eyes widened as he spun on his heel and moved from the doorway.

Jethro brushed his dirty blond hair from his eyes and whispered, "They're southeast of the center. We need to move if we want to catch them."

Their group rushed through the village, stepping over fallen Scythians at every turn. His brother had obviously moved quickly. Stealthily as well—there'd been no sounds of battle. As they approached the town's center they halted, remaining hidden in the shadows while Jethro called out a signal. Some of his tension left his body when they heard his brother's answering call.

As Tehl and his men approached the fire-lit square, he saw five Scythians kneeling on the ground before his brother, surrounded by the Elite. Samuel, who had been pacing, paused when he caught sight of them and then strolled up to Tehl, feigning casualty. His tension returned, followed by a healthy dose of adrenaline. Something was wrong.

"We have a problem."

A short statement—and not one that boded well.

"There are Scythians in the trees across the river, over the Mort Wall, observing us, yet so far they have done nothing to come to the aid of their kin." His brother jerked his head toward their captives. "I can't put my finger on it, but something is wrong. They were defeated far too easily."

That gave Tehl a real pause. Scythians were notorious for fighting until death rather than be taken captive. Their soldiers were not trained to be passive. He squinted over Sam's shoulder at the brawny group of warriors, their dark eyes staring back seemingly void of all emotion. His brother was right, something was amiss in this situation.

"A trap?"

"No," Sam said in a low tone. "The area has been scouted and there are no others. It seems those watching from the Scythian riverside are alone."

Tehl scanned the dense forest for any hint of the soldiers his brother spoke of but could detect no signs of movement, not until the moonlight caught the tip of an arrow. Why hadn't they attacked? He and his men were within the archer's range. What were they waiting for?

Tehl caught his brother's eye and spoke under his breath. "Maybe we should give them a show and draw them out?"

Sam nodded, and Tehl stalked toward the line of warriors, halting just before them. They were truly giants of men. He himself was a tall man, but a few of them topped him by five inches. In addition, each man wore his long black hair exactly the same: knotted back with bone and feathers. The skin of their faces was so flawless it seemed unreal, almost like they'd been hewn from stone.

Unnatural.

Tehl suppressed a shudder. It was actually what led to Scythia's exile from the rest of the world: an unhealthy obsession with perfection—more specifically the perfect warrior—and these statues, kneeling dark-eyed and motionless before him, served as proof that their obsession had not been abandoned.

He moved down the row inspecting each man, noting the swirling designs painted on their skin and their multiple piercings. Coming upon the last one though, Tehl froze.

Not a man. A woman.

Beneath the myriad of scrawling designs, her bronze skin glistened in the firelight. She dropped her head, sending her midnight braid slithering down her back. Tehl stepped closer and grabbed hold of it, giving it a rough tug. Her face tipped upward, exposing blank, black eyes tipped up at the corners. He'd never before seen a Scythian woman. He understood them to be guarded jealously by their men. Her face sported sharp, high cheekbones with arched brows and a pouty lower lip. She was a beautiful woman, no doubt about it.

"They're sending women to do warriors' work now?"

Silence met his question.

No response, not even a flicker in her eyes.

Tehl lifted his eyes to the forest, he shouted across the river. "There is no need for hiding. We are warriors, not spies. Tell me, where is Your Honor?" He dropped the woman's braid, holding his breath. Would they take the bait? His eyes darted to the woman and again to the riverside. Eight warriors had emerged from the forest and now stood on the riverbank. An enormous warrior stood at the forefront, regarding them steadily, his black hair hanging down his bare chest.

"Have you nothing to say?" Tehl asked, lifting a brow.

The massive warrior took a step forward and spoke, his deep, accented voice rumbling across the river. "What would you have me say? I was rather enjoying the little show. Don't stop on our account."

'Don't stop on our account.' That statement alone revealed quite a bit. They were unconcerned with his treatment of their captive kin. So why were they here? Tehl's mind ran several scenarios but none seemed to fit.

His brother cleared his throat. "I wasn't aware it was a show we put on." Sam turned and addressed the captured warriors. "You hear that? They care nothing for you. Your own brethren would stand by while you die and enjoy it."

"In death there is honor," was her short reply.

His brother cocked his head, studying the female Scythian and Tehl wondered what he was about. Sam sauntered over to cup her chin, tilting her face first to the left, then to the right.

"Women—always more emotional creatures. You can't even beat it out of them," he spoke just loud enough for his words to carry across the river. "Isn't she beautiful, brother? And so exotic! Look at those cheekbones and plush lips. She could make a man very happy." Sam's gaze skated down her leather breastplate and rested on her flared hips. "And those hips!" Sam whistled. "Perfect for having children. Maybe I should take her as my layman."

Foreign curses and growled threats erupted around them.

Tehl grinned to himself. Leave it to Sam. His brother was playing on the enemy's purist beliefs, for Scythians were sickened more by 'mixed breeding', as they called it, than by death. The man had a devious mind.

Brilliant. Absolutely brilliant.

"I think she could bear you many strong sons," he agreed in a casual tone, as though speaking of the weather. "You and I both know you'd benefit from a few spare heirs."

Finally, the large warrior spoke up. "These men do not concern me, but they chose to cross the Mort Wall and have broken our law. They are now criminals, so I leave their lives in your hands, but we deal differently with our women. Give her to me, and we will depart from Aermia."

Lies. "You mean to tell me the warlord of Scythia had no knowledge of this attack?" Tehl asked, his voice hard.

"This was not sanctioned."

Tehl didn't believe him for one second; they'd been pillaging Aermian lands for months and it was not the work of a ragtag band of thieves either. Each attack had been executed with military precision. Obviously, they weren't simply thieves and murderers, but liars as well.

"I think not." Sam's smile was frosty. "The woman is mine now. I will release the other warriors, and if they make it across the river tied up, they're yours to deal with."

Samuel nodded to his men, and, brusquely, the Elite hefted up the warriors one by one, pushing them into the flowing water. The first immediately sank without resurfacing. The other three labored across, and the first to reach the bank struggled to his feet only to be struck with an arrow to the chest. Tehl's breath whistled out of him as the other two met the same fate.

"Well that's *one* way to deal with disobedience," Sam remarked, disinterestedly.

The warrior shrugged a shoulder. "If they were caught, they're not worthy, anyway. However, it is in your best interest to release the girl so I suggest you do so."

Sam shook his head with an arrogant smile.

The warrior nodded curtly. "So be it."

They melted back into the forest as silently as they had appeared. He scrutinized them as they disappeared, the warrior's parting words ringing in Tehl's head. They bore a note of finality, of warning: tonight's actions would bring consequences. But what was done, was done. They'd have to deal with whatever came of it later.

Sam squatted next to him, facing the woman. "You're important; care to enlighten me as to why?" he asked.

She set her jaw and stared through his brother.

"Yeah, I figured as much." Sam looked to Sethen and Garreth. "She is now your responsibility. Make sure she is not harmed and cannot escape." His brother turned back to the woman and trailed a finger down her cheek. "How do you fit into the puzzle, my dear?"

The Scythian woman jerked her face away and continued to ignore him.

***

Tehl blinked, having been pulled from the previous night's memory by the snapping of a branch. Looking up, he saw the fiery woman from the silo pushing through the tall grass. She reached where he was sitting, and she slumped onto a nearby fallen log. The girl pulled his blade from a sheath at her waist and held it out to him.

"No, keep it." he muttered, returning his attention to the village. She neither spoke nor made a move to leave. Curious, Tehl glanced at her from the corner of his eye, only to catch her staring at him.

"What?" he asked, irritated by the intrusion; he'd been enjoying the silence.

"Thank you. I mean, for the blade... I have never owned anything so fine." She opened her mouth to continue before closing it again. After a pause, she sucked in a deep breath, continuing, "Look. I am sorry for the way I spoke to you last night, my lord. Had I had known it was the crown prince to whom I spoke I would have shown more respect." She again paused. "No, that's a lie. I'd have spoken the same way, but I have been informed there could be dire consequences if I don't apologize, so..." she trailed off and shrugged.

His lips twitched at her rather blunt confession.

"There will be no punishment, Jasmine. You were upset and angry." He allowed his amusement to bleed into his voice as he spoke. "The Crown can spare you, this time at least."

Her shoulders slumped, and her breath whooshed out. "Oh. Good then. I... I have to think about more than myself now."

He remembered the two small children clinging to her the night before. "You lost your husband?" He winced at how tactless that sounded.

Sorrow shrouded her features. "No." She shook her head. "I lost my brother and his wife, my only living relatives. So their twins are mine now."

"How old are they?"

"They just turned two years. I doubt they will remember anything of their parents when they're grown, only my stories of them."

Tehl sympathized; he of all people knew how painful it was to lose family. She pushed her dark brown hair from her face with a watery smile. His eyes narrowed as he scanned her face, realization dawning. Her skin hardly creased, even when smiling. She must be very young. Not much younger than himself. "Exactly how old are *you*? Your face, it's smooth: you can't be over twenty years."

"Has anyone ever told you how blunt you are?" He shrugged, and she sniggered. "I will be nineteen years next week."

She was too young to raise babes alone. How would they survive the winter? Did she even have a place to live? Tehl decided he would arrange matters so that the little family would be taken care of. As he thought, he turned his gaze back to Silva, making a mental list of all the things the villagers would need to rebuild. The remaining farmers and his Elite were already working to clean up the damage. As usual, Sam stood in the middle of it, heading the efforts. His brother looked up and caught his eye. He handed off his shovel and strode their way.

It was time to get to work. Tehl stood stiffly and offered a hand to Jasmine.

"Thank you, my lord." Taking his hand, she stood, groaning and rolling her neck. She spared him a glance and a quick smile before focusing on Sam's approaching figure. "Quite the old pair we make."

Sam's smile widened as he glanced from his brother to Jasmine, eyes lighting up at the sight of her. "And who might this lovely woman be?" Sam flirted with a wink.

Her soft smile dissolved into a scowl.

Samuel took her hand and kissed her knuckles. "I am happy to make your acquaintance, fair lady. I am Commander Samuel of the

Elite. And you are?"

Jasmine jerked her hand from his and wiped it on her skirt, disgusted, muttering something about slobber. Tehl smirked at his brother's odd expression. He couldn't tell if Sam was amused or offended by her reaction.

"It's not that easy to scrub me from your skin, my lady," Samuel teased. Jasmine simply raised her eyes and glared.

Her temper rose, and Tehl's smile widened. Jasmine would put Sam in his place, he could tell. And boy, did she not disappoint.

"I would appreciate it if you kept your hands, and lips, to yourself. Please refrain from touching my person in any way," Jasmine fumed. "I am sure this comes as a shock, but not all women appreciate your kind of attention."

Well, that *was* a first. He'd never seen Sam shot down. One point to Jasmine.

Sam brushed it off though, dismissing Jasmine. "We relocated the people of Silva because of the burned homes. I plan on leaving a few Elite here until the Guard arrives to help with rebuilding. The Mort Wall has weakened, it'd be prudent to establish a post here; thus, Silva will always be protected."

Tehl was about to reply when Jasmine muttered, "Because you did such an amazing job before…"

Sam stiffened and gave the girl a cold look. "You know nothing of war, little girl. I suggest you gaze around your Scythian-free home before casting judgments."

Jasmine flushed with anger. "You know what I see? Loss. Loss of my family, my friends, and my life; and all because you didn't protect us. Our homes were burned to the ground while we were beaten and starved. I lost every member of my family, save the twins, becoming a mother in one night. And you," she seethed, "let the brutes responsible go free."

Samuel's face softened. "They died. Nothing is more final than that. Those Scythians departed from this world; they can't hurt anyone anymore."

"They should have suffered, just like the rest of us have. We will feel the effects of their attack for years." She stepped forward and poked Samuel in the chest. "That is on you!"

"What you're feeling will also pass." Sam's gaze held compassion.

She dropped her eyes and turned her back on him. Jasmine stepped forward and curtsied deeply. "Thank you for the gift, I won't forget your kindness and help." She pushed passed Sam and hustled toward the village square.

Samuel frowned after her. "You never told me your name," Sam shouted. His brother could never leave well enough alone.

Jasmine peeked over her shoulder. "You don't need it."

Tehl turned toward him, a smug grin plastered on his face. "You know what? I don't think she liked you, Sam."

His brother was still watching the young woman walk away. He ran a frustrated hand through his blond curls but quickly shifted, sending a cocky smile his brother's way. "She experienced something horrific. It wasn't me."

Tehl glanced at the petite brunette now smiling at Jaxon. "No, that woman despises you. She didn't act that way toward me or Jaxon." He pointed out Jaxon smiling as Jasmine giggled.

Sam's face darkened as he spied the exchange. When he noticed

Tehl's interest, his face blanked. "She has horrible taste in men, especially if she had this remarkable specimen," he said, motioning from his shoulder to his toes, "before her and still chose Jaxon."

He rolled his eyes at his little brother and shook his head. His eyes swept over the ruined village once more, the smile falling from his face, now sobered. "What happened last night..." He paused, gathering his thoughts. "Something was not right, Sam. No one has ever taken one of them prisoner. *No one,* Sam. It doesn't feel right."

Sam nodded as Tehl spoke. "I've been thinking the same thing. We may have had the element of surprise but that doesn't account for them laying their weapons down. Neither did they resist nor speak when we restrained them. I had been prepared for some kind of trap but then nothing happened. When we discovered the warriors across the river, I thought for sure they'd ambush us and that perhaps that was the plan all along." His brother stared at the log behind him in thought. "Yet, all they did was stand there! It makes little sense. Who sits back and watches their kin get dragged away? Also, those warriors didn't even care, and that is dangerous. Why would they only react to my taunt to their woman?" Sam paced as he continued to work through his thoughts. He covered his face with a hand and took a deep breath through his nose and paused. After a moment, he dropped his hand in frustration. "We've more questions now than we did prior!"

Tehl waited for Sam to finish venting his frustration. Sam barked out a harsh laugh as he stabbed a finger Tehl's way. "And the nerve! You and I both know those warriors weren't rogue. Scythia sent them here for a purpose, I just don't know why. Another damn piece of the puzzle missing," Sam huffed.

"We will figure it out," Tehl replied, placing a hand on his brother's shoulder. "At least we have someone that might shed more light on the situation in Scythia. You got her to respond to you last night; you can do so again. But currently there are other pressing needs. These people need our immediate care and focus."

Sam sighed and nodded. "It would be best if we left two teams here for rebuilding and protection until the Guard arrive." He eyed the surrounding destruction as they returned to the village.

"What of their thane?" Tehl asked.

"They have no protector or keep near. They have always reported to Sanee."

"What?" Tehl frowned. Without a thane, or a post, the people of Silva were left vulnerable. They needed the protection more than any other area as they were right on the Scythian border. Tehl glared at the destroyed homes; every time he felt he'd gotten his feet under him, something set him off balance again. "Gather those set to return with us and inform them we depart in half an hour."

Sam nodded once and strode toward the Elite, already barking out orders. Tehl rolled his kinked neck. It was no wonder his father was driven mad after his mother died. Running a kingdom by yourself was difficult. He had a rebellion to deal with, a Midsummer Festival to plan, and Scythians breathing down his neck. Tehl sighed and straightened up. He could do this. He would do this. He just needed to take it one day at a time.

Chapter Sixteen

TEHL

When the tall gray turrets came into view, Tehl breathed out a sigh of relief. Between his lack of sleep and hours of hard riding, he was sufficiently worn out. It seemed like he'd only blinked and they'd arrived at the inner courtyards. He rubbed his eyes hard. Had he fallen asleep? No, he didn't think so, but he sure didn't remember the last leg of their journey. Tehl brought Wraith to a halt and dropped to the ground. The moment his feet hit the dirt, he groaned—everything in his body seemed to ache. Ruefully, he stretched his lower extremities, chiding himself. He needed to ride more often. He'd been spending too much time in the city.

Leaning against the saddle, he gingerly ran a hand down Wraith's sweaty neck, whispering praise to the exhausted beast.

Wraith cocked an ear, listening as his master spoke. Tehl stroked the downy nose softly and stumbled back a step as Wraith bumped him in the chest with it.

"I know buddy, time to cool down, but don't worry, afterward it'll be oats and carrots for you." Tehl could have sworn Wraith smiled in response. With a smile of his own, he gave a farewell pat to the horse as a young stable boy sporting an unruly mop of orange hair collected the reins and led him away.

Tehl glanced back to the company and saw his brother discretely issuing instructions to Garreth and Jethro, after which two Elite came and collected the Scythian woman, no doubt carting her off to the dungeon.

Returning to Tehl's side, Sam gave him a brief report. "Everything is being taken care of, my lord. Supplies and men are already on their way to Silva. We'll attempt to obtain whatever we can from the female warrior. I'll update you in the morning with anything we learn over the course of tonight."

Tehl nodded. He was more than ready to rid himself of his armor and be done with this day.

He returned to the castle. The lanterns lining its interior walls scattered distorted shadows along the dimly lit corridors and illuminated a figure approaching him from the far end of the hall. It wasn't until the figure neared that he noticed a familiar set of purple eyes. Gavriel. His cousin met him in the middle. Tehl clapped a hand on his cousin's shoulder in greeting and motioned for him to follow.

"Walk with me." Together, they moved toward the royal wing.

"How have the last two days gone? Have you survived court in my absence?"

Gavriel grimaced. "Barely. I don't envy you or your lot in life. I can't fathom how you listen to your officials drone on about such droll things all day, nor the bickering nobles I had to dine with two nights in a row. Don't even get me started on some of the crazy women..."

Tehl smirked at the disturbed look Gav shot him. As he jogged up the stairs, he taunted, "What? You couldn't handle all those ladies vying for your attention?"

"If you could even call them ladies. Several bore a stronger resemblance to bloodhounds than women. I had to scrub twice to get the feeling of wandering hands off me." He shuddered.

Tehl barked out a laugh. "No need to worry, I won't subject you to that again any time soon." As they arrived at his chamber, Tehl turned his head, ready to bid Gavriel goodnight, but caught a whiff of himself. Oh boy, he stunk. "Sam and I will update you in the morning, and I'd appreciate a report from you as well, but for now I think a bath is my top priority."

The smile fell from Gav's face. "Actually, there are things that require your attention immediately, as in tonight."

Tehl tensed. Turning back to his cousin, he inquired, "What does it pertain to?"

"The rebel in the dungeon."

Tehl perked up. Perhaps the woman broke. He smiled. "Did she give you the information we need?"

"*No*, but..."

"Then it's not important; if it can't wait, speak with Sam. I have had a long day. We'll speak in the morning."

Gav's face hardened. "There's been an incident with the girl, Ruby: she's sick. She needs a healer."

"She can have one when she answers our questions," Tehl retorted.

"Tehl, it's serious."

The stress of the last several days combined with his desperate need for sleep increased his frustration. Tehl glared at his cousin and spoke harshly. "If that's the case then it should be easy to make her a deal. She gives us what we need in exchange for a healer. She is a prisoner, not a guest. My orders stand. No bread and just enough water to keep her sustained! Is that all?"

Gav picked an imaginary piece of lint off his shirt and looked up at him, his purple eyes simmering with anger. "Yes, that is all, *Your Highness.*"

His anger melted away with his cousin's mild answer. Shame and embarrassment pricked him over his outburst. As Gavriel sketched a bow and stalked away, he called out to him. "Gav... I'm sorry, but we need her talking—and soon."

His cousin glowered over his shoulder. "If she dies, it will be on your head. Will you be able to shoulder that? I know you. You would never forgive yourself."

Tehl blew out a frustrated breath as he moved into his room. Thinking on his words, guilt pricked him. Gav had a good heart and was only being a decent human being. He didn't deserve such treatment.

His chamberlain entered, distracting him from his thoughts, and began divesting him of his chain mail and leathers. After everything had been removed, he rolled his shoulders, relishing how light he was without them.

"Would you like me to ready a bath for you, Your Highness?" the chamberlain inquired.

Tehl knew he needed one but figured he was so exhausted that he'd probably fall asleep and drown in the tub. "No, that will be all."

The chamberlain bowed and then departed. Tehl looked across the room to the mirror; his face and clothing were streaked with dirt, ash, and sweat. His eyes were bloodshot with his eyes turning a hideous shade of blue green. He trudged over to the washbasin and began scrubbing all the skin he could reach. Once he'd completed that, he peeled off the rest of his soiled clothing, leaving a trail to the bed. His eyes burned as he closed them. All his worries and responsibilities could wait for tomorrow. Time for blessed sleep.

Chapter Seventeen

TEHL

The faint light of dawn painted the ceiling in a soft buttery yellow, rousing the crown prince from his bed. Goosebumps appeared on his arms and torso the moment his feet touched the icy stone floor. He rubbed his tired eyes, wishing he could slip back into bed and stay there. Tehl shuffled to the window and squinted as he watched the new day dawn. He had a mountain of things to do, but before anything else, he needed to deal with the rebel.

Tehl abandoned the peaceful picture his window offered him. It was time to get moving. He threw on a clean pair of trousers and a linen shirt, stumbling as he tried to pull on his boots. He opened his door as quietly as possible and peeked out, glancing down the hall in both directions. Pleased to find it empty, he gave a smile, nodding to the guards stationed at his door, and slipped away. The last thing he needed was to be waylaid. He snaked through the corridors, hoping to remain unnoticed, and exited through the east entrance. The sun caressed his face and he closed his eyes, taking a moment to savor its warmth. The metal ring of swords pulled him from his trance. Tehl opened his eyes and cocked his head, watching Samuel beat Jaxon into submission. Both men had discarded their shirts, skin covered with dirt. Noticing his brother watching, Sam shot him a grin. "Coming to practice, brother?"

"Not this morning. I have other duties demanding my attention."

"If you need my help, you know where I am." Sam winked and turned back to Jaxon.

Tehl dismissed his brother and strode to the dungeon entrance. The guards stationed there snapped to attention with a bow. He dipped his head in acknowledgment and continued down the stairs to the bowels of the castle. Jeffry was slumped at his desk, stroking his mustache, obviously deep in thought. His eyes lifted to Tehl, bitterness filling his face.

Tehl's brows furrowed as he stopped before the old man's desk. "Is everything all right, Jeffry?" The Keeper's scowl deepened. Multiple emotions flickered on the older man's face until it settled into a mix of disappointment and distaste. Confusion swirled through him. What had he done to deserve that look?

"My lord, I have always supported your father, yourself, and your brother because your family has always been honorable and just. You know I consider you part of my family."

"Thank you, Jeffry. You have been faithful in your service and a wonderful friend to my father. My brother and I consider you family as well."

"I'm afraid I hadn't finished, son."

Tehl straightened at Jeffry's bluntness. The Keeper pierced him with another dissatisfied look. What could have upset him to such a degree? He had never been one to take offense easily in the past. Tehl opened his mouth to ask, when Jeffry cut in.

"May I speak plainly?"

Despite the awkward tension between them, a smile crept onto Tehl's face. He'd never known his old friend to speak in any other way. Jeffry was a blunt man.

"You always have before. Even if I said 'no', I doubt that would keep you from telling me, anyway."

Jeffry cracked a brief, crooked smile but quickly sobered. "What you are doing with that woman is wrong, sire. She has caused no trouble, and from my brief talks with her, she is a lovely young woman."

Tehl sent Jeffry an incredulous look and chuckled. He hooked his thumb over his shoulder pointing down the hall. "Are we speaking of the same woman? You don't mean the vicious viper Sam and I brought in here?"

Jeffry straightened and stood up to his full five-foot seven-inch frame. The older man placed his gnarled hands on his desk and leaned forward. "She shouldn't be here."

Tehl couldn't believe it, she had Jeffry fooled. Gavriel was all up in arms over her needing medical care last night. What sort of spell had she cast over everyone while he was away?

By now, more than a bit annoyed, Tehl stared at Jeffry and inquired, "I understand you disagree and your opinion is noted.

However, have my instructions been followed?"

Jeffry stiffened at the dismissal but nodded.

"Just rations of food and water? No blankets? No care as I requested?"

"Yes, we have followed your commands to the letter, my lord."

"Then I appreciate your devotion to your responsibilities despite your personal feelings. Now though, I must see if I can glean any information from our captive." He gave Jeffry a short nod and strode with determination to the cells. He'd only made it three steps when Jeffry spoke from behind him.

"I doubt you'll get anything from her."

Tehl looked over his shoulder with a chilling smile. "I'm sure I'll find a way."

As he continued down the dank hallway, his mind turned over the odd conversation. Jeffry had never been disappointed in him, and he didn't like that he seemed to be now. Curses and pleas were shouted to him as he wound his way toward the woman's cell. He passed one cell only to pause and back up.

The Scythian woman.

She sat in the dead center of her cell staring at nothing. Tehl scrutinized her for a moment, waiting for some reaction to his presence. Nothing. Not even a glance. Wherever she had buried herself within her mind, it was effective. She wasn't mentally present.

Tehl shook his head and moved on. A conundrum, that's what she was. But he would leave the figuring out to Sam; his brother salivated over puzzles, so it made sense to trust him with this one.

At the end of the dim hallway, he veered left and a familiar figure came into view. Gav was asleep against the wall not fifteen paces away. Why was his cousin sleeping down here? Was he that worried?

"He has quite the hero complex, doesn't he?" a low voice whispered in his ear.

Years of training kept Tehl from flinching, and he knew his brother was the only one who still surprised him. He rolled his eyes and turned as Sam emerged from the darkened area between two lanterns. "Was that really necessary?" Tehl quipped.

Sam smiled. "Someone has to keep you on your toes, and I need to keep up on my sneaking skills, so it's dual purpose. Looks like you might need to brush up on your spying skills though."

"That would be nice, but I doubt my advisers will let me out of the castle so soon after being gone for a couple days." Tehl eyed Gav's prone figure and then back to Sam. "Do you have any idea what he's been up to? Did he speak with you at all last night?"

Sam shook his head. "I haven't spoken to him since before we left. I was just as eager as you to speak with dear Ruby this fine morning."

His cousin finally stirred and then hefted his large frame off the ground. Despite the weak lighting, Tehl was able to detect dark smudges under Gav's eyes. When had he slept a full night? The extra responsibilities were taxing everyone, and he now felt even worse about their previous conversation. Tehl opened his mouth to apologize, but Gav held up a hand.

"Your prisoner awaits you," Gav said flatly.

Damn. In letting his temper get the best of him, he'd really mucked things up last night. Tehl sighed. It wasn't the place for apologies; he'd have to make amends later.

Tehl stepped up to the cell bars, his nose wrinkling at the smell. It smelled worse than a healer's tent on a battlefield. Tehl examined the small form in the middle of the floor. She lay curled on her side with her back facing them. As she shifted, she disturbed the faded black cloak covering her, revealing a naked thigh. Tehl froze, his brain scrambling for some explanation. The last he had heard she'd stolen some clothing from the Guard, so how was she naked now?

His head whipped to the side, meeting Gavriel's gaze. "Where are her trousers?" he asked sharply.

"Destroyed," Gav bit out, his body rigid.

Tehl's eyes returned to the pale bruised leg. "How?"

"Ask her yourself, sire."

Tehl clenched his jaw at the sneer in his cousin's voice and cleared his throat. "Time to get up."

The wench didn't move, she ignored him.

He raised his voice. "Answer me, rebel."

Again, she didn't acknowledge him, but continued to lie there. Tehl gritted his teeth and leaned forward, the cold metal biting into his hands as he squeezed the bars. "Listen here, Ruby, you will answer your crown prince and show some respect!"

A third time, she ignored him.

"Unlock it," he demanded to no one in particular.

Sam stepped forward and placed the key in the lock and turned it. Tehl wrenched open the door and prowled around her body, stumbling as he caught sight of her face. It was almost unrecognizable. Her face was purple and swollen, the creases of her lids barely visible. Dried blood had clumped her black locks into snarls around her face.

Tehl leaned over and lifted the cloak, sucking in a sharp breath at her state. Everywhere he looked, her skin was mottled with bruises. She was too pale, almost translucent. His eyes tripped over her torn shirt and bare legs, cataloguing all the cuts that crisscrossed her thighs. Her blood was smeared over her body like a garish painting. He paused at the tourniquet tied around her left thigh.

Thank God someone had done at least that much.

Tehl swallowed thickly and lowered himself to a squat. Her hands were resting limply by her head, wrists oozing blood and yellow pus onto the stone beneath her.

"Gav, *what happened*?" he whispered, his voice hoarse, his eyes on her mutilated wrists.

"One captain took it upon himself to make sure she was interrogated."

Bile burned his throat. He couldn't believe it was one of his own men who did this. Shame and rage filled him. Tehl tore his eyes from the broken girl and stared at his cousin with accusation. "And where were you?"

His cousin's face hardened. "I was taking care of the kingdom as you were hunting Scythians like you commanded me to, my lord."

Tehl grunted, knowing he was being unfair, and turned back to the girl. He reached out and gently brushed the damaged skin around her wrist, still in shock. "All this from her bindings?"

Gav took a deep breath and shook his head. "When Jeffry and I came upon her, they'd already stripped her. She got those because they'd hung her from the ceiling by her wrists. Tehl..." He paused, swallowing. "There was so much blood. I didn't know if she was alive when I pulled her down."

Tehl lifted his hand and placed it on her forehead. She was burning up; a light sheen of sweat dampened her temples and her swollen face. He smoothed her hair from her face and glanced down at her bare thighs. His stomach rolled, and his breath seized. He had to ask. "Was she..." Tehl stuttered, "um, violated?"

Tehl held his breath as he awaited his cousin's response. Gav's expression promised death. The floor dropped out from under him. It had happened under his roof, so *he* was accountable. Prisoner or not, she was still his responsibility and never did he intend *that* sort of interrogation. There were some lines you just didn't cross.

"No," Gavriel growled, passed clenched teeth. "I arrived in time, but that doesn't mean she's unscathed. Take a closer look at her bruises."

He peered at her and reached for her leg. Her body was a map of injuries. Tehl traced one and familiarity struck him. He looked between his hand and the mark.

Handprints.

They were bloody handprints.

Disgust washed over him; such treatment... How could it have happened under his watch? "Why hasn't she been treated then?" he hissed, glaring at her offending bruises. Perhaps if he stared hard enough, he could singe them from her skin altogether.

"Because you ordered me not to. I did what I could for her without committing insubordination."

Gavriel's words cut him like a knife. His anger gave way to a heavier burden—soul-crushing guilt. She was going to die. He'd seen fevers like hers before; it'd be a miracle if she made it another night. While he was sleeping soundly in his bed, she'd lain, dying, on a cold, stone floor. A wet, rattling cough brought his attention back to the pitiful creature before him. Tehl leaned over her and shook her once. "Ruby?" She moaned and began to shiver, but didn't wake. "Sam!" he called without taking his eyes off her. "Get her to a healer."

Sam moved into the cell and knelt by her side. He placed his fingers above her collarbone and leaned over her. He placed his ear near her mouth and listened. After a moment, he rose, regret evident in his eyes. "Tehl, I honestly don't think she'll make it. Her lungs are filled with fluid—whether from the fever or blood from internal damage, I'm not certain."

He should have listened to Gav. Because of his foolishness, the girl would die. "We need a healer. We have to try."

Sam shook his head at him. "It's too late brother, we can only make her comfortable."

Tehl understood, but he wouldn't accept it. There had to be something, anything. A hand squeezed his shoulder. Gavriel. His cousin no doubt blamed him, yet he still offered comfort, though he deserved none.

"Where do you want her moved?" Gav reached down to pick Ruby up.

Something about Gav holding her made him bristle. Tehl brushed aside Gav's hands and scooped her up into his own arms. He cradled the frail body against him and stood. He all but ran from the cell, leaving his brother and cousin behind.

Sam caught up first. "What do you plan on doing for her? You can't care for her, Tehl. Pass her to me, and I will see that she is cared for."

He tightened his grip and picked up his pace. "It's my fault she is in this state so she's now my responsibility." When the Keeper came into view he realized he now understood exactly why Jeffry had been so disgusted. Tehl spared him a glance as he passed. "You were right, old man."

Tehl shot up the stairs, trying not to jostle the girl too much. He burst out of the dungeon, and in the morning light she looked even worse. She needed Jacob right now.

He ran.

Several servants jumped out of his way as he barreled toward the infirmary. It would be all over the palace that he was running through the castle with a naked woman in his arms but, at the moment, he didn't care. All that mattered was getting to the healer in time.

She let out a wet cough and shivered in his arms as Tehl slammed into the infirmary, Sam and Gav right on his tail. Seeing their urgency, Jacob jumped to his feet, rushing to his side before he could blink. The Healer's eyes widened. "What happened here?" Jacob asked clinically.

"Interrogation."

Jacob's face darkened. "Place her on this cot." He motioned with his chin to the right. "Is this your hellcat?"

"Yes," Sam answered, looking lost.

Tehl placed her with care on the cot while Gav cradled her head, and Sam pulled a sheet over her exposed legs. After placing a hand on her forehead, Jacob listened carefully to her breathing. "I will do all that I can but I am not sure if she will survive. The state of her lungs alone…" He shook his head. "I need to strip her and assess injuries. Get out."

Tehl stared down at the shivering girl. She didn't look anything like she had when he met her. She was so vulnerable. "If she recovers, I want her placed in one of the guest quarters." He ignored the looks he received and focused on the Healer rushing around the rebel.

"I don't think that is wise or particularly safe. She may be helpless now but she is still dangerous. You would put anyone who has to deal with her at risk."

He knew the risks. "I'm aware of that, but I don't care right now. It's largely my fault she is dying, and I need to right this wrong. I'd prefer her warm and comfortable when she awakens. We will deal with the danger she poses *if* she survives."

Sam pinched the bridge of his nose. "Well I guess we'll need guards stationed at the infirmary. We don't know what her reaction will be should she regain consciousness." Sam grinned at Jacob, "We wouldn't want anything bad to happen to the good Healer here."

Jacob glared at Sam. "This is not the time, or place, for jesting." Censure and urgency filled the Healer's voice. "Leave, and please find Mira and send her in. Time is of the essence!"

"Of course."

Sam turned on his heel and swept out the door after Gav. Tehl spared the broken girl a parting glance.

Please make it.

Chapter Eighteen

SAGE

Sage floated in a vast sea that burned hot and cold. One moment she was hot and uncomfortable, the next, so cold it felt like she'd been stabbed with a thousand needles. Fingers of mist ran through her hair, whispering words she couldn't understand. Sage sighed, content, thinking the mist must have been a gift from above. But then it shifted, creeping over her body, filling her nose and mouth, stealing her air. She was suffocating. Her body began to sink, and colors swirled above her tauntingly as she slipped farther and farther below the surface.

She was going to die.

A gruff voice called to her from the darkness, whispering that he would make everything right, that he would take care of her. She smiled to herself. It'd be nice to have someone take care of her for a change.

Fire pulsed through her veins and she cried out. She was burning! She writhed in pain, unable to pull away from the heat overtaking her body.

Again, the gruff voice spoke. "We need to get her into the tub, her fever is too high. Fetch more snow from the ice cellar!" Then it softened, and she felt a gentle pressure somewhere on her arm, steadying her. "Be still, Ruby. We're going to cool you down." The voice commanded.

Needles pricked her all over once more, and someone screamed. Who in bloody hell was screaming? She ached for silence, for some reprieve from her torture. *Leave me alone! I'm tired. I'm done. Let me go!*

"Please… Let me die…" Sage pleaded aloud with the darkness.

The gruff voice spoke again. "No. You will not die, Ruby. Do you understand me? Not on my watch."

Irritation filled her. Even now, in death, would they give her no peace?

Sage smiled when the darkness finally surged forward, beckoning. She welcomed it with a gentle sigh, gratefully sinking into its cool embrace.

***

Darkness gave way to light. The flames were gone, but now ice froze her blood. Her teeth clacked together as she shook uncontrollably. Had she died? Why was it so cold? Perhaps everything would go numb soon. Sage opened her eyes and tried to make sense of the myriad of colors flooding her vision. After a moment, the pair of hazel eyes peering down at her with concern came into focus.

"Ruby, dearest, can you hear me? Ruby?" She recognized the gruff voice. She sighed when he put a hand to her cheek; it was a blessedly warm appendage. Like a flower to the sun, she tried turning toward him, wanting to soak up the heat he gave off, but for some reason she couldn't move. She tried to speak, but the shivers wracking her body made it difficult. If she could just tell him she was cold, perhaps he'd warm her up.

"C-c-c-col-d-d-d."

His eyes snapped to the other side of room. "Mira, I need you to climb into bed with her, she needs your body heat. She is shivering far too much for my liking. It would be best if you stripped, I will step out of the room."

Sage registered a soft rustling before a big ball of warmth wrapped itself around her. She pressed her nose into it and sighed. Warm at last.

"I have you, love. That's right, snuggle in nice and close. I will keep you warm," a soft voice crooned.

Then the voice sang to her:

Lullaby, and goodnight, my sweet, the skies are dark but the stars are bright,

May the moon's silvery beams bring you endless sweet dreams.

Close your eyes and slip into your rest, may these dark hours keep you close and give you peace.

Dream until the sky's bright with dawn. Lullaby and goodnight, my sweet, I'll protect you from harm, and you'll wake in my arms.

Finally, warm and at peace, Sage floated away to the tune of the melody.

Chapter Nineteen

TEHL

Tehl sat in his chamber, mesmerized by the dancing flames in the hearth, mulling over recent events. Two days had passed since he'd left Ruby to Jacob's care. He had thrown himself into his duties with uncommon gusto, even giving attention to the details of the Midsummer Festival, selecting decor and pouring over guest lists with enough zeal that even Demari was satisfied. Sam and Gav checked on the rebel daily, bringing back to him bad news each time. She wasn't breathing well, and her fever raged on. And that wasn't the only bad news.

Word had spread that he'd been seen sprinting through the castle holding a mostly naked woman. By the next night, he'd had several men congratulate him at dinner on his new mistress. When

Tehl denied having a mistress, the men had laughed, giving him knowing looks. His blunt words and adamant refusal only piqued their curiosity. Still, gossip was hardly the worst of his problems.

Of primary concern was his war council; they were divided. Half supported a preemptive strike on Scythia while the other half wanted to pretend they posed no threat at all—yet neither was a viable option. He'd listened to them debate for hours over whether to take action. Ultimately however, Aermia would not win a war with Scythia while they continued to battle the civil unrest within their own country. They needed to unite their people first; only then they could deal with Scythia. Tehl had said so, though the mention of the rebellion was most unwelcome to those who preferred to disregard its existence.

Tehl snorted. Stubborn fools. Still, their dissent mattered little at the moment; he had the final say. He knew Scythia would attack; it was only a matter of when. Sam hoped it to be immediate. Tehl didn't put his stock in hope, however; he put it in preparations. For that reason, Tehl had already started work on potential battle plans, although it felt odd to be planning war in one room and a festival in the other. He wondered if one would interfere with the other. Would they already be at war in a month's time? And if so would they survive it? Would there be time for the festival? It had been too long since his people had had something to celebrate. As frivolous as it seemed, he knew they needed this reprieve from their sufferings. He shook his head and stretched, weary of his thoughts.

He felt restless. Maybe he just needed exercise. Tehl lifted himself from his large wing-backed chair, his boots making a soft thud as he crossed the plush rugs of his room. The castle was silent, peaceful. He wandered down the hallways and stairs, pondering little and important matters alike. Servants scurried to and fro, bowing as he passed, then hurrying on, absorbed in their tasks.

Eventually he found himself in the hallway leading to the infirmary. He figured he'd end up here at some point. Time to check on the little rebel. Both guards bowed before one opened the door for him to enter. As soon as he stepped into the sweltering infirmary, his nose was assaulted with eucalyptus. Sweat collected on his brow and between his shoulder blades.

His gaze swept over the room. The girl's cot had been moved, and it now sat close to a roaring fire. Jacob sat, sound asleep, in a rocking chair next to the fire. The older man's shirt was soaked clean through with sweat, a soft snore escaping him. He moved closer but pulled up short when he noticed a blond head alongside the dark one.

What the devil?

A few more steps and Tehl stood before the cot, staring into a pair of tired blue eyes. She stared back, surprised by his presence, but spoke not a word. His eyes slid along the black-haired rebel curled up next to her, clinging to her almost like a barnacle. Her swollen face was pressed into the blonde's neck, an arm slung across her chest. He watched as the blonde's surprise gave way to curiosity. It seemed they both had questions.

"What's all this?" he asked softly.

"She was too cold. We tried everything else to bring her

temperature up, so Jacob asked me to lie near her, share my body heat. It's working: she finally stopped shivering about an hour ago."

"Do you know who she is?" Tehl asked, wondering if she knew the risk she took.

She nodded once. "Jacob told me before we put her in the tub. People overtaken with fever often put up a fight when we put them in the ice." She shrugged. "So it was a good thing I was forewarned; I would never have thought someone so tiny could fight like that! Rather like a lioness. It took both guards, Jacob, *and* myself just to hold her down."

This woman understood the rebel was dangerous *and* a traitor, yet she didn't hesitate to use her own body heat to keep her alive. It was a noble and courageous thing to do, and he respected her for it. "What's your name?" Having forgotten to whisper, Jacob stirred at the sound of his voice, though he didn't awaken.

"Shhh..." the young healer chastised, glancing to Jacob with concern. "He only fell asleep a few minutes ago, and it's the first opportunity he's had since she arrived." She turned back to him and stilled as if just remembering to whom it was she was spoke. "Forgive me, my lord, I was thoughtless when I spoke." She paused. "My name is Mira."

He waved off her apology. "There is nothing to forgive. Mira, you only spoke out of concern for Jacob, and I could never find fault in that."

"What did you do for me, dearie?" Jacob's gruff voice asked, still rough from sleep.

"She was taking care of you." Tehl gave Mira a smile, which she returned with a crooked one.

Jacob reached over, affectionately patting Mira's hand. His hand drifted to touch the rebel woman's forehead, absentmindedly stroking her tangled hair from her face.

"How's she doing?" Tehl inquired.

Jacob took off his spectacles and tried to clean them on his sweaty shirt, only to grimace when he examined them in the firelight. He'd streaked sweat all over them. The Healer plopped his glasses in his lap and squinted up at Tehl. "Bad news is that the infection has a firm hold on her lungs. The good news is her fever is dropping. She is not in immediate danger, but her lungs are still a serious concern. If the fluid doesn't clear, she could easily die."

Tehl grimly regarded the source of his guilt. "Is there anything I can do?" She looked so frail.

"No, there is not." He heard the old man sigh. "In her sleep she's been asking for her mum and papa."

Tehl's head snapped to Jacob. "Has she said anything else?"

Jeffry shook his head before Tehl finished. "Nothing but whimpers. When we put her in the ice bath she started screaming and thrashing." Jacob's face pinched inward. "And she was begging me to let her die. She was out of it though, the fever-induced delirium. If she survives, I doubt she'll remember any of this." As Jacob finished his shoulders slumped, clearly exhausted.

Mira untangled her arm from the girl and touched Jacob's hand. "You have done all you can for her and given her your best. We both have. But now it's up to her to keep fighting, and the herbs we've administered will help her do that. Why don't you go and find a bed for a couple hours? I'll stay here and send for you if anything changes."

Mira's actions warmed Tehl's heart. She was just as worn out as Jacob but was still trying to care for the older man. The Healer opened his mouth to argue when Tehl cut him off. "Go and get some rest friend. I will watch over both girls for the next few hours while you rest. When you come back refreshed, you will be more ready to tackle her sickness."

Jacob stared at him a moment, his tiredness apparent. After a beat, he nodded and hefted himself out of the rocking chair. He shuffled out, touching the girl's forehead and Mira's shoulder as he passed, murmuring goodnight.

Tehl moved to the abandoned rocking chair and took Jacob's place. Sitting this close to the fire had raised his temperature by several degrees he was sure. He only hoped he wouldn't suffocate. He tugged on his collar. It was much too hot for his leather vest. Tehl decided he was better off without it and undid the buttons and peeled it off. Next, he loosened the strings on his shirt but froze when a feminine throat cleared. He lifted his eyes to the twinkling blue ones now staring at his chest. It was his turn to clear his throat.

She lifted her eyes, amusement plain on her face. He fumbled, attempting to re-lace his shirt in embarrassment.

"No need to lace up on my account. It *is* bloody hot in here. I bet those leather pants are cooking you alive."

He dropped his laces and looked at her. "Don't you worry about your reputation though? Here you are alone in a room with a half-dressed man; if someone saw us your reputation would be ruined."

She chuckled, her shoulder shaking with her laughter. Why was that so funny? Most women would be anxious right now.

When she caught sight of the look on his face, she choked back her laughter with a smile. "My reputation was ruined long ago when I started working here with Jacob. Heaven forbid a young woman work near an older man. Do you know that most people think I'm his mistress?" She paused. "If you're worried about propriety, those hulking guards can serve as chaperones. No one's virtue is endangered." Mirth colored her words.

Mira spoke straight with him. She didn't play coy or use double meanings, leaving him to guess at her words. He liked that. "Mira, I think we'll be great friends."

Pink touched her cheeks. He couldn't tell if it was from the dizzying heat or his words, but one thing was sure: she was exhausted, and dark smudges lined her drooping lids.

"Why don't you sleep for a bit? I will watch over the both of you until Jacob returns."

She looked at him with hope. "Truly? That would be heaven. I haven't slept either. If her breathing gets more labored, or there are any other changes, don't hesitate to wake me. Please and thank you." She paused. "Oh and don't forget to stoke the fire." Another pause. "My lord," she tacked on.

"I'll take care of it. Now sleep."

Mira rearranged herself, checking the girl's temperature and adjusting the blanket to cover them both. As soon as she closed her eyes she was asleep, emitting a soft buzz from her nose that made him grin. Tehl settled into the rocking chair, closing his own eyes.

It was sure to be a long night.

The heat slowly lulled him to sleep. He dozed until a rustling disturbed him. Tehl yawned and scooted to the edge of his chair, focusing on the two sleeping girls. The rebel had kicked their blankets off and was now shivering, little goosebumps running up her arms. The pathetic whimper that passed her lips had Tehl frowning. Mira, even in her sleep, scooted over and threw a leg over the girl, but her shivering kept on.

Tehl got up and began laying more wood over the coals. He then crept over to the cot, pulling the blankets up over both girls. Finally, the combination of the stoked fire, and the blanket slowed Ruby's shivering considerably. He settled back into the chair, its dark wood creaking as it bore his full weight. He leaned forward, placing his elbows on his knees and his chin in his hands, keeping an eye on the rebel.

His eyes traced a small patch of light freckles on her button nose. Her long dark lashes rested on her pale cheeks, showcasing the black bags and bruises beneath them. Her dark hair lay across her chin and hung off the cot in tangled, sweaty strands. A pained moan reached his ears, and he found himself reaching out to soothe her, gently removing the hair from her clammy face, smoothing it behind one ear.

He wasn't much familiar with comforting someone, but he remembered how his mother would softly draw on his face whenever he was ill. As a child, he had loved it. He started tracing the rebel's arched eyebrows down to her cheekbones, then her chin. He avoided the broken nose and bruises. Tehl continued this way until she stopped shuddering. As Tehl pulled away, she turned her face into his hand, her lips resting against his palm.

"... Don't leave me papa, I hurt all over."

Her innocent plea made his heart clench. He heard her mumble something else and leaned closer, to hear. Tehl caressed her cheekbone with his thumb and whispered, "I won't leave you, love."

Her lips formed part of a smile as she exhaled a soft, "love you, papa," and then she was once again dead to the world.

Her soft utterance was so different from his first impression of her. She didn't seem like a ruthless traitor. Was she perhaps coerced into this? Even with these thoughts spiraling, he knew it was largely wishful thinking on his part. She was guilty. A rebel.

He shouldn't have checked on her. Something about her was alluring to him whether he wanted it to be or not. His brother was right in his observations—Tehl couldn't think clearly around this girl.

She was a potential informant and that had to be the end of it.

Even so, he never moved his hand from her face.

***

Much later, a deep cough roused him. Tehl raised his head from where it had been resting on the girl's cot. He stared in horror as he realized that during the night he somehow ended up holding her hand. He jerked his hand away and looked toward the door. Jacob was watching the scene with a keen look.

"What?" Tehl mouthed, trying not to wake either girl.

"Nothing, my lord. You took very good care of our girls last night. Thank you."

Jacob walked briskly over and elbowed him out of the way. He placed a hand on the rebel's forehead and smiled, relieved. "Her fever broke." His soft tone had Mira stirring, but not enough to wake her. Jacob moved away, waving for him to follow. "The danger is mostly gone now that the fever's gone. I think she will survive."

Tehl stopped to study the older man. "How soon do you think Sam will be able to speak with her again?"

Jacob frowned, his face darkening briefly, but he quickly smoothed it to a thoughtful expression. "It depends on her recovery and willingness to fight. It's possible she will be physically recovered in two to three weeks' time, my lord. Mentally though? I have no idea."

Tehl took that in stride. "She will fight. It seems it's a favorite pastime for her." Tehl looked back to the sleeping forms. "Please keep Sam or Gavriel informed of her progress."

"As you wish." Jacob bowed.

Leaving her this time was just as difficult as it had been the previous time; he wouldn't visit her again. Sam would have to be the one who discovered her secrets. She called out for her papa, saying that she loved him. Under the influence of the truth serum she had shared a different story.

Secrets. It seemed she had many. Tehl hoped that she could start talking and help them before it was too late.

Chapter Twenty

SAGE

Herbs had teased her nose before she was fully awake. Now, clean white walls glared at her, and Sage squinted, eyes watering as she tried to makes sense of her surroundings. A roaring fire was going next to the cot upon which she was lying, and an empty rocking chair sat nearby.

Memories assaulted her.

Burning.

Drowning.

A gruff voice.

She needed to stop passing out.

Sage drew in a sharp breath, causing her lungs to seize. She gasped, and a burst of harsh rattling coughs racked her body. Each cough sent pain pulsing through her, making her wish she could sink back into oblivion. Slight pressure shifted on her abdomen, startling her. Sage lifted her head, squinting at the arm slung over her waist, a *very* female arm. Her gaze followed the petite arm to the young woman plastered to her side. Puzzled, she admired the heavy golden braid draped across her arm, tracing it back to its owner. Surprised blue eyes stared back at Sage.

"Who in the hell are you?" Sage blurted. "And why are you in my bed?"

The last thing she remembered was someone taking her cuffs off before darkness had swallowed her. The blonde shifted and Sage was suddenly aware of how closely they were tangled together. A blush crept up her neck and onto her cheeks. The woman laid a hand on her forehead and, if Sage hadn't been so tired, she would have jerked from her touch despite the fact it was impersonal.

"Ah. Your fever broke in the night." Relief was clear in the young woman's voice. "To answer your other question, I'm Mira."

Sage pursed her lips, squinting at the girl. "Still doesn't explain why you're clinging to me like a lover."

Mira scooted back, smiling at her, displaying not a shred of embarrassment. She waved a hand, indicating their surroundings. "This is the infirmary; you were brought to us delirious with fever. We used an ice bath several times to drop your fever, but by the time your fever dropped a few degrees you were shaking uncontrollably. We covered you and placed you next to the fire, but it wasn't enough." Mira shrugged. "The only other option was for me to crawl into bed with you in order for you to benefit from my body heat."

Sage appreciated that she kept her explanation succinct and clinical, but she still had so many questions. First, though, she took stock of the woman next to her; it was obvious from her posture and the dark rings under her eyes that she'd hardly slept. The fact that she had been caring for Sage in spite of this meant she owed this woman a great debt of gratitude.

"Thank you." Sage patted Mira's hand. "I'm sure I don't know everything you've done for me, but, from the circles under your eyes, I know it couldn't have been easy. I'm grateful to you." Mira smiled back at her, accepting her thanks with a quick dip of her chin.

Sage scanned the room, noting any exits and various things she might use as weapons should the need arise. A fire poker lay within a few feet of her. Excellent. She dropped her gaze to her hands, playing with a loose blanket thread to feign nonchalance. "How did I end up here?" Sage peered up through her lashes at the young woman.

Mira's lips parted but then she hesitated, as if searching for the right words. It was interesting that she felt the need to censor her explanation. What didn't she want Sage to know? The young healer was most likely a wealth of information, so she'd need to be nice and put the woman at ease. She gave Mira a sheepish smile and noted the girl's posture relax. Perfect.

"Sorry for all the questions, I am just so confused."

She spoke the truth. It baffled her that she'd been placed here, in this warm room, rather than her frigid and dingy cell. So far, they had drugged, starved, and tortured her. Why bring her to an infirmary then? Suddenly, it hit her. It was her information they were after, information she couldn't provide if she was dead.

Sage winced and rubbed her temples as a throbbing pain started behind her eyes. She needed to put those somewhat depressing thoughts aside and focus on what was now her top priority: recovery.

She'd never get out of here alive in this condition.

A harsh and rattling coughing fit seized Sage. Immediately, Mira hopped up, fetching her a glass of water. The healer cradled her head and brought the cup to Sage's cracked lips, carefully pouring the soothing liquid down her parched throat. Sage grumbled an incoherent complaint when, all too quickly, Mira pulled it away.

"If I give you any more you might retch," Mira explained. "You need that to stay in your stomach."

The young healer turned and placed the glass on the bedside desk before speaking. "Though accompanied by his cousin and brother, it was the crown prince himself who carried you up here to be treated. That was three days ago."

The crown prince's dirty hands were on her? She recoiled at the thought. She was also concerned; that kind of attention was dangerous. What had she done to warrant it? She needed to be out of here sooner rather than later. After wiping any hint of her thoughts from her face, she faced Mira and inquired, "How long will I be here?" Hopefully she'd be allowed to stay in the infirmary until her escape. Just the thought of moving had her aching.

Slipping a simple woolen gown over her shift, Mira spoke, "Until you're healed enough so we can safely move you to another room."

"Another room?" Sage probed.

A male voice spoke from behind, startling her. "Indeed, young Ruby. Once you're more stable, we can move you to a more comfortable space for the duration of your recovery." An older man stood close to where she was sitting, grinning down at her. "Orders from the crown prince himself."

It took everything inside her not to recoil at his words. Why would the crown prince want her to be comfortable? She studied the older man as he came closer, placing two fingers on the inside of her wrist. His hands were calloused but gentle. Like many of his profession, he seemed a kind sort of person. Nevertheless, she had to fight the impulse to yank back her arm and move away. He released her hand and leaned over her body, peering into her eyes, and this time Sage shrunk back, snapping, "Does no one in this infirmary understand the concept of personal space?" She swallowed, trying to mask her unease with irritation.

Sympathy shone in his eyes as he straightened. "Healers are curious by nature. We dedicate our lives to discovering better ways to mend and heal—and doing that means getting close and personal. Had the lovely Mira here not been willing to invade your 'personal space', I don't believe you would be with us now."

Sage cringed at how ungrateful that sounded. She offered him a quick smile and rushed to explain. "I meant no offense and deeply appreciate what you both have done for me. I was a bit disoriented and a little surprised at finding myself in a bed, let alone with another person sharing it. And then to have a man touch me who I don't know. It's…off-putting."

He bobbed his head in understanding. "I can't imagine what you are going through my dear. The state you were brought in…" He trailed off, swallowing. "It was inhuman. Mira and I did our best to care for you. We were at your side every moment. You were never left alone." The kindness in his gaze almost undid her. He understood her panic at being left unprotected, especially after what she'd suffered. "Also, my name is Jacob." He gave a courtly bow and popped up, quite spry for someone his age.

Sage forced a wobbly smile on her face and lifted her shaky hand in the air for him to take it. "My name is Ruby. It's a pleasure to meet you." A flash of disappointment flicked across his face but it was gone before she could even be sure she'd seen it. He was all smiles as he kissed the back of her hand like a gentleman.

"Quite the manners, my lady," the Healer remarked.

She tugged her hand from his and examined her nails. "I figured it was only fitting after that gracious bow. And I am no lady, only a girl from the streets," Sage wheezed, already short of breath. It felt like someone had put a wet cloth over her mouth and was forcing her to breathe through it. She began hacking anew, squeezing her eyes shut as tears leaked down her cheeks from the force of coughing.

"Take a deep breath my girl, it will help," Jacob's low voice coaxed. The smell of lavender, eucalyptus, and mint saturated the surrounding air. It took several tries for her to take a deep breath, and eventually her lungs loosened allowing her to breathe. She slit her teary eyes and looked up at the tight-lipped Jacob.

"Am I going to die?" she asked bluntly, her heart pounding weakly. She was already exhausted.

The Healer's face was severe as he stared down at her. "I won't pretend that your situation is not serious, but as I told you before, you'll not die under my care."

His words did elicit a faint echo of familiarity, but she couldn't quite place it. Her eyelids drooped, fatigue grasping her in its claws. "How is it possible that I am so tired? Mira told me I have been sleeping for days."

He slumped into the sturdy rocking chair next to her cot. "Your body is trying to heal itself. Sleep is a very good thing, and you'll probably be doing a lot of it this next week. Close your eyes, Ruby. Mira and I will watch over you."

The idea of them watching her as she slept discomfited her, and apprehension crept over her. She'd be so vulnerable. Sage tried to reel in her thoughts and looked between the two healers. She sensed nothing dangerous. For three days, these two had diligently cared for her, and she'd come to no harm at their hands. As much as she hated turning her back on the older man, she wanted to face the door. That way she could see anyone who tried to sneak up on her. Better the devil you know than the devil you don't. She gave Mira a sleepy smile and, after snuggling into the blankets, drifted off.

Chapter Twenty-One

SAGE

Sage's eyes flew open. Something had awoken her. As the hair on her neck rose, she realized something about her surroundings was different. Firelight writhed with the shadows on the walls in a twisted dance of black and yellow. She looked around and made out the crown of Mira's blond head peeking out of a blanket on the cot next to hers, snoring lightly. Exhaling, Sage tried to calm herself. Nothing was amiss; it had only been a bad dream. She shuddered, forcing the unpleasant images from her mind. She turned and faced the fire, hoping it would drive the chills away. Her eyes drifted to the Healer sitting in the chair, and her heart leapt to her throat.

It wasn't Jacob in the chair.

For a moment, she was paralyzed, but then she was scrambling backward violently, putting as much distance as possible between herself and the strange man. Her legs caught in the blankets, and she stumbled to the floor, coughing as she fell.

The intruder rushed toward her, and a scream caught in her throat as she fought to free herself from the web of bedding. She had to get away! Panicking, Sage pulled herself across the floor, nails clawing at the stone. Large hands gripped her waist, and she cried out; she couldn't go through this again. He needed to stop touching her. Now. Sage raked her hands up his arms and pinched with all her might, drawing blood. "Someone help me!" she yelled.

Both guards crashed through the door, but her heart sank when they hesitated. They weren't going to help her. Sage's stomach soured; she was going to be sick.

"Vicious little wench! I'm only trying to help," his voice rumbled against her back. "Calm down, it's Sam."

She didn't care who he was, she continued resisting him with all she had. He cursed. An ear-piercing shriek passed her lips as he hauled her up from the floor. He dropped her on the cot, and she stilled, thankful at least that his hands were no longer on her. She opened her eyes and saw it was the young prince standing before her, watching her intently.

Before she knew what she was doing, her fist smashed into his face. His head snapped to the side, and he worked his jaw. Terror filled her, and she was rooted to the spot. What would he do? He swung around, his dark blue eyes meeting hers. Her skin crawled at his nearness so she did the first thing that came to mind: she coughed into his face.

Instantly, he recoiled, his face twisted in disgust. Her victory was short lived though as another vicious coughing bout seized her. A dainty hand appeared before her nose with a bottle of scented oil.

"Deep breaths, Ruby, you need to take deep breaths. No need to fear. I won't let anything happen to you," Mira spoke in a calm and encouraging tone, rubbing a soothing hand between her shoulder blades.

Sage did what she was told, never taking her eyes from the enemy. Despite her fear, Mira's comment struck her as funny. What could a petite little woman accomplish against the much larger man? If she had to guess, she'd say he was nearly the same height as his brother, over six feet. Between coughs, she managed a sharp laugh. "Mira." *Wheeze.* "He could do whatever he wanted." Sage looked over her shoulder at the sweet healer and patted her shoulder. "I appreciate the thought, though."

Sage returned her gaze to the dangerous man in their presence. Samuel Ramses. A man of many titles; *Prince Samuel. Commander Samuel.* And then the label known only by a few: *Spymaster Samuel.*

It seemed he was also her jailor, tormentor, and, very likely, the harbinger of her death.

His extended proximity still perturbed her. Since their first encounter he'd not shown a single genuine emotion. She suspected he was all façade. Even now, he sat casually, but his eyes told a different story. They held a measure of wariness. The spymaster stared back at her, taking in her assessment of him. Hatred rolled through her, bleeding onto her face. "You here for round two?"

A little glimmer of emotion flashed in his eyes, but disappeared just as quickly. "No." He dropped his eyes to the fire next to him.

"Maybe more drugs this time?" Sage snarled. She shouldn't be provoking him, but she couldn't help it. She hated being cornered.

His jaw clenched as he whipped his head her way. "No, I have no intention of drugging you, Ruby. I also have no intention of harming you."

She barked out a laugh. She was tired, cranky, and fed up with being afraid. "'Intention' is an interesting word, is it not? Everyone has good *intentions* until they don't. So forgive me if I don't put stock in anything that comes out of your lying trap," she spat. Mira gasped at her offensive words.

Sage was done with the situation. What game was he playing? Would he hurt Mira too? She had no doubt that all the men of this place had been born into privilege—spoiled and able to do and take whatever they pleased. Such men had no business wielding power.

"Ruby. You must believe me when I tell you that neither my brother nor myself sanctioned what happened to you."

She allowed her disbelief to show on her face. Was he here to cast off the blame from his family? Why bother? They must want her cooperation badly, she thought.

Furious, her anxiety temporarily evaporated. "How dare you come in here to shirk the blame. You," she spat, pointing a shaking finger at him, "are a liar and a coward." Mira squeezed her shoulder, as if to quiet her, but there was no stopping her now. If she would die, she wasn't going quietly. "If that was the truth, it was still *your* men. You are the one who drugged me so I couldn't protect myself from…" Her voice broke. Tears flooded her eyes. Sage glared through the watery glaze. "You will *never* be absolved of your crimes."

Compassion filled his face.

Disbelief rolled through her—like she would believe he felt remorse over his actions. His emotions weren't genuine, just another mask to get what he wanted. The spymaster reached out to her, and she jerked back, bumping into Mira. "Don't touch me!" she hissed, her lungs tightened painfully as she tried to catch her breath.

"I think it would be best if you left, my prince." Mira stated, not a suggestion but a command.

"I won't leave. I have orders to watch over Ruby and make sure she is protected."

Sage's mind spun. "Protection? Where was your protection when, when…" She stumbled for the right word. "When they stripped me down and used me for their amusement?" she rasped, her face hardening. "Oh, that's right, I needed protection from *you*. So forgive me if I won't count on your protection. None of this is for *my* protection but to make sure your asset doesn't escape your clutches."

The spymaster's face sharpened, and his eyes glistened with anger. "What do you mean they *used you for their own amusement?*" he asked in a deceptively soft voice.

She shivered at his dark tone. Sage knew where his mind had gone with that question. "A man does not have to force himself on a woman to hurt her. Words can cause as much damage as blades and fists. To my knowledge—" Sage choked on the words, not able to force them from her throat. She swallowed and donned her blank mask, her heart beating wildly in her chest. Sage forced herself to look at the young healer for confirmation.

Mira's pale face pinched, and she jerked her head once.

"You don't have that on your conscience..." Sage sneered and turned back at the commander. Pity. Pity was written all over his face. Panic clawed her chest as his blues eyes delved into her, like he saw every inch of pain swirling just beneath her surface, threatening to break through. Sage fisted her hands in her lap, her broken nails digging into her palms. She would not weep in front of him.

"I am so sorry."

Her dam broke.

Grief and shame choked her, sucking the fight right out of her. It was too much; her pain wouldn't be contained any longer. Sparkling drops dripped down her bruised face in rivulets. Sage closed her eyes, shutting out everyone. She was weak.

Large arms wrapped around her pressing her into a wide hard chest. "Let it all out, darling."

Her breath seized.

He caged her.

Trapped her.

Sage writhed against him. "Get your filthy paws off me!" she screamed, blinded by her tears. He tightened his grip and whispered things she couldn't understand through her panic. The world spun. She couldn't breathe. Her heart would burst. He needed to stop touching her.

"My lord, you are making her worse, please let go of her," Mira pleaded.

"No, Mira, she needs this." His tone of voice brooked no argument. "Let it out, Ruby, it's okay."

No, nothing was okay.

Her enemy held her.

Sage couldn't protect herself.

She was damaged.

Weak.

Sage cried harder, trembling as he held her steady. Something broke open inside her, and she wasn't sure how to put it back together. Samuel's large hand tunneled under her hair and rubbed the back of her skull. Sage cried herself out and hiccupped, her throat raw. She lay limply against the spymaster's wet chest, thoroughly wrung out. It was then she noticed Mira had moved to her other side, tenderly combing her fingers through Sage's hair, singing.

She stared at the fire, wishing she could burn away everything she was feeling. Emptiness and pain were her companions. The spymaster's breath tickled the hair at her crown. She needed him to stop touching her skin. Sage pulled every last drop of strength and courage she possessed and begged. "Please have mercy, let go of me. Every touch feels like *them*."

"It's okay, Ruby. Those men have been taken care of and they can't hurt you here. We will protect you. My brother has ordered it. If you would prefer me not to be here, I can send Gavriel."

A hazy memory of purple eyes and a man unchaining her resurfaced. Her savior. "I like Gavriel."

A chuckle rumbled in his chest, vibrating her cheek. "Most do; he is a good man."

He gave her a little squeeze, which unsettled her, her skin prickling. She *really* wished he would let her go. If she wasn't so weak from illness, she'd have the strength to make him let go. She hated being weak, but every muscle in her body was tired. Her stomach growled, breaking the silence that had settled upon them.

"It sounds like you're in need of some breakfast." His arms released her and Sage avoided his eyes by scrutinizing the fire. "I know you don't trust me, but please at least trust this will all work out." The spymaster's attention shifted to the young healer. "I will send someone with her breakfast, and Gavriel will stay tonight." He patted her shoulder. "Speedy recovery to you."

Sage shrugged his hand off, ignoring him. He sighed as he stood. She listened as he crossed the room and exited, his footsteps fading down the hall. Sage's eyes returned to Mira. "What'd he mean, breakfast?" she questioned.

"You've slept a full day, it's nearly dawn. The sun should rise any minute."

She had lost an entire day. What day was it? "Where is Jacob?" she wondered out loud.

Mira folded the blankets, placing them on her cot. "Prince Samuel sent him to bed last night before he settled here for the evening. We will move you to your new room today."

She didn't want to leave the infirmary. It was safer here than anywhere else.

Mira continued, "I will stay with you until you're healthy enough to leave."

Equal parts of sadness and jealousy swirled through her at Mira's naïvety. She would never leave this place. Even if she gave up information, the Crown wouldn't think of releasing a valuable asset. Escape was her only option.

Jacob swept in, smelling of herbs and disturbing her thoughts. He stepped in front of the fire, a warm smile on his face. "It's fantastic to see you sitting up by yourself! Progress is a wonderful thing. I have other good news. A chamber is ready for you and Mira to relocate to today." He gestured to the guards standing nearby. "These gentlemen will help move you to your new abode, and Mira will help settle you in. I'll check up on you daily, but Mira will be your support until we can boot that sickness from your lungs. Garreth, if you please, pick up the lovely miss Ruby and follow me."

As the soldier approached, she forced herself to hold her ground and not scramble away. She focused on his face, telling herself over and over that he was not her torturer, though she went rigid the moment his hand touched her.

"Easy there, love," his deep voice whispered. "I am just going to carry you; no harm will befall you. My arms are going underneath your shoulders and knees and that's all; I won't move them."

He plucked her from the cot and cradled her in his arms. Her eyes closed. Even though she chanted in her head that he would not harm her, the terror was still there. She dug deep for some humor in the situation. Sage finally settled on: "I am not your love."

"I suppose not." Despite having her eyes closed she could hear the smile in his voice.

Her eyelids stayed tightly shut. Sage knew they went up three flights of stairs, made a left turn, and then a right. A door creaked, and she was placed on something soft. By the time she opened her eyes, the guard was already heading out the door, and Jacob and Mira were the room's only other occupants. She cleared her throat. "Thank you."

Just before leaving, the guard looked over his shoulder with a wink. "My pleasure, love." Then the door closed.

"Stubborn man," she grumbled to herself.

Her new cage was stunning, more beautiful than she ever could have expected. She'd been placed on a giant four-poster bed that was crafted from the pale aqua wood of the jardintin tree. They only grew in the coral sands of Blested Beach, and their wood was rare and highly prized. White, gauzy curtains were draped from post to post, floating around the bed. Rich, dark blue carpets covered the stone floor and deep cushioned chairs were scattered around the spacious room in a sea of colors. A large fireplace occupied the wall adjacent her bed, its mantle comprised of purple shells, shimmering abalone, and dainty starfish. Next to the fireplace, two large doors of pale wood overlooked the sea, their tops filled with glass forming a window. Royal blue drapes of brocade bracketed the doors, their base embroidered with exotic fish.

The room embodied opulence.

Sage ran her hand along the crisp white coverlet upon which she sat. Compared to her pristine surroundings, she looked just like the street rat she professed to be.

"How do you like your new home?" Jacob asked.

"It's gorgeous. I've experienced nothing like it, and there's only one thing that could make it better."

"What would that be my dear?" Jacob asked curiously.

"A bath," she said. Sage glanced at her hands and grimaced. "I feel like I'll leave a trail of filth everywhere I go."

A giggle snuck out of Mira, and she placed a hand across her mouth, attempting to cover it. The sound loosened something in Sage, bringing a genuine smile to her face.

"I am sure you will have to burn this shift," she said, pointing to Sage's sweat covered linen.

The Healer chuckled and nodded his head. "Mira will draw you a bath, and I will let the kitchen know where to send your breakfast. I'll be in tonight to check on you before I find my own bed. Enjoy your day, my dear." Jacob patted her hand and quit the room.

Sage watched as Mira first stoked the fire, then buzzed around the suite, getting things settled. She slumped into the pillows, surprised to see a mosaic on the ceiling. It was a beautiful array of blues, greens, and yellows; it was like she was beneath the sea, looking up at its surface. "So, what do we do now?"

"We get you healthy."

Sage rolled her eyes, then craned her neck to see the blonde. "Yes, I know, but will we be able to leave the room when I can walk?"

Mira's face became guarded.

That was a no.

"It will be some time before you regain your strength. Let's concern ourselves with that when the time comes."

"So basically, no then?"

Mira sent her an apologetic smile and disappeared into the bathroom. "Just wait until you see this bathroom," Mira called, her voice echoing.

She stared at the ceiling, with the sound of running water in the background. Sage had been nowhere with working plumbing. How did it all work? When she took her bath, she would have to inspect the pipes.

Mira bustled out, brushing damp strands from her face. In another setting, she and Mira would have been friends. She was a sweet caring woman, when the time came to make her escape, she'd do everything in her power to make sure Mira wasn't blamed.

"Bath time?" she asked, excited at the prospect.

Mira grinned at her. "I have no desire to continue dealing with your smell as I try to sleep. It's time to get you washed up."

Sage grinned back at her. Oh yeah. Mira would be a great friend and ally in this horrid place.

Chapter Twenty-Two

TEHL

Tehl's days melted into each other. Each day would start out with monotonous planning for the Midsummer Festival—discussions that would inevitably dissolve into arguments over colors, decorations, or budgets. There was also the usual comment regarding his mother's role in times past, which always frustrated him. Did they not realize he missed her as well? Without fail, he always ended the meetings with a headache—or the impulse to run screaming from the room.

Once *that* nightmare ended, he would be pulled into the war council where again, sensible discussion dissolved into arguments over whose idea should be acted upon. It was ridiculous. They were all suggesting the same thing, just in different ways. It boiled down to this: everyone wanted to either go to war or send spies to Scythia.

However, the moment a man of theirs stepped foot on Scythian soil, it'd be considered an act of war. This point sparked a heated debate among the council, on whether it was worth the risk. Sam believed it was, as did Tehl, though the former worried that, were their spy to be discovered, Scythia would make an immediate retaliatory strike. And, as Sam had yet to extract even a word from the Scythian woman, they didn't have the information needed to make their chances of success feasible. No, they would have to wait to spy on the enemy nation until they had more of an idea of what they'd be getting into once they were over there.

Finally, Tehl ended each day entertaining his court at dinner in the place of his father. The never-ending stream of scantily clad debutants throwing themselves at him was tiresome. He couldn't quite figure out why they did that squished-lips thing. They resembled fish. When he'd asked Lady Rose about it, her expression of outrage practically singed his hair off. She'd then snapped her fan shut and stomped away in a bustle of rustling skirts; this too, confused him, as it was an honest and impersonal question. He didn't understand why it was so offensive. He would want to know if he was making a face that was so incredibly unattractive.

Ladies of noble birth preened and simpered before him everywhere he went. It perplexed him that they would put themselves in a compromising situation simply to get his attention, since they knew he could marry none of them. The old law dictating

Royalty must marry only those of common birth kept Aermia united. Each group would thus be represented by their own member of the monarchy: one for the nobility and one for the citizens.

Even as he made his way from the training area each morning to his personal dining room, young women seemed to stop him at every point. That morning Tehl tried to be more inconspicuous, hoping to reach breakfast *sometime* before noonday. He scoped out the corridor, searching for any sign of a woman, and saw none, until he spied one of his Elite, Garreth, walking briskly toward him with a young woman in his arms, Mira trailing behind him. The healer gave him a small smile and Garreth nodded respectfully as they passed.

Tehl's breath stilled when he saw the young woman's face. It was the rebel. Her hair tumbled out of its braid and stuck to her damp face. The pallor of her skin made her black hair seem as though it had sucked in all the surrounding color. What struck him most was her face. Her cheeks were sucked in, her brow furrowed, as though she were in terrible agony. Her hands clutched Garreth's tunic so tightly that her knuckles were white.

Garreth jogged up the stairs and vanished from his view. Why was she in so much pain? Where were Garreth and Mira taking her? He needed to ask Sam; his brother always knew what was going on these days.

Tehl jogged to the dining room surprised to find his brother crunching on some bacon there, alone. Tehl had left the training yard before Sam, yet here he sat, already eating. How did he manage it? Tehl shook his head in mirth and flopped down into his chair.

"How did you get here before me? I left before you did; and don't tell me your skills are better than mine." He eyed his brother while snatching up an apple pastry.

Sam cracked a smile and threw one muscular leg over the chair arm. His brother plucked a raspberry off his plate, inspecting it closely. "I *am* better than you, I walked right by you." Sam's familiar blue eyes snapped to his. "You were gawking at Ruby."

Tehl tensed at his brother's comment. "Ruby? On a first name basis, are we? I thought she was an asset, and that we didn't use her name." He sat back, crossed his arms, waiting for his brother's retort.

Sam tossed the berry into his mouth and chewed thoughtfully. "She is not an ordinary asset. With what she has gone through she deserves to be called by her name. I've been thinking. If we treat her differently, she may become not a prisoner but an ally. We need someone like her. She has surprising battle skills, not to mention a strong will that rivals yours. She could be the key to ending the rebellion, not with brute force, but with us all uniting against Scythia." Sam paused, tapping his finger on his chin. "It would take careful maneuvering."

So that's what this little speech was about: he wanted the rebel to spy for him. "I assume your 'maneuvering' has already begun." A smug smile crept across his brother's face that answered his question. Tehl snagged a fluffy biscuit for himself, buttering its surface thoughtfully.

"So, I can thank you for having her moved this morning, I take it?" He watched Sam out of the corner of his eye while drizzling honey on the flakey biscuit.

Sam leaned his head back and steepled his hands underneath his chin. "Her fever broke, so it was time we had her moved somewhere more secure."

Tehl bit into his biscuit and let the sweet and buttery goodness melt in his mouth. A groan slipped out. What did the cook put in these? They were delicious. He examined the golden biscuit as though it would solve the kingdom's problems.

"Trying to get that biscuit to tell you all its secrets, brother?" His brother's voice held laughter. Tehl spared Sam a glance, and his brother wiggled his eyebrows. "Did you even listen to a word I said?"

Tehl smiled sheepishly.

Sam sighed and began muttering to himself. His lips fought a smile; there was nothing more Sam hated than to have to repeat himself. Sam blew out an annoyed breath and continued. "As I was saying...before you and your biscuit got intimately acquainted...I had her moved into one of the smaller suites in our wing."

Tehl spat out his biscuit and watched as it smacked Sam right on the cheek. Sam reached up and brushed the gooey pastry off his face in disgust. His brother meticulously wiped his hand on his napkin and pinned him with a glare. "Now that was just rude," he murmured.

Tehl sniggered at the disgust on his brother's face. The longer he stared at Sam, the funnier it became. Gut-wrenching laughter boomed out of him as Sam's face pinched even more. "Sorry, but it's funny..." he said between peals of laughter.

At that, Sam's irritated expression broke. Before long, his brother was laughing as hard as he was. Tehl took a gasping breath and grinned. "I haven't done something like that since I was a child."

Sam mirrored his grin with a devilish glint in his eye. "It's all right, I will get you back sooner or later," he stated casually.

That remark wiped the smirk from the crown prince's face.

Sam was the master of pranks.

Sam's smile turned predatory, like a leviathan smiling at a seal.

Never show fear.

Tehl straightened his shoulders, feigning confidence. "We'll see about that."

He ran his hand thoughtfully along the dark stubble on his cheek. Sam did nothing without good reason. "So you moved a dangerous rebel into the royal wing, not the guest quarters?"

Sam squinted. "That's what I just said."

Tehl mulled it over. It made sense to keep her close to them so they could watch her. There would be less chance of someone meeting her then. Not to mention if she tried to escape it would be significantly harder for her to do so. There weren't many rooms available. The only ones were...

His gaze locked with his brothers. "You know how this will look right? An unattached woman living in our wing? Those rooms were used for mistresses in the past and the occasional visiting family member. Everyone knows she's not family."

Sam's lips formed a smirk.

Realization dawned on him. "That's what you want them to assume."

Sam swung his leg to the floor and scooted to the edge of his seat. "Precisely. You were seen running through the palace with a half-naked girl in your arms and your two closest friends trailing you. Rumors are already circling about whom the new mistress belongs to. Many had already tried to get into the infirmary to meet her out of curiosity. This way no one can get to her except those we allow. Our court assumes she is involved with one of us, so it won't seem odd for her to be staying close by. It is better than the alternative, having any of them knowing the truth," Sam said. "She draws attention everywhere she goes. We need to control how she is perceived by others. People rarely look past the surface. They see what they expect to see. Gav and I have been noted entering at night and leaving the infirmary in the morning. By keeping her inaccessible it will keep our court guessing and thus focused on the wrong thing."

It was a logical plan. He didn't like her being so close, but it seemed like the best option. The rebel would hate being thought of as his mistress. He liked the idea, but the long-term consequences concerned him. "Her reputation will be ruined," he worried.

Sam scoffed. "Her reputation was ruined when you flashed most of her body to most of the people residing in the castle. There've also been the nightly visits from Gav, you, and me. Not to mention, we don't know who she is. She's in character, a cover. Ruby will cease to exist when she leaves."

"You think she will escape?" Tehl asked.

"It's just a matter of time, Tehl. Be thankful she's as sick as she is. I will keep the Elite on her at all times but she's good. Once she is healed, there isn't any place that could hold her..." Sam trailed off. "If we can get her on our side, she would make the perfect spy. She's unlike anyone I have come across." Sam's voice was full of awe.

For some reason, that rankled Tehl. He brushed it aside, pinching a grape between his fingers. "Can we turn her?"

Sam considered this for a moment, staring blankly at the wall behind him. "I think so. She is not an anarchist. She legitimately wants to help her kingdom. She's been led to believe the Crown is doing nothing for its people. If we show her what we do, and how we are dealing with Scythia, it may soften her enough to give her pause over her chosen ties with those of the rebellion."

Frankly, Tehl had his doubts about anything being able to 'soften' the vivacious girl, but it was worth a try. He shrugged.

Footsteps caught both their attention, and a moment later their cousin came into view. Gav dropped into the chair next to Tehl and began picking out an assortment of fruit, pastries, cheeses, and meats.

"Good morning," Gav said cheerily before digging into the feast before him.

Sam stood and circled his own chair, gripping the top of it. "Good, we are all here. I explained the situation to Tehl, but you need to be informed of the developments." Gav focused his attention on Sam, continuing to shovel eggs into his mouth. "If anyone asks you about your new mistress, be evasive but don't deny that you have one."

Gav paused mid-bite, his eggs slipping from his fork comically. Gav gaped at the two of them. "What new mistress? What the devil are you talking about? I've never had a mistress, and I certainly never will. And why would anyone ask me about it?" Gav spluttered.

Sam winced. "Members of the court, and servants, saw each of us enter the infirmary for the night. They drew their own conclusions. They are not sure which one of us she belongs to. There are some who believe she belongs to *all* of us."

Gavriel set his fork down, his nose flaring as he drew in a deep breath. "You mean to tell me that our court assumed that all three of us had her? Why would you ever tolerate such an obscene conclusion?" Gav's voice dipped down lower.

Tehl held up his hands in innocence. "I have been trying to convince them for the last few days that she is not mine," he said.

Gav pinned Sam with his gaze. "This was your idea?"

"Yes." No remorse.

Gav glowered at his breakfast. "I can understand how this would tactically be the best choice."

Sam beamed. "Thank you, I am glad you see it that way. I—"

"I wasn't finished," Gav cut him off. "This will brand her. You know what they will call her right?" He looked to both of them. "They will consider her a whore. She'll lose any chance of a regular life with a good man."

"I anticipated that. No one has seen her face, nor does anyone know anything about her. Even if any of the information leaks, her name is fake. I searched high and low for information about who she is. I haven't found a single thing about her. When 'Ruby' disappears so will that reputation."

"What happens if we get her to switch and work with us? She will be seen around the palace," Tehl interjected.

"That's why she is in the royal wing. We can control who sees her. Anyone who saw her face when you took her to the infirmary won't recognize her once she heals. Even since we pulled her from the dungeon, she looks different. Gav, you have seen her, what do you think?"

Tehl glanced over to Gav and watched as he pushed his food around his plate.

"She looks like a different person from when we pulled her from the dungeon, it's true, and she is still covered in cuts and bruises. When she is fully healed, she won't be recognized by anyone except the ones who have had close contact with her—like Jeffry, Jacob, and Mira. Who are the servants that are taking care of her meals and chambers?"

Sam piped up. "I chose a special few who worked with our mother and are discreet. Also, the same four Elite have guarded the infirmary for the last couple of days. They are trustworthy, I have no doubts in their loyalty to us."

"You realize if they think she is one of ours you must stop entertaining female company. Can you do that?" Gav challenged, a sardonic lift to one eyebrow.

Sam carelessly waved away his question. "It won't be a problem.

Besides, even if I still kept my female company, it would keep people guessing. They would wonder if I was just a scoundrel stepping out on my mistress, or if she belonged to one of you." Gav wrinkled his nose and resumed eating. "Any more concerns?" Sam inquired.

Both men grunted 'no', and Gavriel resumed eating. Tehl watched him eat in morbid fascination. Was his cousin chewing his food? He was inhaling it. One moment there was a pile on his plate, and the next there was none. "Little hungry, cousin?" Tehl teased.

Gav scowled at him and wiped his mouth. "I didn't get to eat dinner last night, and then I practiced with the Elite this morning. Don't judge me, I am starving. At least I don't have honey and biscuit stuck to my face," he retorted sourly.

Tehl brushed his cheek, his fingers sticking to the honey. He viciously scrubbed at it with his palm. "Why didn't you tell me, Sam? You would let me leave like that?"

Sam tugged on his pierced right ear. "I thought it was funny. Gavriel said nothing either until you teased him."

Tehl huffed at his brother, dropping his gaze to the table. Sam's plan was reasonable, and it didn't have any holes in it that he saw, but it still didn't sit right with him. He hated the idea of anyone thinking he had a mistress, let alone one he would share with other men. Possessiveness surged through him at the idea. When he found the right woman, he would never share. She would be his and his alone.

Sam strolled to the end of the table and looked out of the window at the cerulean ocean. "Gavriel, I told the girl you would stay with her from now on," he said absently.

Gav cradled the back of his head with his laced fingers. "Why is that? We were taking turns."

"She doesn't like me."

Gav snickered but turned it into a cough at the black look Sam gave him. "I don't know how that is possible," Gav deadpanned.

"She wants you."

Gav stilled for a moment. "Why?"

"She remembers you pulling her down from the chains, I suppose she associates you with safety. Last night..." Sadness passed over Sam's face. "She was terrified of me when she saw me—she scrambled back so fast she fell to the floor. She didn't possess enough energy to run, so she crawled away from me. I wanted to rip someone's head off when I left. She is a complete wreck. She needs your calming personality, Gav."

Gavriel's face softened. "I understand. I will watch over her, and who knows. Perhaps she will open up if she feels safe."

"If she sees you as a savior or a friend she may soften. You are what we need to get her to switch sides or even just act as an intermediate between the Crown and the rebellion. She could stop a civil war." Sam paced as he spoke and then looked straight at Tehl. "I have news you won't be happy about. The captain awaiting judgment for his crimes against Ruby has disappeared."

The silence was deafening. A pin-drop could have been heard.

He got away.

The sick bastard got away.

"Did I hear you correctly?" Gav hissed in his soft, scary voice.

Gavriel was about to lose his temper, and it would be a sight to behold. "You let him get away?"

"I didn't *let* him do anything." Sam's voice whipped through the air. "He was publicly stripped of his title and locked in his rooms awaiting judgment." His brother's fists clenched, and small tremors shook his arms. "I visited him this morning to exact some old-fashioned justice after I left that poor girl in the infirmary. But he was gone. My people are searching, but so far there has been nothing."

Tehl's blood boiled. It wasn't Sam's fault. Tehl knew his brother blamed himself. He took a moment and reined in his temper.

His brother's anguished eyes met his as he continued, "I promised her she would be safe from him this morning. That he would be punished."

Serge *would* be punished. Tehl would make sure of it.

Gav rested his elbows on the table and his head in his hands. His shoulders heaved with ragged breaths. Tehl hadn't seen Gav this upset since Emma died.

Tehl gave his cousin a moment to collect himself and centered his attention on Sam. "Use any resources necessary. He needs to be found. He is a danger to Sanee."

"I agree. If you will excuse me, I would like to go hunting myself. I will see you at the war preparation meeting this afternoon." With that, Sam pushed off the wall and stalked toward the exit.

"Brother," he called after him. Sam paused, looking at him expectantly. "When you find him...bring him to me."

Sam gave him a wicked smile and a slight bow. "It will be done, my prince."

"And so the plot thickens," Gav mused. "My question is, why would he run? His punishment would have been severe, but he wouldn't have hung. Serge wasn't known as cowardly so this doesn't fit with his character. He was of the Guard, not the Elite so I can't figure out how he made it past them. Most would have been found by Sam's spies by now. It doesn't bode well that they're turning up nothing. We've got to be missing something."

"As much as I would like to pursue it myself, Sam is the best. He will find him." Tehl rapped his knuckles on the table and pushed back his chair. It was time to start his day. He would have to put this aside and trust Sam to do his job.

Tehl scratched the back of his neck, and his nose wrinkled. "I need a bath before I get hounded about the Midsummer Festival. I will meet you at the meeting."

"One thing before you go. Is it necessary I stay with her during the night? Her rooms are close to ours—if anything were to happen, we would hear it."

"I don't need you there for protection; but I do want you there so she can feel safe and secure."

He examined Tehl as he mulled it over. His cousin rolled his neck as he stood. "I understand. I'll do my best." Gav clapped him on the shoulder as he left.

Tehl hoped this went as planned. He was tired of feeling one step behind.

Chapter Twenty-Three

SAGE

A salty sea breeze ruffled Sage's hair, loosening strands from her braid. She sat on her balcony, watching the gulls heckle and chase each other playfully. As the cool air kissed her bare arms, it left a trail of goosebumps in its wake. She tightened her shawl about her, enjoying the summer's day.

Mira sat beside her, humming a little tune as she sewed. Over the last few days, she'd established a sort of routine. Gavriel left before she woke each day, so she enjoyed a quiet breakfast with the healer before stepping into her bath. Afterward, Mira would rub her with special oils to help open her lungs while she let her hair dry by the fire. It was around this time that the sweet healer turned evil, forcing Sage to walk the rooms until her legs shook.

After this torture, Mira would read to her until lunch, and then they'd eat together. Once Sage had a full belly, she would inevitably fall asleep.

She still wasn't sure if it was due to her body healing itself or Mira slipping something into her tea.

When she woke, Mira would move her out to the balcony, and that was her favorite part of the day.

She had learned a lot about Mira. She'd told her about growing up with her family until she became an orphan at the tender age of eleven. She became a ward of the Crown and ended up in the palace. Jacob's wife had taken notice of her, deciding to take the young girl under her wing. Jacob too, had opened his arms to her, and together they basically raised Mira. Growing up watching Jacob help people had cultivated within her a desire to help as well, and that's how the little blonde became the only woman healer of their nation.

Mira asked Sage questions here and there, but she never probed. She tried to answer Mira's questions as honestly as possible.

Once the sun began to sink below the horizon they would move inside and have dinner. Sage would stare into the fire, missing her family and pondering her escape. Once she climbed into bed, Gavriel would magically appear. He was always kind and never made her uncomfortable. Sage didn't love that he stayed the night in her room, but he placed his cot so it sat on the far side of the room. She was also comforted by the fact that she kept a stolen knife stashed beneath her pillow. She would never be helpless again.

Right before she fell asleep, Jacob would shuffle in to check on her. Sage swore he was made of kindness, jokes, and smiles, ever full of exuberance, joy, and just a pinch of mischief.

She could barely make out someone muttering, so she pulled her eyes from the rolling waves, looking instead to the interrupter of her thoughts. "What did you say, Mira?"

Concern marred Mira's face. "I called your name twice before you answered. Are you all right?"

"I am fine." Sage smiled softly. "I was deep in thought, that's all."

"Anything you want to share?"

"Nothing important, just wishful thinking. I am a little stir crazy, and I envy the gulls and their freedom. Sometimes I wish I could fly, too." Sage peered through her lashes at her companion, hopeful. "I am better today. My lungs aren't giving me as much trouble as they have been. I am strong enough for a short walk."

Mira shook her head. "You aren't ready now, but in two or three days you should be. I will talk to Jacob and get his opinion, and perhaps we can go from there. How does that sound?"

Sage pushed down her resentment, knowing her friend was not the true source of it. She forced a smile onto her face. "That sounds reasonable, thank you, Mira."

Jacob would first talk to the crown prince of her request to get out and walk. Embittered at the level of control that tyrant had over every aspect of her life had her heaving out a frustrated breath.

She returned her gaze to the bobbing ships in the ocean and the oyster fishermen preparing to sail back into the harbor. At that moment, she heard the creak of her door and the heavy tread of boots moving through her room toward them.

"That must be Jacob, I knew he would come early," Mira explained, rolling her eyes. "We're out he—" Mira choked on her own sentence.

Sage glanced at her tongue-tied friend to see what had startled her. Mira hastily dropped her sewing to the ground, sinking into a curtsy. Sage tensed, knowing whoever was approaching was not someone she wanted to see. She hadn't seen Mira that flustered before. Sage focused on the double doors, battling her terror. She would not become a victim. A huge, rugged older man filled her balcony doorway. His steel dark blue gaze swept over her, pausing on the curtseying healer at his feet.

"Your Majesty, please forgive me!" Mira cried.

Sage's eyes widened, and her heart flew to her throat.

It was the king.

The king.

King Marq.

"It's nothing, please leave us." His voice was gruff and deep.

Sage shivered and stared pleadingly at the healer, who hadn't taken her eyes from the king since he first stepped foot on the terrace.

"Yes, Your Majesty." Mira stood and met her eyes, flashing her an apologetic smile before scurrying out of the room.

Traitor.

Sage vaguely heard the door close behind Mira as she stared at her friend's empty chair, numbness seeping into her limbs. What did his visit mean? What could he want? She rubbed her eyes and blinked up at him. He still stood on her balcony; she wasn't imagining things.

The king of Aermia was in her room.

He glided confidently from the doorway to the balcony, resting his large, weathered hands on the stone railing. Other than the initial glance, he had yet to look at her.

She couldn't help but stare. He was nothing like she imagined. She'd expected a hunched-over old man, but that couldn't be further from the truth. He stood tall, wrinkles etching his face and silver streaking his blond hair. Tanned muscular forearms peeped out of his rolled up sleeves. How similar he and his sons were.

All in all, he was an exceptionally handsome man despite his age. He must have made a striking figure in his youth. Sage had always thought the princes' good looks came from their mother, since her beauty had been famed throughout Aermia, but obviously they took after their father as well.

This was the man that had deserted her country.

He was the traitor.

Sage felt ill. She'd been harboring a glimmer of hope that there was a valid reason for the negligence of their king in his duty toward Aermia, but he stood before her strong and virile, seemingly unscathed by time and illness. He had no more right to rule than she did, despite his royal blood. She checked her growing resentment, fixing her face into a neutral mask.

"Looked your fill yet, darling?"

His softly spoken words snapped her out of her gawking. Painstakingly, she stood and dipped into a wobbly curtsy. "My king,

I am sorry if I have given offense. I did not mean to stare, but it is not every day the king himself waltzes into one's rooms." She observed him through her lashes to see if her sly needling bothered him.

His full mouth twitched and a small smile graced his face. "Your rooms? I was under the impression that you were staying in my home."

Arrogant. Like father, like son.

A tart reply was poised on the tip of her tongue when he spun to face her, resting a hip on the sturdy railing. His blue eyes were hauntingly familiar; another trait his sons had inherited. He wiggled his eyebrows, his eyes sparkling.

He was teasing her.

The *king* of Aermia was teasing her.

Well *that* threw her off balance. Her world tipped on its axis. Was this really happening? What was going on?

"Touché, my king," she conceded, dipping her chin once. Her legs quivered, but Sage locked them and stood tall. His gaze ran along the contours of her face. She tensed when his eyes scanned her body, right down to her bare feet peeking out from under her nightgown. Sage shoved aside her anxiety and met his bright blue eyes. They crinkled at the corners as he smiled down at her, his two dimples popping.

He was beautiful, and that was downright offensive.

The king gestured to her feet. "My Ivy always hated wearing shoes too. She hated the confined dress code. She changed once we married, and it was a damn miracle she wore anything proper to court. She often left her hair unbound, with bits of shell and sea glass woven through it."

Her heart squeezed at the longing she heard in his voice. "She was a lovely woman, the whole kingdom misses her, sire."

The smile on the king's face faded and grief took its place. She fluttered her hands at her side, lost for words.

Weariness weighed on her, and her legs shook with the effort to stay standing. She braced a hand on her chair, gesturing to the empty one next to her. "Would you like to sit down, Your Majesty?"

"Thank you."

Sage waited for him to seat himself and then sank into her own chair, relieved to be off her feet. He didn't speak, merely gazing out at the sea. Awkward minutes passed, and Sage tried not to shift uncomfortably in her seat. She spied on him from the corner of her eye, scrutinizing his profile. From her reports, he was a renowned hermit, so why the visit? Information? More torture? Would he harm her?

Dread trickled down her spine. She was alone with a massive man.

Stupid, stupid, stupid!

She should have strapped on her stolen knife. The bed was too far. Pressure on her balled hand startled her from her frantic thoughts. Her emerald eyes widened as the king's large hand squeezed hers.

"Calm down, darling. I'll not hurt you."

He already had.

The king patted her hand twice before relinquishing it. She

watched him rest beside her, his hands laced together over his stomach.

The entire situation was surreal. Here she was attempting to dethrone him, and he sat there like they were bosom buddies.

"With your permission I would like to be blunt, Your Majesty."

He cocked his head, gray-blond curls tumbling across his forehead. "Be my guest."

"I don't understand what prompted your visit. It's confusing. I am humbled by your presence, but I feel it might be improper for you to be spending your time with a girl from the streets."

Maybe he would take her hint and leave.

"You do realize my wife was a fisherman's daughter?" the king drawled.

"Yes."

"Your station matters not a whit to me. Hard work from both the common and noble classes is what makes Aermia a successful kingdom."

She wasn't expecting that. He would not leave that easily. Time to try another tactic. "I am a thief," Sage challenged.

"That's what I have been told, but I don't believe a word of it."

He smirked at her, and Serge's smirk flashed through her mind. Shivering, she pulled her shawl tighter around her as if it could protect her from the horrible memories.

The king's face pinched as he caught her expression. He faced the ocean and threw his boots onto the balcony edge. Once his gaze moved from her person, the air trapped tightly in her lungs released in a soft hiss.

Sage endeavored to remember what he had said. He didn't believe her. "What do you know about me?"

He tipped his head back, letting out a bark of laughter, the sound of it scattering the gulls in the wind.

"I know the story you told my men and sons: your name is Ruby, your family abandoned you, two of your brothers are pirates, and that you have been living on the streets for some time. You steal to survive, but that's not who you are."

"Who am I?" Sage raised both eyebrows in a mute prompt.

"You are courageous, strong, and kind."

"What?" Suspicion slithered through her. He was up to something.

"You had the opportunity to kill my son and some of the Elite, but you did not. That suggests you're not one to revel in violence," he paused and breathed deeply. "Even when you were... I won't say 'interrogated' because that was not an interrogation. It was a violation..."

He knew? He was the king, of course he knew.

"You never stopped fighting," he continued, steel lacing his tone. "They did not break you, no matter what you may be feeling now."

Her eyes dampened. His sons sanctioned it. The king didn't know.

"Everyone to cross your path has been treated by you with kindness and appreciation. You have not taken advantage of anyone." His faded sapphire eyes flashed to her green ones. "You have a good heart."

He was sincere.

Sage blinked.

The king meant what he said.

Her emotions bounced everywhere. Pain, fear, helplessness, gratitude, shock, and embarrassment flooded her. Her family appreciated her, but no one had ever said something of that magnitude to her. Sage struggled with what she had been told and what she was currently experiencing. "How do you know all of this?"

"I may not be visible but that does not mean I am not around." A sheepish smile crossed his face. "Also, Jeffry and Jacob have always been close friends."

"Jeffry and Jacob?" Sage parroted back. "The Keeper and the Healer?"

His eyes gleamed. "The same. They're twins."

"Really?" In her mind, twins were supposed to look alike. They had a wicked sense of humor in common, but that was pretty much where it ended. "Jacob never said anything."

"Not all of us share everything. I would think that'd be something you'd understand." His solemn eyes rested on her.

"I don't understand what you mean, sire," she fibbed, scrunching her face up in confusion.

He regarded her evenly. "You are an excellent liar."

She kept her body loose and gave him an offended look even as her heart sped up.

The king held up a hand. "In different circumstances, I believe you would be an honest person. From your character, I would stake my life on you protecting someone."

"I think you are seeing things that aren't there, my king. My name is Ruby," she said firmly, turning to admire the setting sun and the kaleidoscope of colors it cast on the evening sky.

"Sure it is, darling," the king retorted.

"I am not your 'darling'," she muttered in a low tone.

The bellowing laughter that burst out of the hulking king suited him. The sound comforted her just as much as it frightened her.

"You are feisty, and I like it. I have enjoyed our time together. I'll be visiting again soon." He nimbly shot out of his chair, hovering next to her. Sage scrambled out of her seat putting a little more distance between them.

"May I?"

She followed his eyes to her hand, where it was fisted in her shawl.

He had asked.

The king of Aermia was asking, not taking. She grudgingly let him lift her shaking hand. He pressed his lips to the back. "Until tomorrow, then."

He spun on his heel, disappearing through the double doors. Sage flopped into her chair and stared, sightless, at the weathered stone beneath her feet. Her head spun. He was nothing like she pictured. She had been told he was a selfish old man, but the man with whom she talked did not seem to be so in any way. Nothing was as it should be these days.

Nothing could have prepared her for this.

Nothing was black and white anymore.

Chapter Twenty-Four

SAGE

Mira rushed onto the balcony, her skirts rustling with every step, bewilderment evident in her features. Sage was pretty sure her own face mirrored the young healer's.

"Was that truly the king?" Sage had to ask. The answer was obvious, but it seemed so farfetched to think he willingly spent part of his afternoon sitting with her. Mira's head bobbed so emphatically that her blond hair bounced around her face.

Sage blew out a breath, lifting the few stray hairs tickling her face. She opened her mouth but nothing came out. She waved a hand to Mira, as if that could explain everything, and placed her chin in her palm, waiting for Mira to say something.

Mira opened and closed her mouth like a fish. Finally, she settled on, "Are you all right?"

Mira's concern for her warmed Sage's heart. She smiled, grateful to have the healer supporting her. Mira must have had a million questions, yet her first question was on her wellbeing. "I am fine. Confused, but fine. What did I do to warrant his company? Does he visit everyone who enters the infirmary?"

"No," Mira shook her blond head. "I haven't seen him in over a year and I don't understand why he would come to you. He doesn't even show up to welcome important visitors."

Sage arched a brow, and Mira's cheeks pinked at her careless words.

"Not to say you aren't important," Mira rushed out.

Sage attempted to tuck her grin away, but the dismay on Mira's face made her lose it. She sniggered.

Mira chuckled, slapping her on the arm. "You vain thing. I wasn't trying to be mean." Mira took on a curious look. "Indulge me though. What did the king want?"

"I don't know. We talked little, mostly just staring out at the ocean and listening to its waves. Maybe he just wanted company?" Sage shrugged. "He said he was coming back tomorrow."

"WHAT?" Mira screeched.

Sage pulled on her ears playfully. "Ladies are capable of such sounds?"

Mira didn't smile.

Her smile dropped. "What? What's wrong?"

Mira stood up and paced the small space. "Does this look like it's fit to entertain the king?" She gestured to the worn but clean chairs on which they were sitting.

"He didn't seem to mind when he was here," Sage interjected. "I doubt his focus was on the furniture."

Mira mumbled to herself, counting on one hand.

"What are you doing?"

"I am making a list. There is a lot to be done before he returns tomorrow..."

Mira spouted off a long list of things to be changed or accomplished before the king's following visit. It was spoken so quickly that Sage caught only a few of her self-imposed tasks: scrub the stone, new furniture, food, waitstaff. Sage shook her head. Mira was overthinking it.

Sage hoisted herself out of her chair and into the healer's path. She grasped Mira's biceps, shaking her once. "Listen. Calm down. I have a feeling that wouldn't please him at all."

Mira opened her mouth to argue but Sage cut her off. "I'm sure you know much more about palace etiquette than someone such as myself, but I got the impression he enjoyed the simplicity of today. Little is needed. From what I gathered, he has been seen little these last few years. He obviously wants to be left alone, so no waitstaff. I agree on the refreshments though. It's a wonderful idea as men can *always* eat."

The blonde pursed her lips as she contemplated. "Men do love food," she finally conceded. Mira noted the setting sun and hustled her back into their suite. "Let's start a fire and get you all toasty."

Sage closed the doors to the balcony, drawing the heavy curtains across the windows, and clambered into the enormous bed. She quaked underneath the covers while Mira coaxed the fire back to life. Sage ground her teeth together in frustration. It wasn't even that cold outside and yet she shivered like it was the middle of winter. She owed Mira her life.

"Thank you, Mira."

"It's nothing, Ruby."

Sage was really starting to hate that name. She wished she could give Mira her real name. It seemed like ages since she was truly herself.

Her mind flitted to her family. What were they doing at this moment? Had they stopped searching for her? Tears pricked her eyes as she thought of the fear and pain her family must be experiencing. She had disappeared from their lives over two weeks ago. Sage needed to keep focused on regaining her health; she would not break down. She had to keep up this pretense until she managed escape. Sage shoved down her sadness and turned her thoughts to the day's unusual visit. No matter how charming the king was, his visits didn't bode well for her.

"Mira?"

"What is it?" Mira sat on the bed next to her.

Sage swallowed hard, hoping this gamble would pay off. "I am worried about the attention this will bring me if others know about the king's visits. I feel like it'd be best if we kept everything discreet."

Mira studied her face and clasped her hand. "I agree. When the king left, he demanded the guards' silence but not mine. However, I see the wisdom in keeping silent, so I shall. Gavriel reports back to the princes though, so we need to be careful to leave out any mention of his visits in the evenings."

"You would do that for me?"

"I would do it for both of you. You may be just what the king needs right now." Mira stood and moved toward the door. "I'll go and find us some dinner."

"This means a lot to me. I won't ever forget your kindness, Mira," Sage said with sincerity, every word from her heart.

Mira winked over her shoulder, exiting the chamber. "Next time, you can take care of me when I'm ill."

Guilt coursed through her, knowing she wouldn't be here when Mira got sick. Hopefully, she would be far away and could leave this all behind her, but something told Sage that leaving Mira would be much harder than she'd initially imagined.

Knuckles wrapped on the door as it swung open.

"That was quick, Mira. Did you run all..." Sage sat up, surprised.

Gavriel strolled through the door, his black hair windswept, his violet eyes warm.

She twisted to the windows, noting the faint light filtering through them. "You're early."

A spark of anxiety crept up on her. She had never been alone with him before. Why the change? Sage swallowed and tried to be rational. Gavriel hadn't hurt her. He'd always been kind. He saved her.

Gav wouldn't hurt her.

"Well, I had little to do this evening, and I wanted to escape dining with the court. Thus, I decided to beg for sanctuary." He cast her a sheepish grin.

"By all means, enter and enjoy the comfort of my Crown-appointed abode." Sage gestured to the opulent suite.

Gavriel jostled something under his arm while he moved to his cot, his back to her. She peeked out of the corner of her eye, covertly examining the parcel.

"Would you like to see what it is I brought you?" he said, not turning around.

How did he know she was looking? He must have eyes on the back of his head, just like her mother.

"I would," she said. "I must admit my curiosity is piqued."

Avoiding any sudden movements, he made his way over to her, a spring in his step, placing the parcel on her bed.

If any other man had done so, she'd have scampered away, but there was something so soothing about Gavriel. This man could have left her to die, but he didn't. He chose to help her. She had nothing to fear from him.

Carefully, she unwrapped the parcel. Inside, she found a stunning chessboard. "A game?"

She tipped her head up staring into his gorgeous violet eyes. *The man had no right to look that devastatingly handsome.*

"I beg your pardon?"

"What?" She blinked.

He rubbed his nose, flashing her a shy smile. "Um...about my eyes."

Sage squished her eyes close, mortified. Of all the things to say out loud. A nervous chuckled escaped her. "Oh, hell, I can't believe

I said that out loud." She wanted to bang her head against the wall.

He waved a hand at her as if to wash away her embarrassment.

"It's true, though. You are gorgeous. I have never seen eyes like yours before."

Seriously.

Someone needed to bind her mouth shut.

It was his turn to give her an embarrassed smile. "Why thank you."

"But I can't accept this," Sage sighed dramatically. "What would your court think of you bringing a thief gifts? It simply isn't done!"

"I'll just tell them that my eyes didn't woo you, so I had to bring you gifts to capture your heart," he teased.

The awkwardness melted away with their combined laughter.

Gavriel bowed to her. "So, my lady, would you like to play a game of chess with me?"

"Of course, my lord, that sounds positively delightful!" she simpered. A smile played about his lips as he set up the board.

That started what was to become a nightly tradition of theirs. They gossiped, laughed, and teased Mira, whose frequent response was a playful scowl over the top of her book.

But Sage still dreaded going to bed. Everyone settled down and fell into an easy sleep, save her. She would stare at the ceiling, willing herself to stay awake, until sleep claimed her anyway.

Nightmares assaulted her.

Sharp blades. Terror. Leering faces. Torn clothing. Humiliation. Pain. Rough, bruising hands. Helplessness. Shame.

The first time, she woke up screaming, Gav had his arms

wrapped tightly around her. Mira was whispering, but Sage didn't understand what she was saying.

There was only terror.

And hysteria.

Gavriel rocked her, his lips on her temple, murmuring to her she was safe. Eventually, the hysteria turned into soul-shattering sobs. Gav's arms were no longer a cage but a sanctuary, and so she snuggled into them, crying herself asleep.

The next day, she was so embarrassed that she avoided any eye contact with Gav at all, but the stubborn man wouldn't let her get away with it.

Three little words.

You're not alone.

It turned out that Gav, too, suffered from nightmares because of his wife's accident. He wished someone had been there to comfort him on those nights. Gav brushed the hair from her face, just like her father always had. "There is no reason to be embarrassed, Ruby. What happened to you was traumatic, and it's okay to be vulnerable sometimes. I can help fight your demons."

Sage teared up with his compassionate promise. She never expected to have someone care for her in the palace of all places. She couldn't believe how lucky she was to have gained two such devoted friends. Mira and Gavriel were something special. She wished she could take them with her when the time came for her to depart.

Chapter Twenty-Five

SAGE

Between her afternoon visits with the king and Gavriel's company in the evenings, Sage's days were more diverting and seemed to move a little quicker. Neither man was anything like she'd expected him to be.

She had accepted the king's visits, but still didn't know what to make of them. He insisted she call him Marq, and it was odd using his given name instead of his title. She still expected someone to reprimand her every time she said it.

Each day she spent with him it became increasingly evident that something wasn't right. Some days, he was teeming with energy and stories. Others, he stared morosely out to sea, like he had nothing to live for. Sage didn't know which persona she would greet each day. Marq lost track of time and memories. It frustrated him when he recovered from one of his episodes.

It was heartbreaking to watch. He may have been physically strong, but his mental state was deteriorating. The king hadn't abandoned Aermia like she had been led to believe; he was sick, but not in the usual way. Whatever it was, it could not be seen or examined. From the stories he told, however, she realized how much he loved his people. It was sad that he had not the capabilities to even care for himself, let alone a kingdom.

How had his sons kept his current state a secret for so long? How would the rebellion use that information? That question plagued her. She didn't know what she would do with the information. Despite her best efforts, the king had grown on her. He didn't deserve what they had planned for him. It wasn't a crime to grow older. Sage still didn't care for his sons, but she had softened toward Marq. She didn't know what to do. She needed to think.

And think she did.

Sage had been trapped in her suite for two weeks. She needed to get out, even if it was only a walk, before she lost her mind.

Her sanctuary was her balcony overlooking the sea.

Sage stretched her poor, abused legs out and propped her feet on the railing. At least they were healing. The sun warmed her deliciously as she plotted how to trick Mira into letting her out.

Any time she brought the idea up, the blond healer would change the subject or make excuses about her health. True, Sage wasn't completely healed, but she knew her own body and she could handle a walk. Her coughing had abated during the day and was now only an issue at night.

"I haven't seen a prettier sight since my dear Ivy," a deep voice purred.

She jerked, but relaxed once she recognized the voice. Sage cracked her eyes open sleepily, wearing a lazy grin. "You are a shameless flirt! What would your sons say if they heard you speaking like that?"

He flashed her a wolfish grin and plopped down in the seat he had adopted for himself. "They would probably be disappointed that I beat them to it." A pause. "Sam would give me his blessing though, once he stopped nursing his own wounded pride."

A peal of laughter erupted from her, which seemed to please him. His grin deepened. It was good to laugh. Freeing, almost.

"I don't doubt that for one moment. I never know quite what to expect from him." Sage had seen Sam here and there, but he never stayed long, and she appreciated that. He still made her uncomfortable. She didn't think it was the man himself so much as the fact he was a sizeable man, one who could hurt her if he chose, and it was that which unsettled her.

"I have news which I believe will brighten up your day."

Sage reached out, clasping the king's rough hand. "Just having you here considerably brightens my day, Marq."

"And you call me the flirt," the king said, smoothly. He leaned toward her like he had a secret. "What would you say if I told you I was going to steal you away for a walk?"

Sage squealed, unable to help it. "I would say you were my

favorite person in the entire kingdom. Plus, you would save me from an early death of boredom. Please don't be teasing me, my poor heart couldn't handle the disappointment."

"Your wish is my command." Marq sprung up from the chair and held out his arm.

Sage graced him with a blinding smile and allowed him to take her arm. She barely kept from bouncing on her toes. She was to be free, even if it was just for a bit.

Mira and the guards stood outside the door. Various degrees of surprise showed on their faces when she followed in the king's wake. All of them bowed deeply as they passed, and Sage struggled not to pick up her pace. Someone surely would send her back into her gilded cage. A soft, sweet voice made Marq pause. And there it was. Mira.

"Excuse me, Your Majesty, she's not well enough to be out. If she exerts herself too much, it will aggravate her injuries."

The king looked over his shoulder and spoke. "We're not going for a strenuous hike in the mountains, only for a walk. She will lose her damn mind being trapped in those rooms any longer. We both appreciate your concern, and I promise to take good care of her. Good day."

Having dismissed them, the king strode forward with purpose. Sage craned her neck and met Mira's worried blue eyes. "I am all right," she mouthed, smiling encouragingly before facing forward and catching up to His Highness.

"So where are we going?" Sage inquired curiously. If she had been able to skip, she would have.

"It's a surprise."

His face betrayed nothing. Marq led her down the long hallway to the last door on the right. The door swung on silent hinges, revealing another suite as elaborate as hers. She was a little disappointed that she wasn't going for a longer walk but she figured beggars couldn't be choosers, so she pasted on a smile, appreciative of the king's kindness. Marq glanced at her face and chortled. "What's so funny?"

He pointed at her face. "The look on your face was priceless. Don't worry, *this* is not your surprise." He turned and walked toward an immense bookcase and pushed a silver-leafed book inward, until there was a faint click. The bookcase rolled to the side, exposing an empty doorway.

Her feet carried her to the king's side. She ran a hand along the stone looking for the catch. "A secret entrance? Where does it lead?"

"Follow me, and you will find out."

King Marq lit a lantern and began descending the stone steps. Unease crept over her. Was this some kind of trap? It would be foolhardy to blindly trust him. She turned it over in her mind. Had Marq truly wanted to harm her it was within his power to do so, even more so because their alone time afforded him many opportunities to do whatever he pleased—yet he'd never given her cause for fear. She realized it was more the situation than the man himself that discomfited her, and even that was lessened by the small weight at her ankle. After the king had caught her off guard that first day, Sage had made sure to always have her little knife on her.

"Are you coming?" His words echoed up to her.

Sage stepped into the dark stone stairwell, her decision made. The king waited until she'd reached him before continuing down the spiraling steps. Each of her ragged breaths felt overly loud in the closed space. Time ceased to exist in the shadowy stone staircase. Every once in a while, they passed darkened doorways. When she asked where they led, the only answer she received was, "Here and there."

She shrugged it off; everyone had secrets.

Forest-green lichens crept up the walls the farther they descended. Sage's legs shook with each step, causing her to brace a hand against the wall. Something slimy squished between her fingers and down her hand. Disgusted, Sage jerked her hand back. What was that? She shook her hand, ready to break down and ask how much farther they had to go, but, before she got the chance, Marq spoke.

"Watch your step, the stones are quite slippery."

Sage rolled her eyes at his back.

"I saw that," he chided.

What? How could he have seen her face? Spoken like a true parent.

His low chuckle filled the air. "No, I didn't, but I *did* raise two boys."

She smiled at his response. It sounded like something her papa would say. The crashing of waves on stone snagged her attention. She looked around, trying to locate the sound, hope filling her. "Is that what I think it is?" she whispered.

The king looked up at her, eyes glittering with excitement. "Come and see for yourself."

Sage almost fell on her face in her haste to scramble down the remaining stairs. Marq steadied and aided her the next few steps as they entered a cave. Sage stared in awe at the starfish that clung to the cove walls. She had a special fondness for the little sea creatures. Her heart stopped when they wound around a large porous rock and she spotted a rough archway pouring sunlight into the dim hidden cove. Their speed picked up as they burst out of the cave.

Her feet sunk into the damp sand, filling her slippers up. She was on the beach, the bloody beach! She yanked off her slippers and wiggled her toes in the sand, a bright smile lighting her face. The king watched her with a silly smile of his own, taking in each of her expressions.

Joy and appreciation filled her. Momentarily forgetting his station, and her suspicions, she grabbed him in a fierce hug. "Thank you so much!" Sage whispered into his shirt. She stretched up on her toes and kissed his whiskered cheek before stepping out of his arms.

She looked up at him only to see the oddest expression cross his face. Suddenly self-conscious, she dropped her eyes to the golden sand beneath her and took another step back. "Uh... I'm sorry," she mumbled. He had told her to call him Marq, it was true, however, his casual behavior did not negate the fact that he was still their sovereign and *not* her grandfather. She needed to keep that in mind.

"Ruby!" he admonished, his boots entering her view. A large, calloused finger slid under her chin, forcing her to meet his eyes. A wealth of emotions simmered there. "It has been a long time since someone has embraced me with genuine affection. Thank you for such a gift."

His sturdy arms embraced her tenderly. Warmth and affection filled her as she took in his words. Maybe, just maybe, she'd found a kindred spirit in the Aermian king.

After releasing her, she was shocked to see him plop down in the sand and strip off his boots and stockings. He rolled up his trousers and stood. "Shall we, my darling?"

Sage rolled her eyes at him—she would never break him of that. "Despite that nickname, we shall, my king."

He led them straight to the ocean. Sage lifted her skirt as the warm water raced past her toward the pristine beach. Her eyes closed as she tipped back her face and raised her arms above her head, savoring the sun's warm embrace. The briny sea breeze ruffled her clothing, making the linen slap against her legs. She wished to capture this moment and remember it always. This was freedom. Freedom and peace.

"I love the sea," she said, not opening her eyes. "As a little girl, I always wanted to be of the Sirenidae. My grandmother used to tell me fantastic stories about swimming with them when she was a girl. Do you think the Sirenidae still exist?"

Sage twisted to face the older man, opening her eyes. A mixture of love and wistfulness shone in his face.

"What is it?" It was times like these he would turn inward, shutting everyone out. She gave him an encouraging smile.

"I met Ivy here. She was so beautiful I didn't think her real. I tripped just trying to get to her," he grinned absently at the memory. "She stood exactly as you are now, face to the sun, arms stretched out, the waves caressing her ankles. I thought she was a mirage that would disappear before my eyes." He crossed his arms and kicked at the waves. "The truth was a lot less fantastical. She was the daughter of an oyster fisherman. Tired of waiting for him to return one day, she wandered onto this beach looking for sea turtles. That moment is etched into my memory. She was the most beautiful creature I have ever laid eyes upon."

The love and devotion in his voice brought tears to her eyes. *That* was what love should be like.

"I have never heard that story before. Thank you for sharing it with me, I will cherish it," Sage whispered, meaning every word.

His eyes emptied, the light extinguished. Her heart clenched at his desolate expression. Today was a good day, and she would not let him disappear.

An idea formed and so she plotted. She could be thrown into the dungeon for this, but it would be worth it. Sage swung her foot back and kicked a volley of water over the king. He yelped in surprise, eyes widening. Water dripped from his graying blond curls onto his startled face.

Life flickered back into him, and then there was something in his eyes that gave her pause. Feigning nonchalance, she balanced on the balls of her feet and shrugged one shoulder. "Your face was a little red, I thought you might need to cool off."

There was definitely a deviling gleam in his blue eyes. His face twisted into a mischievous grin, one she had almost certainly seen on Sam's face; like father like son.

"My dear lady, you look overheated yourself. Allow me to refresh you," he growled leaping toward her.

The sand shifted beneath her feet, impeding her escape. A wave of water slapped her in the face, leaving her sputtering.

"That's it! I *will* have my vengeance!" she shouted, flinging saltwater at the ambushing king. Sage only got one good splash in before he struck again, practically drowning her. Sage lifted her hands up in surrender. "I yield, I yield!"

"So, you yield and therefore agree that I am the most skilled water warrior you've yet crossed paths with?" He puffed his chest in mock pride.

She pushed her dripping hair from her face and wiped the saltwater from her stinging eyes. Sage placed her fist over her heart and bowed with a flourish. "I bow to your superior water warrior skills, Your Majesty."

They eyed each other as she stood. The oddity of the situation hit her. If she ever told this story, she was certain no one would believe her.

He chuckled briefly before composing himself. Almost immediately, however, another chuckle escaped. He then pointed to her head. "You seem to have something in your hair."

Sage patted her head and encountered something slimy. Seaweed. She had seaweed in her hair. She looked back at Marq in time to see him struggling to keep a straight face. "Is this funny, sire?"

His lips twitched once before his laughter rumbled out, joined by her own giggles. Once they had both reigned themselves in, she asked, "What would you like to do now, my king?"

"My king? Your Majesty? Sire? We are well past all that. Please, call me Marq, darling."

"I will call you Marq, the day you stop calling me your darling, my king."

"Touché." the king dipped his head. Marq straightened and gazed at an outcropping of black porous rocks. "How would you like to go starfish hunting? Ivy was always fond of it."

"That sounds like just what I need this afternoon."

Much to her delight, they found all manner of interesting things. Crabs, starfish, sea anemones, sand dollars, and gorgeous sea glass rested in the tide pools; they found every color of the rainbow. When was the last time she'd laughed and smiled so much?

As the sun sank, they began strolling back to the castle. She tilted her head back and observed the immense gilded prison looming above them. She had half a mind to run screaming in the other direction, but she discarded the idea as soon as it formed. Though frail in mind, the king was strong. In her state, she would make it only a few paces before he caught her.

She glanced his way and caught him studying her in that intense way he was prone to from time to time. She smiled weakly and dropped her eyes. "Is there something on your mind, my king?"

"Did you have a nice time this afternoon?" The vulnerability was clear in his voice and it hurt her heart.

"I can't remember the last time I have enjoyed myself this much." Her honesty surprised herself. "Thank you for such a wonderful adventure this afternoon. I will treasure this memory." And she meant it.

"The same for me, my darling," Marq admitted. "Thank you for humoring an old man."

Sage raised her chin and winked flirtatiously at Marq. Right before her eyes, Marq Ramses, king of Aermia, blushed.

"What is this?" she exclaimed, pointing to his pink cheeks. "Are you blushing, Your Majesty?"

"I don't know what you are referring to. Men don't blush, especially not kings. I must have gotten too much sun."

"As you say, my king." Sage tucked away her grin.

"Your words say one thing but your tone says something very different." He squinted at her. "Don't forget that I've two sons well versed in sarcasm."

"You are quite right."

Her smile dimmed. His two sons. Monsters. Sam no doubt was proficient in the art of sarcasm, the crown prince however... A chill ran down her spine. In her meager experience, he didn't have a humorous bone in his body. Probably no joyful ones either.

The unlikely duo reached the entrance to the stairwell and began their trek up the slick stairs. Every step slurped obnoxiously in the narrow space. Sage wished she had put her slippers back on as the algae and seawater squished between her toes, but it was too late now. She then noticed that Marq had yet to put his boots back on as well. She squared her shoulders. If the king could do it, then so could she.

Sage sent up a quick prayer of thanks when they reached dry stairs. She flexed her toes with each step to alleviate the cramping from trying to keep her balance. The dark algae covering the walls ended at that point too. How odd. "Why does the algae stop here?"

"The tide comes in and fills the stairwell to this point."

Her eyes widened in understanding. She had wondered why they left this passage unprotected, but it made sense. Even the best swimmer couldn't hold his breath long enough to swim up all those stairs once this place flooded. The stairwell seemed to shrink around her, so she picked up her skirts and scampered after the king.

With each step, her breathing sawed in and out. After another couple of flights her legs quivered with each step, but still she pushed on. Finally, a wracking cough seized her, and she gasped for air.

Marq swung the lantern around. "Are you all right?"

She waved a hand at him and then placed both hands on her knees. "I will be okay," she wheezed. "I need a little break. My legs feel like jelly."

He frowned at her and pursed his lips. "We might have overdone it today. I know a shortcut we can use."

He waited for Sage to catch her breath before starting back up the stairs like a mountain goat. Sage mumbled curses and continued, slogging after him. To her relief, they climbed only fifteen more stairs before he glided into a new tunnel.

Grit and dust stuck to the bottom of her feet as she followed. Beady eyes gleamed at her from the abandoned hallway. She sincerely hoped that whatever happened to live down here left her alone, specifically creatures of the eight-legged variety. She gave each web they passed a wide berth.

King Marq halted as the hallway came to a dead end. He probed the wall until she heard a faint click. Soft light filtered in when the king poked his head out the door, looking left and then right. He waved her forward and shut the door behind her. She memorized their hiding spot with a keen mind.

It was a perfect way to escape.

The king peeked around the corner and then flashed her a smile full of mischief. "It's been years since I snuck around with a young lady. It's clear, let's make our escape."

They casually wandered from their spot, each mirroring the other's grin. They had only taken a couple steps when a doorway opened, and a sea of men spilled out, spotting them.

Chapter Twenty-Six

SAGE

Fear and anxiety overcame her as the group rushed over. A series of bowing and scraping vaguely registered, and she tried to take a step back from the king's side. His hand slipped around hers and tightened. Her breathing turned ragged. So many men. She needed to get away. She wasn't safe.

One by one, the pairs of eyes focused on her, making her skin prickle. Each look held its own special horror. She was surrounded. She needed to leave. Sage frantically searched for an escape route when her eyes caught a familiar gaze.

Gavriel.

She barely registered the spymaster standing beside him before focusing on Gav. If she could only get to Gav, she would be safe. She dropped her gaze to her hand in the king's grasp. Her fingers were white. She couldn't feel them. Her eyes dropped farther to her feet, and Sage grimaced at her dirty, bare feet next to the king's hairy ones. What a sight she and the king must make. Both windswept, looking tumbled.

Tumbled.

Oh no.

She tried to slam the door closed on her nightmares but they fought back.

Bile crept up her throat at the memory of grabbing hands. Her vision swam, turning the floor to a puddle of colors. Giant, black blobs entered her line of sight. A large hand stretched toward her, palm up. A buzzing filled her ears, and black spots danced across her eyes.

"My lady, it is so nice to see you again."

Gav. Thank the stars, it was Gav.

Sage blinked as he took her hand and placed a light kiss on the back of it before kissing her cheek. "Take a deep breath, Ruby. These men will not harm you. Sam and I will let nothing bad happen to you," he whispered in her ear. "Breathe, you need to breathe."

Sage's breath rushed out of her at his softly spoken command. She didn't even know she'd been holding her breath. Sage closed her eyes and tried to will the fear away. It didn't abate completely, but with Gav at her side it was more manageable. She was not the victim. Sage lifted her head in increments until she met his unique eyes.

"You're looking so well, my lady." His gaze swept over her, missing nothing.

"Thank you, my lord. The healers took excellent care of me. The sea breeze and sun were exactly what I needed this afternoon."

"Indeed."

His penetrating look was uncomfortable. She shifted her eyes from his face to Sam's grinning one.

Sam stepped forward and dipped into a courtly bow. "My lady, I praise the stars to be able to see you again so soon."

Whispers erupted around them at his comment. Sam smiled down at her smugly. A glimmer of irritation worked through her. What was he talking about?

Sage pasted on a sweet smile. "If only I could say the same," she mumbled so low that only Sam heard it. His lips twitched at her insult.

Insufferable man.

"The pleasure is all mine, Your Highness," she simpered, sounding like an idiot.

It was as if a silent signal had been given. The surrounding men pushed forward to greet her, her anxiety ratcheting, but as Gav had promised, both Sam and Gav positioned themselves so that none of the men touched her.

"What the devil are you all doing standing in the doorway? Don't you have things to do?" The irate voice carried over the melee.

The crown prince.

Sage cringed and huddled closer to Marq, a small whimper escaping her. A hand tightened on her own, making her realize she hadn't released his hand. She drew strength from the king as the prince's frustrated voice moved toward them.

He was the reason she was left in that cell. His men were the ones who had brutally attacked her. She suffered and had nightmares each night because of him. A spark of rage ignited inside her, burning her dread to ash. She would not cower. Sage dug deep from a place she didn't know she still had. She straightened to her full height, a few inches over five feet, shored her nerves, and cleared all emotion from her face.

The spymaster's watchful eyes intensified, cataloguing each of her movements. That man saw too much. She needed to keep an eye on him, but her thoughts ceased when the crown prince came into view, her breath stuttering as if she'd been kicked in the stomach.

His powerful figure cut a swath through the men. Wide shoulders and a powerful chest led down to sculpted waist and strong thighs.

Imposing. That was the word that came to mind when looking at him. He was taller and stronger than his father.

Sage's eyes snapped back to his face. High cheekbones faded into a hint of dark stubble shading his chiseled jaw. Thick, wavy hair framed piercing eyes. Eyes that were locked on her.

Alluring.

There was something about his inky hair and midnight eyes that appealed to her, though she knew better than to trust that. Beneath that beauty held cruelty, and Sage would never forget that.

His face registered his shock before he schooled his features. He lengthened his stride, stopping mere paces away. Sage locked her shaking knees, attempting to hold onto the anger, which kept her fear at bay, and not scamper away.

"Your Majesty. It is good to see you." He bowed to his father respectfully.

King Marq stepped closer to his eldest son and slapped him on the shoulder, dragging her with him.

"It is good to see you as well, my son. This young lady has been a source of much amusement of late. We had a stimulating afternoon. I haven't truly enjoyed someone's company in far too long." Marq touched her hair, his fingers trailing over the silky strands until they brushed her shoulder.

Her eyes snapped to the king who smirked at his son. What was he doing? He had never touched her like that. Stimulating company? Even to her, those words sounded suggestive. She scanned the group of men, gauging their reactions. Many knowing looks sent their way made her want to puke all over the floor.

Her gaze returned to the crown prince. Anger was plain on his face. Disgust. Sage returned his glare with one of complete indifference, but her mask was cracking. She needed to leave. Now.

The king turned to her like he had read her mind. She gave him a relieved smile when he kissed her hand prettily. He would take her back to the room unscathed.

"Thank you for the wonderful afternoon. I will see you soon, my darling."

What?

Sage blinked and then stared at him in confusion. The king

dropped her hand and thrust her into his eldest son's arms. Her whole body froze as the crown prince reflexively caught her, his giant hands wrapping around her biceps. The hair rose on her arms when the prince's thumbs swept across her exposed skin. When would this hell end?

"Please accompany her back to her chamber."

She meant to plead with Marq, but the words stuck in her throat. Sage sent him a pleading look, which he returned with a bright smile before sauntering off with most of the men. He'd left her with the enemy. He'd betrayed her.

Why would he do that?

Fear, betrayal, and confusion tangled inside her. The large body in front of her shifted, causing her to jerk backward and snap out of her thoughts. Her eyes flicked to the man holding her hostage. A cry gurgled in her throat at the anger there.

He released her abruptly and held his elbow out to her stiffly. "If it pleases you, I will escort you back."

Everything screamed at her to run. But to where? She had nowhere to go. Her emerald eyes darted around, taking in the few remaining men who were eyeing her with curiosity. A warm hand settled in the middle of her back.

"Accept his offer, Ruby. It's for your safety." Gav whispered.

Safety? Sage wanted to laugh. She would never be safe with him. She eyed the crown prince's elbow like one would a snake. She didn't want to touch any part of him, but logic filtered through. If she went quietly, maybe she could get away. If she insulted the crown prince in front of witnesses, there would no doubt be consequences.

Sage took one step and paused. Gavriel nudged her in encouragement. She gathered her courage and shuffled to the prince's side. Her fingers rested lightly on his sleeve, his arm hard as ice. "I thank you, my lord."

He drifted forward, Sam and Gav alongside them. Courtiers passed them, tittering and whispering into each other's ears or behind fans. Sage ignored the stares that crawled across her skin. She was led through a twist of hallways and rooms, finally arriving at a grand staircase that split in two. Sage cringed inwardly at having to hike up another set of stairs.

She'd only wanted a walk.

"What was that?" the prince hissed.

"Nothing, sire."

The prince set a grueling pace up the white and gold marble steps. After the first set, her legs trembled so badly that she wobbled and almost tumbled down the stairs. The crown prince cursed, slipping an arm around her back. She would have thrown it off if she could have stayed on her feet. Once again, he picked up his speed, dragging her up two more flights of steps. His grip tightened around her back so that his fingers were brushing against the swell of her right breast.

Her mind flashed back to unwanted caressing hands and cold eyes. She flung herself out of his arms when they hit the landing. Sage lurched to the side, swaying, before she caught her balance and stormed toward her door. She needed a bath. She could still feel his skin against hers.

A large hand slid around her wrist like a manacle. Without thought she lashed out at her attacker, punching. The crown prince caught her fist in his palm, snarling at her.

She tugged on her arms but he held on. "Let go of me!" Frantically, she pulled on both of her hands locked in his grip. He prowled toward her, making her scramble backward. A solid object pressed into her back. A wall. She was trapped.

Dark blue eyes glared into green ones. "What were you doing with my father?" he snarled.

"None of your business."

The pace of her breathing escalated with his closeness. She had promised herself she would never let herself get in this position again, and yet here she was. She was better than this. Swiftly, she smashed her knee upward, and color drained from the prince's face. Sage pivoted under his arm and swept her leg out, knocking him onto his back. She ripped the knife from her ankle and pounced on him. Sage straddled his chest, her knees pinning his arms, with her knife tip pricking his neck.

"Don't you ever try that with me again! I don't care if you're the next king. If you touch me without my permission, I will kill you! Do you hear me?" she screamed. "I don't care if I swing for this, but I never want to be forced to suffer your touch again! Do you understand me?" she growled, pressing her stolen blade harder into his neck.

"He can't answer with your knife pressed against his neck." Gav's calm voice wrapped around her. "You need to step back, Ruby. I won't let anything happen to you, but you need to let him go."

Gav moved closer, but she never took her eyes off the crown prince. What was she doing? She wasn't an assassin. His midnight eyes tracked the single tear that dripped down her face and plopped onto his cheek.

"No more," she whispered brokenly. She was lifted off him and into Gavriel's arms. Sage looked up, meeting her friend's violet eyes. "Please take me to my room."

Gavriel wrapped her up and led her to her suite. A scratchy voice made her falter.

"I promise."

She looked over her shoulder with a single nod of acknowledgement. "Remember that you do."

Sage wavered when both guards turned to her. She inspected both of them and arranged her face into a weak smile. She knew them. Sage ignored their pity-filled eyes and entered her suite, for once happy to be in her cage.

Mira stood up from her chair, dumping her book on the floor. "You have been gone for hours! Did you overdo it? Why are you wet and dirty? Never mind, I will draw a bath right now."

Sage shrugged out of Gavriel's arms and rushed into Mira's. "Thank you for being a good friend," she whispered into the healer's neck.

Sage dropped her arms and moved to the balcony to watch as the last of the sun's rays faded. Gav and Mira whispered to one another but her mind was a thousand miles away.

It was time.

Something had caught her attention when she arrived at the door: a guard was twisting his ring on his finger. It caught her attention because it was something she, too, did when deep in thought. The ring's exquisite design intrigued her.

A dragon pierced by its own sword.

So similar to the family crest that you wouldn't notice the detail, unless you peered at it closely. Her time in this prison was finished. The rebellion was here.

At last, she would escape.

Chapter Twenty-Seven

TEHL

Tehl glared at the ceiling. He was such an idiot. What was he thinking grabbing her like that? He hadn't thought at all. Tehl blew out a breath as Sam leaned over him, his blond brows wiggling.

"The family jewels still attached brother? They're kind of important, something about heirs…"

"Not sure Sam, bruised for sure though. Would you check on them for me?" he joked through his pain.

Sam's faced soured. "I fear I must decline; I love you, but not that much." His brother held a hand out. "I will, however, help you up. That much I can manage."

Pulling onto his knees, nausea washed over him. Tehl hunched over and heaved. He had never been hit that hard between the legs before. Tehl swiped at the sweat on his forehead before holding his head in his hands.

Rapid footsteps stomped toward them—an angry staccato.

"What the bloody hell were you thinking?" his cousin exploded, shaking a fist at him.

Tehl pushed to his feet, bile burning his throat.

"It's a good thing she kicked you as hard as she did or I would've had a go at you!" Gavriel's eye narrowed on him. "You're damn lucky."

"She has impeccable aim, for sure," Sam piped up, unhelpfully, from the wall.

"Shut your mouth, Sam." Gavriel stabbed a finger Sam's direction. "You're just as guilty for not doing anything!"

"Well, I never!" Sam gasped.

Gav gave Sam a black look then turned his rage back on Tehl. "Did you, or did you not, both ask me to befriend the girl to gain her cooperation?"

"I did," Tehl gritted out.

"With the stunt you pulled, I doubt she would give us a blanket even if we were freezing to death. I have been earning her trust bit by bit, but do you think she will listen to anything I say now?" Gav ran his hands through his hair then stabbed a finger at him. "Not only did you destroy any chance of her working with us, but you frightened her. Ruby has suffered here." Gav's eyes darted between them. "Hell, you both are aware of the nightmares she has every night. I try to calm her, and they've lessened in the last week, but I would bet my horse she has terrors again tonight. *Think* before you act."

Remorse filled Tehl. He had avoided the rebel because of this very problem. He didn't think when he was around her; everything became muddled. "I'm sorry, but imagine my surprise when I spotted her among my advisers in a wet nightdress. She held *my* father's hand as though she did it every night. She looked tumbled, don't deny it." Anger licked at the remorse burning it away. "She should've been in her room."

Gavriel's lips thinned.

Sam sauntered over to them. "What I would like to know is how she's acquainted with our father. Did you see how chummy he was with her? He was smiling at her like he used to before Mum died. How did they meet Gav?"

"I haven't the foggiest. Mira, her healer, was the only other one aware of his visits."

"Visits?" How many times had his father come to her?

"Evidently he snuck in almost two weeks ago and surprised them both. He had the Elite and the healer sworn to secrecy. He's been visiting her for a couple of hours every afternoon."

"Do you mean visiting or *visiting*?" Sam queried.

Tehl stiffened. Had she seduced his father?

"When he introduced her, did his tone imply the latter?" Sam questioned.

Gav shook his head. "No, Ruby spoke to Mira about her afternoons with your father. They talked. Marq told her stories about your mum and the sea. They're companions, nothing more."

"I thought you were getting pretty close to her." Tehl's brows furrowed. "You weren't aware of his visits? Ruby said nothing to you?"

His cousin's jaw clenched. "She never told me though she had plenty of time. She didn't trust me with this."

"Ruby wasn't sworn to secrecy?" Sam probed.

"The rebel wasn't sworn to secrecy, but she said nothing."

"Why?" Sam asked skeptically. "She could gain many things from her connection to him. It was obvious my father has affection for her. What is she after?"

Gav continued to glare Sam's way. "Ruby's worried the king's attention would bring more of *our* focus." His cousin turned his glare on him. "She didn't want *you* coming to question her."

His own eyes narrowed. "If she hadn't betrayed the Crown, she would have no reason to fear me. My question is this: what does my father want with her? We have no idea what she's fed him or what he's told her. She's dangerous. Sam—" His eyes cut to his brother. "Any new information on her?"

Sam sighed in frustration. "No, no one knows anything. Either that or they're just unwilling to give her up. I have picked up one lead, but it will be a few days before I know anything."

"Okay then. Keep me posted on that. In the meantime, I need to visit our father." Tehl wrinkled his nose. He was not looking forward to that. "Gav, when you asked her to step away she did because she trusted you." He let his cousin absorb that for a moment before continuing. "She still trusts you, as do I. I need you to continue to keep watch over her."

Gavriel nodded. Tehl next addressed Sam. "I have no clue what you're doing with your sneaks; that's your realm to deal with, but keep an eye out. The rebel's been here for three weeks. Someone will come for her, and soon, I'm sure of it. When they do…" Tehl trailed off, exchanging a knowing smile with his brother. "In the meantime, Sam, I need you to gain an oath of silence from the Elite guarding her door."

"Apparently, they are already excellent at keeping secrets," Gav cut in.

"On that note…" Sam winked and stalked toward the Elite.

Tehl hung his head, staring at the carpets beneath his boots knowing what his cousin would say next. His eyes traced the blue scales of a mermaid woven into the rug, awaiting the inevitable speech.

"This situation could have been avoided."

There it was.

"Damn it, Tehl."

"I don't have eloquent words and manners like you, Gavriel. I may be able to read people, but I'm never sure how I should react to their emotions." He paused, frustrated. "I can't change who I am." He rolled his neck and faced his cousin. "What would you do if you were in my position?"

"You won't like it."

"Still, I want to hear it. If it will help me be a better king for Aermia, then I will do my duty."

"You need a wife." Blunt.

Tehl blinked at him trying to figure out if he heard right. "A wife?" he parroted. What did that have to do with anything?

"Yes, a wife. You need someone to round your sharp edges and make you more approachable. Someone that will complement and enhance your abilities, support you in your role. Plus, the things you hate are all tasks that your mother oversaw. When you marry, your queen will assume those responsibilities." Gav's face morphed into a devilish grin. "She will also help you with the whole heir business. Baby-making is always fun, and I can tell you *that* from experience."

He smirked at Gavriel's last comment. "Heirs?"

Gav's smile widened, and he nodded. "Heirs."

Tehl shook his head at his cousin. "I will consider it. Thank you for your advice."

Tehl patted his cousin on the shoulder and headed down the corridor. Would a woman make that big a difference? Gavriel never gave bad advice and his family had keenly felt the loss of his mum and Emma. Their presence certainly made a difference.

But where would he ever find a bride? He didn't have time to hunt for one. Tehl filed it away for later. He needed to deal with his father.

If he could find him.

***

Although he'd searched all of his father's usual haunts, he'd yet to encounter him. Marq Ramses had an uncanny ability to disappear when someone was looking for him. Tehl's time had run out. It was time for dinner.

He grudgingly made his way toward the great hall. A loud shriek echoed through the doorway, followed by the buzz of many voices.

Tehl hesitated in the doorway, wishing escape was possible. He'd rather eat with the Elite or out in one of the pastures. At least with the animals he could enjoy some measure of peace and quiet.

He braced himself and strode into the great hall with his head high and shoulders back. The sound of a hundred chairs scraping the floor reverberated in the open space.

Made-up faces flashed him painted smiles, their eyes predatory. Men and women dipped in intricate bows and curtsies as he brushed by.

He leapt up the two stairs to the dais and faced his court. "Be seated and enjoy your dinner," he commanded in a loud voice before sitting.

Gav was sitting on his left but Sam's seat was empty. "Figures," he grumbled to himself.

"What was that, Your Highness?" said a young woman, two chairs down.

He looked at her for a moment and then realized his voice had carried farther than intended.

Tehl cleared his throat and sent her a brittle smile. "Nothing, my lady."

She lowered her eyelashes and simpered in her seat. He wanted to roll his eyes at her coy glances. She was anything but bashful. Caeja, councilmen Jaren's daughter, had thrown herself at him many times already; it seemed ridiculous to play shy now. Sam's running theory on their motives was disturbing. His brother figured that, though they knew he couldn't marry them, most of them didn't care. He said they were probably all hoping to get pregnant, so it'd be their child on the throne one day. His nose wrinkled at the idea, and he realized he was still staring at Caeja. Her cheeks pinked, whether from embarrassment or anger he didn't know, but he quickly wiped his face clear of expression.

Tehl focused on his food and only spoke when asked a question. He tried to keep his answers short so that no one drew him into conversation. Once he finished, he sprawled in his chair and watched the delicate political dance around him—every look, laugh, touch, or joke was a means to an end.

His mind drifted back to what Gav had said earlier.

A wife.

She could probably steer through the court waters better than he could. Plus, if he had a wife maybe some of these women would leave him alone. Tehl almost snorted at the thought.

Yeah, right. The women of his court had no shame.

The more he considered marriage though, the more he liked the idea. His thoughts had already turned to children of late, so if he married soon it was possible that within the year, he could welcome a child of his own into this world.

Tehl stood and retired for the night, thankful to leave behind the lights, people, and music. In his suite, he paced, restlessness plaguing him. He was too wound up from the day's activities to fall asleep. He needed to spend a while on the ledge.

He brushed aside his tapestry to display a hidden door that complained as he pried it open. He then picked up his lantern and slipped into the black tunnel.

These hidden, dank hallways had always intrigued him, ever

since he was a child. He had fond memories of hiding in places where his mum would be, then jumping out to scare her. She would scream, swat him on the shoulder, and kiss his head. Tehl smiled at the memories as he came upon the tiny gray door that led to his sanctuary. He had to hunch over just to fit through. On the other side, a cool sea breeze ruffled his hair as he waited for his eyes to adjust to the dark.

Moonlight glimmered on the black sea, only to be shattered by the frothy white waves and luminescent algae growing on the rocks beneath the surface. He edged along the castle wall to a large ledge that overlooked the sea. It amazed him how the ocean never looked the same. It was always changing, and yet, constant.

He loved this spot. It was the ideal place to sit and ponder life. No one had ever found him here, not even Sam. If they knew about it, they left him alone. Peace. Joy. Contentment. In his mind, that was what his ledge represented.

Closing his eyes, he leaned his head against the stone wall behind him. Little bats called to each other in the night, bringing a smile to his face. Many abhorred the small creatures of the night, but Tehl had grown fond of them over the years since they'd made their nests beneath his ledge. He left them in peace, and they left him in peace.

A pebble skittered across the stone, and his eyes popped open at the disturbance. He jolted when he recognized his father squeezing himself through the little door.

Marq Ramses skirted along the wall and plopped down beside his son. Tehl gawked at his father, bewildered. The king never failed to surprise him.

He hadn't wanted to be found earlier, so why was his father seeking him out?

Marq's lips quirked upward. Without looking at him, his father murmured, "I wanted to join you. And, as for not wanting to be found, well... I am always around, you just need to search harder."

He blinked at his father, realizing that he had spoken his thoughts aloud. Tehl shook his head and turned back to the frothy black waves. He had a million questions for his father, but they could wait. Now was the time for peace. They sat in companionable silence for some time, the ocean waves lapping below.

"Your mum used to sit out here."

Tehl shifted, glimpsing his father from the corner of his eye. His expression was so bittersweet that he ached for his mum.

"Any time she felt overwhelmed or tried to work through a problem, she would sit here, sometimes for hours. I always worried about her falling but she'd just pat my cheek and tell me to stop being such a worry wart." His father smiled. "Then she had you and your brother. From the day she held you in her arms things changed for her. She was still herself, but much more cautious; she had her precious boys to care for. Then, one day, you discovered this ledge."

"I thought I was the first and only one to discover it."

The king shook his head. "This was your mother's place well before it was yours. I have lived here my entire life, yet I never knew it existed—not before her. She was in the palace but a week before she discovered it." He fluttered his hand out, encompassing the cove. "Your mum was so afraid when she realized you'd found her cove. She wanted to forbid you from ever coming back; that's how scared she was. She was worried you'd hurt yourself or fall."

His father clasped him on the shoulder. "I stood up for you. A person needs a place to decompress, especially a prince. I also reminded your mum I never forbade her to come here, though I, too, always worried." Laughter rumbled deep in his father's chest. "I received a nasty look for that one, let me tell you. She pursed her pretty little lips like she'd eaten a hundred lemons. After a while though, she nodded her head and dropped the subject. But later, I noticed a pattern. Every time you disappeared, so would she. So one day I followed her. It turned out, she had snuck down the stairway behind you, and there she sat, watching you from the stairs. She understood you needed your time, but she also wanted to make sure you were safeguarded." His father's eyes crinkled. "Thus, I retraced my steps and never mentioned it."

Tehl swallowed around the large lump in his throat. "She watched over me *every time*?"

His father nodded. "You were never alone. She loved you with everything she had and hoped to protect you as much as possible from the world. She was a wonderful mother. The kingdom is a darker place without her," he choked out, pain in his eyes.

Tehl gave his father some privacy, returning his gaze to the inky sea. Why would someone subject themselves to that kind of pain? Having that sort of love could destroy a person, so he wanted no part of it. He wanted a companion, but not for love, there was too much risk in that. His mind drifted to the rebel, her clinging to his father for dear life. It seemed his father might have a new ladylove. What was his father thinking? She was a traitor, not to mention too young for the king.

Way too young.

She had to be near *his* age. It was absurd.

"What were you doing with that girl today, father? She was in a nightdress—hardly the proper attire to entertain the king," he demanded.

His father scrutinized him, but Tehl kept his face serene, letting his father examine him.

"Son, no matter how mildly you spoke those words, it reeked of jealousy. Does Ruby interest you?"

"Answering my question with a question, that's telling in itself. As for your question, no, I don't have a claim on the girl, nor do I want one. Why are you taken with that slip of a girl? She's nothing compared to mum."

His mum was tall with lithe grace and ethereal beauty, whereas the girl was short, all curves and mystery. Her emerald green eyes flashed through his mind. He'd never seen prettier eyes. Tehl frowned at his thoughts and glowered at the waves. Nothing about her should appeal to him at all.

Tehl turned his frustration on his father. "Again, why were you parading your indiscretion around today?"

Silence answered him.

"Mum would be disgusted with your behavior. She hated men who took mistresses." Tehl laughed without humor. "But who am I to tell you how to treat your light-skirts? Do you even know who you hopped into bed with?"

The look on his father's face had cowed many a man, but not Tehl. He kept his gaze steady. His father drew in a deep breath and let it out again, speaking between clenched teeth. "Firstly, 'that girl' has a name. Learn it and give her some damn respect. She is no light-skirt. She's as beautiful as your mother, both inside and out. That being said, I have never replaced your mother and wouldn't even think of doing so with someone at least half my age, no matter how charming she may be. Even *if* she was my mistress," the king growled, "it would be no concern of yours. I am the king and can do as I damn well please. I am not required to dole out explanations to you. You, on the other hand, have much to answer for."

"What?" He was working himself to the bone to keep Aermia from falling to pieces, what complaint could his father have?

"That poor creature has been locked up for weeks because of you. My only motive today was to give her an afternoon of happiness, as is my right."

Was his father that naïve?

"You realize she is deceiving you?" Tehl asked incredulously.

"No more than anyone else."

She had his father fooled.

He replayed his father's words when something dawned on him. "How did you know I had her locked up?"

The king's face seemed to say: *'Seriously?'* "I've been the king longer than you've been alive. I can still keep track of what goes on in my home, even if I am not always a part of it."

Tehl pinched the bridge of his nose. He came to this spot for peace but all he was getting was a headache. "So you're telling me it doesn't matter to you that she's a traitor to the Crown, and in league with the rebellion? She's dangerous and yet you'd let her go free?"

"Ruby's not free. She is up in her suite at this very moment."

"That is not the point! She could have escaped today!" His voice rose with each word. "She is all we have to help us settle this rebellion before it turns to civil war. To mention nothing of the fact that, with Scythia practically knocking at our door, discontent is the *last* thing we need right now! I don't understand why you would take the risk. She is trouble! Trouble crammed into an alluring package."

A smug smile crept up his father's face.

"Stop looking at me like that. Any man would notice," Tehl muttered.

"You would need to be dead not to notice." His father winked. "And yes, to answer your question, I knew she was with the rebellion. My curiosity was piqued after speaking with Jeffry."

Tehl winced. Her time in the dungeon wasn't something he wished on anyone. "I..." He paused, at a loss for words. "I am responsible for what happened. What befell her shouldn't have happened."

A large hand rested on his neck. "We can do only so much, son. Our people choose to obey us. When they don't, we must deal with the consequences of their actions as justly as we can. That being said—" His father's tone turned to ice. "The man responsible ought to die."

That was one thing they agreed upon. "I couldn't agree more, and when we find him, which we will, he will regret ever touching her."

Tehl leaned his head against the wall, watching the billowy silver clouds drift across the darkened sky. The bloodthirsty part of him was excited to find Serge and finish this business. Another part of him, however, couldn't stop focusing on the beguiling yet irritating rebel currently locked in his home.

"What do you think of her?" He cracked one eye open and glanced at his father. "You must like her if you visit her every day."

His father stared out at the ocean. He was quiet for so long Tehl thought perhaps he wouldn't answer.

"She isn't what I'd expected," was the soft reply. "Ruby has been puzzling and interesting because, although she did hide things from me, she was also completely honest about others. She has shown courage, kindness, strength, and compassion. I was also surprised to find she actually wants the best for our people and truly cares for them as a whole." His father met his eyes. "She's not the enemy. Mark my words, she could give you what you need and more."

Tehl leaned forward and clasped his hands loosely between his knees. "Did you learn anything useful from her?"

"Nothing she didn't want me to." The king smirked. "She has just as many faces as Sam. She has been well trained; I hope that whoever she is working with will negotiate, as they're sure to be a formidable enemy."

"If she is anything like Sam we need to proceed with extreme caution. Her betrayal could ruin Aermia."

"I consider myself a good judge of character and my gut says, given the opportunity, she would do what is best for the people no matter the 'side' she is on at the time. We must show her that ours is the best for Aermia."

"Gav is working on it as we speak. She doesn't care for Sam though, and she *loathes* me."

His father cocked his head in a silent question.

Tehl straightened his back and then stared anywhere but at his father. "I handled her roughly, threatened her family, and threatened to ravish her before we imprisoned her."

At his father's sharp inhale, he faltered before soldiering on. "Then I ordered limited food and water. I forgot about her when I went to the border after the Scythian invasion. When we arrived home, she had already been attacked. She believes I set those men on her." He put a hand over his mouth and mumbled, "I even ended up backing her against a wall when she tried to walk away from me today. I didn't know I had much of a temper until I met her." Tehl threw a rock, irked. "On top of all that, Gav tells me I need a wife, which after planning the Midsummer Festival, I am inclined to agree with."

The lullaby of the night descended after his statement. Waves thundered below, harmonizing with the soft fluttering of bat wings and his father's quiet breaths.

"It sounds like a lot of upheaval."

Acceptance.

There was no judgment or condemnation in his father's tone.

Tehl slumped against the stone wall, the tension leaving his body.

"A wife? I swear you told me there would never be one a couple of weeks ago."

"Circumstances change, father. I can't do this by myself. I need help. Sam and Gav are doing what they can, but I need a consort."

His father nodded in understanding. "I know what you mean, after your mother died... I just couldn't. Still can't. I am sorry I'm not what you need."

The king aged before his eyes. Tehl's heart ached at the change. Part of Marq Ramses had died along with his wife, leaving only a glimmer of the man he grew up with. This broken man had taken over his father after his mother's death.

His father levered himself up and looked down on him, infinite sadness sucking the life from the blue eyes so like his own. "I will do my best to help when you need me. Good night, son."

The king picked his way across the rocky ledge to the door way.

I need you now was on the tip on his tongue but he bit back the words. For a while tonight, before he'd slipped into melancholy, his father had been his old self. It was as if the king was in a deep hole and Tehl had no idea how to dig him out.

He tilted his head back and gazed at the luminous stars above him. They winked like fireflies in a darkened meadow. A wife. He wondered again where he was going to find one. His brother was right; he lacked social skills. He had the constitution of a bear some days, so who would want to live with that? He needed to make it happen.

Chapter Twenty-Eight

SAGE

Sage sat on the floor, staring into the crackling fire before her. She ran her hands through the luxurious carpets, her mind running a mile a minute. She'd now been in the castle over three weeks. Her eyes slid to her companions: Mira was rocking in her chair, reading about some herb, and Gav sat on his cot writing letters. She was going to leave them; she had to.

She looked to the two people who had taken such good care of her; as unlikely as it had seemed, the three of them had become good friends. A rebel, a healer, and a prince. Sage smirked. It sounded like the beginning of a bad joke. Her smile faded a touch as guilt stabbed her. She had to leave them.

Gav looked up from his furious scratching with an easy smile, meeting her eyes. Her own smile froze on her face. She dropped her eyes so his probing ones couldn't read her thoughts.

She was a liar.

A fake.

Sage felt sick.

She was a traitor of the highest order.

They had been nothing but kind. She had to figure out how to leave without implicating either of them. The Elite rebel with the ring would start his shift early the next morning, so she had until dawn for her goodbyes.

Her thoughts moved to the sleeping draught she'd stashed in her dress. When she was moved to this room, Mira had dosed her with the sleeping draught to ease her pain and help her sleep. The problem was that once she took it, she couldn't wake up from the nightmares, so she hated taking it. Each day, when Mira was using the privy, she would pour some into a different bottle and dilute the one that Mira was using. The pain was worse, but it was worth it if it meant waking from her terrible dreams.

A soft sigh drew her attention to Mira, slumped in her chair, looking exhausted. A surge of affection bubbled inside her for the sweet woman who had pulled her from the edge of death.

Gav set aside his correspondence and stood, gesturing to the chessboard.

"Would you like to play?"

She smirked at him. "Are you ready to lose again?"

Gav scoffed, eyes twinkling. "A woman has never beaten me." He puffed up his chest, strutted over to the wall, and struck a pose.

She giggled at Gav's uncharacteristic playfulness. A petite snort caught her attention, and she stared at Mira, eyes wide. The poor girl covered her face in embarrassment, unable to completely cover her beet-red cheeks. Mira attempted to hold in her laughter, but the harder she tried, the worse her little snorts became.

Sage jabbed a finger at her friend, laughter spilling out of her. "What," she gasped, "was *that*?"

Mira shook her head, a blond hair covering her face like a curtain, lamenting, "I try to control it but sometimes it simply will *not* be controlled!"

"Do not worry, my lady, your secret is safe with me." Gav sent Mira a friendly smile, along with a wink, and patted her on the shoulder like a man. He flopped down onto the other end of the bed and set up the board.

Sage stood up and stretched her hands above her head with a soft groan, arching her back like a cat. "I am in the mood for some lavender mint tea. Would either of you like some?"

She made her way over to the hutch upon which sat the honey, tea, and an assortment of cookies and cakes, all the while praying they both said 'yes'. She closed her eyes in relief as a chorus of yesses sounded behind her.

Slouching, she pulled out her draught from her gaping dress. She was thankful that it was sweet; mixed with the tea and honey they wouldn't taste it. She put a couple teaspoons of tea leaves into each cup, as well as a few drops of the draught, then slipped the small bottle back in her bodice.

"Honey?"

Please want honey, please want honey, please want honey, she chanted in her head. A masculine and feminine 'yes', Sage thanked the stars.

Sage spooned some into each cup, and then moved to the pot hanging over the fire and carefully poured water into each cup, stirring them until the tea was so fragrant her mouth watered. She handed a one to Mira and then Gav. As they lifted the tea to their lips, she had a sudden urge to snatch the cups away or knock them to the floor. Instead, she stifled the feeling and sipped at her own tea, silent.

"Thank you, Ruby, I needed this. It's delicious." Gavriel's smile skewered her heart.

Mira mumbled her thanks as well and settled back into her rocking chair with her book.

"Shall we?" Sage pointed to the game.

Gav lay on his side smiling impishly. That was her answer. Sage rolled her eyes and chose black, even though it meant she'd given away the first move. She studied his move and countered.

When she looked up from the board, Gav was studying her, intensely. Her heart stuttered, and her palms began to sweat. Did he suspect her betrayal?

Be calm, he can't know.

"I am sorry for what happened today with the crown prince. He meant no harm."

She wasn't expecting that.

Gav moved his next piece and captured her rook. "He may be rough around the edges but he is actually a good person. Tehl will make a powerful king."

Rage and bitterness welled inside her. Sage wanted to ignore his comment, to act like she hadn't heard his words, but she couldn't. "You mean to tell me," she said through gritted teeth, "that the man who threatened to ravage me, hurt my family, starved me, and then had me attacked is a good person? Forgive me if I don't agree."

"He never had you attacked," Gav replied, his voice soft.

"No." Sage cut him off, slashing a hand through the air. "Do not defend him. I don't want to hear it. Even *if* he didn't sanction it, it still happened under *his* roof by *his* men. How can he expect to rule a kingdom if he can't control what happens in his own home?"

"I understand but he isn't—"

Heat filled her cheeks as frustration built up inside her. How could Gav defend such a monster? Tears tracked a path down her cheeks as Sage dropped her blurry eyes to the game board, trying to get a hold of herself.

"You *know* how I suffer at night," she whispered. "Nothing would ever convince me he is a good man. The crown prince is a pretty monster who holds too much power." Sage moved a piece and balled her hands into tight fists.

Gav's tanned hand touched hers softly, imparting comfort. She squeezed his hand once, then swiped at her tears. She met his grave eyes with a watery smile. "I understand that you owe your loyalty to your cousin and that you love him. You are a wonderful person, Gavriel. You see the best in people, but we can't agree on this subject. It's best for you and I if you don't mention him."

He released an aggravated sigh and held up one hand. "One

more thing, then I will let it rest. Just remember to never judge a book by its cover. You might be surprised by what you find inside."

"You're right." She paused waiting for him to look up at her. When his eyes met hers, she murmured. "His cover is exquisite, but I have seen what is inside. It's a nightmare. Like I said before, he's a beautiful monster."

Gav blanched at her statement but recovered. She knew she was being harsh, but it was the truth, and he needed to hear it. Focusing back on the board, he moved a piece, and she looked down to find he had her king trapped.

"How did you do that," she muttered.

"With lots of diversions," he teased.

Sage glared at him and swatted his shoulder, her grin undermining its effect. This was her last night with them and she wouldn't ruin it. A thump drew their attention to Mira. She had fallen sound asleep in her chair, her book askew on the floor.

Gav shook his head and looked back at her. "I guess it is time for bed."

"That it is." She stood and curtsied. "I concede to your excellent strategizing skills, my lord."

Sage picked up Mira's book as Gavriel put away the game.

"Mira, love, we need to get you to bed," Sage crooned.

Mira growled something unintelligible and snuggled further into the chair. Tenderly, Sage pushed her friend's fine blond hair from her face. She would most likely never see this woman again. She swallowed, a lump forming in her throat. "Gav," she called. "I will need you to carry her to bed. She won't get out of this chair herself."

Gav chuckled, hoisting Mira out of the chair like she weighed nothing. Gently, he lowered her friend into the bed. Sage nudged him out of the way, tucking her in. She placed a small kiss on Mira's forehead and whispered, "Good night, sweet girl."

Sage crept from the side of the bed, turning to the fire. Gav stood, watching her haloed by firelight. His dark form glided to her. Sage squeaked when his muscular arms engulfed her suddenly. One of his hands slid into her hair, pressing her face against his firm chest.

"I am sorry I brought my cousin up and that it upset you so. I'll try not to do so again."

Her mouth parted in surprise as his lips touched the crown of her head. Sage tipped her head back, staring into his glittering eyes full of affection. It killed her knowing they would be on opposite sides come tomorrow. She lifted onto her toes to press a delicate kiss on his cheek. "Thank you for being what I need you to be." She cradled his cheek and Gav's eyes closed as he leaned into her palm. "Your wife was a lucky woman." Sage meant every word.

His throat convulsed, and he released a shuddering breath. Sage rubbed her thumb along his cheekbone once more before releasing him. She stepped from the circle of his arms moving away. Gavriel's hand gripped hers, halting her. Sage examined her small hand in his, running her eyes from his muscular arm to his wide shoulders and, finally, to stare at his profile.

"Thank you." His voice was gruff. "Ruby, I..." Anguish and confusion was clear in his voice.

"You have a lot to offer, brother." His head snapped to her at the endearment. "Most of us miss *someone* and we all have to learn to let go. One day you will be able to move from the guilt. And maybe you will find someone again."

His dear purple eyes swept across her face as if he was searching for something. She drew in a breath, squeezing his hand. "I am not that someone, Gav. I am, however, your friend. Just as you are mine." She gave him a small smile.

He mulled that over for a bit, eventually returning her smile. "That you are. I suppose you're right, sis."

His returning her endearment filled her with joy. 'Brother' and 'sister' were the highest honor you could bestow upon someone other than blood kin. With those titles you claimed them as a companion for life. Sage's smile spread so wide that her cheeks hurt, Gav's expression mirroring hers.

"Not that I haven't enjoyed our heart-to-heart, but I really ought to head to bed," she hinted.

Sage let go of his hand, and he ruffled her hair as he walked to his own cot. She scowled at him, placing her hands on her hips. "None of that, though!"

"Not a chance, sis. We're siblings now, that's just what we do."

"Out!" Sage stabbed a finger at the door.

Gav winked and left the room, still smirking.

Sage changed her dress in a rush, switching it for one of Mira's plain ones. She then clambered into bed, pulling the covers to her chin. A few minutes passed before Gav snuck back to his cot. Blankets rustled as he tried to find a comfortable position.

"Good night, Gav."

"Night, Ruby."

Shame washed over her at the use of her fake name. They had practically adopted each other yet he didn't even know her. She was a fraud, a fake. She wished she could tell him, but it was too dangerous now. It wasn't just about her. If she said anything it would endanger both her family and friends.

She didn't want to leave without giving him something honest though.

"Gav?" she whispered to the dark.

"Yeah," he groggily replied.

"My brothers used to call me 'Sai' when I was little. You're welcome to call me that."

The room was quiet, save Mira's soft breaths and the crackle of the fire. Had he fallen asleep?

"Sai it is then dear sister. What is it short for?"

"It's not, just a nickname," Sage evaded.

"Okay. Sweet dreams, Sai," Gav slurred.

It wasn't long before loud snores came from Gav's cot. Sage stared at the ceiling for another hour before deciding to test the depth of her friends' slumber. Sage jumped off the bed and stomped to the bathroom. Nothing. She grabbed the cold doorknob and slammed the heavy bathroom door. The sharp noise thundered through the room. Still nothing. They didn't even stir.

Sage trudged back to bed feeling equal parts of triumphant and somber. She would be free in a matter of hours, but would leave behind friends she had come to treasure. Someday she would try to find a way to make it right between them.

Sage slipped back into bed and forced her eyes closed. Her perspective had changed with her time here. Not everything about the Crown was evil and there were no absolutes. The crown prince was still an arrogant brute, it was true, but she had softened toward everyone else, even the king. Her heart clenched at the thought of Marq. She would protect him. The older man had suffered enough. With that thought, she drifted off.

***

Light knocking at the door roused her. She eyed her companions, still sleeping soundly, and snuck from bed. Carefully, Sage pried the door open. The Elite from the previous day stood before her.

"There's not much time, we have to move now. I take it you took care of your companions?" he asked in a hushed voice.

She nodded once, taking a final peek at her cherished friends. Now that it was here, the thought of escape was bittersweet. Hopefully they would understand her actions. Sage closed the door and looked to the guard expectantly.

He shoved a worn, brown cloak and cane into her arms. "Put the cloak on and use it to conceal the cane."

Sage regarded the two Elite sleeping on either side of her door. "Did you expose yourself?" she asked, clasping the cloak. She tucked the cane away, awaiting his answer.

"No, but the night is still young." He gestured to the sleeping Elite. "I had them drugged."

She smirked up at him. "Great spies think alike."

An amused grin played at his mouth as they slipped silently down the corridor. With each twist and turn, room or staircase,

Sage catalogued everything. She had seen little of the castle apart from her suite and the infirmary. She filed each detail away so she could create a map later.

Her partner paused to scan the large, open hallway before them. When he was sure the coast was clear, he waved her forward. As they moved through the main corridor, she spied the doorway leading to the courtyard and her heartbeat sped up. Sage's pace picked up, exceeding her guide's. Her breath whooshed out at the sight of a dark blue sky and twinkling stars. A hand snatched her cloak, stopping her in her tracks.

"Slow down," the Elite admonished. "Pull your hood up around your face, and lean on the cane like you're aged. Make sure your braid is hidden, as it would give us away immediately."

She did as he said, hunching over, and hobbling outside.

"Old mother, let me help you."

He lifted her other hand up and placed it into the crook of his elbow. The pace was excruciatingly slow; the sky was already starting to lighten. They needed to move. Should she make a run for it? Her comrade tightened his grip on her hand as if he had guessed her thoughts.

Finally, they reached the gate. They were going to make it.

"What are you doing up this early?" The voice shattered the quiet of the early morning. "I thought the Elite usually slept in 'til the sun was high in the sky."

Her muscles coiled, preparing to sprint. Sage had come this far. She was not going back.

"I am helping the old mother to the gate."

The guard on the wall above them smiled. "Will you need any assistance outside the gate, old mother?" he inquired kindly.

In the scratchiest voice, Sage uttered, "No, young man, but thank you for your kind offer. These old bones aren't as young as they used to be, but I can still get myself around. A good day to you."

Her partner waved to the guard as they began their painstaking shuffle through the gate and into Sanee. With the tall, gray stone walls behind her, joy and elation filled her. She longed to sprint and stretch her legs. But soon. Very soon. For the next half hour, they wound down the hill and into the city.

The rebel moved her into a shadowy alley. "Rafe expects you. Goodbye, Blade." He sketched a bow and disappeared from sight.

Sage shook her head at the nickname. Rafe called her the rebellion's blade only once! And for some reason, it stuck.

She ditched the cane and straightened, rubbing her smarting back. She desperately wanted to see her family, but she knew she needed to find Rafe first. Time to find out what they'd all been up to this last month.

Chapter Twenty-Nine

TEHL

Tehl stared with narrowed eyes at the many papers littering his desk. No matter what he did, it seemed like they multiplied every time he blinked. This had to be the worst of his responsibilities, the paperwork. It always came in unrelenting waves. He picked up a petition that had something to do with the Midsummer Festival. Tehl read the same line five times before dropping it onto his desk and slumping into his seat with his eyes closed.

He had slept fitfully the previous night, spending most of it just staring at the ceiling. His conversation with his father kept running over and over in his mind. Nothing seemed clear, but one thing stood out to him. As much as he was loath to admit it, he was in the wrong when it came to the girl. His handling of the situation from beginning to end had been a long series of mistakes. Which meant he had to apologize. To a rebel. To a traitor. His day couldn't get much worse.

His back pinched, interrupting his thoughts. He'd sat on that ledge for so long that his whole body ached. Maybe he was just getting old. He snorted and raised his arms above his head, stretching from left to right. A groan of pleasure escaped him and he wondered why stretching felt so good. Hell if he knew, but he was pleased his back had lessened its throbbing.

Tehl straightened and assessed the mountain of documents before him. He needed to get someone to help him in here.

The emerging sunrise poured light into the room, warming him. Tehl yawned loudly and blinked to clear his watering eyes. He needed to stop moping around and get down to business. He eyed the stack of letters concerning the festival like how a mouse eyes a snake. Before he could do anything with them, a quick rap sounded on the door. Damn, they found him already. He would hang himself if he had to discuss anything even remotely connected with decor.

"Enter," he called gruffly.

Sam, Gav, and Mira, the blond healer, entered his office. Tehl's smile dissolved at the distraught look on Mira's face. She looked like someone died. His eyes bounced to Sam, his brother meticulously straightening his shirt. Gav's face was beet-red. Something was wrong.

"What happened?"

No one answered him at first, and his eyes snapped back to Mira. She twisted her hands in her skirt, staring at her feet with tears dripping quietly down her face. The room was still and tense, and his heart pounded wildly as several thoughts flashed through his mind.

"Is it," he croaked, and then cleared his throat. "Is it, father?"

"No." Nothing else. Sam's tone was emotionless.

What the hell happened? Tehl stood up and leaned on his desk. "Stars above! Someone tell me what is going on before I go mad."

"She's gone."

Two words only.

Two words that froze him.

There was no doubt in his mind who *she* was. "Do you know where she went?" he rasped.

Sam shook his head, obviously irritated. It was the first expression he had shown since walking through the door. "We don't. The Guard stationed at the gate did not see her leave. She could still be here in the castle but I doubt it. Someone with her training and skills would be long gone by now. If you like, we will still search the palace, but it will take a couple days to search the grounds too," his brother huffed. "The only thing we know for sure is she had help."

Tehl stared down at his piles of papers. She was gone. His chance to prevent a civil war, peacefully, was gone.

In an uncharacteristic display of anger, he shoved himself to his feet and threw everything off his desk. Breathing hard, he looked down at the clean wooden surface. He needed to reel it in; anger solved nothing. How did she get past Gav?

Tehl zeroed in on Gav. "How did you let this happen?" he

snarled.

Gav's fists clenched and small tremors rocked his forearms. "I did everything thing you asked," he hissed.

Oh hell. Tehl took a step back. His cousin was beyond angry, furious even. If Gav hissed, it was time to walk the other way. His cousin hadn't been this temperamental since he was a boy, barely on the cusp of manhood.

"I stayed with her since day one." Gav stabbed a finger at him. "I slept in her room *every* night, cared for her, befriended her, and watched over her. I even let others assume she was my mistress, all to protect her! Don't you dare put this on me!"

Gavriel was right.

Tehl held up a hand. "I am sorry for implying that this is your fault. It's not. Thank you. This hasn't been easy on you."

He walked around the desk and leaned against it, crossing his arms. Mira still hadn't looked up from the floor.

"Mira," Tehl called, trying to blot out the anger in his voice. "How did she escape?"

She peeked at him with tear filled eyes. "I don't know. She gave no hint she would be leaving."

"Was there anything unusual about last night?"

"No, not at all. It was like any other night, we ate, spent time by the fire, and I read while Gav and Ruby played chess. At some point, I fell asleep and Ruby tucked me in."

"Sai," Gav cut in.

"What?" Mira's face scrunched in confusion.

"*Sai.* Before bed she told me to call her Sai."

Tehl cocked his head and studied his cousin. Gav shifted and pinked a little bit. Interesting. That was not typical behavior. "What about you?"

"We talked while we played our game. Then we tucked Mira into bed. She hugged me, kissed me on the cheek, and, uh, called me brother. Then we went to bed."

His brain snagged on kiss. Why the hell was she kissing Gavriel? Was she trying to seduce him?

"Don't give me that look, Tehl. It wasn't like that."

Tehl wiped away whatever look was currently displaying his emotions.

"What was it like then?" Sam challenged. "She has only wanted you. Yesterday, she was close to murdering Tehl, but you talked her down. Please explain that. Exactly how close are you two?"

Mira glared at Sam. "Your tone makes it sound like they were having some clandestine affair. I've been present the whole time. Nothing of that sort ever happened." Her eyes flickered to Gav then back to Sam. "She was comfortable with Gavriel because he took care of her and soothed her at night when she'd wake from the night terrors *your* men inspired," she accused, furious.

Her narrowed eyes pierced him in his spot, "As for you, she might still be here if it weren't for you. She was shaken after that stunt you pulled yesterday. Most of her experience at this castle has been a nightmare. What made you think she would change her mind and stay here to help you?"

All three men stared at the normally meek woman. She had a little fire in her. It took a moment for her anger to die out. Her eyes widened, and she sunk down into a deep curtsy. "Forgive my strong words, Your Highnesses."

Tehl liked Mira, she was an intriguing blend of meekness and steel.

"Mira, there's nothing to forgive. But satisfy my curiosity, how do you know we need her help?"

She quirked an eyebrow. "Just because I am a woman it does not mean I can't see or hear. You've not been as quiet and discreet in my presence as you perhaps thought. But I've kept your secrets, and I will continue to do so."

"Thank you, Mira. If we need you further, I will send for you. Have a wonderful day."

Her gaze narrowed at his dismissal, but she only gave a slight nod, curtsying before she left, the door clicking shut behind her.

"We need her to be found, but use discretion. I doubt anything will turn up, but without her, drastic measures will need to be taken when dealing with the rebellion." Tehl sighed. "Most importantly, we need to find who helped her. Her escape means that there are spies among us, in our home even. The rebellion leaders are not stupid. If they were willing to give up that knowledge just to free her, she is even more important than we guessed. Did she say what Sai stood for?"

"No, she didn't, though I asked, but she avoided the question. She trusted me and that's the only reason she gave me her nickname. I think she wanted me to have a real piece of her as a parting gift. I should have seen it." Gav rubbed a hand across his forehead in agitation. "She called me 'brother'," Gav mumbled to himself.

Sam stepped to Gav's side and clasped him on the shoulder. "She's a spy, most of what she said to you was probably fiction. She needed your trust."

Gav shook his head. "I am not naïve. Some of what she told me wasn't real but I feel she told me as much of the truth as she could, given the circumstances. She wasn't playing a game. She meant it." Gav gazed at him steadily. "I returned her sentiment. I called her my sister."

Tehl's eyes bulged out of his head. Gav was willing to admit deep affection for her, and considered her a member of their family even. He couldn't believe it.

"Truly?"

"I did. I spent almost a month with her. I helped nurse her back to health and held her in the middle of the night. You made me her guardian, and I took the responsibility seriously. How could you expect me not to get attached? She also cherishes Mira though. If Sai returns, it will be for her. We'll need to keep eyes on her."

"Is Mira a threat? Would she help Ruby or Sai—whoever she is?" Tehl asked frankly.

"No, she would not betray the Crown, she is loyal. What I meant is that if Sai got hurt or in trouble, she would go to Mira, and Mira would help her."

Tehl straightened, moving to the window. "We don't have time to search for her this week. In seven days the Midsummer Festival will start. Nobility will arrive from all over Aermia and," he hesitated, "I received word that a Methian prince will join us for the festival."

Sam and Gavriel gaped at him.

Sam recovered first. "They haven't visited our kingdom in almost one hundred years Tehl. Why now? A coincidence? I think not." Sam asked, always pragmatic. "Do you think this bodes ill for us?"

"I can only guess. We treat them like guests, but we watch them like enemies. We need every available member of the Elite at our disposal this week. Sam, I need you to use some of your people to search for the girl. If you don't find her in the next two days, hold off the search until after the festival has finished. We have too many things pulling at our attention as it is. Hopefully, we'll come out of this umolested."

"Well, I certainly want to be molested by many pretty women." Sam's eyes gleamed.

"Really, Sam? At a time like this?"

Samuel held his arms out in a what-can-you-do gesture. "Brother, you left yourself wide open. I mean, who uses the word 'molested' anymore? Why not 'unscathed' or 'unharmed'?"

"Whatever," Tehl grouched. "Don't you have some information-gathering and rebel-catching to do?"

Sam's lips spread into a mischievous smile. "I do, my lord. I will attend my duties immediately. Good day, sire." Sam clicked his heels together and swept from the room.

"He has style. And he always manages to find the humor in a situation," his cousin remarked. Gav stared out the window for a moment and then surprised him, "I decided to move my daughter here, so I have some arrangements to make, but if you need me all you need to do is ask."

"That is the best news I've had in weeks!" He grinned at the thought of having their miniature relative running around the castle. "When should we expect her?"

"Within the next couple of weeks. Do you need me for anything else?"

Tehl glanced back at the obscene pile of papers and back to his cousin, a silent plea in his eyes.

"Not going to happen, Tehl. I will see you at dinner." Gav backed out of the room, a crooked smile on his face.

"Respect. Does no one show the Crown respect these days?" Tehl asked himself.

Gav chuckled, closing the door. Tehl glanced distastefully at the pile of correspondence, making no move to touch the letters. Stalling. That's what he was doing, stalling. He sank into his chair and began organizing the papers. He definitely would need coffee to get through all this.

Chapter Thirty

SAGE

She roamed the city, turning down random streets and alleyways to be certain there was no one following her. Sage peeked around a building and down the lane, spotting only a fisherman, a handful of washwomen, and a stumbling drunk. The washwomen seemed to be getting an early start to the day's activities while the man was no doubt sobering up from an already forgotten night.

The smell of freshly baked bread teased her nose. Sage's stomach rumble loudly, and she winced; sneaking around was pointless if her stomach gave her away. She needed food.

Sage tugged on her cloak, double-checking its hood was well in place. She took a last glance behind her, scanning the alley. Blessedly, still no signs of pursuit. She entered the lane, seamlessly blending into the group of washerwomen.

Her eyes darted left and right, searching for signs of danger. When the Crown came looking for her, and she was sure they would, they'd be looking for a woman on her own. They'd probably not take notice of the lowly washerwomen. People often saw only what they expected to see.

Whenever one of the women would look her way she would give them a polite smile—friendly enough that they wouldn't think her rude, but not warm enough to invite conversation. Together, they meandered down the slick cobbled road when a familiar sight greeted her.

A dreary, worn down fishing shack. It blended well alongside the various other dilapidated structures. To anybody looking, it was a typical lower class home, but it actually held many important secrets. A sense of excitement overcame her, and she barely kept her feet from sprinting toward it. Instead, she discreetly separated herself from the group, approaching the battered edifice. Sage slipped into the narrow space between her gray shanty and another hole parading as a home. She scraped her hand against the rotting wood until she met with a rickety door in need of a new fresco. Sage shoved on the door until it swung inward on soundless hinges. She stepped in, shutting it behind her.

She blinked several times as her eyes adjusted to the dark interior. It smelled like dust and molding cloth. Old furniture and faded carpets were haphazardly strewn about the space. As she stepped into the kitchen, she noted the lack of dirt on the floor. Sage tiptoed into a spacious pantry and, again, shut the door behind her.

She probed the wall and found the catch, hidden behind ancient jars of peaches and pickled herrings. A soft click sounded, and a hidden door sprung open. A proud grin curled her lips as she entered. The door was pure genius; no one looked for a door that was a part of the actual shelving.

Sage hunched over, creeping into the bitty space. The door swung shut on its own, trapping her in the dark. She took a calming breath and walked forward four steps. Lifting her hands in front of her, she reached for the spiral staircase hidden there. Cool iron touched her fingertips. Sage shuffled until her slippers met the unyielding metal stairway. She glided down the stairs without hesitation, missing not a step. She reached the bottom and strode directly forward, the placement of her feet exact. The place was rigged with traps; one wrong step and you would find yourself in a pit of jagged rocks. A door met her hand, and she rapped once, paused, and then knocked again three times swiftly and two times slowly.

She hadn't minded the dark before but something about standing in it now had sweat breaking out on the back of her neck. The inky darkness pressed into her, and an onslaught of dark memories washed over her, making her gasp. Chains. Brown eyes. Pain. Fear.

Sage clenched her eyes closed and tried to slow her breathing as her anxiety rose. "You are not there. This is not that place. No one can hurt you. You are free," she whispered to herself, trying to keep the panic at bay.

"Pass phrase," a deep voice demanded from behind the wooden door.

An image of a blade pressing along her torso flashed behind her closed lids. Sage braced both hands on the thick door to keep upright. She panted heavily as she fought the urge to run up the stairs in search of comforting light. She took a shallow breath, and managed to say, "It's Blade."

"That's not possible," the voice argued.

Irritation combined with her terror caused her to lash out, kicking at the door. "God damn it, Hayjen! Open the bloody door!" She was teetering on the edge of hysteria.

The door yanked open, and she stumbled forward into the arms of a giant man. Already feeling trapped in the darkness, the sudden contact from this man had her entire body trembling.

He needed to stop touching her. *Now.*

Instinctually, Sage slammed her knee up into his groin, and he doubled over in pain. She twisted and stabbed her elbow into his face, his head snapping back. Sage planted her foot on his stomach kicking him into the wall.

"What the bloomin' hell was that for?" he wheezed, his large body sliding down the wall.

It was like she was trapped inside herself as she watched herself attack this man for no reason. The sound of his voice penetrated her panic, ringing with familiarity. She had attacked her friend. Hesitantly, she rose from her defensive crouch, taking a tentative step toward him.

"Hayjen?" she whispered.

Her old friend glared at her from his spot on the floor. "Sweetheart, who else could it possibly be?" he lisped through his newly acquired split lip.

She squatted in front of him, staying out of reach, and offered a sincere apology. "It has been a rough couple of weeks. I am so sorry."

"Where have you been? You just disappeared one day. We searched but no one discovered any hint as to your whereabouts." He scanned her from head to toe, snagging on her wrist. Self-consciously she pulled her sleeve down, and his ice blue eyes snapped to hers. "Where did that come from?" he barked out the words, his voice menacing.

For a split second, a horrid flashback was her reality, and she again experienced the pressure of the chains and the warmth of her own blood dripping down her body. She shuddered, shaking her head to dislodge the memory, and forced herself to meet his penetrating gaze. "That's what I need to discuss with Rafe. Can you take me to him?"

Hayjen scrutinized her for another moment before grunting. Sage took that as a 'yes' and stood, stiffly offering her hand to the bear of a man. His meaty hand clasped hers as she hauled him to his feet. Sage made to release his hand but his tightened around hers.

"One minute," he mumbled.

She trembled in his grip when he lifted her hand to his face. She bit her cheek, mortified with her own weakness. Hayjen would never hurt her yet here she was cowering like he was an enemy. It sickened her.

Lightly, he drew a finger along the uneven skin that had finally begun to heal. "You will carry these scars for the rest of your life, and I am sorry for it. But you aren't the only one." He dropped her hand and pushed up his shirt sleeves, displaying thick wrists bearing scars remarkably similar to her own. Her eyes sought his, and she saw just how much he understood her pain. No pity, but respect. They shared a special kind of camaraderie born from their fellow suffering and survival.

"Rafe will not like it." Hayjen nodded to her wrists. "He has been in a foul mood of late."

The comment made Sage crack a smile; his anger was legendary. Rafe didn't lose his temper often, but when he did, it was a sight to behold. The man's wrath could make a Nagalian sand storm seem like a small burst of wind. Hayjen gestured for her to follow and began navigating the winding corridors.

For anyone who didn't know their way around, it was a disorienting labyrinth of tunnels. Every once in a while, her nose would catch the scent of sea salt on a draft. Some of the tunnels connected with the ocean; an easy escape if the location was compromised. She would take the leviathan—the giant carnivorous fish—over the Elite any day.

She winced at her disingenuous thoughts. If she'd learned one thing during her "stay" at the castle it was that nothing was black and white. Not everyone had been horrible, and she had been surprised with the kindness displayed to her. Stealing away without saying goodbye to Mira, Gav, and the king pained her.

Angry male voices carried from down the corridor, spiking her pulse. She shoved down her agitation as well as the accompanying guilt. It was something she'd have to deal with later. Hayjen swung to his right through a doorway and stepped to the side as she breached the doorway.

The scene they came upon as they entered astonished her.

There had to be at least twenty-five men crammed into the tiny space. Rafe had his back to her and was listening to a thin older man, named Mason, who was waving his hands wildly as he tried to get his point across. People were talking over one another, and stabbing fingers at each other.

What's going on?

All the loud male voices unnerved her, and goosebumps broke out on her arms. Sage rubbed them vigorously trying to rid herself of the sensation. No one had yet noticed her. She took a deep breath and crossed her arms to hide their shaking and fortified herself for what she knew needed to be done. Sage struck a casual pose on the wall, and projected her voice, using the smokiest tone she could manage: "Gentlemen! Gentlemen! This is no way to act in the presence of a lady. Have you all forgotten your manners while I've been away?"

Silence descended and twenty-five heads swiveled her way. The quiet was deafening. Her heart beat frantically in her chest, and nausea tried to overwhelm her, but Sage pushed through it, focusing on Rafe's back so she wouldn't have to look into all those eyes and panic.

The rebellion's leader tensed, and he turned to face her. His luminescent amber eyes zeroed in on her, a wealth of emotion displayed there. Looking at him, she had a sudden realization. After everything that had happened the last few weeks, she had expected him to appear different in some way because she felt so different herself, yet here he was, looking exactly the same. Seeing his long scar and unruly wine colored hair, exactly as she remembered it, comforted her somehow

She was home.

"Little one," he breathed out the fond nickname. Her heart flew to her throat as he rushed up to her and swept her into his arms. His familiar spicy scent washed over her as he hugged her tighter.

This was as close to family she'd been in almost a month. "My family?" she choked into his chest.

"They have been taken care of. They never stopped searching for you. Every time they posted a drawing of you we had to pull it down. We didn't want the Crown getting anywhere close to them."

Grateful tears ran down her face and onto his shirt. He had protected her family, keeping them safe when she could not. She was safe. She was *finally* safe.

"Let it out, little one. Let it out. I have you," Rafe soothed.

She was only vaguely aware that she started crying. She'd held in so many of her emotions for so long that there was no stopping it. Everything she'd bottled up came out in a rush. After a bit, she pulled back and looked into Rafe's face, the sight so dear to her. He clasped her cheeks with large hands and brushed away any evidence of her tears.

"You're safe now." He leaned down and pressed a tender kiss to the crown of her head, tucking her tightly against his chest once again, like he was afraid she would slip away. A soothing rumble began in his chest, relaxing her.

A stray thought popped into her head. Did grown men purr? Was that what he was doing? She would have to ask her mum about it later.

Rafe lifted her, squeezing tighter, and she raised her head from his shoulder, looking to the silent group of men. Sage stared into their faces, embarrassment colored her cheeks. Maybe she could take a page from Sam's book and use humor to cut the awkwardness. She crossed her eyes and gave them a silly grin. Most returned it with one of their own.

Mission accomplished.

She tapped Rafe on the shoulder to put her down when she spotted a familiar pair of eyes. Her whole body froze as she continued to stare into the eyes of the person who featured in her nightmares every night. Sage would never forget him: the monster masquerading as a man.

She could barely breathe. A dull roar sounded in her ears, her head fuzzy. The walls closed in on her. As her feet touched the ground, the breath rushed out of her. She couldn't see him any longer but she swore she still felt him, if that was even possible. What was he doing here? Panting, she tried to pull herself together.

"What's wrong? You need to take another breath. You're shaking."

The shaking didn't stop though. It only worsened.

Hayjen stepped up next to her and pulled her sleeves up to display her injuries. "This might have something to do with the way she is reacting."

Sage stared down at her wrists, eyes stinging, ashamed of the scars but too panicked to do anything about it. A hand tilted her chin up, and she met burning amber eyes. "Are there more?"

She closed her eyes and dug for courage. Sage took a breath and looked Rafe straight in the face. "Yes, there are many more." She wet her lips before continuing. "You have a spy in your midst."

Genuine shocked crossed both men's faces. "Who?" Rafe

demanded.

"Serge," she took a breath and continued in a hushed tone: "That was the name he went by. The plain fellow. Brown hair, brown eyes, incredibly tall. He is staring at us now. He was a captain of the Guard at the palace." Her voice never wavered or cracked. A small success.

Rafe spun, pointing at the culprit. "Is that the man you saw?"

Her eyes flew to him, a scant fifteen feet away, not able to turn her gaze away. Terror filled her. Rafe snapped his fingers in front of her face, and she blinked, looking back at him.

"He is not a spy Sage, he works for us. We planted him in the Guard so we'd have eyes inside the dungeon and on the spymaster. He gave us the information on your whereabouts so we could get you out. His name is Rhys."

"Us?" Sage mumbled to herself. Rhys. The name was familiar, but she'd never met the elusive member of the rebellion's circle. He had been on an assignment since she joined. The room blurred, and the ground heaved beneath her feet. She stumbled back, into Rafe. Everything was off kilter. Serge was a spy. "*You* sent him?"

"Yes," he drawled.

Her gaze bounced from Rafe to Serge—or Rhys, or whatever his name was. Something broke inside her. Anger and hate warred with her terror before the former overcame the latter. Determination filled her. They were separated only by a round table. He was so close, a wicked smile adorning his face. It didn't matter whom he'd sided with. He was a horrible human being, and he should never be allowed to harm anyone else. She would make sure of it.

Sage snatched Rafe's dagger from his waist and spun out of his arms. She launched herself onto the table, sprinting toward the man who'd haunted her. Only a couple more feet and she'd reach him. Strong hands grasped her ankles, yanking her feet out from under her. She threw the blade with a feral cry as she crashed down into the table. Her elbow smarted, but she didn't care. Her eyes never left the monster bleeding in front of her.

She missed.

She'd missed his heart and had struck his shoulder.

Sage fought to move forward but was wrenched across the wooden table by powerful arms. The whole room erupted into a chorus of shouts as men rushed to help their downed man. Sage struggled harder, but no matter what she did the arms circling her would not let go.

Desperation filled her. "You sick, twisted piece of garbage! You are the evil in our world!" Rafe had moved a step back from the table, so, seeing an opening, Sage lifted her legs and pushed off the table trying to knock him off her. "Mark my words, you wretch! You'll die!" she screamed.

"Stop!" Rafe bellowed in her ear.

"Never," she promised. "Put me down. That animal doesn't deserve to live."

"I don't think so. Not after the stunt you just pulled. Why would you attack one of our brothers?"

She stilled, disgusted with his word choice. "Brother?" Her icy voice was deadly calm. The venomous tone caught the attention of those closest to them. "Brother?" Sage hissed again. "Do brothers chain their families to the ceiling? Or torture them for hours? Or…"

She swallowed bile and continued, "or try to rape their sisters?"

Rafe's arms had slackened at her last statement. Sage used his shock to her advantage and tucked her chin, pushing his forearm over her head in one swift motion. In less than five seconds, she was out of his hold and backing away. "*You*! You sent him to me."

Rafe's face was filled with pity. She didn't need his pity. Sage shook her head, her long braid whipping around her head. This was his fault. Betrayed emerald eyes met remorse-filled amber ones. The entire time she'd been blaming the Crown for her suffering, it wasn't the Crown's doing after all; it was her own so-called brotherhood.

"I was keeping my cover! Someone had to interrogate you, and I was protecting you from much worse things. The Crown is corrupt so stop being so ungrateful for what I did for the cause." After he'd finished, his face contorted in pain, bringing her a small amount of satisfaction.

"You! Shut your damn mouth!" Rafe thundered, sending a deadly glare Rhys's way.

His voice sent shivers along her flesh. Sage sucked in a breath and stared down her personal demon, numbness settling over her. "You almost killed me," she said, her tone flat. "I'm sure I could do without your special form of protection. The Crown protected me, not you. If *this* is what you all are—" She waved a hand, indicating the remaining men. "If *this* is how you operate, I want no part in it. The princes' rule is a far cry above anything you lot would accomplish."

"Then the rumors are true, you are a whore. Mistress to the king, the princes, or perhaps all of them, at least from what I'm told,"

Rhy's sneered.

Suddenly, the anger was back, and she saw red as she sprung toward the snake spouting lies, but a solid arm wrapped around her middle. She looked into the ice blue eyes; Hayjen. She dropped her eyes and stared straight ahead, frustrated that she was stalled once again.

Hayjen leaned down to her ear, whispering, "It is not the right time. We *will* take care of him, I vow it. But it must be when the time is right. Don't let him get to you now. Take a deep breath and match your breathing to mine."

Trusting him, she tried to do as he said, breathing in time with him.

The viper on the ground smirked at her as someone tended to his wound. "Never fear, though, you won't be required to entertain the old man for secrets, not anymore. Instead you can be the instrument we need. Poetic justice if you ask me, he won't ever see it coming from his lover."

"What is he talking about?" she questioned Hayjen.

"He's talking about the king's assassination on the night of the Midsummer Festival. They plan to use you to get it done."

Her gaze clashed with Rafe's. "Regicide? *That's* your plan?" She looked around the room, but most of the men avoided eye contact. Cowards. "We are supposed to be trying to help the people! We're not assassins. This is wrong, and you ought to know that. We can't build our regime on the blood of the royal family!"

"It will be done." Rafe stated, his voice ringing with finality. "We voted, and the decision was made. It will happen with or without your help."

She snarled at him and squeezed Hayjen's arm, willing him to let her go. How could they do this? Her friend released her, and she stalked over to Rafe, staring into his rugged face. She searched his eyes, but all she saw was determination. She was so confused. How could he sanction this?

"This is wrong," she whispered, for his ears only. "You know it is."

His jaw tightened, but he gave no answer. It seemed he was unwilling to change from this terrible course.

Disappointment filled her. It was not supposed to be like this. She had thought them her friends, her family even, yet if she didn't do something they would kill another of her friends. Her mind reeled.

Sage realized she had only one choice.

Perhaps if she accepted she would have a chance at thwarting their plan. "I will go along with this but once it's done, I am out. I never want to see you again." She squeezed her eyes shut. After a beat, she opened them, looking up at Rafe with all the condemnation in her soul. "You make me sick."

She turned on her heel and stormed from the room, a symphony of male voices shouting behind her. She wound through the narrow tunnels until she came to a stairway. The dimly lit walls felt like they were closing in on her. She had to get out.

She sprinted up the dirty steps and burst into a dim cave echoing with the sounds of thundering waves. Sage's breaths came in sharp pants, the sea breeze doing nothing for her rising nausea. She leaned over, braced her hands on her knees, and began heaving. The cave spun around her and somehow, she ended up on her hands and knees as she continued retching, her stomach emptying completely before it subsided.

Weakly, she wiped her hand across her mouth and focused on getting up off the ground. Large hands gripped her waist, startling her, and a piercing scream tore from her throat. A spicy scent tickled her nose. Rafe. It was only Rafe. Despite what her mind knew, in her current state her body still recoiled. She slapped his hands away and spun to face him. She eyed his casual stance and took a couple wary steps back, never taking her eyes from him.

"Are you all right?" his deep voice rumbled.

What a dumb question. Why would she be all right?

She couldn't bear the sight of him. He made her ill. Tears flooded her eyes, and she had to suck her lips into her mouth to keep them from trembling. He had betrayed her, more than anyone she'd ever known. It would have been less painful had he physically stabbed her. She examined her ruined slippers, trying to get her reaction under control.

"Sage, I—"

"Don't!" Sage cut him off. "Nothing you say justifies what just happened." She pointed to the stairwell. "You are supposed to be a protector. Our way of life isn't that safe, but I didn't expect that the danger would come from you!" she spat the words out. "You sent him to me, that nightmare...that monster! He's wicked and soulless! His acts would haunt even the strongest of men."

Rafe held his hands out before her. "I didn't know," Rafe pleaded. "We weren't aware of what he'd done. Justice will be served."

"You did nothing in there, Rafe! Nothing! I haven't been able to sleep a full night in almost a month because of what he did. Are those the type of people we are working with? That man should be dead or, at the very least, rotting in a dungeon."

"He will be dealt with, I promise, little one." As Rafe took a step closer, she took a matching step back. His hands closed into fists at his sides. "I will not hurt you."

"You already have," his face fell, but she continued. "But it won't happen again." She dusted off Mira's old dress and switched the subject. "You really plan to kill the king?"

Rafe turned to the waves crashing against the black rocks below them. "It needs to be done. Have you forgotten all he has done to Aermia and its people?"

"I have not." She knew all too well how much the people were suffering. "That doesn't make it right though."

"Have you been compromised, Sage?" Rafe turned, his eyes hard, probing. It was as if he wanted to see into her mind, searching for secrets.

"No, I have not."

"Then how is it," he said, taking a slow step toward her, "that you went from hating him four weeks ago to defending him now?" He took another step, and another, until he was only a foot away, his gaze intense. She didn't move. She would be damned if he cowed her. "Does he have some sway over you? You need to tell me the truth, Sage, and I will not judge you for anything you might have done to stay safe. I understand what it is like, living among the enemy. Are any of the rumors true?"

It took her a second to figure out what he was implying. Sage slapped him hard across the face, fueled by righteous indignation.

"How dare you!" she hissed. "I would never do that! I am no whore," she sneered, "and you know nothing."

Rafe never flinched, his amber eyes serious. A red imprint shone in his cheek.

That must have stung like the devil.

A slight growl rumbled in his chest, and he finally succeeded in intimidating her. There was always something wild about Rafe. Primitive almost. Restrained aggression. She took a step back.

"Well then, little one, explain it to me. If you hold no affection for the king, what changed your mind?"

Should she tell him about the king's mind? Would it convince him to stay the rebellion's hand? It was a gamble but it could save Marq's life. "He's sick."

Rafe snorted. "Well then, it will be easier to get rid of him."

Sage looked at him in horror. "That's not what I meant." She tapped her head. "He's sick in here. He is not mentally all there."

"How would you know this? My best spies can't get close to him." His dark brows arched in question.

Sage debated telling him about Marq's visits but knew gossip would reach his ears sooner or later so she might as well use the information to her advantage. "He visited me every day."

"Why?" he barked.

"Honestly? I think he was lonely, and curious about me as well. They may not have had proof, but they suspected me of working with the rebellion. However, he always treated me with kindness and respect. When he was lucid, I could see what made him such a good ruler. I agree with you, he shouldn't being 'ruling'. But it's not *him* we should worry about, it's the princes. They are smart and powerful. *They* have the ability to see through your plans." She paused. "That's why it won't work. If they saw me, I'd be locked up before I uttered 'swamp apples'."

Rafe cocked his head, a sly smile on his face. "They won't be able to touch you, Sage."

"How do you mean?"

"I meant what I said. You will go as my consort to the festival."

Why did he have to speak in riddles?

"Out with it Rafe." She was tired of talking to him, all she wanted to do was get home and see her family.

"You will go as my escort to the festival, they will have no choice but to leave you alone." He paused. "I am going as the Methian prince."

What? The Methian's hadn't visited in years. Had he lost his mind? That would never work.

Rafe continued: "The Methians accepted an invitation to the festivities this year. They would have arrived in time for only the last couple days of the festival, but something will happen on their journey, and we will go in their place. The Crown won't dare touch you if you're with me. They wouldn't dare offend the Methians."

She tried to poke holes in his plan but nothing came to mind. "What happens to their real prince and his entourage? Are you going to murder them as well? The Methians have always been known for their prowess in battle, they won't go down without a fight."

Rafe clasped his hands behind his back and looked down at her. "It is nothing to concern yourself with, it has been taken care of."

Sage dropped her chin, bitterness welling inside her. She hated not having the full plan. It was something they commonly did after all—if no one person had all the information the entire plan could never be given up. She understood this, but it still rankled.

All at once, exhaustion hit her. The day had barely begun, but it already felt like a lifetime had passed since she'd played chess with Gav. She was done right now. "I need to see my family." She turned her back on him, moving toward the ascending staircase.

"You will be debriefed in a couple of days. Later this week, I will send someone to measure you for your costume for the festival. Be ready."

Not a question, a demand. Sage looked over her shoulder and lied to Rafe for the first time since meeting him. "I gave you my word, and I meant it. The king is sick, and maybe you're right, it might be a blessing to put him out of his misery. I'll be ready when you come for me, just know that I meant what I said, I am truly done after this. You will leave me and my family alone henceforth."

Rafe sighed. "Little one..."

"Those are my terms if you want my cooperation. I want your word."

Rafe stared at her and nodded once. "I promise."

"Thank you." With that, Sage turned her back on one of people she had thought of as a true friend.

Chapter Thirty-One

SAGE

Sage hiked up the stairs, feeling pinpricks of guilt with every step. She hated that she had to lie to Rafe. She'd accompany him to the festival, but that was it. She would not harm the king, it was a line she wouldn't cross. She needed to warn one of the princes, or even Mira, if she could only get to them.

She reached a platform with the ladder at its end and began ascending its rungs. Hand over hand, she climbed until she reached a hatch. Shoving it up and open, sunlight poured in, and she was momentarily blinded. Its rays warmed her, driving away the damp chill from the cave. She hauled herself into the brightly lit space: a small tool shed in the fishing district. Sage glanced through its windows and checked for anyone watching that might spot her exit. No one; the coast was clear. She pulled her hood up and began moving through the outer rim of the district. It still amazed her how extensive this tunnel system was; she had moved underground about a mile from start to finish. The vast combination of caves and tunnels was an excellent asset to the rebellion, one they frequently made use of.

Sage picked up her pace as she wound through alleys and markets. The closer she got to home, the more she wanted to run. When their smithy finally came into view her heart galloped wildly. She had been dreaming about coming back for weeks, and now she couldn't believe she was here at long last. Unseen, she slipped to the back of the forge. The heat was staggering when she entered the room, but even that felt like home. Her poor papa was sitting on a bench, hunched over a dagger, inspecting it.

"Papa?" she called.

His faded eyes wandered to her and froze. He rubbed his eyes and blinked several times. "Sage, my little shadow, please be here. Please be real."

His plea just about broke her heart. "Papa, it's me. I'm really here." It killed her that he thought she was nothing more than a figment of his imagination. Sage rushed to him and fell to her knees in front of him. "Papa, I made it home," she croaked, wrapping her arms around his middle.

A large hand settled on the back of her head and stroked her hair, the comforting gesture breaking loose a sob she didn't know she'd been holding in.

"My sweet girl, my sweet, sweet girl. My baby girl." His voice cracked with emotion. "I am so happy you are here. What happened? Are you all right? We never stopped looking for you, we knew you didn't elope. But it was as if you'd vanished into thin air. Where have you been?"

She looked up into his anguished face. He had aged so much in a month. His hair looked grayer, his green eyes a little duller, black bags circling them. He tenderly wiped her tears away, which only made her sob harder. She hadn't thought she'd ever see him again, she realized. It was hard to believe she'd made it home.

He gave her a warm smile and crushed her against his chest, speaking softly. "Shhhh...it will all be okay," he crooned into her hair. He rocked her until her tears ran out and her hiccups had all but stopped. She took one more sniff of his smoky shirt before sitting back on her heels.

"Where have you been?" he asked again, his eyes grave.

Sage dropped her gaze to his boots. "I've been very ill and have been healing for the past couple of weeks. The healers didn't think I would survive. I would have come home as soon as I woke but I was so weak." Sage paused, debating how much she should reveal.

"Is there nothing you can tell me?"

Her papa knew her well.

"I was being held captive. I am so sorry for the pain I've caused, but no, it would endanger you all if I say more. The less you're privy to, the better."

"Can you at least tell me who took you and why?"

Sage stared at his top button deciding. He needed to understand the threat to their family. "The Crown took me because they thought I was associated with the rebellion."

He slipped a finger under her chin and lifted her head, so she had to meet his eyes. "And are you?"

She closed her eyes for a moment and swallowed hard. She would never lie to her papa. Just as quietly as he asked, she answered, "Yes." She refused to open her eyes and see his reaction, so afraid he would be disappointed with her.

"Open your eyes, my sweet girl."

She cracked them and breathed a sigh of relief. It was only love on his face.

"Sage, I know you would do nothing to harm our family. You have more kindness, love, and compassion than most people of my acquaintance. I am sure whatever you did, you did it because you care about our people and this nation. I can't find any fault in that, I just want you to stay safe."

"Me too, Papa. I have one more loose end to tie up, but then I will be done with it all. I promise."

He studied her for a moment and then kissed her forehead. "Okay, if that is what you want."

"It is," she said with conviction. "It's not what I imagined it to be. Nothing is as clear as I once thought." Sage paused before changing the subject. "Is Mum inside?"

He shook his head, "No, she is at the market. She will be home later and so will your brothers. Why don't you go rest until then?"

"I am fine, Papa," she argued. "I can help you with whatever you need." She looked at the scattered projects around him.

"No. You are so pale I am surprised you haven't passed out. You need your rest. Plus, if your mum found out she'd have my neck," he said dryly. He hefted himself from the bench and lifted Sage to her feet. His arms engulfed her in another bone-crushing embrace.

"I love you so much."

"I love you, too, Papa."

He released her and shuffled into their home. She followed and noted that everything *looked* the same but *felt* so completely different. Her papa opened the door to her room, and she glided through it, stopping in the center to examine everything. Not one item was out of place, and not even a speck of dust had come to rest on the furniture.

"Your mum said you would return, despite what everyone else said. She wanted to make sure it was ready for you when you did." He clasped his hands and scrutinized her. "Do you need anything?"

"No, Papa. Just some rest."

He patted her arm and then departed, closing the door behind him. Sage kicked off her soiled slippers and collapsed onto her bed. It was a lot lumpier than the luxurious one she'd had at the palace but this one was familiar, home. For the first time in weeks she truly felt safe. The last thing she saw before closing her eyes were the faded yellow stars on her ceiling, stars her mum had painted long ago. As soon as she shut her eyes, she was asleep.

***

Sage jolted awake, breathing hard, a dagger in her hand. Her whole body was covered in a thin film of sweat. She registered a touch on her arm and quickly placed the blade's tip on the offending hand in warning.

"It's okay, love, shhhhhhh... It's just me, put the dagger down. You're safe. You've no need to be afraid." Her mother's voice carried to her through the darkness.

Sage trembled as her eyes adjusted to the dark. "Mum?" She turned in the direction of gentle voice. A small pool of moonlight highlighted Gwen's cheekbones and dark eyes. "Are you really here? I'm not dreaming?"

"Yeah, baby." Her mum's hand stroked her hair as she spoke. "You were having a nightmare... I came in when I heard you. Sage." Her voice broke. "Love, I am so happy you're home. I've missed you so much. We looked, and looked, and looked, but there was no trace of you." Glimmering tears spilled down her mum's cheeks.

Sage dropped the dagger. "I am so sorry, Mum." And she truly was.

"Papa told me what the two of you discussed earlier. I am so relieved that you're safe. We are so thankful to have you home. I love you so much, baby."

She pulled Sage into her arms and hugged her like she'd never let go. Her mum gave the best hugs. They were love, warmth, and comfort all rolled into one. Gwen released her, pushing Sage's midnight hair from her face, running a hand down a dyed lock.

"I was surprised to see a black head sleeping in this bed rather than the little brown one I've always known," she whispered, a smile in her voice. Gwen dropped her hand and looked straight into Sage's eyes. She could tell her mum was fighting to keep her emotions off her face.

"Sage," she said, her voice quiet but firm. "I put you in your nightdress so you'd not sleep in those dirty clothes." Her mum paused. "I saw them."

Her heart sank. Sage made it a point not to look closely at the marks on her body...the brands of her humiliation. She couldn't shake the sense of powerlessness that they inflicted. She hated that her mum had seen them. It was something she'd hoped to never discuss because the shame just about choked the life out of her. She ought to say something, but she just...she just couldn't. She occupied her hands by smoothing imaginary wrinkles on the bed, searching for something to say.

"Sage, look at me."

Her eyes raised, and Sage saw more compassion and love in her mum's expression than she could handle. "I know you must have questions but I...I *can't* do this right now. If I do, the nightmares will be..." Trailing off, she reached out and clasped her mum's hand as a tear dripped down her face. It gutted her that, in hurting her, Serge had also hurt her mum. "Please, Mum. I love you, and I promise that, when I can, I will come to you."

Gwen nodded and cupped her cheek. "Okay, love. I understand. I...I have seen nothing like that before. I can't imagine what must have taken place and how bad it must have been for you..." Her mum choked on a sob. "Oh, my sweet girl, if you need me at all, you have only to ask."

Sage's smile wobbled as fatigue crept back into her body. Her room didn't seem so comfortable now that it was cloaked in darkness and shadows. She didn't want to be alone; gulping down her pride, she gave her mum a beseeching look. "Mum, would you stay here with me?"

Her mum answered by crawling into bed. Sage stared at her, her eyes and heart filling with gratitude.

"Nothing will hurt you. Your papa, brothers, and I will all care for you." Her mum patted the bed and Sage scooted down, facing her. She ran her fingers through Sage's hair, singing a gentle lullaby like she had done when her daughter was just a little girl. She closed her eyes and drifted off to the comfort of her mum's clear notes sweeping through the air.

***

The next day was spent lazing about with her family. She played games with her brothers, helped her father finish a few projects, and picked flowers with her mum. They studiously ignored the fact that she'd been taken captive, and it wasn't until later that night, as the two of them washed dishes, that her mum even broached the subject of her disappearance.

Laying down the pot she'd been scrubbing on, her mum touched her arm. Sage set her rag down and steeled herself for the conversation that would happen.

Gwen's smile was warm, though there was sadness in her eyes. "We are so happy to have you home. There aren't enough words to express how thankful we are." Her mum looked down at the floor, deep in thought. She took a fortifying breath and looked up, her hazel eyes peering into Sage's face. "There have been rumors since you disappeared. *We* knew you would never run away or elope, but honestly? That's what most are assuming, that you're compromised." Her mum didn't soften the blow. "Brace yourself for some backlash from all this. It's unfair and cruel, but there is nothing we can do but push through it."

"Who's saying I'm not compromised?" Sage bit out.

Even though she hadsuspected something like that would be the case the reality of it still hit her hard. Sage had been kidnapped, attacked, and humiliated, yet she would have to bear the disdain, as if it was her fault. Even if she left the rebellion, the consequences of that situation could affect the rest of her life. The joke was on her. She had escaped, but she wasn't free.

The expression on her mum's face made her wince. The last thing she wanted was to hurt her. Chagrined that'd she'd allowed her bitterness to seep into this conversation with her mum, she immediately moved forward and clasped her mum soapy hands. "I am sorry. I didn't mean that, I'm still adjusting to everything. I want to work through it, but for now, let's be done with this." Sage pecked her mum on the cheek and turned to the large wooden table, and began to scrub viciously.

Her mum's gaze was heavy on her back, and Sage prayed that she would just let the subject drop. When the water sloshed in the sink behind her, she exhaled a sigh of relief.

As they continued their chores, Sage couldn't help the fat tear that plopped onto the table as she scrubbed. She wanted a family. She wanted a husband who would love her in the same way her father loved her mum. Now though, she had lost any chance of that. Her chances died the day she got caught in that alley. This was the only time she would mourn for that future. She was the one who'd decided to join the rebellion, knowing full well there could be consequences. Now she had to live with them. As soon as the tears stopped, she wiped them away, as if they'd never been there. If only other things were so simple to remedy.

Chapter Thirty-Two

SAGE

Sage spent the rest of the week attempting to regain a sense of normalcy in her life. She helped her father in the forge during the day and celebrated the Midsummer Festival at night. The first time she left the house, their neighbors and friends refused to look at her, sneering and gossiping behind her back, but, by the end of the first week, their fascination had dwindled. Whispers still followed in her wake but she had at least a little reprieve from the open censure she'd received initially.

There were only a few interruptions to her life. At one point, Rafe dropped her a mixture with which she could remove much of the squid ink from her hair. The first time she looked in the mirror and saw her own brunette hair, she felt more grounded, like she was a step closer to her true self. A couple days later, a seamstress swept in, took measurements for her costume for the festival's finale, and then bustled right back out. Apart from that one instance, she mostly ignored the rebellion and the plans for assassination until the last day arrived, and then her panic set in. She still hadn't figured out how she would save the king but she had to try. When her costume arrived, Sage placed it on her bed and her mother, catching sight of it, sat down heavily, her jaw slack.

Sage understood the reaction. Never in her life had she seen something so fine. It must have cost a fortune. Every year prior, she'd gone as a maid of the sea, or something else similar, but the magnificent costume wasn't something she could have imagined, even in her wildest dreams.

The bustier was a pale and shimmering aquamarine silk. Tiny, dyed seed pearls accented the edge of the cups forming intricate waves. Two delicate ties wound around the neck, the material fading from soft aquamarine to a silver that was almost white. On the ends of the straps dangled white, blue, silver, and green shells, pearls, and sea glass. A finely woven, silver net lay next to it on the bed, glimmering like early morning dew on a spider's web.

What was that for? It certainly wouldn't cover much.

Moving on, she examined the skirt. The shimmering transparent silk was hand painted with every hue of blue and green found in the ocean. Each individual thin strip of the skirt started off pale but intensified to a much deeper color as it reached the bottom. She couldn't help herself; she ran her hand along the symphony of colors, her eyes widening as she realized the colors weren't woven together. Each sliver of color was a separate piece of material! She raised the skirt, examining and watching it undulate before her. It reminded her of a jellyfish gliding in the ocean. Even though the length of the skirt seemed modest, her legs would peep out with every move.

She shook her head and carefully laid it back down. She turned around to her mum. "I can't wear that."

Gwen stared at her for a beat, then back to the garment. Her mum's lips pursed, and she looked back at Sage. "It's not *so* bad..." she trailed off.

Sage snorted. "My legs, midriff, and entire back will be on display. It will only give more fodder for the gossip mill, Mum. I don't want to humiliate Papa and you."

Her mum smiled wryly as she crossed the room, approaching Sage. "I won't pretend that I don't wish there was a lot more fabric to the dress, but you and I both know that with where you're going, it will help you fit right in." Her mum's hazel eyes met hers. "This is a disguise, love. You won't humiliate us. You will look regal in that dress, it's fit for a queen. All we want is for you to come home safe to us. That's it. If this disguise is what's required for that to happen, then so be it."

Sage searched her mum's eyes for any doubts or condemnation but she found nothing. Sagging with relief she returned her gaze to the dress. "Quite the disguise," she muttered to herself.

Gwen rubbed her hands together. "Let's get started then."

***

By the time her mum finished with her hair and some minimal

cosmetics, her back and butt were smarting. Sage had forgotten how much time it took to get ready for such a fancy affair. She stood up with a groan, twisting from left to right to sooth her aching back. "Ugh... I am *so* old."

Her mum's response was a slap on the butt as she chuckled. "You're not old until you have grown children, love. Now strip and hold still while we get that thing on you and get it all arranged."

Sage did as she was commanded, ridding herself of the much humbler garments she usually wore. Her mother's sharp inhale had her eyes snapping to her face, but she was busy with the skirt. "Everything okay?" she inquired.

"Mmhmm."

She eyed her mum curiously. How odd. She shrugged it off and stepped into the skirt aided by her mum. The silk kissed her legs as it moved, tickling her skin. She giggled, reaching down to scratch her calf. Her mum smiled, twirling her finger at Sage, indicating she should turn around. Sage plucked the bustier from the bed and held it in place. Her mum brushed her hair aside and tied the straps around her neck and back. It pushed her chest up so high she thought her breasts would smother her. There were no hiding those.

"Oh, let me fetch the sandals and jewelry." Her mum bustled from the room and Sage turned, viewing herself in the mirror.

The woman staring back looked nothing like her. The colors complimented her green eyes so well that they sparkled like emerald jewels. The stark contrast of white starfish combs made her brown hair seem even darker. She would never be tiny and delicate because of the physical work she did in the forge, but her voluptuous chest, tiny waist, and curvy hips made up well for her muscular arms and broad shoulders.

She stepped closer to the mirror, and all her joy drained right out of her. Faint pink lines marred the otherwise smooth skin on her stomach. Sage bit her lip and pushed her left leg out to examine the damage. One of the ragged lines was so long it wrapped completely around her thigh. She reached down to touch it, and the scars on her wrists glared up at her.

She was ruined. There was no way she could wear this to the palace.

A sudden noise startled her into looking up and she caught her mother's gaze in the mirror. Sage couldn't mask the pain that shone in her eyes. Her mum placed the jeweled sandals and a pile of jewelry on the bed next to her, coming to stand behind her. Clasping her arms, she soothed, "You are enchanting, baby." Her mum reached down and caressed her wrist. "Everyone has scars, love. Some wear theirs on the inside, and some bear them on the outside. But you know what? Those that allow the world to see their scars and move forward are the bravest and best of us. That is true courage."

Sage teared up, touched by her mum's simple words. Gwen squeezed her wrist once and reached down to the pile of treasure lying on her bed. She picked out two wide silver cuffs with seahorses and a few pearls on them. "As you know, your father made these for me when we were betrothed. They are not as fine as what you are wearing, but I guessed you might like them. Then you will carry a piece of your family with you and help you take courage."

"I would be honored to wear them," Sage choked out.

Her mum clasped them on her wrist and, although they didn't completely cover the scars, they did help her feel less self-conscious. Sage reached down and fingered the large scar that ran diagonally across her abdomen. "Is there anything we can do to cover this?"

Gwen scrunched up her nose, deep in thought. A smile broke out on her face. "I have an idea."

She gingerly picked up the fine silver netting and set to work. Right below the tie on her right shoulder her mum pinned the netting, draping it to the center of her chest and pinned it there with a pearl. She then draped it down Sage's stomach and tied it in an intricate knot, attaching it to her left hip but allowing the rest of the material to drape down. She'd worked a miracle in a matter of moments! Her scars were now much less visible. She felt more comfortable having a little more covering.

"Well? What do you think?" her mum asked enthusiastically, her words coming out in rush.

"It's so beautiful, Mum. Thank you."

Her mum beamed at her and retrieved the sandals. "Your carriage should be here any moment. Let's get these sandals on."

Her mum was still fussing over her when the carriage arrived. After what seemed like forever, she was ready and putting on her finest cloak. Just before departing, she placed her leg on the bed and methodically placed her daggers into their thigh sheaths. She then dropped her skirts and swished around, eyeing herself in the mirror. Even with all the slits, you couldn't spot her weapons. She grinned at the expression on her mum's face and hugged her goodbye. "Mum. I have to be prepared. Don't worry too much. I love you, and I will be home later tonight."

Her mother clutched her hand. "You better be, love. I will rip Sanee apart looking for you if you disappear on us again." Her mum's face was serious. Sage didn't doubt for a second she really would do just that.

"I promise, Mum."

She dropped her mum's hands and exited her room. Her father sat on a bench by the front door, his green eyes crinkling when he spotted her. "You are lovely."

She stretched up on her tiptoes and kissed him on the cheek. "Thank you, Papa."

He touched her cheek and affectionately rubbed his thumb along her cheekbone. "Keep your head and be cautious."

"I will."

Her father opened the door, and she peeked out, surveying the area. No one was paying them any heed. A cloaked man emerged and opened the carriage door, and so, sparing a last glance to her parents, she slipped into the carriage. She shot a quick glance to the man holding the door and amber eyes peered in at her.

She sat quickly, with Rafe entering right behind her. He tapped the ceiling, and the carriage lurched forward. She tilted her head away from the window, hiding her face. Instead of moving into the city they traveled deeper into the country, entering a copse of trees, which hid another carriage. Rafe hopped out of their carriage and opened the door of the one alongside, holding out his hand to her. "My lady."

Sage took the hand he offered, stepped down, and then right back up into the other conveyance. As soon as they were both inside, the driver started back toward Sanee. "Smart," she mused, watching the sun set on the horizon. "Hiding the Methian's carriage out here and conveying us to it from within the city? Good move, especially since no one will note an unmarked carriage heading to the country. Very clever, Rafe. "

"I thought you might like that, little one." She could hear the smile in his voice.

He had no right to call her that anymore. He had betrayed her. "I am not your 'little one', my lord. If you recall, I am a lady of station."

She frowned at him when he merely chuckled. "Forgive me, my lady, I meant no offense by it." Another more muffled snigger followed his comment.

There was no way they could keep up this ruse, especially in front of actual dignitaries. "They will throw us out or lock us up as soon as we speak. You know that right?"

"I think not." Rafe was silent for a moment. "How do you like your costume?"

She pushed back her hood and glared at him. "It is beautiful to be sure, but it's also entirely inappropriate."

Rafe flipped his hood down as well, leaning toward her. "It's more modest than what you will see there, I give you my word.

And," he enunciated, "it is entirely appropriate for someone of your station." He shifted in his seat and then asked, almost self-consciously, "Did you truly dislike it?"

She smiled and patted his leg. "It is incredible. I have never seen painted silk like this. The colors are unreal. The fabric-maker must have been quite skilled, it's as if he took the sea and imprinted onto the material. I reckon I'll never see the seamstress again but make sure she knows she did a fantastic job." She paused. "And Rafe? Thank you."

He nodded once, looking out the window. As they entered the city and made their way up the hill, Sage drew her hood to once again cover her face. Ahead of them was the palace, and unease rolled through her even looking at it. She still had no clue how she could save the king. Lost in her thoughts, she didn't realize they'd already covered the distance. It wasn't until the carriage stopped that she looked up, a million butterflies taking flight in her stomach. She swallowed back the nausea that accompanied them and took several shallow breaths in an effort to alleviate her anxiety. Salty air wafted through the door as Rafe held a hand out to her. Her eyes bounced from his outstretched palm to him and back again.

Get it together! she scolded herself.

Sage grasped his hand and gracefully descended the stairs, murmuring a soft, "Thank you, Your Highness."

Rafe bowed and tucked her hand into his arm, leading her up the steps and into the palace foyer. Well-dressed servants were directing people here and there. Voices and soft music echoed from her left. A servant bowed to Rafe and guided them to the anteroom outside of the ballroom. As she moved, the shells, sea glass, and pearls hanging from the back on her top tinkled in a melody of sound.

Sage murmured a quiet, "Thank you," as the servant divested her of her cloak. As she straightened her netting and brushed her skirt out, a choking sound caught her attention. Sage glanced to Rafe as he sidled closer to her, looking utterly transfixed. "Little one," his voice deepened. "There just aren't words. You are breathtaking."

A blush crept up her neck and into her cheeks. She tugged at her cuffs, self-conscious. His hand reached down and touched the edge of her scarred wrist peeking out from underneath the cuff. She grimaced. He missed nothing.

"Are there more?" he whispered.

She eyed the servants milling around them and bobbed her head once.

He stiffened. "We will talk about this later."

Sage batted her eyelashes at him. "No, we won't, Your Highness. I'm done." She placed her hand in the crook of his arm and faced toward the herald. Rafe's gaze burned into her until their names were called. They both straightened as the door opened. She pasted a demure smile on her face.

Into the dragons' nest we go.

Chapter Thirty-Three

TEHL

His head was pounding.

Adjusting his crown, Tehl moved the blasted starfish, so it'd stop poking him in the ear. Slowly, he stretched his neck and scanned the sea of costumed people. The air buzzed with excitement. Tehl wished he had their energy. For him, this week had been brutal. Between getting ready for tonight, leading each festivity every day, and the late nights and early mornings that were usual to festivities, he was already dead on his feet.

He shifted in his chair and peered at his brother. Sam was eyeing a pretty redhead across the way, winking at her before moving onto catch the eye of another young woman. Same old Sam.

Catching his expression, his brother shrugged and gave him a smirk before turning to lazily glass the room. "Don't give me that look. It's my responsibility to have enough fun for the both of us. You obviously look like you'd rather be anywhere else."

Tehl frowned and tugged at his costume. Generally, he didn't mind being bare-chested, but here it left him feeling like he was being hunted, surrounded by leviathans. Sam had no problem with being ogled though. It seemed like his goal was to show as much skin as possible. "Are you aiming to add more women to your harem with that getup?" Tehl quipped.

"God, I'd better." Sam grinned, a wicked gleam in his eye.

One of the noble families made their way toward the dais to pay their respects. If it hadn't been for the constant greeting from guests, he'd likely be asleep in the chair. Tehl straightened, swapping pleasantries. Their youngest son, perhaps three by the looks of him, was scowling and tugging on his own costume. The poor little guy looked as miserable as Tehl felt so he searched a nearby platter for something to improve the little man's night. As he did so, he heard Sam and a duchess chattering about the lovely decorations.

Good. After all the stupid work I put into picking them out, they should *be impressed.*

He spied a lemon tartlet that might tempt the boy. Plucking it from the platter, he stepped down to the duke and his family. Each bowed or curtsied, and the little one wobbled, frowning at the floor.

"What is your name, young man?"

Big brown eyes peered at him from a round face. "Xavie, my prince." The duke cleared his throat and the little boy's eyes darted to his father. The duke smiled, puffing out his chest a little so Xavie straightened and puffed out his chest. "I mean *Xzavier*, my lord."

Tehl bit back a smile at how the boy had tried to deepen his voice. "Is it uncomfortable to be a lion, Xzavier?"

Xavie scratched at his neck where the scruff must have tickled him. "Well...it itches like the dickens," he spouted, pulling on it.

"Xzavier!" his mum scolded. "Where did you learn that phrase?"

The little boy slid a glance to the duke before looking quickly to the floor. The duke smashed his lips together to keep from laughing while his wife blushed and discreetly swatted him on the arm.

Tehl focused back on the Xzavier. "My costume is bothering me too. You know what helps me get through it?"

"What?" he asked curiously.

"Sweet treats," he replied, offering the lemon tart to the boy. He swore Xavie's eyes widened to twice their usual size and glazed over. Chubby little fingers reached for it, but then hesitated.

"Go on," Tehl reassured, "it's for you."

The little fingers swiftly plucked it from his hand, cradling it in his little palms like the most precious of treasures. "Thank you!" He squealed, rushing to show his mum his newfound prize. She wiggled her brows at him, enjoying his enthusiasm. Tehl stood, grinning down at the little Xavie who returned it tenfold. After the duke and duchess had withdrawn, Tehl padded up the steps to the dais, returning to his seat.

Sam clasped him on the shoulder. "Well done, brother. You notice the needs of others, it will make you a good ruler one day."

Tehl shrugged off the compliment and focused on the people milling about.

"The Methians have yet to arrive." He had awaited them all week. They had received word there had been a delay due to weather, so he had no clue when to expect them, and that put him on edge.

"Crown Prince Rafeth of Methi and Lady Salbei," the Herald's voice echoed.

"Well, well. Speak of the devil," Sam whispered.

Tehl scrutinized the couple descending the staircase into his ballroom. The prince was a tall, muscled man with wide shoulders and a trim waist. A long scar ran from his eyebrow to his chin, giving him a dark, dangerous air. The prince ran a hand through his rakish hair, the glossy auburn waves, so dark they were almost black. Numerous pairs of female eyes tracked his approach.

"Damn," Sam whispered, "there goes half my harem."

If he wasn't so tense, he would have laughed at his brother's woe-begotten tone. Tehl turned his attention to the woman who accompanied the Methian prince.

A sirenidae.

Tehl barely managed not to gape.

A damn sirenidae sent from the sea to tempt him.

A sea of blue and green showcased her fine figure, her nipped in waist and flaring hips accentuated by her seductive skirt. As she glided down the stairs, it undulated like the sea itself. Every step she took provided tantalizing glimpses of her legs. Her shiny, dark brown hair caressed her chest and fell a couple inches above her navel. His gaze dropped to her petite sandaled feet; even those were attractive. He had to give it to the Methian prince; he sure knew how to pick women.

"My God," Sam breathed. "I would sell my soul for one night with that stunning creature."

For once, Tehl completely agreed with his brother. If only she would lift her head. He slid his gaze back to the Methian prince who was currently staring at him as he whispered something in her ear. Their gazes locked, his eyes feral as he glared at Tehl.

Point taken, she was his.

Sam's sharp inhale caught his attention. He looked to Sam with raised brows.

"Bloody hell," Sam cursed. Sam glanced at him and then back to the approaching couple, so Tehl too turned his attention back to the foreigners when a pair of striking emerald green eyes met his boldly.

Familiar eyes—nothing foreign about them.

Recognition dawned. He blinked a couple times to make sure he was seeing clearly.

It was the rebel. *She* was the Methian prince's companion.

What the hell? How was she acquainted with the Methian prince? Was she their spy or was she spying on him as well? Questions popped up in his mind, one after another but, with some effort, he pushed his questions aside. Now was not the time.

Let the games begin.

They stopped at the foot of the dais, and the room quieted as whispers circulated around them. Tehl stood and nodded his head to the other prince. "Welcome to my home, Your Majesty. I am glad you have traveled safely to our kingdom. I hope you shall enjoy your stay with us."

Prince Rafeth bowed. "I thank you for your invitation. We were happy to receive it and be afforded the opportunity to visit your beautiful kingdom."

Tehl caught sight of Gavriel on his left. His cousin stood stock-still, staring at his supposed friend, the mysterious Sai. She stared back at him with not even a glimmer of recognition.

The prince's eyes narrowed at his interest but he swept his arm out to introduce the woman. "Let me introduce Lady Salbei, my companion."

She smiled at them and dropped her gaze to the floor, shyly. Oh, she was good. That girl didn't have a shy bone in her body. She executed a perfect curtsey and hovered there.

Sam slipped down the stairs to lift her from the ground. He picked up her hand and kissed it. "My pleasure to meet you, my lady," he mumbled against her skin, oozing charm.

"The pleasure is all mine," she purred back, dark lashes fluttering.

Sam winked at her, and Rafeth shifted closer to her side. The prince was not stupid; he knew when another man was trying to encroach on his territory. His brother needed to be careful this time. Tehl, however, needed to play host.

"We would be delighted if you would sit at our table and enjoy refreshments. One of my servants will direct you." A servant appeared at their side and bowed low.

The prince nodded graciously. "We will humbly accept your invitation." He turned and offered his elbow to the rebel at his side. "My lady."

Tehl sat on his throne and took their measure as they followed the servant to the courtyard. He about swallowed his tongue at the naked skin bared to his eyes. Her back was completely bare save four delicate ties holding her top together. Her hips swayed as she walked, leaving a trail of drooling men in her wake.

"What an interesting twist," Sam murmured. "Who knew she cleaned up so well? You know, I like my women devious... If I could just sneak her away from the prince..." his brother trailed off, probably thinking of a way to steal her virtue. "Do you think he knows?"

"Knows what?" Tehl asked quietly.

"Who she is."

"I couldn't say," Tehl said. "I don't know what to think. In the last month of trying, we still have learned nothing about her. We already knew she wasn't some street rat, but it appears she's the Methian prince's companion."

"She is not someone new to him either," his brother remarked in a low tone. "I could tell from the way they moved together, and his reaction to your stare and my wink. Their relationship is real."

"Is she a spy for the Methians? Or is she a plant for the rebellion?" he asked under his breath.

Sam's lips tipped up. "It's a mystery I intend to untangle. I will keep our new guests occupied." Sam sauntered down the stairs, smiling and winking at female passersby. No matter their age, they blushed and smiled back.

Tehl ignored his brother's antics and looked to his cousin. Gav seemed rooted to the same spot, scowling at the floor.

"She didn't even acknowledge me," Gav gritted out, looking up at him with fire in his eyes. "Never once did her expression flicker. I even questioned my own eyes for a second until I spotted the scars."

"Scars?" He hadn't noticed any scars.

Gav scoffed at him. "Of course you didn't notice them. You were too busy ogling her, right along with most other men in this room."

Tehl shot him a dirty look but quickly smoothed it when their exchange garnered attention. "We will figure this out. Sam is gathering information as we speak."

Gavriel snorted. "Maybe halfway to helping her out of her skirt."

Tehl brushed that comment away, along with the accompanying uncomfortable stab of jealousy. A servant entered, bowing before him. "Dinner is ready, Your Majesty."

Tehl descended the stairs, the crowd parting for him, bowing as he walked by. Swiftly, he made his way outside and toward a table that was raised above the rest. Reaching it, he turned to face the crowd below him. He picked up a goblet of wine and raised it to the people. "Good people of Aermia, I stand before you, in the king's stead, to start the festivities this eve. I am not one for speeches, so…" He paused and smiled. "Let the festivities begin!"

The crowd roared back at him as he set his goblet down, and music filled the air. He surveyed the jovial crowd as they *oohed* and *ahhed* over all the work that had gone into tonight; His staff had done well. There were candles in little glass jars hung on ropes high above their heads. They winked in the darkening sky like stars. Large, dark blue lanterns sat on carved wooden columns, illuminating the area in soft light. Exotic orchids perfumed the air, spicy and sweet.

Soon though, other scents filled the air, those of roasted meat, herbed bread, and rich gravy. Hordes of his staff moved into the courtyard and up to his table, laying out a beautiful banquet.

"Thank you," he said to those working around him.

Despite his hunger, he focused on the people surrounding him. There were a couple of his advisers, some visiting nobility, Gavriel, Sam, the Methian prince, and the rebel. He still couldn't get any name to stick to her. Rebel? Ruby? Sai? Lady Salbei? Who was she?

His companions for the evening gazed at him expectantly. "Please sit. Prince Rafeth, Lady Salbei, it would please me greatly to have you dine with me." He gestured to the seats on his right sit.

Rather than place himself between her and Tehl, Prince Rafeth guided Lady Salbei to the seat next to him, which he thought odd. He glanced at Sam from the corner of his eye, noting that his eyes narrowed ever so slightly. His brother had noted it as well. Sam and Gav sat on his left and across from the foreign prince.

Tehl took a bite of the roasted rosemary red potatoes, savoring the herbed butter. He swallowed and looked at the prince. "With everything that befell you on your journey I'm glad you've made it here unscathed."

"It's fortunate we made it here at all. We kept getting delayed. Once we made it past your border, however, it was nothing but smooth sailing."

"Do you sail?" Tehl asked, trying to keep the conversation flowing. "I would love to hear about your homeland."

"I enjoy sailing every once in a while." The prince gestured toward the sea. "Our sea is nothing like yours, the water is gray and turbulent most of the time. Our forests are our real source of pride. There are trees as far as the eye can see, and everything is lush and green. To those unfamiliar, I've heard seeing it for the first time seems unreal. The lakes are so clear you can spot fish swimming at thirty feet down."

"How do you farm?" Gav asked, intrigued.

The prince twisted his wine goblet between his fingers. "We have areas that have been cleared over the years, usually near lakes and springs, and that's where we grow our food."

"What about cities?" Sam probed.

The prince watched Sam for a moment before he answered. "We, of course, have cities but not where you would expect them."

Tehl tucked his grin away, knowing that answer would bother Sam.

"Where?" Sam asked, his curiosity shining through.

Rafeth caught the twitch of Tehl's lips and shot him a grin before turning back to Sam. "Our cities are in the mountains themselves."

"You mean *in* the mountains?" Sam asked, incredulous. "That would take years of work."

Rafeth shrugged, "You're not wrong. Our homes were carved out of the mountains hundreds of years ago."

Sam gaped at him for a moment before recovering. "How interesting."

Gav's voice whipped through the air. "My lady, where are you from?"

Lady Salbei smiled at Gav, eyes bright. "I am from Aermia."

"How did you ever come to meet Prince Rafeth?" Gav pressed.

She looked up at the Methian prince with a sweet smile. He picked her hand up and kissed it. "Would you like to tell the story, little one, or shall I?"

The rebel blushed turning back to the table.

She had to be the best actress Tehl had ever met.

She blushed on command.

Incredible.

"I lived in a little village along the Methian border in the providence of Challaraies. My parents died when I was quite young and my grams raised me. She lived in a cottage about a mile outside of the village, too far to run for help if we needed it. So we needed to protect ourselves." She paused taking a breath. "Grams's father had been in the Guard most of his life and was stationed in this little village. Over time he married and had three daughters. He decided just because he had girls didn't mean they didn't need to have skills so he taught them how to use a sword and bow. Grams passed it on, teaching me what she could."

She cleared her throat and the Methian prince handed her his goblet. "Thank you," she smiled gratefully at him. She took a quick sip and resumed her story. "Growing up, I loved being able to use both a sword and bow. But the sword was always my favorite."

Her eyes sparkled at the shocked older men at the end of the table. "I practiced every day and loved every moment. As I grew, I had to take on more responsibilities because it got to be too much for Grams. One day when I was about twelve, I was exploring and I found the most beautiful meadow with a gurgling spring. It was clearer than anything I had ever seen and so full of fish. From then on, I hiked there every day. I would set up my fishing nets and then work with my sword. Years passed, and that meadow became my second home. I even made friends with the local animals." She smirked at them. "But that is a story for another time."

She picked up her story, but he wasn't paying attention her

words, only to where her hand unconsciously ran along the edge of her costume, where pearls met lovely skin. He jerked his gaze away and scowled. What was wrong with him?

Tehl glance around the table and smirked, he wasn't the only one. The other men were just as entranced as he had been. The Methian prince's eyes were locked on her, full of banked desire. He looked at her almost coveting, like she was his most prized treasure. She noticed none of it though, so lost in her story. Tehl tuned back in.

"The forest stilled, silent." She dropped her hand, and the men held their breath, eyes focused on her. "I knew I wasn't alone. I scanned my surroundings trying to figure out where it was coming from. The hair on the back of my neck stood up because I could feel that something watched. I clapped and hollered but still nothing, so I knew it couldn't have been a bear. I thought perhaps my stalker was of the feline variety."

Curses sounded around the table, and she grinned slyly at them. "Despite my best efforts, I found nothing. So I braced myself for an attack. Finally, when I couldn't handle the silence any longer, I shouted, 'I know you're there so come out and face me.' To my surprise, it was a man who stepped out." Tehl looked from the prince to her.

Prince Rafeth chuckled. "Her swordplay was a thing of beauty. Every move was like water, such fluidity I hadn't seen in a very long time. Not to mention she herself was stunning, so fierce but so tiny. One of the first things out of my mouth was 'little one'. It popped out before thinking about it."

She shook her head ruefully. "Needless to say, I was not pleased with his appearance, nor his nickname, so I commanded him to leave my meadow. But all he did was laugh and said it was not my meadow, but his."

"You were on Methian land?" a baron asked from the end of the table.

"She was," Prince Rafeth replied.

"All those years I had been fishing and hunting on their land." She smiled sheepishly.

The Methian prince ran his thumb along the top of her hand and sent her a secret smile. He didn't like how Rafeth looked at her. Tehl frowned at himself. It must be residual guilt from the events several weeks before. He shook it off and focused back on the couple.

"It wasn't long before his visits became a regular event. We even began to train together. I learned a lot from him." She smiled at the Methian prince with true admiration.

She was a good actress, he would grant her that, but the emotion shining through was real. Their affection for each other was a reality. And the way the prince touched her, both with possession and interest...that was *definitely* real.

"Is that how you came by your scars?" Gav questioned looking her straight in the eyes.

The table stilled, silent as most of the men glared at Gavriel. Tehl couldn't believe his cousin would ask that. Why would he make her relive that?

Sam even looked taken aback by Gav's question. If looks could kill, Gav would be dead. The Methian prince had retribution written across his face as his hand clenched the rebel's. She looked over at the prince and gave him a small smile before cocking her head, staring evenly at Gav.

With intent, she untangled her hand from the prince and calmly removed each one of her cuffs laying them side-by-side on the table. She placed both hands on the table for all the men to see. "That's what torture looks like, my lords," she said in a low tone. She looked each man in the eye until she lifted her wrists up in front of her face and twisted them. "This is what happens when bad men have power."

She stood up and brushed aside the delicate silver netting hiding her navel. A six-inch scar marred the smooth skin. "I was hung from a ceiling and then cut for their amusement." She dropped the netting back in place and lifted her sandaled foot to the arm of the chair. Her skirt rippled away leaving her calf and thigh exposed. A map of cuts wrapped from the outside to the inside.

It wasn't the first time Tehl seen them, but it still sickened him. The rebel had experienced many horrors in his dungeon. A slight tremor ran through her arm as she ran her finger along a few of the scars.

"Was justice served?" one of his advisers growled.

She paused and looked down the table at his adviser, sending him a vicious smile. "Not yet. But it will be."

The Methian prince's eyes were focused on her scarred thigh. "My lady, perhaps showing all your scars off at the table isn't the best of manners."

She dropped her foot and didn't spare the prince any attention. The rebel stared at Gav. "I am sorry if I have embarrassed you, my lord, but beastly questions call for beastly actions."

Immediately, he could see the guilt in Garvriel's face. Standing abruptly, he bowed to her. "Forgive me, my lady. It was unseemly and unfeeling of me."

The rebel clasped her simple silver cuffs on her wrists and pieced Gav with her gaze. "Nothing to forgive, my lord." She squared her shoulders and curtsied to Tehl. "I shall go and freshen up. If you will excuse me, my lords." She swept down the stairs like a queen, head held high.

Tehl scooted his chair back, ready to go after her. "I believe apologies need to be made to your lady. Enjoy your dinner." He strode away before anyone could argue.

Again, the dancing crowd parted for him as he tried to catch up to her. Her skirt waved and taunted him as she turned a corner ahead of him. She was going the opposite way of the powder rooms. He stalked her down a couple hallways until he figured out where she was going. He cut through one office and ended up right behind her. "My la..."

She gasped and spun with a kick. Reflexively, he caught her leg and jerked her against him. She flailed backward, toppling them into the wall.

His face was smashed into her neck, and her hair tickled his nose. Her pulse raced against his lips. He tried to move his right hand, but her hair caught in his rings, not to mention it was sandwiched between the stone wall and the curve of her lower back. The more he moved the more tangled it seem to get, she hissed out a pained breath when he accidentally yanked on her hair. "Sorry," he mumbled. He focused on his other hand and found it still clenching her thigh. "If I let you go, will you hit me?"

"Yes," she spat. Her words held much vehemence, and she ruffled the hair at the top of his head.

"Okay then. Until you calm down, this is where you will stay." Tehl spread his fingers and widened his grip on her thigh. Soft skin pressed into his calloused hand. Were all women this soft? And where was that cinnamon smell coming from?

Hunting for it, he ran his nose along the column of her neck. The aroma was stronger behind her ear, intoxicating. His mouth watered. Tehl wanted to run his tongue along her tender throat. His hand shifted on her thigh, and his thumb met the end of her sheathed blade. Tehl snapped back to reality. She wasn't just a warm, soft body; she was dangerous. He scowled at the faint tremors wracking her body.

"P—please, don't touch me," she stuttered out.

Guilt flooded him at what she must be experiencing with him practically mauling her. But then anger burned through his veins, overriding the guilt.

She was the one who attacked him.

She was the one creeping around his home.

She was the traitor.

He opened his mouth, and drunken voices nearing made both of them squint down the corridor. Tehl dropped her leg, jerking back, only to drag her with him.

"Let go," she seethed, pulling away from him.

"I am stuck," he growled right back at her, trying to untangle himself from her hair.

"Oh, God," she whispered. He looked away from the knot of her hair in his rings to see the color had drained out of her face. "No one can find us like this. It would humiliate Rafe." Her eyes darted left and then right. "There's nowhere to go." Her eyes darted rapidly from Tehl, to the wall, and back to the approaching voices. "We need to distract them." Her brow furrowed and then blanked as her tremors worsened. "You need to embrace me."

"What?" How would that solve any of their problems? They would be found no matter what. That would make him appear like he was seducing the Methian prince's woman.

"Listen to them. They're drunk. They won't remember anything come morning, or even in a matter minutes. Plus, you can hide my face that way."

His face soured.

"Believe me." She glared up at him, eyes full of hate. "I don't want any part of you touching me. Do you have any better ideas?" Hope shone in her eyes.

He didn't—there was no escape, and they were out of time. He grabbed the back of her head with his tangled hand and her hip with his other.

"Take a step back."

"What?"

"We don't have time to argue. Move."

The rebel glared, and pressed back against the wall.

"Now, shift to the side."

Her eyes narrowed to slits. "No."

Tehl ground his teeth. "This was your idea," he reminded, "I am not the villain here, I'm trying to shield you."

She hesitated for a moment and then reluctantly obeyed. He leaned into her and placed his forearm against the wall, blocking anyone's view of her face from the hallway. Her body shuddered against his as a group of rowdy men rounded the corner.

Their slurred voices made her shudder harder. Her eyes were glazed over, like she was somewhere else. Tehl looked at the frightened creature before him, pity filling him. Softly, he pulled a couple locks of her tangled hair forward and stroked it.

"I will not hurt you, and I won't let any of those men hurt you, either. It will be okay," he soothed. Her eyes locked on his, filled with fright. "Shhh...it's all right, love." He let go of her hair and cupped her cheek. "Trust me." That seemed to get to her, she blinked a couple times and then snorted.

Well at least he had broken through her terror.

She darted a glance to the loud group of men who were making crude comments and then back to his face, panic in her eyes. He watched her solemnly as he ran his thumb across her bottom lip coaxing her mouth open. Small panicked breaths puffed out of her lips but at least it didn't sound like she would pass out anymore.

He tipped her chin up and rested his forehead against hers. "I am going to kiss you, so don't stab me," he warned her. He sure didn't want her to start screaming and have those men think he was assaulting the Methian prince's lady.

Ever so careful, he brushed his lips along hers: once, twice, and then just pressed them there, staring into her wide green eyes. She stiffened further; even her lips were hard against his. He moved his head back and narrowed his eyes at her. "You need to kiss me back so they don't think I'm ravaging you in the hallway."

Her hands shook as they crept up his chest and hesitantly sunk into his hair. Her nails scraped against his scalp, sending shivers down his spine. He tilted her head back and nuzzled her cheek, running his lips along her cheekbone, gently across her lower lip, and up her other cheek.

He inhaled a deep breath of cinnamon and was surprised when her hold tightened on him, just a bit, guiding him back to her lips. A soft kiss danced across his lips, fleetingly. She tilted her head and pressed her curves against him in a way that made his hands want to wander, but the reminder of the daggers hidden on her person, and his own beliefs kept them in place.

Tehl held her against the wall and angled her head so he could get better access, her breath catching in astonishment. He couldn't get enough of her taste, or the feel of her in his arms. He wanted more.

Tehl slid his lips sensuously against her full ones, over and over, trying to coax her into opening. When that didn't work, he traced his tongue along her bow of her top lip to her plush bottom one. That got a response out of her. She pulled on his hair, and he groaned, beseeching her for entrance. Pain exploded on his bottom lip. He jerked back and glowered at her. She'd bitten him.

Whispering wrenched his attention from the woman is his arms. He eyed with disdain the lewd inebriated men blatantly staring. When they recognized his face, theirs paled, all bravado forgotten. "Forgive us, Your Highness," they chorused.

"Leave us," he commanded, his tone icy.

There was a flurry of clumsy bowing and drunken scrambling down the corridor. Her small hand slipped to his bare chest and pushed hard. Tehl stumbled back a few steps and a sharp cry sprang from her lips. His body missed being pressed against her already. He glared at her, pushing aside his ridiculous response to their kiss.

Tehl raised an eyebrow. "Didn't think that through did you, my lady?"

She straightened her skirt and look up at him with fury filled eyes. "It worked perfectly, I didn't want you to be touching my person anymore and you are not," she said primly. "I count that a success."

Tehl rolled his eyes and tried to untangle her hair from his person. "Are you going to tell me what you are doing wandering around here?"

Chapter Thirty-Four

SAGE

Sage stilled, everything she had rehearsed flew right out of her mind. It was all she could do not to throw him off of her when he pressed closer. It felt just as when Serge, or should she say Rhys, had his hands all over her. She shuddered and focused back on the irritated prince in front of her.

She watched his large fingers fumble with unknotting her hair from his rings, and she blew out a breath at his incompetence. Sage pushed his hand away.

"By all means, take the lead," he said sarcastically.

Sage bit back her retort, knowing she needed him to listen to her. Her skin prickled from his gaze. There was nothing she wanted more than to disappear from this place and never set eyes on the crown prince ever again. She focused on unwinding the hair and was blunt. "Marq is in danger, someone will try to kill him tonight."

He inhaled sharply. Sage didn't lift her eyes from her task, worried that her anxiety would get the best of her. Was he shocked that she used his father's name or that he was in danger?

"Who?" His voice was bland.

Was his tone a good sign or bad?

Her muscles coiled, and she casually slipped into a defensive position. She took a deep breath. "Me."

Silence.

Sage looked into his eyes as emotions crossed his face: shock, concern, fear, anger.

"I never planned on hurting him nor will I in the future. He was nothing but gracious and kind." Sage glanced down and stared at his sandaled feet. "He doesn't deserve to die for being sick," she whispered. She lifted her head and met his hard eyes. They looked like chips of sapphires, frigid but beautiful. "I couldn't care less what happens to you, but I will not let harm come to your father."

Questions poured out from him in a frustrated rush. "How did you come by this information? Who sent you? Why would they send you if you will not harm him?"

All logical questions, but she would only actually answer the last one. She grimaced as she yanked the last of her hair from his rings and straightened. She stepped back, out of his reach, and his eyes tracked the movement knowingly.

"It is none of your business who I am, or whom I am working with." His face flushed with anger. Time for her to get to the point.

"Logically," she began, "I was the best choice. Your father is a known hermit, yet he visited me every day for weeks. They figured we had a special relationship and that he would seek me out tonight." The words were bitter on her tongue.

The crown prince crossed his arms, thoughtful. "They intended to send you back into the arms of your enemy? I assume they know what happened, so if they still sent you that in itself is telling. What noble masters you serve."

Her heart clenched—that was exactly what her so-called brothers did. Rafe sat downstairs, celebrating, all the while knowing what he had sent her to do.

"Can't you see how wrong that is?"

The sympathy in his tone surprised and almost undid her. Sage blinked hard and got a hold of herself. The crown prince paced in front of her as she stared at the floor. "You're right."

His pacing stopped, so she pressed on, "My own so-called brothers were willing to send me back here, despite everything that took place. I only want what is best for Aermia, bloodshed and death is not the answer. They didn't listen though. If I didn't take the job someone else would have. At least this way I can protect him."

"How do you plan to do that? If you don't try someone will replace you, Ruby." He paused. "Or Salbei or whatever your name is."

"You can call me Sai," she offered.

"God save me from spies," he muttered as he spun and crossed his arms, muscles bulging. Sage eyed him warily, balancing on the balls of her feet. He was a big man, but she was faster. She'd outrun him if necessary.

"I don't trust you but I can see that, for once, you are being honest. Your affection for my father is obvious so tell me, what do you plan to do?"

This time she paced, the only sound the whispering of the silk swishing along her legs. "You need to stage an attack."

The crown prince regarded her shrewdly. "You want me to pretend there was an attack on my father?" He threw his hands in the air. "Are you out of your mind? I have the Methian prince sitting in my courtyard along with hundreds of people. Do you know how will they react? The kind of chaos that would ensue?"

"I didn't mean to make a huge scene. I'll return to the table. A while later you can rush through the crowd and get Sam and Gav's attention, the three of you leaving early. Most of them still suspect you have a mistress upstairs you're not sharing with the world. To others watching it might look like more than it is," she hinted.

"You are being watched?"

"Yes," she admitted.

The crown prince let out a harsh laugh. "I can't believe I am going along with this, but I honestly can't see any other option if we're out of time. I will not take a chance with my father's life."

"Then I will leave you to it. You have much to accomplish with little time, good evening." She backed away until she reached another corridor.

"If you are betraying me in any way, you will never see the light of a day again," he uttered, menace clear.

Her heart sped up at the threat, but she gave him her back, anyway. She was not a coward.

Pausing, Sage considered him over her shoulder and winked. "You would have to find me first." She sprinted down the hall, rounded another corner before slowing down, once again resuming Lady Salbei's persona. She neared the courtyard and sent up a prayer. Stars above, let this plan work.

***

The plan worked.

She returned to the table to be greeted by many admirers. It made her uncomfortable but she was still flabbergasted at how a little flash of skin and a sad story could turn some of the gruffest men into a puddle of goo.

Rafe seemed to be enjoying himself more since she returned, holding her hand, kissing her temple, or stroking her arm. She was impressed with his acting abilities. If she hadn't known any better, she would have thought him truly besotted with her.

A little after midnight, the crown prince came thundering through the crowd. Even though Sage despised everything about him, he was still a thing to behold. His black hair shone underneath a silver crown and she couldn't help but notice the hungry looks women gave him, their eyes devouring his bare chest and arms. He powered up to their table and nodded to his guests. He whispered in Gavriel's ear and then Sam's.

Sam stood and roamed over to her side, a smile creeping across his face that would make any woman's knees weak. He lifted her hand and gave it a lingering kiss. Completely inappropriate and completely Sam.

"It has been a pleasure to bask in your presence, my lady," he whispered across her flesh. "I cannot wait for us to get better acquainted."

Sage barely stopped herself from rolling her eyes and wiping her hand on her skirt. A low grumble came from Rafe that put a sly smile on Sam's face. Sam looked at her, his eyes smoldering. "Until we meet again, my sweet."

The three royals bid everyone good night. She studied Rafe out of the corner of her eye as he scrutinized their departure. His amber eyes caught hers, a strange glint in them. "My lady, I believe it is time I retire for the night." A sensuous smile slipped across his lips. "The journey and all of this excitement must have tired you as well."

She faked a yawn behind her hand. Rafe raised himself out of his chair and offered his hand to her. Sage smiled at him and let him help her up. She bid all the gentlemen goodnight when a gruff voice from the end of the table piped up. She zeroed in on the older man with the ruddy complexion and wiry gray hair.

"My lady, if I might be so bold as to say so, to my old eyes your scars enhance your beauty." Everyone's attention at the table concentrate on him. The older man straightened in his chair and sent her a kind smile. "They show your courage, bravery, honor, and willingness to fight back. Fierceness is a fine quality in a woman." His gaze ran over Rafe, evaluating him, before his faded gray eyes moved back to her. "If you ever find yourself in need of a husband feel free to call upon me."

Sage's cheeks heated with his remark though she knew the comment was good-natured. She smiled her first real smile of the night and dipped her head to him. "I will keep that in mind."

Rafe's tensed next to her. "She will not find herself in that position though, I assure you," he said stiffly. Sniggers turned into coughs when he turned his glare on everyone. She had to stifle one herself and look away from the older man's twinkling eyes. Rafe bid them goodnight and rushed them toward the castle. He beckoned a servant who helped them locate their rooms.

When they first arrived at their guest quarters, the comfortable rooms made her feel right at home, but only for a moment. She quickly brushed it off, keeping in mind to whom these rooms belonged.

A large bed with luxurious carpets and tapestries adorned the walls and floor. The warm hearth invited her closer, so she stared at the flames, waiting for Rafe to start asking questions. She heard him flip the lock and then he was beside her, staring with her into the flames.

"Is it done?" he asked in a low tone.

"Yes." Simple. To the point. It *was* done, though not what he expected. However, there was finality in her actions; what she had done could not be reversed.

Rafe turned and stared at her profile. She stood still trying not to fidget. She hoped he couldn't read on her face what she had done. What was he looking for? How was she supposed to act after killing someone? Sage decided numb seemed like a good place to start so she tried to emulate it.

"How are you?"

She kept her face expressionless, but inside she raged.

How was she?

Really?

He wanted to know how she was after stealing an innocent man's life? What an inconsiderate and stupid question.

She twisted her neck and stared at him. "I feel nothing."

"Oh, little one. I wish I could take this burden from you." Rafe reached out and cupped her face with one hand. She almost flinched but stayed still. His amber eyes filled with anguish at her expression, and he pulled her into his arms.

She held herself stiff and kept focused on the dancing flames. "How soon are we to leave?" she asked flatly.

Rafe's hands continued to rub tiny circles on her lower back. "I have a messenger delivering a missive in a couple hours that will imply I need to return to my kingdom immediately." His hands slowly skated up her back to her shoulders.

Her eyes flew to his when he caressed the nape of her neck. His eyes probed her like he was trying to figure out a puzzle. The color of his eyes still startled her sometimes, like tonight. The amber almost glowed in the firelight. His thumbs rubbed across her collarbones, sending goosebumps along her arms. She pretended she didn't notice his attention tracking the little bumps.

"You looked ethereal tonight. I couldn't have imagined something more beautiful, even had I tried. It was like the sea had conjured you to tempt me to her depths. You caught the eyes of most of the men tonight."

"Wasn't that the idea?"

Rafe chuckled darkly. "That was the general idea, right up until I saw the way you looked when you took off your cloak. I thought by the end of tonight that I might have to fight off those princes and the older man at the end of the table." He smiled at her, smug. "But they all knew you were mine. No one would take a Methian prince's woman."

Now that got a reaction out of her. Her eyes jolted to his, her eyebrows creasing. "You played your part well, possessive lover and all. But Lady Salbei isn't yours because she doesn't exist, and as you know, I belong to no one." Sage brushed his hands off her and began to walk away.

"What did the crown prince say to you?"

Sage halted and squinted at him over her shoulder. "I only spoke with him at the table. What are you talking about?"

"He said he would find you and apologize for what happened at dinner."

Sage feigned surprise. "Well, he never found me." Rafe nodded, believing her lie. "I am tired. Wake me when we are to leave."

***

When the missive came, leaving was easier than she expected. They made their apologies to some of the advisers and to Gavriel. He kept casting looks at her that reeked of betrayal, and it ate at her heart. Rafe said their goodbyes and hastily moved her to their carriage but Sage looked over her shoulder and caught Gav's eyes. Just before disappearing into the dark carriage she looked at him directly, mouthing, *Forgive me, brother.*

The returning ride was the same as their initial departure. They rode far into the country, switched carriages and began their ride back to the city. She stared at the moonlit grasses, moving like ocean waves in the gentle breeze. "Where is the other carriage going?" she questioned.

"It will pick up the real prince and take him back to Methi where he won't remember a thing."

She ignored Rafe the rest of the ride and pondered the choices she had made since she joined the rebellion. Whether right or wrong, she had certainly grown wiser because of it.

Before she knew it, they were in front of her home. She straightened her cowl and peered at Rafe from underneath it, her eyes straining to pick him out in the dark. Sage reached across the gap between them and grasped his hand.

"Thank you for the training you gave me. I will always be thankful for what you taught me but this is the last time you we'll see each other. I am done, Rafe."

"You're sure this is what you want, little one?" His face was grim.

"Yes." Her tone brooked no argument.

He caressed her palm and his hood dipped. "If that is what you want, then fine. But this won't be the last time I see you."

Sage stared him down. "Yes. It will," she said sternly. "Any association with you puts my family in danger. I am not willing to risk it anymore. That's what I mean when I say we are done."

His betrayal had cut her deeply. She would never let someone use her to hurt someone else. She swallowed thickly and let loose the words he needed to hear. "I thought you were my friend, Rafe.

But friends don't send their loved one back into a hell from which they escaped, nor do they sanction murder for the greater good. They don't send people to torture them and then protect the wrong doers."

Rafe growled.

Sage held up a hand. "I am done." She stood up and tipped back his hood, exposing his magnetic eyes. She kissed his scar and whispered a farewell against his cheek before leaving him to the darkness.

Chapter Thirty-Five

TEHL

Tehl tried to work out the kink in his shoulder, slowly rotating it in a wide arch. The last day of the festival was a far cry from what he'd planned for. He hadn't slept at all the previous night.

Why was it so much harder to stage an attempted poisoning and subsequent rescue than to actually poison someone and then rescue them?

Despite all the revelry followed by hard work and the plotting the night before, he had responsibilities to take care of so he couldn't let his exhaustion keep him from them. He rubbed at his shoulder, thinking of the new developments this morning. The Methian prince and the mysterious Sai had crossed the border into their own kingdom early this morning, and Tehl still didn't know what to think about it. She'd slipped through their fingers yet again. Although she'd made the right choice last night, she still was no friend of the Crown. She was still a traitor. There were just too many questions surrounding the entire situation. Reaching any concrete conclusions was difficult with the little information they had, and trying to piece it together was already giving him a headache. Sam was the spy, not him.

"Getting old brother?" Sam's words interrupted his thoughts.

Speak of the devil and he will find you. Tehl spun to his brother as he stretched his shoulder once more. "Not any more so than you. Didn't I just hear you complaining in the ring? Something about needing beauty sleep?" Tehl quipped.

Sam shrugged, sending him an unrepentant grin. He ran a hand through his blond curls. "I understand you have a busy day before you, but I need to pick up my armor this morning, and I thought perhaps you'd like to join me?"

He couldn't remember the last time he wandered the city with his brother, not for any duty but just for the pure joy of it. A boyish smile formed as he contemplated the idea, and Sam's smile mirrored Tehl's once he agreed. His brother gestured to a cloak lying on the fence encompassing the training ground.

"Prepared, were we?" Tehl joked, retrieving the items.

"Hopeful. And, of course, *always* prepared," came Sam's glib reply.

They both slid their hoods up and snuck out of the courtyard, entering Sanee. For a while, they wandered around, without real purpose, picking up smoked fish here and a pastry there. It was relaxing for Tehl to simply be, to enjoy the moment of complete freedom with his brother. They stopped by a seamstress, picking up some new linen shirts, and then went to a cobbler for new boots. They found new tack for Sam's horse as well as other random things that interested them. Tehl also enjoyed watching Sam interact with people, smiling and laughing, asking after their children and grandchildren.

As they left the last little shop Tehl studied his brother. "I've enjoyed this, but I have to ask, why are we making these purchases in Sanee when we employ people at the palace to do all of these things?"

Sam shrugged and looked down the lane. "True, but these people need it more."

That struck Tehl.

He had always been proud of his brother but never before seen the true depths of his generosity and foresight. Samuel cared for the people as much as he did. "How long have you been doing this?"

"Since I was a boy, probably around sixteen, so maybe nine years. Mum always said to help when we saw a need. At first, I tried to give them money, but they would often donate it to the poor, despite needing it themselves." Sam shrugged. "So I came up with another idea. They wouldn't turn down work, so I began commissioning the things I needed from them."

"Do they know who you are?"

"No, just a wealthy nobleman. The people around the fishing district rarely mingle with those living near the castle. It's been easy to keep my identity a secret."

Tehl liked the idea. "I might follow your example."

Sam smiled. "It only makes sense that you, like everyone else, would want to imitate me."

He rolled his eyes at the cocky reply and gave his brother's shoulder a shove. "Do you have everything you need?"

"One more stop, and then we can head home. I commissioned a sword." Sam's eyes widened with excitement. "I am close with the family that runs the forge. Years ago, I actually ran around with the smith's sons causing mischief until they began to work on merchant ships."

Only his brother would have a secret identity and secret set of friends. "Will we meet them today?"

Sam shook his head. "No they'll be working, but you'll get to meet Colm, their father."

His brother led him down a couple dirt lanes to a forge at the edge of the city where they entered a storefront. Inside, a middle-aged man was cleaning blades and displaying them. Sam greeted the older man with a hug and began chatting.

Tehl glanced around at the odd collection of things: axles for wagons, horseshoes, and axes interspersed with short blades, and swords of various lengths and styles. His brother's yip of excitement peaked his curiosity. He abandoned the daggers he'd been examining and moved to Sam's side.

The older man held out a broadsword that awed Tehl in its beauty. The magnificent blade had been crafted with Aermia's symbol perched on its hilt. The fierce black dragon draped itself around it, sapphires glittered for its eyes and the scales shone like obsidian. Tehl leaned closer.

Black seed pearls, how clever.

Sam reverently took the sword and placed two fingers underneath the hilt to test it. The balance was perfect.

Sam handed it to him, smiling giddily. "She is one of a kind, is she not?" his brother asked, his blue eyes gleaming. "Colm, you've outdone yourself."

Tehl gently touched his finger to the edge and a drop of blood welled instantly. Tehl grinned at the smith. "I suddenly find myself in need of a sword as well."

"Thank you." The smith held his hand out. "The name's Colm Blackwell. Any friend of Sam's is welcome here."

"I'm his brother," Tehl tipped his head toward Sam.

The smith smiled. "So you're the illusive brother, the one with the 'serious side'."

Tehl shrugged, his lips tipping up.

"Sam, would you like this wrapped?" Colm held his hand out for the sword. Tehl placed the stunning sword in the man's hands.

"Yes, please. And I have to say. I've seen your work over the years but this is truly something else. The craftsmanship, the attention to detail, and the artistry are each remarkable. The dragon looks so lifelike I feel like he might fly away any moment," Sam flattered.

Tehl smiled at the older man and gave him a nod of respect. "Your craftsmanship is unique. I have seen nothing like it. You do your trade proud."

Colm paused and studied them thoughtfully. "I've known

you a long time Sam so humor me for a moment. What is your opinion on women working in a trade?"

Sam's brows furrowed for a moment before clearing as he seemed to reach some understanding. "If they can accomplish the task, why should they not be able to do what they want?"

Tehl contemplated the cogs working in Sam's brain and tried to identify the reason for the change in subject.

The swordsmith turned his attention on him. "And what of you?"

Tehl cocked his head, wondering what the man was getting at, but answered anyway. "Women are the stronger of the two sexes. They give life and deal with us on a daily basis."

Colm laughed at that for a moment before sobering. "Sam, I am sure the boys have told you that Sage helps me in the forge."

"Indeed."

"Well, in reality, she does more that assist me. I cannot take credit for your sword," he said in a low tone. "My daughter created it."

Tehl looked at the man and then to his brother. Sam blinked a couple of times, then a slow smile bloomed on his face. "Is Sage here? After all these years, I still haven't met her. Are you hiding her or something?"

The swordsmith smirked. "Any man who knew you would hide their daughter."

Sam chuckled but didn't deny it. "Why keep her talents a secret though?"

"Most men think their sword will be defective, weak, or

worthless if crafted by a woman." Colm's face hardened.

"What rubbish," Sam added.

"Damn straight. She is the best swordsmith in all Aermia. We receive commissions from all over and great swordsmen now wield some of the best blades, all made by a woman."

"Can we meet her? I would love to pay my compliments to her in person, and of course, satisfy my curiosity."

Colm grinned at that. "You have an overabundance of curiosity. Sage," he hollered. "Would you please come help me for a moment?"

"Mmhmmm..." a feminine voice sounded from the back.

Tehl and Sam's attention focused on the light steps heading their way. The curtain pulled back, announcing a curvy brunette's entrance. Her head was down as she brushed her skirt off.

"What did you need, Papa—" Her question cut off when she looked up, eyes locking with Tehl.

Bright green eyes.

The rebel.

She was right under their noses the whole time.

Finally, a true name. Not the rebel, Ruby, Lady Salbei, or the mysterious Sai.

Sage.

It fitted her.

Tehl stepped next to Sam as they both stared her down.

"Why hello, Sage," Sam purred.

To be continued...
In Book 2 of the Aermian Feuds, Crown's Shield

Crown's Shield

Would you like a sneak-peek of Crown's Shield? Sign up for my newsletter *for a sneak- peak of Crown's Shield, new release alerts, giveaways, and more!*

Reader reviews play an important role in a books success by helping other reader's discover new stories they might enjoy. Please consider taking a moment to leave a review for Rebel's Blade *on Amazon!*

I love hearing from bookish peeps so if you want to say hi, ask a question, or report an issue with the ebook send me an email at conact@frostkay.net.

Find out more about me and my books here:
Website: www.frostkay.net
Amazon: www.amazon.com/author/frostkay
Facebook: http://www.facebook.com/Author-Frost-Kay
Twitter: www.twitter.com/FrostKayAuthor
Instagram: http://www.instagram.com/frost.kay.author

About the Author

Frost is a lover of all thing book. She frequently imagines stories while she is baking, so there's always a surplus of goodies to be found in her home. Her love of the written word started from an early age because of her mama's passion for reading. Not one day passed without stories. Frost frequently geeks out over her favorite authors and is prone to fangirling. She has a penchant for red lipstick, and a not so secret love of sour skittles. She lives with her four hellions in Southern Idaho.

Where to find Frost:

Facebook

Website

Twitter

Instagram

Acknowledgements

Stars above, Rebel's Blade has been an incredible journey.

There are so many elements to indie publishing. I always thought a novel was born a big beautiful piece of art. Let me be the first to tell you, it's not. Only with the helping hands of many others does a story become a master piece.

To my friends. You guys rock! Thanks for putting up with my bookish self, and for bringing the wine...mostly for the wine. Lol.

To my lovely author friends. I wouldn't have survived without you. Your advice, willingness to answer my million and one questions, and encouragement when I felt like throwing my laptop against the wall, meant the world.

To my BDWAB peeps. Girls, you know who you are. Y'all have pushed, supported, and given me love when I was down, thank you. Lots of love.

To my Betas. Wow, just wow. You gave Rebel's Blade your valuable time and honesty, which is harder than you'd expect. Thank you. You're worth your weight in gold.

To my Editor, Ashley. You are one of a kind. Thank you for the late nights, your valuable insight, and again, your honesty. A book is only as good as is edits in my opinion. You helped turn my idea into something special. Love you sister from another mother.

To my cover designer, Amy. You are the best. Enough said.

To the readers who took a chance on The Aermian Feuds, I hope you enjoyed reading Rebel's Blade as much as I loved writing it. Sage, Tehl, Rafe, Sam, and Gav have so many more adventures that I can't wait to share with you.

To the hubs. Seriously, you're the best. Taking the wee beasties out for ice cream when I needed to push through a scene helped more than you know. I am lucky to have you in my life. Love you.

~Frost Kay~

CPSIA information can be obtained
at www.ICGtesting.com
Printed in the USA
BVHW031249020321
601493BV00023B/1775/J